Praise
HOW TO FAIL

"In this steamy romance, Naya Turner is an overachieving math professor blowing off work stress with a night on the town, which leads to a night with a dapper stranger. And then another, and another. She's smitten by the time she realizes there's a professional complication, and the relationship could put her job at risk. Williams blends rom-com fun with more weighty topics in her winsome debut."  —*The Washington Post*

"Denise Williams's *How to Fail at Flirting* is absolutely SPECTACULAR! Ripe with serious, real-life drama, teeming with playful banter, rich with toe-curling passion, full of heart-melting romance. . . . Her debut grabbed me on page one and held me enthralled until the end, when I promptly started rereading to enjoy the deliciousness again."  —*USA Today* bestselling author Priscilla Oliveras

"*How to Fail at Flirting* is a charming and compelling debut from Denise Williams that's as moving as it is romantic. Williams brings the banter, heat, and swoons, while also giving us a character who learns that standing up for herself is as important—and terrifying—as allowing herself to fall in love. Put 'Read *How to Fail at Flirting*' at the top of your to-do list!"  —Jen DeLuca

"Naya and Jake's relationship is both sexy and sweet as these two people, who love their work but are not skilled at socializing or romance, find their way forward. Academia is vividly portrayed, and readers will await the next book from Williams, a talented debut author and a PhD herself."  —*Booklist*

"*How to Fail at Flirting* is a powerhouse romance. Not only is it funny and charming and steamy, but it possesses an emotional depth that touched my heart. Naya is a beautiful and relatable main character who is hard-working, loyal, spirited, and determined to move on from an abusive relationship. It was thrilling to see her find her power in her personal life, her career, and through her romance with Jake. And I cheered when she claimed the happily ever after she so deserved." —Sarah Smith

"Williams's debut weaves a charming, romantic love story about a heroine rediscovering her voice and standing up for her passions."

—*USA Today* bestselling author Andie J. Christopher

"*How to Fail at Flirting* delivers on every level. It's funny, sexy, heartwarming, and emotional. With its engaging, lovable characters, fresh plot, and compelling narrative, I did not want to put it down! It's in my top reads of the year for sure!"

—*New York Times* bestselling author Samantha Young

"The warmth in Denise Williams's writing is unmistakable, as is her wit. She tackles difficult subjects, difficult emotions, with such empathy and thoughtfulness. Best of all: Jake is just the type of hero I love—sexy, smart, sweet, and smitten." —Olivia Dade

Praise for

# THE FASTEST WAY TO FALL

"Denise Williams effortlessly weaves the journey of a fat woman rediscovering and redefining her strength in a heartwarming, intimate, validating, and relatable way. Williams's ability to pen the swooniest of romances will keep your heart pumping as Britta and Wes race alongside each other, and will have you rooting for them every step to the finish line in *The Fastest Way to Fall*." —Cassandra Newbould

"Funny, flirtatious, and full of heart, *The Fastest Way to Fall* is an absolute winner! I loved tagging along with upbeat and utterly relatable Britta as she tries new things, gets strong, and meets her perfect match in Wes. I fell head over heels and never wanted it to end." —Libby Hubscher

# The FASTEST Way to FALL

## DENISE WILLIAMS

Jove
New York

A JOVE BOOK
Published by Berkley
An imprint of Penguin Random House LLC
penguinrandomhouse.com

Library of Congress Cataloging-in-Publication Data

Names: Williams, Denise, 1982- author.
Title: The fastest way to fall / Denise Williams.
Description: First Edition. | New York: Jove, 2021.
Identifiers: LCCN 2021010370 (print) | LCCN 2021010371 (ebook) |
ISBN 9780593101926 (trade paperback) | ISBN 9780593101933 (ebook)
Subjects: GSAFD: Love stories.
Classification: LCC PS3623.I556497 F37 2021 (print) | LCC PS3623.I556497 (ebook) |
DDC 813/.6—dc23
LC record available at https://lccn.loc.gov/2021010370
LC ebook record available at https://lccn.loc.gov/2021010371

First Edition: November 2021

Printed in the United States of America
1st Printing

Book design by Alison Cnockaert

# Author's Note

Dear reader,

I am excited to share this story, and I hope you enjoy reading *The Fastest Way to Fall*. Wes is pretty hard not to love, and I enjoyed every minute of living inside the couple's chemistry. You'll follow two people as they grow, fall in love, and find happily ever after with each other and within themselves. That said, I'd like to take this note to tell you more about the heroine, Britta.

When we are inundated with messages about an obesity epidemic alongside those about body positivity, when bullying and fat-shaming exist in tandem with celebrity role models embracing their bodies, why write about a fat character doing anything but living their best life with no mind to their size? I love those stories where confident, self-affirmed fat people find love and take the world by storm—they're inspirational, and even aspirational, but that's not the story I know how to tell. I know how to tell the story of someone taking the world by storm, finding love, and doing so while navigating the sometimes choppy waters of being a fat woman.

I've been fat my entire life, and I spent so much of my time giving others power to dictate what they thought my relationship with my body should be. When the idea for this book came to me, it was the book I needed to read. I started writing this story for myself at twenty-four, when, brokenhearted and freshly dumped, I feared no one would find me attractive again. I wrote it for me on my wedding day, when I was at my biggest and had never felt or looked better. I wrote it for the me of twenty-seven, who fell in love with the gym and became enamored with what her body was capable of, and the me of today, who keeps meaning to get back on the treadmill. I wrote it for the me of tomorrow, who might need a reminder she's strong and beautiful.

I wanted to tell a story about one real woman falling in love with someone who helped her feel strong and made her want to be stronger. You'll read about Britta's journey to defining what strength means for her, and that includes the shoulders-back, boobs-forward, winning-at-life days and the shoulders-slumped days when a win seems impossible. Love has a funny way of boosting the former and making the latter more manageable.

I spoke with so many people about their experiences, and I hope I have done service to their perspectives. This is not a story about weight loss or changing to find love, but if you find stories that include discussions of body image, exercise, fitness, or nutrition triggering, please take care when reading. While our own experiences with fat phobia, bullying, and body awareness differ, the dangers of disordered eating, crash dieting, and unsafe exercise practices are clear. For resources on these, see the list at the back of the book. I hope you'll stick with Britta and Wes's love story.

Best,
Denise

*Please note, this story contains reference to drug and alcohol abuse by a side character and brief reference to off-page disordered eating and exercise.*

For Bethany, who is strong and beautiful.

# 1

BRITTA

I HUSTLED DOWN the hall, late and waterlogged. *It would rain today of all days.*

With a graceless slip on the slick tile of the conference room, I hit the floor with a surprised cry, and my umbrella sprayed water into the air. My skirt rode up my thighs as the box of donuts I'd carried skidded across the polished wood floor, coming to rest by my boss's Louboutins. Around me, conversation stopped, and I lingered in a cocoon of awkward silence.

Normally, the box was empty and stuffed in the trash before our boss arrived, already full from her kale smoothie or whatever Paleo-adjacent, keto-friendly, sugar-free organic breakfast food was trending. Everyone would enjoy the treat, and I'd maintain my status as popular and much-adored coworker, but the rain had other plans for my reputation and dignity that morning. Maricela's manicured fingers slipped under the table to pick up the pink box.

"Britta, you made it." Claire Morales's voice broke the silence, and a chuckle went around the conference table. She sat back in smug satisfaction.

That's what I told myself, anyway. From my spot on the floor next to my dripping umbrella, I couldn't see anything except her impossibly high heels. For a fleeting moment, I wondered how good their traction was and if she might have her own run-in with the slippery floor.

"I like to make an entrance," I mumbled, trying to stand without flashing anyone. Helen, the instructor for the over-sixty hip-hop dance class I'd accidentally joined at the local gym, would say, "If you got it, flaunt it," which I tended to agree with. However, I doubted I needed to flaunt my cute underwear for the entire staff of *Best Life*, the millennial-focused lifestyle magazine where I'd worked as an editorial assistant for four years.

"Britta, are you okay?" Maricela Dominguez-Van Eiken looked the part of someone who ran a lifestyle empire. Straight posture, dark hair curled and cascading, a perfectly organized planner settled perpendicular to the newest iPhone and a rose gold water bottle. She'd built *Best Life* from the ground and turned it into a lucrative, trendsetting company designed to help people live well. Kale smoothies aside, she had impeccable taste and just seemed to have her life together. *What's that like?*

I rubbed my knee and rotated the wrist I'd landed on, catching Claire's smirk from across the room. "I'm okay." *Just a little mortified.* "Sorry I'm late."

She nodded and passed the box of donuts to the person on her left. It began a slow rotation around the room. Pair after pair of hungry eyes lingered on the treats as my colleagues waved their hands to pass. No one would take one after she demurred.

"It's the third Friday of the month." She tapped her index finger to her collar—her *impress me* gesture. Each month, Maricela sought new ideas from the entire team. After four years, I *needed* to stand out. I was a good writer, but I'd never gotten the chance to flex those skills for *Best Life*. I wondered if I might be able to contribute more to the world than background research on face creams or the inside scoop on whether escape rooms were over and what the next big trend would be.

"I have an idea." With one finger raised, I chimed in. All eyes, once again, landed on me. "FitMi Fitness is a new app that's been gaining popularity and is supposed to be incredibly body positive. Unlike other apps that focus just on tracking weight loss and counting calories, this one has real people serving as coaches, and the experience is very individualized." I kept an eye on my boss, who loved the intentional marriages of technology and human interaction. I wouldn't have been surprised if she had a secret "tech+people" tattoo somewhere on her body. "What if I join and document my journey? I'd talk about the app, but also everything I'm going through."

I didn't have to look around the room to know I was the only one who'd be described as plus-size. If she liked the idea, I was the one person who could write it. I'd learned early in life I was supposed to be ashamed of what my mom called my "extra fluff" and my sister called my "cushion for the pushin'." It wasn't until I got to college that I accepted I was fun, smart, and . . . fat, and that last one wasn't the only thing that defined me. When I found FitMi, my wheels started turning with this idea. I was positive the unique perspective I could bring, plus the human and technology integration, was a sure winner.

Maricela was nodding again but had moved her finger from her collarbone to tap her chin.

*Shit, she hates it.*

"Thank you, Britta. I'd like to see something more original than a weight loss piece, though. I'd want a stronger connection to wellness with there being so much body-shaming in the world already. But bring us the next idea." She called on someone else, and I squelched the urge to sink into my chair and hide. It wasn't the first time I'd had an idea shot down—everyone did—but I'd been positive this one would be the bump I needed to earn a place on the staff as a feature writer. Maricela had already moved on when I thought of counterpoints to her concerns, namely that I didn't want to lose weight through the program. I glanced across the table. Claire had made no secret of her goals, and with one feature writer position available, we'd both been trying to stand out. Hopefully, she didn't have some great idea to pitch.

Claire caught my eye, her expression pensive before she tapped at something on her phone, and I turned my attention back to the discussion about homemade mud masks and trending scents.

After graduating from college, I'd hunted for jobs, desperate to prove to my family that my English and journalism double major wasn't a one-way ticket to unemployment. I was confident I'd find a job where I could write stirring pieces that would change minds and hearts. I was wrong, and I jumped at the editorial assistant position at *Best Life*. Four years later, I'd learned not to roll my eyes during meetings. Though we generated a lot of helpful and insightful content, my heart wasn't always in it. Some days, it felt like I'd veered so far from my original plans of being a writer, I wasn't sure I'd ever get back.

"Great idea. Put together a plan for road testing the masks, and let's get it up for part of the Valentine's Day Alone series. Britta can assist." I'd zoned out, but a senior staff member flashed me a big smile. I'd have to figure out what I'd missed later.

"Anything else?" Maricela looked around the table and paused at Claire's raised hand.

"I have one," she said, her voice even and annoyingly casual. "It's a different angle on Britta's idea. There is another app that is just starting to add coaches. I could join that one while Britta joins FitMi, and we'd do the project together but broaden the scope to focus not on changing bodies but on the entire fitness experience."

I looked to Maricela. *Please let her finger be traveling to her chin.* No such luck. It was still tapping at her collarbone. She was interested in Claire's spin. "What sets this second app apart? How would dual participation improve upon the idea?"

Claire's shoulders squared. "The app is a lot like the others out there, but they take a different approach. It's called HottrYou. Their philosophy is about owning hotness throughout the process."

Our boss's finger drifted toward her chin as her lips pursed. "This is an interesting take, but I don't love the visual of a petite woman writing about being hot and a plus-size woman writing about being fit."

A hundred responses flew through my head, all landing somewhere between tears and declaring I would write about being hot, too. Luckily, my rival spoke before I did, and with a more measured tone than I'd planned.

"On the surface, I agree. However, there's a unique take here. Or rather, a very common take. We all have relationships with our bodies, don't we?" She glanced around the room, where most people were nodding. "And I'm comfortable writing about it."

I nodded and leaned forward, resting my arms on the conference table. "And I love seeing women who are big and happy with their bodies. I love reading stories about people deciding to make a change and losing a bunch of weight. Both can be inspirational, but neither is my story. Fat people can be interested in exercise and fitness without it meaning they don't like themselves. I think I could tell that story, and I think it would land with our audience. Imagine a series focused on a fitness and nutrition experience where the goal isn't thinness or weight at all."

Maricela glanced at her notes, finger hovering between her chin and collarbone.

Claire joined me again, our impromptu tag-team approach seeming to work. "The project would be about relationship with one's body. And, if the apps are focused only on looks or only on weight loss or fall short on their promises, we'll point it out, so readers know. I think it's a win-win."

Maricela glanced down at her tablet, and after a few taps and swipes, she smiled. "Okay, put together a plan. Let's try it."

As we moved on with the agenda, Claire eyed me coolly, clearly conflicted about the idea of sharing the spotlight but also aware this could be the way one of us found ourselves on the writing staff. We'd been in competition since we started, both eager to do well and stand out, and both ready to move up at *Best Life*.

She was a talented writer, and when she spoke about her body, she sounded genuine. I swallowed, realizing the extent to which I'd have to step it up and make myself vulnerable. Despite my impassioned plea and how much I loved the dance class with Helen and the other women, exercising wasn't my passion. I assumed I'd have to eat better and hit the gym for a few months to do this project, but I wasn't wanting or expecting something paradigm altering to happen. Still, if I got it right, it would be big for my career, and I could fake passion long enough to make the project work. Nothing was going to get in the way of success with this assignment and earning that spot as a feature writer. In that spirit, I flashed a wide grin at Claire.

*Game on.*

# 2

## WES

I SCROLLED THROUGH my weather app to get a sense of the week ahead. The ten-day forecast called for rain, sleet, and bitter cold, not that I'd be anywhere besides my apartment, the gym, or the office for the foreseeable future. *Work out. Meetings. Paperwork. Sleep. Repeat.*

Mason, our vice president of communications at FitMi, waved his arm toward the floor-to-ceiling windows overlooking the gloomy expanse of Chicago. "Like a fucking monsoon out there, am I right?" He took a quick gulp from a disposable coffee cup without looking away from his phone.

"Yeah." I grabbed my water bottle. Mason had delivered on everything he'd promised when negotiating his ridiculously high salary the year before, but I still couldn't stand the guy. Taking a swig, I glanced at my watch and fell into one of the conference room chairs, ready to get started with another meeting. At least this meeting was small. Recently, the list of people I could tolerate had grown very short.

My assistant stepped into the room, the subtle scents of cocoa butter and cherries tickling my nose. "Cord will be here in five."

Mason cocked his head and flashed a toothy smile. "Hi, Pearl. It's nice to see you today."

I wasn't sure why, but Pearl didn't like him. I'd asked her multiple times if he'd done something to her, if he'd been harassing or bothering her, and she'd always said no. Still . . . *Douche.*

She raised an eyebrow but otherwise ignored Mason and handed me a manila folder. "You have that conference call at ten. Here's the prep you wanted, and I left the résumés on your desk for the operations position. You need anything else?"

I thumbed through the meticulously organized research on new FitMi users. Our growth was unreal. We were having a hard time recruiting enough qualified coaches to keep up with demand. While I loved the success of our app, I'd never wanted a desk job. I missed working with clients in the park or teaching self-defense classes.

My roommate, my girlfriend, and I came up with the idea for the app in college. Back then, I was studying exercise science, Cord was earning a degree in computer programming, and Kelsey was in management. We'd spent months searching the crowded market to see where we could fit. Even finding a name not already in use was a challenge, and it took us years of hustling to make the company a reality. I'd taught exercise classes and worked as a personal trainer, Cord had made his way up the corporate food chain in IT departments, and Kelsey had powered through her MBA. Nights and weekends meant work sessions in our cramped apartment. Those days felt like a long time ago.

"Nothing else. Thanks," I said to Pearl.

Mason kept on smiling. "I'm good, too."

Pearl shot him a withering stare. She was taller than him and slender with dark, smooth skin and hair in box braids. I was certain she could knock him out if it came to it.

Mason's voice grated on me from across the room. "You know, Pearl, I'm not a bad guy. You don't always have to shoot imaginary daggers at me."

"I'd use real ones, but your suit's so pretty, I'd hate to get it bloody." Pearl turned on her heel and called over her shoulder, "I'm not rescheduling that call again, Wes, so be on time."

"I don't think she realizes I'm a VP," Mason muttered once Pearl was out of earshot.

"She realizes—she just doesn't like you. Pearl is nice to everyone. What did you do?"

"Nothing. I'm being pleasant. It's not my fault she doesn't like me."

"If a woman treats a man like she treats you, there's a reason. Fix it. It's not the kind of place we run."

"I get it. We're a girl-power, everyone-is-beautiful, fat-can-be-fun kind of place," Mason said with a mocking edge to his voice. "I know. I engineered the brand, remember?"

The app had taken off overnight, and I never got the crash course in being an executive. For example, how was I supposed to deal with a vice president whose glib tone and habit of checking his phone mid-conversation set my teeth on edge?

Cord pushed through the door then, holding a Big Gulp, and tossed his wet umbrella into the corner. "What'd I miss?"

Mason set his device aside, finally. "Wes was just reminding me of the company's mission."

"I bet." Cord shot me a *WTF* look across the table. "Sorry I'm late—issue with the servers. So, what's—"

Mason's phone vibrated across the table, and he scrambled to answer it. "Give me a minute." He held up a dismissive finger and stepped out the door.

I cut my gaze to my friend. "What would it take to fire him?"

"Cause and probably a severance package the size of Wisconsin. What happened?" Cord leaned back in his chair in a way that made him look like a sitcom dad ready to solve problems and dispense wisdom.

"He isn't on board with what we do."

"Not sure that, alone, is a fireable offense. What did he say?" Cord sipped from the bucket of Mountain Dew. I had given up reminding him we ran a health and fitness company years ago.

I repeated Mason's words back with air quotes. "Who says that shit? He doesn't get us."

"Sure, he does." Cord shrugged. "He's just a dick." My buddy was the laid-back, agreeable person everyone should have as a best friend and business partner. The things that kept me riled up seemed to roll off him.

Mason made me twitchy. That, and I was drowning in all the work that used to be a welcome distraction. I glanced at my phone, where my text message remained unanswered. *Plus, it's February.*

"Pearl doesn't like him," I added, noticing the way Cord's expression sharpened at her name. To say Cord had a crush on Pearl was the understatement of the decade. When he talked about her, he'd get that look in his eye, like when he worked through a coding problem. I thought Mason's bugging her would push his buttons, but he relaxed his shoulders. "He dated her sister, Shea, and it didn't end well."

"Do we need to kill him?"

Cord chuckled. "If Shea is anything like Pearl, I'm sure Mason did not walk away from that unscathed. Pearl is just protective of her sister." Cord looked down at his phone, probably to avoid me asking him when the two of them had gotten so chummy.

"Sorry about that," Mason announced as he reentered the room, clapping his hands together and taking his seat. "Good news. A friend over in marketing at *Best Life* gave me a heads-up they want to do a feature, following one of their staff through the FitMi program."

*Best Life* was trendy, but I'd never seen them hawking unsafe diets or unhealthy messages—and while FitMi was doing well, that kind of exposure could launch us into the stratosphere.

"She said they'll have someone sign up and try out a coach. I'm thinking we find out who it is and make sure they get the VIP treatment."

"Back up. How do you know her?" Cord had pulled out his tablet and was, no doubt, searching for *Best Life*.

"Natalie and I . . . go way back." Mason's smirk made his meaning easy to decode, but he explained anyway because he was a douche. "We fooled around years ago, but she's cool."

"She's the one who'll be trying out the app?" *The future of our company would teeter on some woman Mason screwed and likely screwed over.*

"Nah, some big girl she works with. Natalie is already hot. This tight little body and the nicest—"

"We get it," Cord said curtly. "And don't talk about women like that here. When is she joining?"

Mason waved a hand dismissively. "Soon. Brock's our highest-rated coach, right? We just did that social media campaign with him. Let's pair them." Mason glanced at his phone again.

His suggestion rubbed me the wrong way. "Let's assign her using the matching algorithm, like everyone else."

Mason tapped at something on his screen while he spoke, avoiding eye contact. "Why not give them our best?"

"I don't want them promoting us if they don't get a real experience."

"Let me talk to Natalie and see what they want. I'll email you." Without another word to us, he was on his phone again. His voice filled the room as his call connected before the door closed. "Hey, Nat. Few questions for you . . ."

Cord took another drink. "Well. That could be good."

I glanced out the window, but streaks of rain completely obscured the view. "Yeah. I guess."

"What's up with you? You're way more out of sorts about him than normal."

I shrugged. "Just lots going on. This management stuff was always supposed to be Kelsey's role."

"Well, she's not here, and it's on us, but you can still coach," Cord replied in the why-didn't-you-already-figure-this-out tone he often adopted with me. "Take on a client or two. It's the part you enjoy, anyway. Then you'll stop whining." He smirked, and I flipped him off.

Kelsey was the only one of us with knowledge on how to actually run the business. It had been a complete surprise when she abandoned us and ended her six-year relationship with me at the same time.

"Kels isn't coming back, man. She's beyond moved on." He rapped his knuckles on the conference table. "Might as well accept it."

"I'm not waiting for Kelsey to come back," I protested, crossing my arms over my chest. "I'm just . . ." *Frustrated. Bored. Angry.* The unanswered text mocked me. "Tired."

"Do what you want, man." He pointed to the manila folder in front of me. "Did Pearl remind you about the résumés?"

"Of course I did." Pearl stood in the doorway.

Cord whipped around, straightened out of his slouch, and gave an awkward smile.

"Hi, Cord. Glad you made it." She shifted her gaze to me, and out of the corner of my eye, I saw Cord's dopey grin unchanged as he listened to her. "Wes, one of the coaching supervisors is on the phone; she says it's urgent."

"I'll take it in my office," I said, standing. "And I'll look at the résumés."

Cord was right about needing to move on with hiring someone, seeing as my ex-girlfriend—the person I thought I'd spend my personal and professional life with—was CEO of HottrYou, our fiercest competitor.

# 3

BRITTA

I HOISTED THE stack of plates from the cupboard and set them gingerly on Ben's kitchen counter next to the roll of Bubble Wrap. "Maricela okayed my pitch," I said, smiling up at my friend, whose gaze was focused on his phone.

"Pitch?" He walked toward me without looking up.

"You know, the one I told you about."

*Wrap.*

*Stack.*

*Silence.* "About the fitness app?"

*Wrap.*

*Stack.*

*Silence.*

"Oh yeah, of course." Ben finally shoved his phone in his pocket and flashed me a smile. "The weight loss thing."

"Not weight loss, but the fitness thing," I corrected, though I wasn't sure he heard me.

"You're going to do it?" Ben flattened a strip of packing tape across a cardboard box, his white T-shirt riding up to reveal a sliver of tan skin between his shirt and jeans.

Maricela had hired him as an editorial assistant at the same time as

Claire and me, but soon he'd worked his way into a position running a popular segment of *Best Life* that appealed mostly to men. After a few years, Ben worked magic, made a big name for himself, and, in no time, had an offer to host a reality show on the *Home* network. He described the show as a straight *Queer Eye* meets *This Old House* with a few touches of *The Bachelor* thrown in.

It took all of three minutes for my crush on Ben to bloom, with his wavy blond hair and thick glasses over his big green eyes. I would have done anything to spend time with him, and though I didn't like this desperate feeling, I wasn't able to stop myself. That included devoting a Friday night to helping him pack for his move across town.

I paused my flatware wrapping to stare at his long fingers as he worked. *He has hands like a lumberjack who moisturizes.*

"I don't have a choice now. You should have seen the look on Claire's face. She definitely would prefer to do this alone." I'd never admit it, but I was kind of glad she'd be posting, too. I liked the idea of someone besides me baring their soul on the *Best Life* social platforms.

Ben straightened and reached for his phone. "Claire'll get over it."

"Have you met Claire?" I waited for him to take his eyes off his phone so we could exchange a smile or a wink, but he didn't look up while tapping out a text.

"True," he mumbled into the screen. After a few seconds of awkward silence, he added, "Maybe don't leave your coffee unattended."

I laughed at his dry sense of humor, though the laugh was more from habit than finding him funny. I'd racked my brain about how to cross the bridge from friendship to more, and I hadn't come up with any good strategies other than always laughing at his jokes.

He spoke over his shoulder while reaching for another box, his gaze darting down my body. "Besides, it makes much more sense for you to do it together—she's a great writer and you're hilarious. You'll complement each other."

"Definitely." He wasn't wrong—Claire was a good writer, and I *was* funny. I just always hoped he'd see more in me than humor. I focused on the plates in my hand, securing another stack in Bubble Wrap.

"Don't get me wrong. You're way cooler." Ben stacked books in a box resting on his coffee table.

"If you mix that box with pillows, it will make it easier to move." The subject change did little to untangle the double helix of disappointment and hope.

"Good idea." He grabbed the burnt orange pillows from his couch. "Anyway, I'm proud of you, Britt. Taking on a project Maricela's excited about and losing a few pounds. It's a double win."

"Um, thanks. Really not about losing weight, though." I wanted to disappear into the Bubble Wrap, in part at his flippant comment, but also because he hadn't listened the first time I said it. I sealed the box of kitchen items and plastered on a happy smile. "This room's about done. Should we start on your bedroom?"

Ben glanced at his special edition Apple watch with the designer band. "Thanks, but I need to call it a night. I'm meeting people in about an hour."

*Oh.*

"Britt. You're the best." He crossed the room. I hoped he'd wrap me in a friendly hug and remind me he cared. His long arms around my shoulders always sent a tiny spark through me as I inhaled his woodsy cologne. This time, he reached over the box to give me a high five. "What would I do without you?"

———

FACING THE LIKELIHOOD that Ben wasn't into me, despite my wishing and hoping, wasn't high on my to-do list, so after leaving his place, I got a little drunk. Not the best coping mechanism, but it worked. When I felt appropriately loose, I stripped down to my underwear in front of my bedroom mirror. If I was going to step into a public forum and join a fitness app, I wanted to take personal inventory of my physical attributes before the Internet did it for me. I started making a list of my features.

*I have beautiful eyes.* Big, dark brown, and with long lashes. My skin was the color of sand after the waves receded, the perfect middle ground between my mom's pale, freckled face and my dad, who described himself generously as a slightly more handsome Idris Elba. I used to wish for blue eyes like my friends in our small town, but now I loved my eyes. When she was alive, my grandma always told me I looked like a rounder version of Lena Horne. I batted my eyes and did my best impression in the mirror.

*Arms.* I held out my hands to my sides and jiggled, watching the flesh undulate. *Is it weird that I'm captivated by this?* I always liked how the skin on my shoulders was smooth and clear, and I was ready for warmer, tank top–worthy weather.

*These are perfectly proportioned toes.* I glanced down at my feet, each little piggy in line, with well-appointed polish.

*I have an amazing rack.* They were too big to be especially perky, but cleavage for days, and they inspired enthusiasm in other ways.

I admired the curve of my ass in the mirror, giving it a smack for good measure and sipping my wine. *Sheer perfection.*

With a nod, I gave myself one last look and walked to the desk. After pouring another glass of merlot, I opened my laptop. The FitMi home page filled the screen.

I clicked the register button and entered my information on the web form.

I fingered the stem of my wineglass and took a deep breath as a questionnaire filled the screen. I gulped down the last of the drink. *Here we go.* After a slew of health warnings, a page of several open-ended questions greeted me.

**What is your primary motivation for joining FitMi? Please check all that apply.**

I reviewed the options: increasing activity, losing weight (see note), strengthening and toning muscles, improving athleticism, gaining nutrition knowledge, addressing a medical concern (please specify), other (please specify). *I want a promotion, and my crush sees me as one of the guys . . . Would that fall under "other"?* I selected increasing activity and gaining nutrition knowledge but scrolled back to check losing weight. I wanted to explore what someone would experience if they checked that and if FitMi was as body positive as it claimed. A message appeared.

**We respect every client's goals, but FitMi coaches will not focus on weight with you. We will focus on helping you reach your goals related to activity and/or nutrition. If you plan to continue, your coach will discuss our philosophy with you in more detail.**

I copied and pasted the text into a document. Something similar had been on their website, but I made note of a few questions to ask.

**Do you have any medical conditions?** No.

*This isn't so bad.* As I hit next to move on, a long list of medical conditions appeared, and I was prompted to check yes or no for heart conditions, high blood pressure, diabetes, cancer, thyroid issues, and a host of things I'd never heard of. I considered pouring another glass or just bringing the bottle of wine to my lips as I clicked no on each item individually, the long list of possible illnesses intimidating.

**How much sleep do you get per day?** 8 hours.

*It's usually closer to five between the time I stop reading and when I hit the snooze alarm, but I strive for eight and that should count.*

**Describe your daily nutrition.** I don't eat as many vegetables and fruits as I should, but if caramel macchiatos, French fries, and peanut butter M&M's are all in different food groups, then I am doing A-OK.

**What are your exercise habits?** Outside of attending a biweekly over-sixty hip-hop dance class I accidentally joined, not doing it.

*Should I lie just a little?* I erased the end and instead typed: My regular exercise includes a good amount of walking to get from place to place in the city. *That lie might be too big. I take the 'L' or an Uber more often than not.* I erased my response again and retyped my original answer. I planned to tell the world I wanted to be more active, and it wouldn't help to lie here. I nodded, then answered a few more questions about favorite foods.

**Do you smoke or use other tobacco products?** Never.

**How often do you consume alcohol?**

I glanced at my wineglass and the almost empty bottle on the counter. *Probably won't be telling the world about that.* A glass of wine or a bottle of beer once or twice a week.

**What do you do for a living?**

I had to be as true to real life as possible to give this an honest review, but even with three glasses of merlot in me, I had enough sense not to allude to *Best Life* or journalism, so I typed "assistant" instead.

**What are your specific short- and long-term goals?**

It had been over a year since I'd been with anyone, and even then, I didn't always feel fully comfortable naked. It wasn't something I'd ever shared before. Taking another big drink of wine and deciding to be honest, I typed "to look and feel good naked."

**Is there anything you've always wanted to do that your health and/ or perception of your body has held you back from doing?** Jumping out of a plane.

*Something about mass and velocity and all the townspeople below.* I thought about adding my joke but figured it might not be the place for self-deprecating humor. It was one of the few things my weight had kept me from doing, and I'd been sad in college when I learned there was a weight limit.

I reread my answers, fingers hovering over the track pad. *Just do it.* I clicked the button to submit the form. I guess I expected the *Rocky* theme to blare from my speakers, but I received a confirmation saying my registration would be reviewed and I'd be assigned to a coach within one business day.

*Here we go.*

# 4

## WES

"WHOA." THE CHAIR squeaked as Cord spun, holding my phone. "Kelsey wants to get together?"

I grunted from where I was doing sit-ups on the floor of his office. It was the third message in two weeks, and I hadn't responded.

"Are you going to meet with her?"

"Are you planning meetings with any of *your* ex-girlfriends?"

"My exes don't run rival companies. What do you have to lose?"

*Just my pride, my resolve to move on, and maybe my lunch.* I didn't answer, instead ramping up the speed of my reps.

Cord huffed, returning to his phone screen. "Fine. But do *something*, 'cause I am tired of this version of you."

"This version of me?" I finished a set before switching to cross-body crunches. My abs contracted as I pulled my elbow to my knee. We'd just finished a conference call with some of our investors and our head of accounting. Good news all around, and everyone was making money, but I'd struggled to stay involved in the conversation. Lately, my head always seemed to be somewhere else, and the quick ab workout gave me something to do.

"Yes. This twitchy version. Like a caged animal that's pissed off. What's going on? Is it Kels? Something with your mom?"

*No, it's February.* "Nothing."

"You're a shitty liar." Cord returned to his keyboard, one worn sneaker propped on his denim-clad knee. With him in jeans, a T-shirt, and Chucks and me in workout clothes and sneakers, we could have starred in a movie called *The Unlikely CEOs.*

I finished the last set and fell back onto the thin carpet, staring up at the exposed ductwork in our trendy downtown office space. The Realtor had told us it added edge and sophistication—it reminded me of living in crappy, unfinished basement apartments where everything always smelled damp.

Freshman year, Cord and I were roommates in the most run-down and cheapest dorm on campus. He was there because he hadn't gotten around to submitting his housing contract until the last minute. I was there because it was the least expensive option I still couldn't afford, even with my football scholarship.

He handed me a water bottle. "You can't ignore her forever."

"I can ignore her today."

He fixed me with a deadpan expression. "Mature."

My body readjusted after the quick workout, and I sat up, flipping him off.

"You just did *Eight Minute Abs* on the floor of my office after spacing out during a meeting with the money guys." A twinge of frustration had seeped into his voice.

*Fuck.* The rough, notched surface of the bricks was cool against the back of my head, and I took another slow breath. "Sorry. I'll get my head back in the game."

Cord shrugged and brushed the hair from his forehead. "I know."

Pearl popped her head past Cord's open door, and I noticed him straighten in his chair, which made me bite back a smirk.

"Hey." Cord's voice came out higher than normal, and he cleared his throat before repeating it in his regular register.

"Hi, Cord." If she noticed him acting like a middle schooler with a crush, she had the grace to ignore it. Instead, she gave him a warm smile, and I swear his chest puffed out. "You need anything before I go, Wes?"

I waved. "Have a nice weekend, Pearl."

She waved back, flashing another smile at Cord, who called after her, his voice too loud. "Have a good night!"

Despite my bad mood, I reached out a hand to offer him a high five he didn't return. "Those tutorials on talking to women are paying off."

"Fuck you," he said, dropping his head to his hands.

"I'm just giving you shit, man." I settled back, enjoying my friend's mild misery.

"Anyway." He stood and clapped me on the shoulder. "Pick up a client or two. You get less edgy when you're coaching." Cord tossed his messenger bag over his head and shoved his phone in his pocket. "Want to grab a beer?"

"Nah. I'm gonna hang for a while." I took a swig from the water bottle but didn't get up from the floor.

"Okay." He headed for the door. "And, Wes?" Cord paused and faced me again. "I know there's something going on. Offer stands."

"Thanks, man."

Cord held up a hand and disappeared down the hall. I let my head fall back against the wall and stared at the ductwork again. Painted black, it was a step up from the apartments with exposed wires and tape holding the pipes together. When my sister, Libby, was small, she was scared they'd fall on her in the run-down places we'd lived, so I made them into characters in bedtime stories so she wouldn't worry. The tale of Mr. Sparky and the Dusty Cobweb.

For a second, my lips tipped up at the memory, and I released a heavy breath.

*February.*

Scrubbing my palms down my face, I shook my head. *Okay. Enough.* I popped up and strode down the hall to my office, brought my computer to life, and logged into the administrator portal for the app. Cord was right. A client would keep me distracted from everything swirling in my head and the administrative tasks piling up on my desk.

Most new clients were paired with a coach automatically through our matching algorithm, but sometimes people's intake information was reviewed manually if they made special notations or added unique comments. Three new registrations were in the queue to be assigned a coach the next morning, and I skimmed through them—an ex-bodybuilder from Akron, a retired teacher in Scottsdale, and an assistant in Chicago. The bodybuilder wanted to get back into the sport; I clicked the button to assign her to a coach we'd just hired who competed in natural bodybuilding competitions. I clicked the button to assign the teacher to me. SamTheMan6 had diabetes and a rare heart condition, so I sent the standard welcome email and added a note to have the client confirm they'd checked in with a doctor before coaching began. I dragged the mouse to x out of the system, but the assistant's profile lingered on the screen.

I scrolled through her demographic information and the first few responses. *Nonsmoker . . . wants to eat better . . . exercise more.* Seemed standard, and I wasn't sure what had kicked her application out of the automated process. I hovered over the button to assign her to someone else.

**What are your specific short- and long-term goals?** To look and feel good naked.

**What does being healthy mean to you?** To look and feel good naked after eating a salad.

**Comments:** I can work with anyone, except a Packers fan. I'd hate to have beef with my coach from the beginning.

I laughed out loud in the quiet office.

I reread her answers and chuckled again before clicking the button to assign myself as Bmoney34's coach. *I can handle two clients.*

---

**From:** FitMiCoachWes1
**To:** Bmoney34
**Sent:** February 1, 7:12 p.m.

Bmoney34,

Welcome to FitMi Fitness! I am your coach, and my name is Wes (he/him/his pronouns). I'm excited to help you reach your goals. Please read the message below for important information about your registration and our programs—that will give you a good idea of what to expect.

I have a degree in exercise science and ten years' experience coaching and teaching fitness and nutrition. You can reach me through the system on our website or through the mobile app.

Let's get moving.

Wes

P.S. I'm a Bears fan from way back.

# 5

**BRITTA**

**LIKED BY BETHANYHM AND 659 OTHERS**

Have you heard about this new diet?

Underwear that camouflages your thighs?

Selfie poses to thin your face?

I've heard about them all. Spoiler alert: No one sticks to that diet
and it probably doesn't work anyway, the underwear cuts off circu-
lation, and your friends know what you look like in real life, so who
cares? That brings me to now. I'm Britta. I'm a writer, a coffee lover,
a devourer of books, and I'm fat. I know that's a scary word
for many people, but I try not to give it that power. This project
is not about me avoiding or running away from being fat. It's
not about chasing some arbitrary ideal body or anything like that.
Truth is, I want to be more active and I want to eat better, so
I'm about to sign up for a fitness app, request a personal trainer,
and invite you to watch how it pans out. I imagine there will be

tears, crushing defeat, and swearing along the way, but I promise to tell you the truth at every step. You can celebrate with me at the end.

So, have you heard about @FitMiFitness? #BestLife #TeamBritta

---

**From:** Bmoney34
**To:** FitMiCoachWes1
**Sent:** February 1, 9:18 p.m.

Wes,

I'm surprised the website connected us so fast. I submitted my registration a couple hours ago. It's nice to meet you.

I've never had a coach or trainer before. Are you going to make me eat kale and do yoga?

Bmoney34 makes me sound like a white rapper from the '90s, but it's been my go-to handle since the sixth grade. You can call me B.

B

P.S.—I hope you're not judging my quick response on a Friday night. I promise I have a life.

---

**From:** FitMiCoachWes1
**To:** Bmoney34
**Sent:** February 1, 9:27 p.m.

B,

To your questions, I won't make you do anything. You decide—I just help you find the options. If you're interested in yoga and kale, though, I've got stuff.

In terms of where to start, keep track of what you eat and how much exercise you do for the next week. Here's a link to the tracking resources in the app. You can send me the results, and we'll formulate a plan. There's no right or wrong here.

What questions do you have?

Wes

P.S. Don't knock white rappers from the '90s. Where would we be as a country without the dope rhymes of Vanilla Ice? Also, no judgment. I'm writing you back on a Friday night.

---

**From:** Bmoney34
**To:** FitMiCoachWes1
**Sent:** February 1, 9:34 p.m.

Wes,

I don't have to diet right away? This sounds like a trick . . .

Where would we be without Vanilla Ice? A profound question. He taught us so much as a nation. I think I like

you. Until you recommend kale smoothies. At that point,
you're dead to me. I'll start tracking tomorrow. You'll know
I'm lying if I say I ordered fruit and yogurt from Dunkin',
right?

B

---

**From:** FitMiCoachWes1
**To:** Bmoney34
**Sent:** February 1, 9:42 p.m.

B,

Diets rarely work, and I suspect you already know that, but I
will help you make choices about food that work for your life.
I find it's better to spend the first few days paying attention to
what you already do—it's easy to ignore what we put in our
bodies when we're not paying attention, so tracking what you
eat and how much you exercise now is where we'll start. As you
go, make note of how you feel (i.e., energized, tired, happy, etc.).
It will give us a baseline.

Also, you indicated wanting to lose weight on the registration
form—many of our clients do, but I want to make sure you
know we don't focus on that with coaching. It can happen
when people exercise more and eat well, but my focus will
not be the numbers on the scale, but on you moving more
and feeling good. This is challenging for some people who
have been conditioned to believe that the numbers are
the only things that matter—let me know if you have
questions.

I look forward to helping you meet your goals, and I'll remember
the thing about the kale smoothies.

Wes

P.S. Who gets fruit at Dunkin'?

I closed my laptop and headed for the kitchen to rinse out my glass.
Turned out my new coach had jokes, which was a relief. Filling out the
form and that first exchange had given me an idea for my next post, and
I returned to my laptop, flipped it open, and began to write. If, on the off
chance I one day won the Pulitzer for this piece, no one would need to be
the wiser that I started it while a little drunk and in my underwear.

# 6

## WES

"HEY." AARON TIPPED his chin up as I approached courtside and sat beside him. "We've got next."

Aaron's wife had been a personal training client, and I always wondered what kind of man could hold his own with Felicia. Turned out, no man ever tried, but Aaron seemed to enjoy being next to her while she bent the world to her will. I'd been playing basketball with him and some guys he worked with for about a year.

I tucked my phone in my pocket. "How's it going?"

He shook his head and bounced the ball from palm to palm. "You hiring over at FitMi?"

"Last I checked, we weren't short any high school assistant principals, and I think your wife might kill you if you left after spending all that time finishing your master's. What's up?" I liked these games. The guys were laid-back, and it was probably good to hang out with someone other than Cord after we'd spent so much time getting FitMi off the ground. Coaching again had helped, and one of my new clients was kind of a trip—but Cord was right, I wasn't myself lately, and I hated having him worry about it. Luckily, these guys didn't know me well enough to ask any probing questions.

Aaron stood, stretching as we talked. "Same old story. Budget cuts.

We had this entire new initiative planned for juniors and seniors that was going to help with the cuts we've already had to make in the P.E. program." Aaron paused and waved to Jake, who made his way toward us. "But." Aaron stopped talking and just made cutting motions with his fingers.

"Talking about your vasectomy again?" Jake set his gym bag on the bench and nodded toward the other guys. "I doubt Wes is any more interested in the play-by-play than I was."

Aaron flipped him off. "This funny guy."

"Naya thinks so." Jake checked his phone and then set it in his bag. I liked him for my friend—nice guy, career oriented, and he was even good with Aaron and Felicia's kids, which was no easy task, as those kids had energy for days. I had never met anyone worse at basketball, though.

Aaron tossed him the ball, which he barely caught. "I think she means you smell funny. I'd say you look funny, but damn it if you're not a handsome bastard."

Jake laughed and tossed the ball back as the players on the court finished their game and our group began a shift forward. We stood at center court, waiting for the last few guys to join us.

"So, they cut your physical education funding?" I palmed the ball. Aaron hadn't finished his story, but I'd loved my P.E. courses in school. I'd spent as much time as I could with my coach and around the school gym.

"Most of the little music, art, and P.E. funding we still had," Aaron said. "It's a mess. We had this peer health education program in the works, but that's not going to happen now. Shame, too. It was a good idea."

"Yeah," I said, more to myself than anyone else, as Aaron got us organized into teams.

WHEN WE WALKED off the court and I checked my phone, I had a missed call I ignored, a text from Kelsey, and a FitMi notification. I paused for a second, thumb hovering over the preview.

The notification from the FitMi app read *Bmoney34 logged three meals.* It had been so long since I'd used the app as a coach, I'd forgotten to turn off the notifications, but I was glad she was jumping in. The other new client had been hit-or-miss, but I tapped the icon to send B a "good work" message. A text remained on my screen, and not the one I'd been hoping for.

**Kelsey:** I know you're ignoring me out of spite. This is important, though.

"Haven't seen you much. Work okay?" Jake's voice cut into my thoughts, and I hit delete before tucking my phone in my pocket.

"Yeah. All great. Busy." I'd missed the last few games. "How's the new place?"

"Not so new—we've been there over a year, but come over some night for dinner or cards or something."

Wow. Almost a year. I'd spent a lot of time with them for a while, and then I just kind of . . . stopped. *Maybe there's more going on with me than just it being February.*

Aaron joined us, waving to a few of the other guys. "Wes, don't let him sucker you in. What he lacks in basketball skill, he makes up for in poker. He'll take all your money."

"I barely have any left after playing with Felicia last time," I said.

"Who do you think taught me?" Jake's phone buzzed in his hand, and he apologized for needing to take it, heading for the exit.

I walked with Aaron while the squeak of shoes and the *thud, thud, thud* of basketballs hitting the courts sounded all around us. The entire game, I'd been thinking about Aaron's program. I knew nothing about kids, but I'd wanted to be a teacher at one point, wanted to be like my coach. "That program that was cut at your school. How much would you need to save it?"

"The actual cost for the program isn't much, but the bigger issue is the staff time. We lost someone we're not going to replace, and the two people who were going to run it and train the peer leaders now have to be doing other things."

Despite the coat I'd pulled on, the frigid February air hit me like a brick to the chest, a brick made of ice that exploded on impact. Next to me, Aaron swore under his breath.

"Gotcha," I said. "So, it's human resources you need."

"People and time are harder to come by," he said, pulling his keys from his pocket.

"Maybe we can help."

"Your company?"

"Maybe," I said, wheels already spinning. "Can you send me more information and I'll look into it?"

When I climbed into my own car, waiting for the window to defrost and the heat to kick in, my phone pinged. *Bmoney34 liked your message.* I smiled, sitting in the freezing car and thinking about some new possibilities for getting back to what I enjoyed.

# 7

A FEW DAYS after my initial conversation with Wes, I added the contents of my lunch to my food journal on the app.

Salad with light ranch dressing, cheese, and croutons

Cheeseburger with ketchup, mustard

Onion rings and sauce (note: no idea what it is. Probably just fat mixed with magic)

Diet Coke

"What are you doing?"

I glanced up from my phone to see RJ's cocked eyebrow.

"It's that app I'm reviewing," I said, popping an onion ring into my mouth. "I signed up over the weekend, and I have to keep a log of what I eat this week."

"I get that." My friend took a forkful of her own salad. "But don't you have to eat a certain way? Like, shouldn't you be insisting that I take some of your onion rings?"

"I'm supposed to set my baseline and pay attention to what I eat now." When I took a bite of my salad, ranch dressing dripped off my fork into a little puddle on the table. "I'm starting here," I said, motioning to my onion rings and then to her plate. "And you're the one who said you wanted to eat more vegetables this year."

"Maybe I should have set a baseline first, though." RJ stretched her long arm across the table and plucked an onion ring from my plate.

"Anyway, the whole reason I pitched the story in the first place was because of you."

"Me? Why?" She reached for another onion ring, but I swatted her hand away.

Sometimes it was hard to reconcile the RJ I knew in college with the suit-clad, badass attorney in front of me. We and our college roommates, Kat and Del, had been inseparable and were always getting into something spontaneous. Now RJ was a lawyer, Kat was a teacher and a mom, and Del—well, it seemed he'd be in school forever, but someday he'd have letters after his name. "Remember? We tried to get your cousin to go to the gym with us for the dance class." RJ had originally talked me into trying Zumba, but we got the rooms mixed up, and the sixty-plus dancers had welcomed us in. I watched RJ's gears turn. "She said she was embarrassed to go to the gym, like thin people would judge her and fat people would think she didn't like herself? It got me thinking about how I'd felt that way, too. I wondered how many other people probably do as well. Like, if you're fat, exercise has to be this big statement instead of something you do like everyone else."

"Well, damn. Look at you changing the world, girl." RJ sipped her water. "I think that's awesome, and you know what else?" She leaned in, lowering her voice, and I mirrored her body language.

"What?"

Her fingers darted between us, and she snatched another onion ring off my plate, popping it into her mouth and then holding up her hands in mock surrender. "I don't want you to feel alone."

"Next time, I'm calling Kat," I said.

"Psh! Good luck. You could try Del, and he'd eat more off your plate than I would while reminding you he's a poor graduate student. You're stuck with me." RJ returned to her salad. "So, you're working with a trainer?"

"Yeah. He seems like a cool guy."

I'd had a clear picture of the person who did that job, and it was someone between my high school gym teacher and the nurse at my doctor's office who clucked her tongue every time I stepped on the scale. He'd been nice, though.

"To baselines, then." RJ raised her glass of ice water.

I raised my Diet Coke. "Cheers!"

# 8

WES

I SAT BACK at my desk, closing the emails from Aaron about the program they'd planned, and fiddling with a pen. I'd been reading, researching, and jotting down ideas for over an hour, and FitMi pitching in where the program needed help looked doable. I asked Pearl to set something up with Cord before clicking over to the coaching portal, scrolling through the message thread with B from the day before, and replying to a question from my other client. Cord had been right; even a week into working with clients again, I felt like I had a better hold on things. There was something else, too. The teacher, Sam, was nice enough, but I laughed when I read B's emails. I laughed a lot.

---

**From:** Bmoney34
**To:** FitMiCoachWes1
**Sent:** February 7, 9:22 a.m.

Coach Wes,

THE FASTEST WAY TO FALL

I updated my food journal for the week. You got the full truth on what I ate. What should I do while you read it and judge me?

B

P.S.—What does a FitMi coach wear to work? Do you dress like a gym teacher? This has been on my mind.

---

**From:** FitMiCoachWes1
**To:** Bmoney34
**Sent:** February 7, 1:16 p.m.

B,

I'm not judging you. I never would. This is all about making an informed plan. There's no one size that fits all with nutrition and exercise. What trends did you notice? Did anything surprise you?

Here's a couple potential changes based on how you reported feeling.

— Based on your journal and your goals, you seem to want food and nutrition that helps you build more balanced meals. I curated some recipes and food suggestions for you to check out. You can access them here.

— Keep healthy snacks around. A protein bar or a handful of almonds in your desk is more convenient than the trip to the vending machine to get M&M's. Here's a link to a resource we have on healthy and convenient snacking.

— On that subject, peanut butter M&M's seem to be a go-to

snack? C'mon . . . if you're going to go sweet, pick a better candy. Have you never had a Kit Kat?

What about exercise? How did it feel? I sent you some ways to get started. Keep track again this week—we'll check in and see how you're doing.

Wes

P.S. How does a gym teacher dress, and why has this been on your mind?

---

**From:** Bmoney34
**To:** FitMiCoachWes1
**Sent:** February 7, 6:38 p.m.

Coach Wes,

I'm picturing tube socks, polyester shorts, and a whistle around your neck. Close? I was worried you'd be a clone of my high school gym teacher. I'm just trying to put an image with your horrible taste in candy. Kit Kat? I thought you said you went to college—didn't they teach you anything?

To your question, aside from walking to the curb to meet my Lyft or rushing for the train, I didn't do much exercising this week. Did I fail my assignment?

B

P.S. Can coffee count as water? I'll give you my firstborn child if you don't make me give up coffee.

---

**From:** FitMiCoachWes1
**To:** Bmoney34
**Sent:** February 7, 6:45 p.m.

B,

You didn't fail. It's a process, and you won't get everything right on the first try—don't expect yourself to. Also, there is no one right way. Let me help you find a plan where you can stay motivated. What kind of exercise do you enjoy? You mentioned the dance class, which is excellent. Do you want to do that more? In the meantime, I want you to try at least three of the everyday suggestions (taking the stairs, getting up from your desk, etc.) for the next few days and one cardio option.

I won't make you give up anything, but here's some <u>information</u> we have on caffeine consumption if you're interested.

Wes

P.S. I don't own tube socks, but P.E. was my favorite subject in school.

Pearl popped her head into my open door. "Mason's here. You have a few minutes?"

"Sure."

"C'mon," Pearl said, motioning to Mason.

He sauntered in and called over his shoulder, "You're going to love me. Eventually!"

Her response of "Unlikely" faded as Mason pushed the door closed, unfazed by Pearl's disdain.

"We have a problem. HottrYou just launched their new campaign."

Mason slid his tablet, where the website for our biggest competitor loaded, across my desk, and he tapped a video.

A deep voice spoke as the screen slowly filled with fitness models in bathing suits. *"There's a hot body in all of us. We'll help you unlock it. But no two bodies are the same—how do you know where to focus? We can help. HottrYou team members will work with you to create a plan. Your hot body is ready to meet the world. Let us help you show it off."*

"This is the first time they're promoting coaches even though we heard rumors they were looking into it." Mason's summary was unnecessary. "How do you and Cord want to play this? You've never wanted to hit below the belt with them, but . . ." Mason pointed to the screen again, his words hanging in the air.

"Do we need to respond? They're pitching something different from us—this is all about physical appearance. Nothing about health."

"I think you're giving consumers too much credit. *We* know it's different—to most people, it doesn't sound different. We could launch a counter ad—a play on theirs that's subtle. Or we push that we already do this. Do we have enough coaches available to handle an influx?"

I shook my head. We were having trouble getting enough qualified people to fill the positions, so I wondered where Kelsey was finding staff.

"If you eased back on the standards, we could recruit more people." He'd already made this point repeatedly behind closed doors. "HottrYou is recruiting, no experience necessary."

"We hire people with training, experience, or degrees. In a perfect world, all three."

Cord pushed through the door, breathless. "I got your text. What's going on?"

I thumbed over Mason's tablet while he explained the situation to Cord. The recruitment ad for their HottrYou Buddies—*what a stupid name*—advertised no experience necessary.

"I was just telling Wes that if we lower our standards for coaches—"

"No go." Cord didn't look up from his screen. "Clients could get hurt, and we could get sued. It's not worth it."

Mason squared his shoulders, and a muscle ticked in his jaw. We'd been round and round on this issue. "Okay. Well, we have to do something. They're coming for us."

Cord set down his phone and gnawed on the side of his thumbnail. "Can we do nothing and just let it play out?"

Mason gave us both a deadpan expression. "Their message is that everyone can be hot. Ours is that everyone can be healthy. Theirs is better."

"Fuck," I muttered. "Can you put together options we can discuss? I don't want to start a war with Kelsey."

"She already started it, man." Mason tapped something on his phone, probably marching orders to his small team. He stood but paused before opening the door. "We'll have ideas by end of day."

I pounded my fist into the desk a few times. "I can't believe she's adding coaches."

Cord met my gaze across the room. "She's competitive. I'm surprised it took this long. You think this is what she's been calling about?"

I ignored his question. "She's hiring unqualified people."

Cord ran his fingers through his surfer blond hair and puffed out his cheeks before releasing a slow exhale and eyeing me skeptically when I silenced my buzzing phone. "Her?"

I didn't need to look at the screen to know I didn't want to answer. "No."

"All right, let's see what Mason's team comes up with." Cord stepped into the hall with a two-finger wave. "You need to call her back. Think about it."

# 9

BRITTA

"It's my first live post, and today I'm getting personal. Real talk. Exercise and big breasts don't always go together. Now, I love my boobs, but sometimes they get in the way. Of what? Get ready. I have a list.

"For starters, buttoning shirts. The shirt gap is real unless you keep a stash of clothing tape and safety pins handy. Also, eating. This might just be me, but rarely do I finish eating anything without needing to fish at least a few remnants out of my bra or brush them off my chest.

"Then walking through a crowd. Squeezing past other people inevitably means dragging my chest against them. Sounds sexy? It's not. Now it's time for me and my boobs to go to the gym. Hit me with your sports bra recommendations. I'm going to need them."

In theory, the open-office concept meant collaboration, communication, and creating a work family. The reality was Jordan's breakfast burrito, Kari's designer dog podcast, and Leigh's hacking cough invading my space. *I want walls.* I read through my research on independent bookstores for one of the writers and hit send. Most of my days were spent in front of my computer gathering information and fact-checking, reviewing pieces, and whatever else Maricela or the other editors needed. I glanced around the office space, the same familiar faces hunched over the keyboard or chatting at workstations. I plugged in my earbuds, opened my laptop, and pulled up the thread between me and Wes.

His avatar was a generic blank profile photo, and I wondered what he looked like. Maybe dark and brooding or perhaps more like a boy next door. Sometimes I pictured Michael B. Jordan, and others Zac Efron.

A shadow caught the corner of my vision, and I spun. Claire stood behind me, arms crossed over her svelte frame. I'd always been jealous of women who could do that without their boobs getting in the way, and Claire stood tall, her hair pulled back from her face and her clear brown skin looking somehow sun-kissed under the fluorescent lights.

"Hey, Claire," I said, pushing my screen down and noticing an impatient Natalie standing beside her.

"I'd like to see your plan for the app project by Monday—Maricela wants us to promote the hell out of it, so we're on a tight timeline now that Claire's company went public with their coaching." Natalie looked between us. "Think you can handle that?"

Claire flashed a wide smile. "I've already started creating content."

I met her expression with my own grin. "That's great. So have I."

Our false niceties left Natalie rolling her eyes before she tapped my cubicle wall, rapping her knuckles twice on the metal endcap. "Monday," she said before walking away.

Claire's smile fell, and she glanced over her shoulder. "She's such a deeply unpleasant woman."

"Agreed." My smile stayed put, though an awkward silence fell between us. "What do you want to call this thing? I was thinking The Body Wars."

Claire pursed her lips in an obvious negative reaction to my idea. "I don't think we want to frame it as a competition. Let's think of something that's a bit more body positive." If she wasn't right, I would have given her a hard time about parroting Maricela's words.

I didn't want to agree, but she had made a good point, and I begrudgingly returned to the desktop file where I'd been brainstorming names. I scrolled down the long list of ideas, most of which were straight-up awful. "What about The Body Project? Body Talk? Um . . . Body for the Win?"

"Body for the Win . . . I like it." She gave me a tight smile, her praise as unfamiliar in her mouth as it would have been in mine.

"Okay. We can pitch it to Natalie."

"There's probably only one opening for a features writer. We'll work together, but . . . let's be clear, we're competing."

"Crystal clear." I was unsurprised by her directness.

"You should know I have no intention of being second best in this. If there's an opportunity to come out on top, I'll take it."

"Same."

Our eyes met and held for a moment, and then she walked back to her desk.

I opened my laptop more aggressively than necessary and cranked up the volume on my phone. I punched in my password, as if each jab of my thumb on the space bar would communicate my rage to the world. The FitMi window was open, and I typed a reply, tapping out the words in time to the heavy bass of the reggaeton song from my playlist.

---

**From:** Bmoney34
**To:** FitMiCoachWes1
**Sent:** February 8, 10:22 a.m.

Coach Wes,

I never answered your question about exercise. After gym class in high school, it stopped being a regular part of my life until the last year. I like the dance class, but the group only meets a few times a month. I have access to a gym, but I've never made much of an effort to do anything there besides the class. I'd prefer to start with other things.

B

P.S. I'm still going to picture you in tube socks.

I clicked on another tab to research energy drinks that claimed to contain minerals. The other windows were manuscripts to review from *Best Life* writers. I was so tired of never being able to shape the story I wanted to tell.

A few minutes later, the FitMi notification flashed.

---

**From:** FitMiCoachWes1
**To:** Bmoney34
**Sent:** February 8, 10:25 a.m.

B,

That's a solid start. For the coming week, plan to do 30 minutes of continuous exercise a day. You could walk, use an exercise bike or treadmill, or swim, if you like. Don't worry about pushing yourself too hard, just get used to moving. Do you have a pedometer? A Fitbit? If not, there's one built into FitMi. Shoot for getting in 10K steps a day as an initial milestone. It's mostly an arbitrary number, but it will kick-start more movement. We'll *step* it up next week.

You can picture me in tube socks. We're all about individuality around here.

Talk to you soon,

Wes

---

**From:** Bmoney34
**To:** FitMiCoachWes1
**Sent:** February 8, 10:31 a.m.

Coach Tube Sock,

"*Step* it up" was bad. You're on joke probation.

B

P.S. My job just got monumentally more stressful, and my normal go-to is a pint of Ben & Jerry's and a rom-com. Any other suggestions?

P.P.S. Suggestions that AREN'T yoga. Don't @ me.

I bit the corner of my lip. Talking to Wes felt like chatting with a friend, a friend whose job was to make me eat more like an adult human. I opened another browser window where I'd begun research on the company to have background for the posts. FitMi was started locally by two guys in Chicago, Christopher Lawson and Cord Matthews. So far, I had found little of interest on either, but everything from reviews on Yelp to social media mentions were overwhelmingly positive.

I was half-heartedly searching my calendar for times to plan the thirty minutes a day when the ping of a new message drew me back and a smile spread across my face.

# 10

## WES

I BRACED MYSELF as the call connected and Mom's raspy voice came over the line. "I didn't think you'd ever call me back."

"Sorry. I was busy. How are you?" Turning my chair away from the desk, I looked out the window at nothing in particular. I struggled to connect the dissonance of it being sunny and bright outside. I wanted gray skies to match my mood.

"Oh, Chris." Only my mom called me by my first name anymore. I'd been "Wes" to everyone else since college.

I tried to pull back my own memories and keep the conversation moving. I didn't want to wallow with her. "What did you take today?"

"You're always in my business."

"You wanted me to call you back, remember?"

"Oh." She sounded far away, her voice quiet.

"Mom?"

"Have you heard from Libby?" She sounded so hopeful, her voice brightening.

"Not in a while." I never knew what had happened between the two of them, but it had been bad enough for Libby to bolt at seventeen. Sometimes taking care of Mom, as much as she would let me, felt like a betrayal to my sister.

"Oh." She sighed, and I pictured her slumping down. "She might come back, Chris. Be patient with Libby. She takes her time."

"Sure, Mom." I wasn't sure why I felt the need to remind her. "It's her birthday today. She's twenty-three now."

"God, I got old. I had two kids by that age. She'll be fine." Her words slurred and then halted, like she'd dropped the phone. "You should find a nice girl. A pretty one who doesn't run."

I didn't have heart-to-heart conversations with my mom. I didn't know what she thought about Libby leaving, but every time she said *She'll be fine* and told me not to worry, I tensed. "Do you need money? Is that why you called?"

"A little wouldn't hurt."

I nodded and told her I'd get it to her. Disconnecting the call, I checked for a reply from Libby for no real reason, and then tossed my phone aside, pushing my palms against my eyes again, the silence of my office overtaking me. I hated that I felt so raw after talking to her. I should have been used to it after so many years.

*What a damned mess. My sister's gone, Mom's barely functioning, and the person I thought I'd spend my life with is trying to destroy my company.*

My desktop notification for the coaching portal pinged. *B.* I still didn't know what to make of her. She was funny. I bet she had a nice smile. As I read her reply, I imagined what it would be like to be with someone who smiled easily. I remembered her question about stress relief. *Dancing is good cardio. I could use some loud music and a warm body against me.*

*C'mon, Wes. Get it fucking together.* I'd never send something like that to a client. There were a few types of men I swore I'd never be. I'd never abandon my kids like my own father had; I'd never use women to meet my own needs. I'd never take advantage of someone who trusted me. I tapped out a real response following a deep breath.

---

**From:** FitMiCoachWes1
**To:** Bmoney34
**Sent:** February 8, 10:50 a.m.

B,

Rough day here, too. I like to run when I'm stressed, but take a hot bath? Go for a walk? Go punch an inanimate object? The ice cream is tasty, so if you want some, check out the serving size information for reference. As for rom-coms, I got nothing. Trust your gut! Here's an <u>article</u> on our site about stress.

Do you want to talk about it?

T.S.

Pearl's voice made me look up from my phone. "Mason said he has options for you and Cord when you're ready. I figured you might want some time after your phone call, so I told him you weren't free until one."

I nodded. "Thank you, Pearl. I appreciate everything. You're . . ." I was going to say something overly emotional that she would wave off. Instead, I corrected and just repeated, "Thank you."

"Need anything else?"

I shook my head. "Thanks."

"You can stop thanking me."

"Never."

"Can you say it with bonus checks, then?"

"That, I can do." She held up a hand when I opened my mouth to thank her and then closed my door.

A notification sounded, and I glanced at the screen.

---

**From:** Bmoney34
**To:** FitMiCoachWes1
**Sent:** February 8, 11:05 a.m.

"T.S." makes you sound like a very classy author of obscure and unreadable books. I like it. I want a cool nickname, too. Get on that, will you, Coach?

I'll walk home and then take a hot bath. Is wine allowed? Please say yes. Your method of running it out sounds awful, but I guess that's why you're the coach and I need one. Hope your day gets better.

No need to bore you with details. I suspect I'm already taking up more of your time than you planned. You can tell me if I am emailing too much. I'm in unfamiliar territory here, but you're the pro. How long have you worked for the company?

B

---

She didn't need to know I ran the company. I didn't want her to treat me any differently. Anyway, it wasn't about me. It was about her reaching her goals. Her goals of looking and feeling good naked. *And now I'm thinking about this smiling stranger I don't even have a picture of in the bathtub, smooth wet skin sinking into bubbles, because I'm going to hell.*

"There might be something wrong with me," I muttered, trying to push the image away. Running would get me out of my head. I had experience compartmentalizing the difficult stuff—there was a special place in my head where I sent Libby, my mom, and Kelsey—and usually staying in work mode kept the feelings at bay. I glanced at the notes on my desk about the potential high school fitness peer education ideas. Between that and coaching again, this was the first time in a long time something even remotely good took my mind off things.

Shaking my head, I grabbed my keys and phone. I had time to go home, change, and get a run in before hearing Mason's ideas on how to deal with HottrYou.

# 11

BRITTA

**Three Things I Like About FitMi So Far**

1. Tracking my food was a pain at first, but it's become a habit now. I never thought this would motivate me, but you get badges in the app when you meet your goals. I love those flippin' badges, plus you can customize everything so it's not one-size-fits-all.

2. The app is easy to use. I'm always turned off by a poorly designed user interface. This one is intuitive and engaging.

3. The coaching. Having someone to help me stay accountable has been what I've needed. He gives me feedback on my food and exercise choices and is supportive without ever making me feel guilty or ashamed or like I don't know anything. I can't say enough about the coaching.

---

**From:** FitMiCoachWes1
**To:** Bmoney34
**Sent:** February 8, 7:17 p.m.

B,

Sorry for the slow reply. It's been a busy day.

Walk and a bath is a good plan. Here's a <u>link</u> to our guide
on alcohol. If you're interested, the main thing to remember
is moderation and that alcohol can leave you dehydrated.
That said, a drunk message from you would be entertaining—
or maybe terrifying since you nicknamed me "Tube Sock" when
sober.

I've been with the company since the beginning, and you're
not taking too much of my time—you're my client. I'm here for
you.

T.S.

I read Wes's message before slipping into my robe. It was almost eight
at night, and I wondered if all the coaches provided this impressive level
of personal service.

---

**From:** Bmoney34
**To:** FitMiCoachWes1
**Sent:** February 8, 7:43 p.m.

Tube Sock!

You would be so proud—not only did I walk home, but I took the long route. I don't remember the last time I did that. It felt good.

Okay, that last part is a lie—I'm sweaty and my feet hurt, but I raise my one glass of pinot grigio to you anyway. My stress didn't go away, but I feel better. I added the blocks of time for exercise to my calendar like you suggested and entered them in the app, so I can get reminders. What's my next homework?

B

P.S. Did your day get better?

The claw-foot tub was a strange extravagance in an otherwise normal apartment. It didn't match the rest of the decor, but having a tub I could sink into was a dream. All I needed was a lover admiring me from the doorway. I struck a particularly mermaidy pose at the thought.

---

**From:** FitMiCoachWes1
**To:** Bmoney34
**Sent:** February 8, 7:51 p.m.

B,

*clinks glass* I'm glad the walk was good. I know it's a shift to start working out every day, but you've got this. Keep track of how much you do and how you feel. Same for food using those meal plan guides I sent. You're doing a good job entering it on the app—make sure you click on my comments.

T.S.

P.S. Thanks for asking. I'll be fine—can't all be good days, right?

I bit my lip, curious what had been so stressful, wondering if I could make him smile with a joke. The best part about using the app so far was talking to Wes. Though I didn't want to sound like a girl with a crush.

---

**From:** Bmoney34
**To:** FitMiCoachWes1
**Sent:** February 8, 8:07 p.m.

T.S.,

If your day got worse, I hope the drink is good, and that it's not your only one.

What would drunk coaching be like, I wonder . . .

B

I leaned back in the tub, and the steam rising off the hot water curled around my neck and loose tendrils of hair stuck to my skin. I closed my eyes, prepared to fantasize about Ben like I usually did, but my mind wandered to what Wes might look like raising a glass to clink with mine. What he might look like at all.

---

**From:** FitMiCoachWes1
**To:** Bmoney34
**Sent:** February 8, 8:19 p.m.

B,

I'm several beers in, so probably a lot like this. Shouldn't have said that, though. You keep calling me Tube Sock, but I haven't given you a nickname yet. What if I call you Bubbles?

Wes

I tied my robe after stepping from the tub and brushed a few wayward strands off my face. My muscles were loose, and the heady scent of the argan oil and vanilla bodywash filled the air. Padding to my bedroom, I reread Wes's latest email and tapped out a reply in that languid state.

---

**From:** Bmoney34
**To:** FitMiCoachWes1
**Sent:** February 8, 8:30 p.m.

I don't mind you messaging me while drinking—helps to see you're human and not some fitness robot.

Bubbles?

---

**From:** FitMiCoachWes1
**To:** Bmoney34
**Sent:** February 8, 8:32 p.m.

You said you were taking a bath. Bubble bath. Bubbles.

No?

---

**From:** Bmoney34
**To:** FitMiCoachWes1

**Sent:** February 8, 8:35 p.m.

Were you thinking about me in the tub, Wes?

I hit send and then immediately cringed at such a flirty response. The lingering shadow of the silly daydream lingered, which was the only explanation I could give myself. *Why did I ask that?* I was about to send a follow-up apologizing when his reply appeared.

---

**From:** FitMiCoachWes1
**To:** Bmoney34
**Sent:** February 8, 8:36 p.m.

Yes.

My breath hitched. His response left me motionless, and my belly fluttered. That response was completely inappropriate, and I should have been upset. I should have been taking a screenshot or jotting down notes for my article. This whole conversation was way out of line, but the shadow of a fantasy lingered on the edge of my mind, and it didn't feel gross or wrong. It felt kind of hot. Before I could come to my senses, another message came in.

---

**From:** FitMiCoachWes1
**To:** Bmoney34
**Sent:** February 8, 8:41 p.m.

B,

Sorry, that came out wrong. I meant I knew you were in the tub, not that I was imagining you in your tub. I'll think of another nickname. Have a good night and good luck with working out tomorrow. Still shoot for 10K steps.

Wes

I set my phone down and opened my drawers to pull out clean clothes. My imagination was a little too overactive, but it was fun to play what-if for a minute.

# 12

## WES

CORD AND I sat against the far wall near a rarely used dartboard. The tables were sticky, the service was awful, and the bar was inhabited by the same regulars who'd probably been coming since the nineties. The people here appreciated cheap drinks and a dearth of young people. I still wasn't sure of the name of the place; the sign outside just read *Bar*.

A light near the door flickered, casting intermittent shadows over a floor already littered with peanut shells and salt from the slushy sidewalks. The floor was never clean, the debris just changed—sand and slush in the winter, stray leaves in the fall, always a series of wet footprints in the spring no matter the weather.

"Who're you texting?" Cord tipped his bottle to his lips, eyebrow raised.

"What?" I set my phone on the table. "No one."

"Yeah, right." Cord pointed to my beer to ask if I wanted another before heading to the bar. I glanced at the screen of my phone, where my last message to B stared back at me. *Shit, I admitted to thinking about her in the bathtub.* I'd been thinking about her, more than I should, especially once she mentioned the tub.

I sent off a correction to B that hopefully made me look like less of a pervert as Cord returned to the table and handed me another cold beer.

"So, what gives?" Cord took a swig from his beer. "All week your head has been somewhere else. You didn't even pay attention to what Mason was telling us. I'm not mad, man. I'm worried. You're usually kind of hyper-focused on work."

"It's Libby's birthday," I said, eyes trained on the pattern of salt and sand pooled by the worn and saturated welcome mat. If you squinted, it formed a rough constellation like the Big Dipper. I followed the path with my eyes.

I didn't talk about my sister often. We'd been so busy with getting the company going the last few years, I thought I was handling her absence better, but I was just getting better at hiding it. I wasn't sure I'd said her name out loud to anyone besides Mom in years.

"Shit," Cord said, his voice barely audible over the Billy Joel song piping through crackling speakers. "Was it sophomore year she left?"

I picked at the label on my beer. "I never knew what else was going on, but she and Mom fought constantly, and she'd developed what I know now was an eating disorder. One day she answered the phone, and the next, she was gone." I'd spent years fearing the worst and searching as best I could. I'd all but given up when I got a text from an unknown number on her birthday, saying she was okay and she missed me. Since then, I'd get those kinds of messages a few times a year, always guarded and careful, but it was something. I'd keep texting that number until it didn't work anymore and then I'd wait for her again. "I haven't heard from her since June."

Eight months was a long time, and work wasn't the welcome distraction it had been in the past.

"Shit, Wes. I'm sorry."

I kept following the pattern in the sand and took a pull from my beer without looking at him. "And then my mom is—well, you know, my mom."

Neither of us spoke. I didn't have to return his gaze to know his brow was knit, trying to figure out the right thing to say.

Cord broke the silence, his voice low again but without a trace of pity. I loved that about the guy. "What do you need?"

"Distraction." I could shake this. I didn't need help or condolences; I just needed to focus on a problem I could fix, and Cord understood.

He leaned one elbow on the table, pivoting on a dime. "Tell me more about this high school thing Pearl said you wanted to talk about."

"Yeah." My shoulders relaxed, and I realized how tense I'd been. "You know my buddy Aaron?"

"Yeah, the one you play basketball with, right?" Cord sat back in his chair, eyeing the small group of trendy twentysomethings who'd stumbled through the front door. I knew they wouldn't stay.

"They wanted to do this peer education thing where older kids lead workshops on fitness for the younger kids who want to learn." Aaron had sent me more information, and the program was a great idea, giving kids a chance to learn and be leaders. Libby had always hated gym class—she'd complain, and I never got it. Eventually, she confessed she hated that she felt judged and forced to focus on her body, when she didn't want to in this very public way. I'd never thought about it like that. The program Aaron described sounded better. "Sort of like a mini version of what our coaches do."

Cord took a pull from his drink, expression unchanged. "Sounds cool. Where would we come in?"

"I'm not sure yet. It's all still coming together, but what would you think of us partnering with them? We could hire someone who would work with the school and train the kids using some of our existing training program. I don't know . . . maybe if it works, it's a service we could provide to schools to do something similar." I was talking faster, motioning with my hands. "You know how often our coaching boils down to undoing shit people have been holding on to since they were kids."

Cord nodded, and I knew what was in that acknowledgment. When we first met, he gave me the cold shoulder, and I figured he was another spoiled, rich asshole like so many of my new classmates. The first semester we lived together, we just tried to stay out of each other's way until he stumbled in drunk one night and thanked me for not being an asshole like the athletes who bullied him in high school. I'd never thought much about what people dealt with until that night. After Libby ran away, I'd thought about it a lot.

"Yeah, and it's not like we're going to expand FitMi to serve minors, so this could be good. We're doing well. You want to do this for free, at least for this school?"

"That's what I was thinking." I was in way over my head. We'd have a thousand details to work out with the school—our insurance, the finances—and that was all before hiring someone to head it up. It would be a ton of work for me in the months ahead, and that was exactly what I wanted.

"Let's do it." He sat back in his chair and glanced down at my phone buzzing on the table.

"Kelsey again?"

I finished the beer and peeled the label. It was a reply from B, and I silenced it. "Nah, but Pearl is arranging a meeting."

"I wonder what she wants."

I did not understand why Kelsey was so eager to talk. Even when we were together, she never wanted to chat. When we first met, Kelsey seemed like the girl I thought I needed—serious, self-sufficient, and cooler than I was. She didn't rely on me for anything, and that felt like a relief for a while after leaving home, but that cool turned colder and colder. We hadn't spoken once since the breakup years earlier.

Cord shook his head. "Kelsey on top of everything else. When you have a bad day, it's an epically shitty day." He held up his beer. "Another?"

I waved a dismissive hand. Another drink would mean feeling even worse in the morning, and this was already more than I usually had. The worry I'd end up like my mom was always resting at the bottom of every drink.

"I got tonight, then." He pushed up from his chair and strode to the bar to close out our tab. I examined my decimated beer label and scratched off the residue. The distraction didn't last long before I unlocked my phone and clicked on the FitMi notification.

---

**From:** Bmoney34
**To:** FitMiCoachWes1
**Sent:** February 8, 8:54 p.m.

You get a pass for having a bad day and being a few beers in. Anyway, I kind of like the name.

Goodnight, Tube Sock

Bubbles

# 13

BRITTA

If any man ever wanted me the way I want this stranger's cream cheese Danish, I'm not sure I'd walk again. I'm getting better at usually choosing foods that give me energy. For example, while lusting after a stranger's pastry full of carby buttery goodness this morning, I took a bite of this very Instagrammable red apple full of nutrients. If I'm being honest, the nutrients didn't measure up, and I debated if feeling a post-Danish sluggishness might not be so bad. #DecisionsDecisions

I SAT AT the *Best Life* conference table, having arrived on time with the donuts. The box was almost empty when our boss arrived. One of the recent FitMi activities had been to read a short article on checking in with your body. It had sounded a little fluffy when Wes suggested it, but it was more about paying attention to physical cues like feeling tired, hungry, and in pain. I'd had the bear claw halfway to my lips when I rethought the decision, because I actually wasn't all that hungry. Instead, I tore off a small piece of the donut and set the rest on a napkin near my notes.

"Good morning," Maricela intoned, as if calling us to worship at the altar of style and grace. Eager congregants that we were, we all sat a little straighter. Natalie gave some updates, including that Body FTW was increasing in popularity with consumers and advertisers. Claire and I shared matching cool smiles. Inside, I was doing a TikTok dance from my chat with Wes that morning.

---

**From:** Bmoney34
**To:** FitMiCoachWes1
**Sent:** February 13, 6:34 a.m.

Wes! I lost 2 pounds! I know, I know—you don't want to focus on the numbers, but it's my first numbers! Two pounds is nothing, but I'm so excited that I had to tell you. I did a little dance in my bathroom. Also, good morning. :)

B

---

**From:** FitMiCoachWes1
**To:** Bmoney34
**Sent:** February 13, 6:39 a.m.

B,

I'm glad you feel good! Are you ready to step it up? New homework: not just 30 minutes of movement a day, 30 minutes of cardio (walking, aerobics, etc., to get your heart rate up). I sent you the information about target heart rate—focus on that and report back. I'm sure your dance class will hit the mark!

Tube Sock

P.S. If your valentine needs some ideas, here's a <u>link</u> to some great alternatives to chocolates.

---

**From:** Bmoney34
**To:** FitMiCoachWes1
**Sent:** February 13, 6:46 a.m.

Alternatives to chocolate sound like cruel and unusual punishment. I'll do a lot for you, Wes, but I draw the line there. But I remember . . . all things in moderation. It's a moot point anyway. No valentine to speak of. Please give real chocolate to the person you're seeing unless they're also some kind of fitness freak, in which case flowers. No roses though—they're boring.

B

---

**From:** FitMiCoachWes1
**To:** Bmoney34
**Sent:** February 13, 6:51 a.m.

B,

No valentine for me, either, but what's better than roses?

W

---

**From:** Bmoney34
**To:** FitMiCoachWes1
**Sent:** February 13, 7:02 a.m.

Wes,

Here's the 411: Anyone can pick out roses. They're predictable. Better options to tell someone what you think of them: lilies (classy), sunflowers (bold), dahlias (unique), ranunculus (soft and girly, but still something different), tulips (cheery), and peonies (they smell awesome). Does that help?

I wasn't sure if he'd responded, since I'd stashed my phone before the meeting. I didn't know how to feel about the relief that washed over me when he said he didn't have a valentine, so I tried to ignore it and focus on the meeting. Tackling Body FTW hadn't lessened the rest of my work, and I had an inbox full of tasks to get through, from reviewing drafts to following up with other departments. I made a quick to-do list on my notes, thinking through what I might write next. I was deciding between a few ideas, but I turned the page when Maricela said my name and asked me to work with the art team on an upcoming photo shoot. Her tone and question were casual, like she asked me to do things like that all the time. I caught Claire's stunned expression in my periphery. "Sure. I'd love to!"

After that, the mental dance routine continued, because everything was coming up Britta, and I allowed my thoughts to wander to Wes being single.

# 14

WES

PEARL LOOKED POINTEDLY at her watch. "You needed to leave five minutes ago."

I pretended to be engrossed in the to-do list I'd made during my last conversation with Aaron. "I know."

"If that were true, you would have left five minutes ago. Cord told me you might do this."

"Since when do you and Cord talk about my appointments?"

She ignored my question and grabbed my messenger bag, snatching my phone and slipping it in. "The car is downstairs."

"Cord should mind his own business," I muttered, pushing to my feet.

"Talk to your best friend about that." I expected her to return to her desk once she'd dragged me from my office, but she stepped onto the elevator with me. "You're a flight risk."

Rolling my eyes, I leaned against the wall of the elevator like a sullen teenager. "Where are we meeting?"

"Margo's. A diner on the South Side."

I clenched my fist at my side. I was familiar with Margo's. Kelsey had picked the location of our first date as well as our last date for our lunch meeting. I thought about canceling on principle alone.

"Who is this woman, Wes?"

I stepped from the elevator and took quick strides across the polished marble floor of the lobby. "The head of HottrYou."

"Yes, of that I'm aware." She kept up with me effortlessly, tall heels clacking. "Who is she to *you*?"

Pearl nodded her head to the black sedan parked fifty feet up the street. Even before opening the outer doors, the chill of the winter day crept over me. It was the cold, or the physical manifestation of how much I didn't want to go to this meeting.

"I'm surprised Cord didn't give you a full report while debriefing you on my schedule." I pushed open the door and stepped into the frigid February day. "She's my ex-girlfriend."

Pearl called after me, "Next time I'll remind Cord to get to the good stuff first."

I sat in the back seat and tapped my fingers against my leg before pulling out my phone as we inched through traffic. Out the window, a man in a heavy gray coat loaded flowers and balloons into the back of a florist delivery van. Red and pink bouquets provided a sharp contrast to the blustery, colorless day. Thinking about B and her flower recommendations, I snapped a photo of the open trunk and attached it to a message.

---

**From:** FitMiCoachWes1

**To:** Bmoney34

**Sent:** February 14, 11:55 a.m.


B,


Lots of roses in this pic. Are you sure about your recommendations? I hope you're having a good day.


Wes

Even as I hit send, I knew I shouldn't. I'd set up the coaching program to avoid impropriety and keep communication professional. I set my phone aside, because I felt myself pulled to break my own rules and I didn't like it. There was something about B that made me not only ignore the voice of reason in my head but permanently mute it.

---

**From:** Bmoney34
**To:** FitMiCoachWes1
**Sent:** February 14, 11:58 a.m.

Wes,

Amateurs. I wouldn't lead you astray. I hope you haven't bought boxes of fiber-loaded, fat-free, sugar-free, flavor-free carob for your friends and loved ones today.

B

P.S. Your weather looks as bad as mine. Where in the country are you? Can I ask that?

*Shit.* Another rule out the window. I always told new coaches to follow three rules related to their identity: Don't give out your real name, don't send photos, and keep your location private. As I thought through how to respond, the car stopped in front of Margo's. I'd have to wait to reply to B. I took a slow, cleansing breath that did nothing to ease the full-body twitchiness coursing through me. Thanking the driver, I reluctantly stepped out.

The faded green awning and chipped gold paint on the window hadn't changed. I wasn't sure why I expected this to be different from the hundreds of other times I'd walked into the space. The smell of coffee and fries was inviting, and the diner buzzed. Nothing about this place was trendy or fancy, but it felt a lot like home. Unfortunately, much like going home, I had no idea what to expect when I got there.

I glanced around until I spotted her. Unlike the diner, everything about Kelsey was different. Her hair, formerly long and the color of milk chocolate, was now blond and cut above her shoulders. Her face looked thinner, and her glasses were gone. I'd always kind of liked her glasses. She waved, and the same smile I'd tried hard to earn all those years crossed her face. The wave of pride I felt when I got one swept over me without my consent.

"Wes." She stood, a fitted dark blue dress and jacket giving her a poise I'd forgotten. She leaned in, wrapping an arm around my back to pull me into a stiff hug.

I inhaled the scent of her shampoo, and the memories of being with her, being close to her, rushed over me.

"Hey, Kelsey."

"It's good to see you." Her voice was clear and businesslike.

We settled into the booth, and a familiar uneasiness crept over me.

"I didn't think you'd ever agree to meet with me," she said, tucking a blond strand behind her ear with a manicured red fingernail. She never used to paint her nails.

"You were persistent."

"Persistence is one of my better qualities."

"I remember."

I looked at the menu, though it was just to keep my hands busy. We had a routine here. She'd order a big, greasy burger with fries. I'd order a grilled chicken sandwich and a salad, and the waitress would give me the side-eye, questioning if she should take my man card before or after bringing the check.

"I'm glad you came."

I continued to study the menu. "What did you want to discuss?"

"It's been a long time. How are you? So much has changed." She set her own menu aside and dabbed at the condensation dripping off her glass.

A waitress approached our table. "What can I get you?"

Kelsey asked for a salad with no dressing and a plain chicken breast, and I ordered a burger.

"I guess things have changed," she said with a smile.

I met her eye then, my expression unmoving. "Guess so." Her comment pushed my unease into something more like distrust.

She tapped her fingers gently against the table. "Yeah, anyway. I'm sure you've seen our new ads. I'd hoped to tell you in person before the latest campaign launched, but you wouldn't call me back."

My silence made her anxious. She hated silence.

"So, we went ahead. But I wanted you guys to understand it's not personal. It's just business."

*Just business.* That's what she said when she broke up with me and left our company in the same week.

She rearranged her water glass. I had an urge to reach over and push it an inch to the left, moving it off-center of her napkin just to disrupt her sense of order. "And our customer bases are so different. But I knew you'd take it personally, even after all this time, and I still care about you, Wes."

I nodded, wishing I was the kind of guy who would get up and just walk out.

"Are you going to say anything?"

I wanted to tell her I didn't think about her anymore, that I didn't call her back because I was too busy living the life she didn't want to share with me, to hit her somewhere it would hurt. Instead, I kept my voice steady. "You're hiring inexperienced coaches. That's a bad idea, Kels."

She shook her head, a tight smile crossing her lips. It wasn't welcoming or kind; it was her I'm-disappointed-in-you expression. "I didn't come here to ask your advice, Wes. I wanted to talk to you."

"Well, we're talking, and I'm telling you it's not safe."

"I realize you have a *degree* in this, but the basics of teaching people to exercise and eat right aren't that complicated. We have a good training program."

She said "degree" as if it wasn't real. As if the five years of biology, anatomy, chemistry, nutrition, biomechanics, and exercise physiology I'd taken were just glorified dodgeball courses.

"It's more than that. There's nuance, and people can get hurt."

The waitress returned with our food, and we stared at each other in silence.

"Noted." Kelsey shook out her napkin. "While we're here, I was hoping we could let bygones be bygones. We're competitors, but we don't have to be enemies. I'd like us to reconnect, to be civil. I—" She paused, drinking water as if the words were stuck in her throat. "I miss you, Wes."

I stared at her without responding.

Kelsey brushed my hand, and the flash of vulnerability fell from her face when I jerked my arm back at the touch.

"Okay." I took a long drink of water. "You're not interested in what I think about your company and you've already made your move. It's been years. What do you want, Kelsey? Why are we here?"

She inhaled as if steeling herself. "I want to apologize."

"Apologize for what?"

"For ending things the way I did. It was . . . I've felt bad about that for a long time."

I'd taken her to Margo's for dinner. Kelsey hated fanfare and big gestures, so I planned to ask her to marry me in our place—our corner of the world—over chocolate milkshakes, her favorite. I'd practiced everything I would say a hundred times, making sure she knew that our family would have everything we'd both grown up without—affection, security, and consistency. I was certain she would say yes, that she'd stay by my side. The tiny diamond ring was the most expensive item I'd ever purchased, and I'd been saving for a year. But when I reached down to make sure the box was still in my pocket and opened my mouth to say "Let's splurge on milkshakes," she spoke instead.

"Wes, I got an offer to work with another app. They have the capital and the investors all lined up, and they want me to lead it. Can you believe it? I'm going to accept the offer." She arranged her water glass so it touched the top of her knife, eyes not leaving mine. "And I think it's best if we end things, too."

Her voice had been so steady, so cool, I was waiting for a punch line. When none came, my hand stilled, fingers around the box. "What? Why?"

"With the two businesses, it would be too complicated, and it's better if I'm alone. Sometimes it feels like I'm all you have, and that's too much pressure, Wes. Plus, this is a huge opportunity for me, and I won't have the time to—"

"We can figure it out, Kels. I don't understand." I hated that my voice sounded pleading and small. "We've been together for six years. Don't . . . don't do this."

She shook her head. "I can't be distracted with someone else's needs. I'm sorry, but you understand, right? It's not personal . . . it's just business."

My voice was deeper than I'd intended when I responded to her apology, the old hurt from earlier slamming into my chest. "It was a long time ago."

"Have you forgiven me?"

"I don't think about you anymore, Kels." Shortly after we broke up, I found out she had started dating some real estate developer. Turned out it wasn't about being alone; it was about not being with me, and it bugged me that that still stung.

She narrowed her gaze. "You're lying, but I'd like you to be in my life again. I . . ." She glanced up at the ceiling like she wasn't sure how to say what she'd come here to. "*Can* you forgive me?"

I rested my hand over my pocket, remembering the box's corners cutting into my palm. The memory of the despair and utter disbelief that had raged in me that night felt fresh, but for a moment, her makeup and new hair color fell away, and I saw Kelsey, sitting in our diner, vulnerable. I didn't want to admit, even to myself, how hearing her words made me feel. To admit how much I wanted them to mean more. Unbidden, my thoughts turned to my client B and what advice she'd give me in this situation. "Yeah, sure."

# 15

BRITTA

**LIKED BY CAROLYYYYYYN AND 726 OTHERS**

A year ago, I thought I had rhythm. I thought I could hold my own on the dance floor. Friends, let me tell you, I had no idea what I was getting into. The women in my hip-hop dance class schooled me. Did I mention I showed up for the 60+ class by accident? They welcomed me anyway, and took pity on me when I messed up the steps, lost the beat, and dropped an f-bomb when I fell on my butt. More than taking pity on me, they cheered me on and invited me to come back. Who is helping you stick to your goals? #SquadGoals #BestLife

WHEN I FINISHED class, sweat running down every crevice on my body, I collapsed on the bench in the corner of the room. Helen's new routine had been a tough one. I didn't expect to have my butt kicked so thoroughly after a year of having taken the class.

Chugging my water, I glanced at the grayed-out mailbox icon—no new messages. Wes hadn't responded since our exchange about the flowers, and I wondered if asking him where he lived was too personal.

Helen, a petite woman in her seventies, joined me and stretched. Her flexibility was amazing, and she loved to tease me. "You're getting better."

I self-consciously started my new stretching routine, trying to remember the video tutorials Wes had encouraged me to emulate. "You think I'm still the weakest link in the class, huh?" I slowed my breath while unsuccessfully swinging my leg up behind me to catch it and stretch my quads.

"Of course, but we've all got forty or fifty years on you."

I watched the woman effortlessly raise her leg. I gave up on my stretch and silently promised Wes I'd do it when I got home.

"You always tell it like it is."

"No other way to tell it." She patted my back and finished her stretch. "I've got to get ready for my date. Get out of here and go enjoy Valentine's Day."

OUTSIDE, COUPLES HOLDING hands strolled down the sidewalks like it was a lovely May evening and not a frigid February night. They were apparently warmed by their love. *Blech.* My gym bag slung over my shoulder, I hurried into the cold to catch a bus.

I wondered what Ben was up to. He didn't like Valentine's Day, saying it was a Hallmark holiday and people made too big a deal of it. I actually loved the idea of a whole day to celebrate love.

My phone pinged then, and I smiled.

---

**From:** FitMiCoachWes1
**To:** Bmoney34
**Sent:** February 14, 7:49 p.m.

B,

Just for you, I got fiber-rich, low-sugar, low-fat, low-flavor Mocko-late instead.

I'm in Chicago, too. Hi, neighbor! How was your Valentine's Day?
Looks like you got a good workout from what you added on the
app.

Wes

---

**From:** Bmoney34
**To:** FitMiCoachWes1
**Sent:** February 14, 7:51 p.m.

Is Mockolate a real thing? I think I've only heard of that from an
old episode of *Friends*.

Good to know you're close by in case I need to ping you if I break
something keeping up with the badass retirees in my hip-hop
dance class.

Uneventful V Day, just work and my hot date with these ladies.
Jealous?

B

P.S. Your company should get a chat function—would be
easier than the email messaging, though you'd get tired of me
faster.

After the short ride to my stop, I hustled to my front door to escape
the cold and swirling wind. I peeled off my clothes once inside my apartment. Though taking off a sweaty sports bra was the kind of challenge
invented by a masochist, I'd earned this state of disgusting. Before I
stepped into the hot shower, I glanced at my phone.

---

**From:** FitMiCoachWes1
**To:** Bmoney34
**Sent:** February 14, 7:53 p.m.

I don't know if Mockolate is a real thing outside of *Friends*. Seems like it should be, though. If I find some, I'll get it for you.

Am I jealous of you bumping and grinding with them? I plead the Fifth.

Good idea on the chat, and I'll mention it to the tech people. I don't think I'd ever get sick of messaging you, though. We can use Chat App, if you want. I'm at WesTheBear.

Mockolately yours,

T.S.

Under the stream of hot water, my muscles relaxed. I weighed his suggestion, debating if moving into a messaging conversation was ethical. There was nothing especially unprofessional about it. We'd still be talking about him coaching me. Chatting just seemed more personal. That's why I'd suggested it—imagining being able to have real-time conversations that felt like conversations versus emailing back and forth. I could keep a conversation on track, and we'd have no reason to veer off into something else. I let the bodywash run into the drain. *Unless he kind of likes me* . . . I squashed the thought. Chatting was just easier; it wasn't like we'd be meeting in person, and it might give me good new material for the project.

When I stepped out and pulled on my robe, I typed in his screen name.

**Bmoney34:** WesTheBear? Are you particularly burly and bearded?

I pulled on a T-shirt and a pair of flannel boxer shorts I'd kept from a boyfriend in college.

**WesTheBear:** Just a Bears fan. Your question illuminates why I've been getting so many invitations for dates on here for so long.

**Bmoney34:** LOL. I'm here to help. I think Tube Sock fits you better, anyway.

**WesTheBear:** I'm not sure that would lessen the weird emails.

**Bmoney34:** It must be so hard to be a man online today. So much unwanted attention.

**WesTheBear:** You have no idea.

**Bmoney34:** Are you still at work?

**WesTheBear:** Home. Why?

**Bmoney34:** Just wondering if you were burning the midnight oil talking to clients.

**WesTheBear:** Just you.

I grinned at his comment, wandering into the kitchen.

**Bmoney34:** Good. I hate sharing.

**WesTheBear:** Kindergarten must have been rough for you.

**Bmoney34:** The absolute worst. If the FitMi plan involves sharing my box of crayons, you have your work cut out for you.

**WesTheBear:** I'll only ask for temporary use of green.

**Bmoney34:** Hmm . . . regular green or one of the fancy ones?

**WesTheBear:** Fancy ones?

**Bmoney34:** Wes, what am I going to do with you? When I hit my next milestone, I'll tell you about the fancy greens. A tit-for-tat thing.

**WesTheBear:** You paid for coaching with real money.

**Bmoney34:** Details.

**WesTheBear:** Speaking of, how'd the class go? Aside from the average age of your fellow dancers.

**Bmoney34:** I always love it! I measured my heart rate like you suggested, and it was pumping.

**WesTheBear:** What was it?

**Bmoney34:** 145. That's good, right?

**WesTheBear:** Right in the target zone.

**Bmoney34:** So, can you help me figure out what in my fridge will make a good dinner? Is that part of the service?

**WesTheBear:** Show me what we're working with.

**Bmoney34:** [Photo attached] Slim pickings. I haven't had time to go grocery shopping. All this produce you have me eating goes bad fast. Your fridge probably looks like an aisle at Whole Foods, huh?

**WesTheBear:** [Photo attached]

I clapped my hand over my mouth and giggled. His open refrigerator contained beer and water, a few bottles of a blue power drink, several yogurt containers, and a jar of mustard.

**Bmoney34:** Should I trust you to give me nutrition advice? Where is your food?

**WesTheBear:** That mustard has some nutrients in it. The yogurt, too, before it expired.

**Bmoney34:** When did it expire?

**WesTheBear:** Let's focus on you.

Wes sent me a link to the site's nutrition section and cookbook. He told me they'd added some of his recipes to the "weeknight meals" section. I was pleasantly surprised to find an easy, tasty dish I could make using some frozen turkey meatballs. We chatted about food and cooking while I made dinner, and I took an artful photo of the finished product.

**Bmoney34:** [Photo attached] What do you think?

**WesTheBear:** Bon appétit *raises a jar of mustard to you*

**Bmoney34:** This is the weirdest Valentine's Day dinner I've ever had.

**Bmoney34:** Not that this is a date or anything, of course.

He hadn't responded, and I blew out a frustrated breath. I would be damned if Claire got to move ahead without me because I'd weirded out my coach. He thankfully ignored the comment, though.

**WesTheBear:** Any reason you didn't upload a photo for your starting image? Lots of people like seeing their progress.

I'd told myself it was to protect my privacy, but it was more than that. I'd never liked seeing before-and-after photos, because looking more like the before than the after photo always made me feel like I had work to do, even when I was perfectly happy with my photo on its own. Claire and I had agreed to not do that for this project, not that I could explain that to Wes.

**Bmoney34:** I didn't have a good photo.

**WesTheBear:** That seems like a poor excuse . . .

**Bmoney34:** Am I that transparent?

**WesTheBear:** I think you have a phone with a camera, is all. It's okay—you don't have to post. Some people like to see the changes as they go through the program—not that you're doing it to change.

**WesTheBear:** I'm sure you're beautiful just as you are.

Aside from my parents and my best friends, no adult had ever called me beautiful, not since my high school boyfriend, Calvin. I wasn't sure how to respond, because my heart hammered.

**Bmoney34:** That's a good line. You should take on a side hustle coaching for a dating site.

**WesTheBear:** My track record is better with fitness. New home-work?

**Bmoney34:** Hit me, Tube Sock.

**WesTheBear:** Stock the fridge again, but this weekend, make a meal plan, and prep as much as possible ahead of time. Here are three links to a <u>shopping guide</u>, a <u>list</u> of easy make-ahead meals, and <u>resources on meal planning</u> in general.

**Bmoney34:** I can do that. Ready for your homework?

**WesTheBear:** Who's the coach here?

**Bmoney34:** Tit for tat, remember?

While I waited for his response and enjoyed the last bite of my tasty dinner, I found the email I'd sent Ben the night before. He hadn't responded to my invitation to watch basketball.

**WesTheBear:** Okay. Tit for tat. What's my homework?

**Bmoney34:** Same assignment. You need more than mustard.

**WesTheBear:** For you, I will buy ketchup.

# 16

## WES

"YOU'RE IN A good mood," Mason commented, sliding a stack of printouts across the table in our office. "And I doubt it has anything to do with the way my team has been *crushing* it in the last month." He raised his voice when he said "crushing," and adopted a singsong tone.

He was an ass, but he was good at his job. In the month since Valentine's Day, we'd run a series of ads featuring our coaches sharing what they learned at different stages of their education and training. It had worked to feature some coaches who were hot, according to Mason's team, despite my initial protests. Since the previous month, our new registrations were up, and we seemed to be outpacing HottrYou.

Mason lowered his voice as if this were a private, male-bonding moment. "C'mon, don't hold out on me. You're finally getting laid, right?"

"Anyway," Cord interjected, reading my expression. "Tell us what's next."

Mason returned to his tablet, speaking as he scrolled. "It would be nice if we had an inside source at HottrYou."

Cord huffed out a short laugh. "Kelsey didn't give anything up when you met with her last month, did she?"

"No." I looked down at the printouts, colorful charts of market share and cost projections. "Not really."

I saw Mason's stare out of the corner of my eye. "Want to elaborate?"
"No."

"C'mon, Wes. I'm trying to do my job here." Mason's ever-present smirk shifted to a frustrated grimace. "Nothing at all we could use?"

"It was personal."

Cord shot me a curious look across the table. I'd been purposefully vague about the meeting with Kelsey. Cord was my best friend, but Kelsey and I shared something different, even after breaking up. She'd grown up like me, with an emotionally abusive mom and her dad in and out of prison. No matter how badly it had ended between us, she'd been there for me back then. We'd darkly called ourselves the fucked-up families club, and it was members only.

"Fine," Mason said. He walked us through the data, detailing how the initiatives were playing out in different markets. When he advised we change our font colors, I tuned out of the conversation. Cord was following along, and I knew I should care, but I just didn't. I jotted down some notes on the legal pad in front of me about ideas for working with the kids. We were running a weeklong training program with them at the end of the summer and then paying some of our coaches to mentor. Through Jake and Naya, we had hired a college student she worked with to help us. Quinn was studying education and was eager to join in. It was all coming together, and we were ready to work with the student leaders within the next couple months.

The screen on my phone flashed, and I grinned before dismissing it. I was sure it was B. No one else messaged me on the app now that the other client I'd taken on had decided not to continue with coaching. I'd gotten used to B's messages, used to that feeling of letting out a breath when I read them.

We'd been chatting a couple times a day for the last few weeks. It always started with exercise or nutrition, healthy habits and new challenges. It always started with coaching like it was supposed to, but I'd glance at the time stamp and realize we'd spent an hour going back and forth. It was too much, and I needed to check whatever this was that drew me to her, but it was hard, because I was genuinely interested in her love of the Bears and her collection of Stephen King novels she reread all the time even though she'd get scared. I wanted to know more about her.

It gave me a weird, full feeling in my chest when she told me about an accomplishment. It made B happy to meet small milestones, and knowing she was proud of herself reminded me I was doing something that mattered. She was always so appreciative.

Glancing up from my phone, I noticed Mason looking at me expectantly. "Yeah, sure," I answered, not knowing what he'd asked. He kept talking, and I glanced back at my phone, subtly tapping the screen.

**Bmoney34:** Today, I saw a squirrel.

**WesTheBear:** Stop the presses.

**Bmoney34:** I wasn't done yet! The squirrel was pawing through a container of salad someone dropped.

"Wes?" Mason's voice cut into my thoughts.

"Sorry, what?"

"The content on *Best Life*, have you been reading it? It's great press, even with them covering both platforms."

I had no idea what he was talking about. More and more, I had these reminders I was unqualified to run this company. "Um, no. I haven't."

Cord chimed in. "I've skimmed bits and pieces. I forget her name, but the woman covering us is funny, and it seems like she's having a good experience."

Mason tapped out something on his phone. "I'd like to see how we can capitalize on other opportunities. Check it out, though. I've got a meeting across town, but I'm sending you the link now." Mason gathered his things and answered a call on the way out the door.

My own phone buzzed.

**Bmoney34:** Reminded me of you.

**Bmoney34:** He really digs salad.

Cord shifted his gaze to me in his patient, I'm-going-to-wait-for-you-to-talk way.

I schooled my expression. "Sorry. Client."

Cord nodded absently. "What did Kelsey want? You never said. It really wasn't about business?"

"She wants to be friends again."

"Friends or *friends*?" Cord's expression said it all. *Stop doing things just to make other people happy.*

"I know what you're going to say. So, don't."

"Okay," he said.

"She feels bad about how she ended things." I paced to the window. "Who knows. Maybe we could be friends."

"Okay."

"It's not like I'm giving her a kidney or something."

"I didn't say anything." Cord sat back in his chair and placed his palms on the table. "Just . . . watch out. I know you want to be distracted right now, but I don't think that's the distraction you want." I glanced at my phone. I knew exactly the distraction I wanted.

# 17

BRITTA

**LIKED BY NOMORENOSEPICKERS AND 965 OTHERS**

Can you believe it's almost April? Springtime means warmer weather and ditching these coats. I can't wait! I'm #TeamFitMi, but I want to post about hotness today. I remember the first time I described myself as hot. I was a sophomore in college, and I said it as a joke. None of my friends laughed like I assumed they would—they thought I was serious, and the conversation kept going. All these years later, I remember that "oh" feeling when they didn't laugh. I realized the joke wasn't funny, that it wasn't a joke at all. I was allowed to call and believe myself hot. I think a lot of us are waiting for permission for that moment, for someone else to validate it. I'm not waiting anymore, but how about you? Reply with "I'm hot," and see how it feels! #TeamBritta #BodyFTW

"LOOK AT YOU!" RJ looked me up and down as we waited for our table. "Do you know how good you look in those jeans?"

"Actually, I do." I struck a pose for my friend. Before arriving, I'd sent

Wes a picture of my pedometer total with eight exclamation points, my brightly painted nails next to the red numbers.

He replied right away—Wes always replied. As expected, he asked me how I felt. I loved it when he asked that.

Next to us, Kat ended the heated conversation she'd been having with her husband. "Sorry about that. What did I miss?" Kat's natural hair was pulled back, an explosion of curls sitting atop her head. She was schooling her expression, though it wasn't like we didn't know her husband was kind of a jackass and had probably just said something to upset her.

"Just that Britta is hot AF," RJ said, waving as Del walked through the door.

Kat smiled, a real smile this time. "Britta has always been hot AF."

"That's what I've been saying," I said, leaning in for a hug and seeing Del rush in the door.

Five years into his PhD in sociology, Del already looked the part of scatterbrained professor. Though always handsome, he was perpetually exhausted, and there was only ever a fifty percent chance his socks would match. "I'm starving. I didn't have time to eat lunch today."

I swatted at him. "Do better." Being around Del was like having a little brother. A grown-ass little brother who couldn't seem to stick with a research topic and was on his way to being a lifelong student.

He gave me a side hug as the hostess led us to our table. "I'll try."

Kat set her menu aside. Really, we always ordered the same thing, so looking was a bit farcical. "So, how is the research going, Del?"

"Ugh," he groaned. "I spent all day debating whether to stick with my current topic or change to something I'm more interested in. My adviser might kill me if I switch again."

"We'll kill you if you switch again," RJ said over the menu.

Del groaned and ran his palm over his face. "Can we talk about something else? Britta, how's your work thing going?"

"Good so far." I told them about the funny piece I'd written on learning the unspoken rules of the locker room, complete with a retelling about the woman who liked to air-dry following her shower. Claire had written about the impostor syndrome of being around lots of fit people. I'd been surprised and a little encouraged that even Claire felt that way sometimes. The previous week, I'd posted about the emotional release of seeing the numbers on the treadmill decrease at the end of a sprint. We were falling into a rhythm of give-and-take that worked. In the third week, we'd both written about our coaches. Mine read like an ode, and I wanted to share it with Wes but couldn't.

Maricela was pleased with both Claire's and my work, but there was only one position available on the writing staff, and so far, Claire's posts generated more traffic than mine. I tried to push down the insecurities that surfaced every time I saw Claire outshining me. Still, Maricela had tasked me with working on the cover shoot, and that was something.

"I never thought I'd enjoy all of this salad and sweating, but it's kind of fun. Wes gives me homework, and you know I love smashing a check-list, so it's working."

Del spoke from behind his menu, adjusting the arms of his glasses. "That's your coach?"

"Yeah, he's great. Supportive."

Kat raised her brows. "Is he cute?"

I pictured him tall and tan or dark-skinned and broad. Sometimes I imagined he wore glasses and polo shirts, and other times I envisioned him with gelled hair and sunglasses. I caught myself studying men while on the 'L,' wondering if the guy reading the *Tribune* or wearing the red sweatshirt was him. *Please don't let him be the greasy guy in the* FBI: Firm Breast Inspector *T-shirt.*

"I have no idea what he looks like." I checked the screen of my phone absently, like his photo might magically appear. "Not that it matters."

Del still didn't look up, but chimed in. "Just make sure you don't end up with some kind of crush on him like that hipster guy."

I harrumphed. "I don't have a crush on Ben. He's a friend, and we're actually having dinner later this week."

Kat and RJ exchanged a worried look before RJ let out a slow "Ohhh-kay."

"What? I promised to cook for him." I thought I did a decent job of keeping my voice and mannerisms cool. Even though Ben had been to my place tons of times with nothing happening, I still hoped that something might blossom between us. I'd wanted that for so long, it was almost a habit. But I'd been thinking about him less since I signed up for coaching and began talking to Wes more.

My friends nodded, saying nothing.

"What?" I bit my lip and examined RJ's face as she looked ever the skeptic. "I'm not getting my hopes up, don't worry."

RJ laughed as the waiter approached. "You'll have to tell us how it goes."

My phone buzzed on the table, a photo of his fridge open and fully stocked appearing under Wes's name. Since our first chat conversation, I'd been teasing him about his lack of real food.

**Wes:** Tit for tat. Thought you'd like to see I was keeping up with my homework.

# 18

## WES

I TRUDGED UP the crumbling concrete stairs and knocked even though I had a key. The paint on the front door was chipped and scuffed.

When I was a kid, we'd moved from crappy apartment to dubious basement until we'd get evicted, pick up our stuff, and start over again somewhere new. I'd tell Libby it was an adventure and make up a story about why we had to leave. She stopped believing the stories in second grade, but I kept telling them for years after that.

Turning the knob, I cursed under my breath that the door was unlocked.

Light from behind me spilled into the dim room. "Mom?" I called, but the house was still. I peeked into her cluttered bedroom and around the corner into the galley kitchen.

I'd told her I was coming over this afternoon to take her to dinner for her birthday. It had been almost a month since I'd been in the cramped house. I paid her rent and utilities, and I'd offered to get her a nicer place, but she refused.

When I dialed her number, a stack of papers and empties on the counter vibrated, her phone lighting up under them. "Perfect," I muttered, tossing the bottles in the trash, sorting through the papers, and throwing out junk. I was about to crumple a receipt from the gas station when I saw my mom's loopy handwriting on the back.

*Ran out. Back soon.*

I tossed the note aside and cleaned off the counter before turning to the sink. I paid someone to clean the place every few weeks, but the garbage multiplied exponentially between visits, so the place remained in perpetual chaos. Cord made fun of me in college because I was adamant about our room being clean—he'd never seen my mom's place. The sink was full of dishes, plus a cookie sheet covered in burned remnants of something. *She baked?*

My phone buzzed. Chat App had been acting up one night, and we'd switched to text messaging but hadn't gone back.

**B:** Need your help. This is a grocery emergency, and since you finally stocked your fridge, I figured you were the man for the job. Do you have a few minutes?

Leaning against the counter, I tapped out a reply and tried to imagine B standing in a produce aisle, panicking.

**Wes:** How can I a-peas you?

**B:** LOL, I'm desperate.

**Wes:** Hit me.

**B:** That Thai chicken recipe you told me about, can you walk me through the tweaks you said you made?

**Wes:** Sure. Emergency, though? Does someone have a gun to your head demanding dinner?

**B:** No, I'm cooking for someone tonight.

**Wes:** Ooh, hot date?

**B:** Kind of.

My thumbs paused, and the muscles across my chest tightened as I worked through why what she said bothered me.

**Wes:** Kind of?

**B:** It's not exactly a date. That's why I need the recipe . . . to wow him.

I rolled my shoulders back to ease the tense muscles. *What? Am I planning to fight this guy?*

**Wes:** Wes to the rescue.

**B:** My hero. Thank you. I'll be quick.

**Wes:** I've got a little time. Here's the <u>link</u> to the original recipe, and I'll send you the changes.

**B:** You are the best!

**B:** Do you have your own hot date?

In my mom's cluttered kitchen that smelled like sour milk and a cheap scented candle, I couldn't fathom a date. *Would B care if I was going out with someone?* "She's a client," I muttered.

**Wes:** Family thing.

**B:** Have fun! I won't bug you anymore.

**Wes:** It's okay.

Before I could stop myself, I added a second message, knowing damn well I shouldn't.

**Wes:** You're never bugging me, and I like talking to you. So, message if you have other questions . . . or emergencies.

A siren sounded down the street, and I stared at the screen, but there was no reply. I wandered into the living room and sat on the couch. The small space was making me itchy, and I wanted to get out of there. I checked my last message to Libby, more out of habit than expecting a response. Then I kept toggling back to the conversation with B, looking for a response. *Mason might be right. I need to get laid, because this is pathetic.*

Still, a growing anxiety filled my gut as minutes passed with no Mom and no reply from B.

The cheap plastic clock on the wall ticked away, and I leaned back into the couch with a frustrated huff. Mom had been gone for at least forty-five minutes. I should have been worried, but I was annoyed, not wanting to be in the house and not wanting to abandon her on her birthday. Waiting for my mom to return from mysterious outings was something with which I had decades of practice. I glanced at my watch and let my head fall back against the couch.

STARTLED AWAKE AT the sound of the screen door clattering shut, I blinked furiously, reacclimating myself to my location. Two figures stumbled toward me in the dim room, the glow from a streetlight illuminating their path.

"Mom?"

"Chris!" She smiled; her eyes were glassy, and her consonants mushy when she spoke. She tried to walk toward me but slumped against the wall instead. "It's my birthday, baby."

The drowsiness fell away as I took in the lanky, sagging man with a gray beard and bloodshot eyes standing behind her. "Who's this?"

"This is . . ." She dreamily raised her palm to the man's chest, her head lolling back with a dewy expression. "I met him at my birthday party."

The man rested his arm on Mom's shoulder, thick half-moons of dirt showing under his long nails.

I stood taller. "You need to leave."

"The fuck I do," he slurred. "Who are you?"

"Chris, baby. He's my friend. And this is my Chris."

I took a step closer to Mom, but I didn't look away from the guy. "What are you on, Mom?"

"It's my birthday, baby. I stopped to get cigarettes, and he took me to a party."

The man was wobbly on his feet and a good four or five inches shorter than me. He smelled like whiskey.

"Leave," I said flatly, shoving the man backward and stepping between them.

"You can have her when I'm done. Nobody tells me what to do, especially not some pretty boy." He stumbled, regained his balance, and sneered at me, struggling to focus on my face, his eyes darting back and forth.

"Get your damn hands off my mother and get the hell out of here." *I don't want to hit this guy.*

"You ain't a kid, and she owes me for the oxy," he said, a smirk crossing his lips. "We'd arranged a . . . trade."

"She's not trading you shit. How much?"

"Baby, no. I have it covered," Mom said, into the wall where she was leaning.

I dug two hundred-dollar bills from my wallet and held them out to the man. "Now leave and stay the hell away from her."

He stuffed the bills in the front pocket of his grubby jeans and slunk back. "Whatever, man. Your mom likes to party. I'll see her again."

"Bye." Mom waved, sliding down the wall to sit on the worn carpet.

"Are you okay?" When I crouched down next to her, she reached for my face, her hands covering both of my cheeks.

"You should have told me you were coming over. It's my birthday."

I wanted to say that we'd made plans for me to take her out just that afternoon, that it was dangerous to bring these guys home, that I'd been worried, and she'd disappeared for hours. The hopeful kid in me wondered how she'd just forgotten her son was waiting. I swallowed it all. "Happy birthday, Mom." I wrapped an arm around her back and helped her to her feet. "Let's get you some water and then you can go to bed."

When she was settled and sleeping it off, I crashed on the couch. I'd make sure she didn't choke on her vomit, like I'd been doing since I was nine. After midnight, I pulled out my phone.

**B:** I think the chicken turned out well. [photo attached]

**B:** Wish me luck!

I pinched the bridge of my nose, tucked the phone away, and sat back on the couch, listening to Mom's snoring and the clock ticking.

*Good luck.*

# 19

BRITTA

"Hi, #TeamBritta. I wish it wasn't the case, but so much of my relationship with my body is tied up in my history with men and feeling desirable (or undesirable). Last week I told you about how I now own the word *hot*, but today I want to tell you about the first boy who made me feel the opposite, like I was the furthest thing from it. My group of friends in high school was inseparable, but one night, only Isaac and I were free to hang out. It was a night like most others, until that moment when Isaac's fingers brushed against mine in the dark movie theater and our hands intertwined. It's been ten years, but I remember those tingles that zipped through me when his fingers stroked my palm. My head swam with the turn of events, and I was sure it was the beginning to some great love story, because holding hands with Isaac was the most romantic moment of my seventeen years, and that story lasted until . . . curfew.

"I don't share this to introduce how I pined over Isaac for years (I didn't) or how that night began a lifelong love of hand-holding (it did). I share it because that night, I felt desirable, attractive, and wanted for the first time in my life. So, the next day when he said it was a mistake, I was certain feeling wanted was a mistake, too. I know I'm not alone in having one of those moments. It took me years to fully shake that and realize his assessment didn't have to shape how I felt about myself."

I GLANCED AT my reflection in the mirror, turning from one direction to another. My jeans hugged my curves. *Damn, I look good.* I thought about texting a photo of myself to Wes but stopped. That would be weird.

My stomach rumbled as the spicy smell of the chicken wafted through my small apartment. Ben wasn't coming over until close to nine, and I was starving. I was usually enjoying my evening snack by that time, and my body protested the wait. Checking myself over one more time, I returned to the kitchen to snap a photo of my handiwork—something safer to send to Wes. I wanted him in my corner tonight. The strange thing was that I'd felt guilty after telling him I was cooking for Ben, this odd feeling I was doing something wrong talking to another guy, which was silly, because of course he wouldn't care. Shortly after I hit send, Ben knocked, and I set my phone aside.

"Hey, you." He propped an arm against the doorframe and held out a bottle of wine, and an easy smile crossed his face. He wore skinny jeans and a black button-down shirt, the sleeves rolled on his forearms. His gaze trailed momentarily to the low vee of my shirt, and I gave myself a mental high five, though I wished his eyes returned to my face a little sooner than they did.

"Hey." I stepped aside and invited him in, but instead of moving around me, he pulled me in for a side hug.

"It smells great," he commented, setting the wine on the counter. "Sorry I had to make it so late. I had a meeting with the showrunner. The network ran that contest a few months ago for someone to be my cohost for an episode, and we're filming this week."

"Oh, I remember that." *I might have entered a few . . . hundred times.* "How's it going?" I asked, pretending to search for the corkscrew.

"Oh, fine." He strode up behind me, casually reaching around to grab the tool. I expected a flutter when he brushed against me, but it didn't come. "It would be more fun with you."

"I bet," I answered, stirring the chicken, my back to him.

"You look good, Britt."

"Thanks," I said, spinning into a curtsy, the wooden spoon in my hand.

"Really good," he murmured, sipping from his wineglass, his gaze traversing my body again. "That weight loss thing is working, then?"

I bristled. "The fitness project is going well. Like I said a while back, it's not about weight loss." I turned again to scoop the chicken mixture onto the cabbage leaves with the hope that he'd pick up on my correction. "Have you seen the posts Claire and I have been putting up?"

"I saw that you were posting." He took a sip from his wine, and I waited for him to share his praise. "I've been so busy, though." He accepted the plate I handed him, and we sat across from each other at my two-person kitchen table. "I'll have to check them out soon."

A thread of disappointment tugged at me. It was such a big deal for me to have content up on the site, and I wanted him to be excited for me. Ben wasn't the cheerleader type, but he'd been in my shoes, and I thought he might be proud. Wes would be proud. I'd teased him about using the same emoji to say "good job"—the confetti one—and he'd started using random emojis. That morning, I'd returned from my class with Helen and the girls to find a snowman, panda, and a fire truck on my screen. I'd grinned to myself.

"I don't need to read it to know it's great, though." Ben lifted the fork to his mouth. "And this is great. I need to let you cook for me more often."

*Not exactly sweet nothings.* "I'm glad you like it."

"I do," he said, meeting my eyes over the wineglass before dipping to my chest again.

After eating, Ben took his wine to the couch and patted the seat for me to sit next to him instead of clearing the dishes. "You can do those later. Come sit with me."

He emptied his glass, and I had the strangest urge to text Wes and get his advice.

"You really *do* look good, Britt," Ben said, his arm stretched out over the back of the couch behind me. The woody scent of his cologne filled my nose as he leaned in and brushed my hair off my shoulder, his index finger trailing down my arm in a way that left goose bumps.

"Imagine how hot you'll be as you keep going," he said, settling his palm on my knee and slowly sliding it up.

I watched his hand and expected a rush of arousal to flood my system. The deluge didn't come, and I tried to make a joke. "I don't know," I said. "I think I've always been hot." I hoped that might give him the opportunity to course-correct his gaffe.

Instead, he chuckled, saying "Sure," and leaned in. I'd imagined a first kiss with Ben hundreds of times, but I wasn't expecting him to kiss so badly, his tongue pushing past my lips and almost jabbing with a snakelike motion that made it difficult to kiss back.

"These tits, Britta. How did I not notice them before?" He palmed my breast; it felt like he was attempting to knead bread and wasn't sure how to do it. He was admiring my body, but I couldn't engage in the cognitive gymnastics to make that feel like enough.

He'd put some kind of wax on his mustache and it was scratchy, and for a flash, I wondered if Wes was clean-shaven and what he would be like against my skin. I couldn't picture him with the overly groomed facial hair Ben had. Wes probably had a day of stubble on his chin, like I found so sexy. *Wes would slow down and make sure I was into what he was doing.* I shook the thought away as the flat of Ben's tongue moved up my neck. *Focus on the guy you've been crushing on for years.* I slid a hand down Ben's chest and pushed him back. "Hey. Let's slow down. We've got all night."

His voice was muffled, mouth still pressed near my skin. "I have a thing around eleven. Let's go to your room. We've got some time." He reached for my hand, still not meeting my eyes. A quick glance over his shoulder showed me it was past ten already.

"Damn, Britta," he said, standing up and not seeming to notice I wasn't eagerly following. "You have no idea how much I need this tonight."

Ben reached for my hand again, nodding to the bedroom, but I countered, trying to pull him back to the couch. "Let's take our time."

I wanted it to be better than that first kiss. I wanted sunshine and fireworks and maybe a few minutes of pleasure in this whole thing. He sat close to me and tried to kiss my neck again, but I leaned away.

"I promised some friends I'd meet them later, but we have twenty minutes or so."

I squashed the bubbling disappointment. "I thought you might want to stay for a while."

He grimaced before sitting up in the chair and leaning forward. "Nah. It's good to know you're down for this, though. I always thought you were a little more uptight."

"What do you mean?"

"Hooking up. Friends with bennies. Casual."

*Okay, couch, you can swallow me up at any moment.*

"I'm . . . not down for that." My voice wavered, but I was determined to be honest. New Britta was bold and danced with seventy-year-old bad-asses. "I mean, I like you a lot."

"Oh, Britt." A serious expression fell into the lines of his half smile, and he dropped my hand. "No. This is fun. I love your tits, and I definitely want your mouth on me. I'd love to play around more; you're cool as hell. You know that TV is so image conscious, though, and you're not the girl I'm expected to be with. It sucks, but that's life in the spotlight, you know?"

Every bit of pride for the muscle I'd built and the milestones I'd reached deflated in that moment, and I was seventeen again, sitting there like a fool.

"Sorry you took it the wrong way, but we're still good, right?" Ben stood but held out his fist for me to bump. "Down for a little more fun before I go, though?"

I stared at him, my heart unwilling to accept the words my brain was processing, and shook my head.

He didn't seem to notice that I didn't meet his fist. "You're right. No time, anyway. I'll let myself out." He winked and patted my shoulder before striding to the door. "Thanks for dinner and . . . everything else. I'll talk to you later." He waved over his shoulder and pulled the door closed behind him.

I sat in the silence of my apartment, the smell of Ben's cologne and the aromas of the curry dinner we'd shared swirling around me, and tears welled in my eyes.

# 20

## WES

"YOU'RE ALIVE." PEARL handed me a pile of messages and eyed me when I walked into work. "What do you need, Wes? A stiff drink?"

It had been a long week, beginning with Mom getting arrested for possession again and then spent dealing with the fallout. She wasn't happy about the house arrest my lawyer had negotiated to keep her out of jail. I looked up from the messages. "Thanks, Pearl. I'm good. I had to cancel some meetings about the kids' program. Could you reschedule those?"

"Already done. You've got a free hour and then a call with the coaching supervisors. The prep is on your desk. After that, you're going to finalize the high school program curriculum with Quinn, and you'll spend most of the afternoon reviewing plans for the new videos before they go live to make sure they meet your standards."

"You filled the day with my favorite things."

"Just worked out that way." Pearl raised one shoulder and shooed me toward my office, a small smile on her face. "Welcome back."

I closed the door behind me and thumbed through the stack of papers, looking forward to my day. I turned in my chair to take in the view. I had an hour, but before I caught up on email, I wanted to reach out to B. I'd told her I had a family emergency and would be offline for a few days, but I'd regretted it, because dealing with everything and not having the distraction of her messages had made it worse. I tapped out a short check-in message and scrolled back through the thread while I waited.

I glanced at the passing clouds and was wondering what emoji combination I'd send her later when Pearl told me I had a visitor.

Before I could answer, Kelsey strode into my office past Pearl and set her coat on a chair. Pearl gave me a wry expression but pulled the door closed when I nodded that it was fine.

"Hey," I said, standing. Kelsey evaluated my expression, and the good mood I'd been feeling since stepping into my office deflated.

"Thanks for seeing me."

"You didn't really give me a choice." I motioned for her to sit, but she wandered to the floor-to-ceiling window instead, pressing a delicate fingertip to the glass. "What's up?"

"This view is incredible." Her breath left a small circle of condensation on the otherwise clear surface. "You guys really made it."

I loved the view from my office, the city spread out around me, the sky feeling closer. It was one of those what-if things we'd talked about when we started out, laying bets wondering what the future held, but I didn't feel like a walk down memory lane with her. "So did you. You're up on the thirtieth floor, aren't you?" I settled back in my desk chair and kicked myself for letting it slip I knew where her office was. The diffused light from the overcast morning lit her pale skin. I was reminded of things I'd seen in her once, loved in her.

"I guess I did." She spoke in an airy voice, stepping back to sit on the edge of my desk, her crossed legs angled toward me. Her pencil skirt rode up above her knee, and she rested one hand on the smooth wooden surface. "Well, kind of."

"Kind of?"

Kelsey's evasive tone was one I knew well from years of half answers. A familiar annoyance clawed at me, but I tried to push it away. *I told her I'd be her friend. I should at least try.*

"I've got a busy day. What did you want to talk about?"

"I need your help." She said it so matter-of-factly, it took me off guard. "We're going under."

"What? Who?" I should have gone on the defense—I knew Kelsey well enough to be suspicious—but I was too surprised to plan my response.

"HottrYou." Kelsey slid off the desk with a sigh and returned to the window. "My crew is good, but they don't have your expertise. We can't compete." She turned, looking at me with affection. Even when we'd been together, she almost never allowed me to see such unguarded emotion. "I didn't realize your passion mattered until I didn't have it around me anymore."

The look was fleeting, just a second or two, but it shook me. On the few occasions she'd shown that soft side when we were together, I'd felt that same disequilibrium, and I hated that she still did that to me, that she still made me care.

I leaned back in my chair, creating space between Kelsey and me. "What are you going to do?"

Her jaw tensed and her expression cooled as she looked out the window. "What do you think I should do?"

"Kels, you're our biggest competitor. Are you actually asking me for advice?" It had come out harsher than I'd meant it to. "Anyway, you know I'm shit with the business side of things."

"I know." She abruptly stepped back from the window and leaned against the edge of my desk again, this time closer to me, one leg crossed over the other inches from my knee. "I have a proposition."

"Okay . . ." This meeting had spun out of my control. "Do you want to sit?"

"I'm fine." She gripped the edge of the desk with both palms. "I think you should merge with HottrYou and bring me on as your head of operations. You never hired a COO, right?"

I pushed back in my chair, creating more distance between us.

"Hear me out." She touched the toe of her black shoe to my foot. "FitMi is the stronger platform, but we still have a large client base looking for what we deliver—the promise of being hot, attractive . . ." She tapped her toe against my calf and slid it for just an inch or two. "Wanted."

"Kels . . ."

"You, me, and Cord. We were a good team, and I would bring the strong parts of HottrYou with me. We consistently outpace you with younger consumers, and our social media game is far superior. This could be mutually beneficial." She looked down, eyes searching mine. "And you and me, we were good together, too. I'd forgotten that."

She settled her hands on either side of my chair and hovered over me, her open shirt at my eyeline and her scent surrounding me. "I messed up," she said, her voice soft, eyes inches from mine. "But I think we could be good again, in business and . . ." She trailed a finger up my forearm, tracing the tattoo. "Elsewhere."

Those soft, teasing touches used to turn me on, and she knew it.

I gently pulled her hands from the chair and stood, our chests brushing for a moment. I walked to the window, and Kelsey huffed, falling into my chair.

"This is a lot to consider, Kels."

She crossed her arms over her chest and raised an eyebrow. "Of course," she said, composed. "I don't expect a decision now."

"Let me talk to Cord about it, okay?"

"Sure," she said, rising to her feet and looking at the watch on her thin wrist. "I should go." She smoothed down her skirt, then held out a palm. She gripped my hand after the shake, though, and pulled in closer. "It could work, Wes."

I nodded and she kissed my cheek. I expected the same rush from all those years before, but I felt nothing except the dry brush of her lips, and without thinking, I glanced at my phone, hoping to see a message from B.

# 21

BRITTA

**LIKED BY BRIGUYATABOOKSTORE AND 882 OTHERS**

I'm a little under the weather today and not my usual witty self, #TeamBritta. Back soon!

CLAIRE'S VOICE CUT through my thoughts. "Are you listening to me?" She cast a dismissive look across the table at me, and heat rose on my cheeks. It had been a week since my night with Ben. The night when I'd gotten what I wanted without getting anything I wanted. I couldn't shake the nagging thoughts. *I don't measure up.*

"Sorry. What were you saying?" We were meeting about Body FTW, but my head wasn't in the game. Claire's work was still outperforming mine. I rarely let that get to me, but I was having trouble fighting the feeling that I didn't measure up anywhere.

The progress I'd been so proud of in the previous days and weeks seemed pathetic. I'd doubled up on my workouts, and having something to push through felt like a good distraction. I'd gone for longer and longer walks and skipped the dance class in favor of a spin class that kicked my butt, but it didn't exactly help me forget. When Ben made it clear I could be dismissed so easily, the rejection had washed over me like a wave, and I never wanted someone to have the ammunition to make me feel like that again. RJ would tell me that was ridiculous, and Del would lecture me on having agency, so I'd ignored their texts. Wes had asked about the changes but returned my message earlier in the week saying he was busy with some personal issues and would be slow to respond for a few days. I'd been equal parts disappointed at not getting to talk to him and relieved I didn't have to explain myself.

Claire rolled her eyes. "I said that we need to mix things up—we could do a week where we're more intentionally critical of the platforms. Point out shortcomings. What do you think?"

"Sure," I said, jotting down *critical* in the notebook in front of me.

"No input?"

"It sounds fine, Claire."

Claire looked me up and down, eyes narrowing. "You never just agree with me. Are you sick?"

"I haven't been sleeping well. Maricela has me working on arranging that photo shoot, and it's been a nightmare. The idea is fine." My head pounded and my stomach felt cavernous, leaving me a little dizzy, but I attempted a smile.

I assumed my body would adjust and could handle the headaches and dizziness temporarily. My hands shook with all the caffeine I'd consumed to make up for the early-morning trip to the gym.

Claire's cold expression thawed. "Are you sure you're okay, Britta? I know we're competing or whatever, but you don't look good."

I didn't have the energy to scan her words for sarcasm. "Maybe I'm coming down with something, too."

"Get out of here. You know Maricela's policy on bringing germs to work."

"Maybe," I mumbled. I felt awful, but I'd lost a few pounds in the last four days. No matter what Wes said, those numbers had to matter and were proof it was working. It wasn't healthy, but I wouldn't do it forever, just enough to get a boost, just until I felt stronger and could push Ben's words out of my head. My cheeks heated as I thought back to my promise to the audience to tell them the truth about this journey and my intentions to love my body. *Do I love it today?* The path I'd jumped onto felt shameful but also seemed like the best option. That said, all I'd heard from anyone else was how I looked tired and sick.

I couldn't bring that into Body FTW, so I kept writing the same way, putting on a smile and only beating myself up in private.

I glanced at my phone, where a message from Wes was waiting.

**Wes:** Sorry I've been MIA. Family stuff. How's it going?

**B:** Hanging in there.

**Wes:** You've been working out like a machine. Anything going on?

**B:** Just pushing myself.

**Wes:** Taking care of yourself, too?

**B:** Been busy. I gotta go. Not feeling well.

I set my phone down and stood, the room swirling around me as my mouth went dry. *When did I last drink water?* I'd had three cups of black coffee that morning. The bitter taste lingered in my mouth. I checked in with Maricela's secretary and let her know I was going home. The energy it took to pack up my things seemed Herculean, and I slumped against the wall as I took the elevator down to the street level. I felt guilty being so clipped with Wes. He was just doing his job.

I ordered a ride, cursing myself for losing the opportunity to get in more steps by walking home. After I climbed into the back seat, I tapped out another message.

**B:** Sorry. I'll talk to you later. Just getting home.

The car pulled up outside my building, and I trudged inside, determined to still get some kind of exercise, since I couldn't imagine hitting the gym feeling like this. I circled around the elevator and stepped into the stairwell, the concrete circling above me in a dizzying tessellation. I started up the stairs to my apartment. My footsteps echoed in the empty stairwell as I made my way higher. My phone buzzed in my hand, and I glanced down.

**Wes:** I'm not trying to nag you. Just concerned. Take it easy and get some rest, ok?

A fresh wave of guilt washed over me. If I told him the truth, he would tell me to be patient and say I was doing great, the way he always did. He'd ask me how I felt and tell me to check in with my body, but he wasn't the one who had touched me and found me lacking. I rounded the landing outside the third floor, my breath coming heavily. I gripped the railing and closed my eyes against the swirling in my head, the dizziness returning.

"What am I doing?" My voice bounced off the concrete walls. I'd wanted Ben forever, but kissing him hadn't even been good. Now I was lying to my coach, the man who occupied more and more of my thoughts. I was not eating enough, and all to feel this horrid, all to prove some point to myself that guys like Ben couldn't hurt me again. It was like a switch flipped in my brain. When I got home, I was going to figure out how to get back on track, maybe ask Wes for help. The dizziness passed and I stepped forward, eager to fall onto my couch and see his words on my screen, but my leg cramped and I lost my balance grabbing for it.

There was a weightless moment, and my body twisted in the air. There was a strange flash of awareness before panic set in. *I'm falling. Falling!* I didn't have time to tense before I hit the concrete, crashing step by step down, but I couldn't get ahold of anything to slow my fall. My head smacked into the last stair before the landing, and I didn't move, afraid I couldn't. I tried to roll to my side, and my body screamed.

I fumbled for my phone, praying it wasn't destroyed. A crack down the screen split it in two, but I could type out *Help* before the edges of my vision darkened.

# 22

WES

CORD KNOCKED ON my door before stepping in. "Welcome back. How's your mom?"

I shrugged and he nodded. "Got it. Let me know when you need help with whatever." Cord pulled the string on his hoodie and sat across from me. "So, do you want to talk about what Kelsey asked?"

"Yeah, I guess we—" My phone buzzed, and I pulled it off my desk. As I stared at the message, my words froze in my throat.

**B:** Help

I typed a quick reply.

**Wes:** What's wrong?

She didn't respond, and I fell into the sound of my pounding heart. I hit the call button. We'd never talked on the phone, but it went straight to voice mail, and I hung up as soon as I heard the automated click.

"What's wrong?" Cord asked, sitting forward in his chair. "Your sister?"

"No, the client. It just says *help*. Something's wrong."

Startled, Cord looked up. "What are you going to do?"

I hit the phone icon, and it went to voice mail again. "This is Britta. Leave a message." *Her real name. How am I supposed to help her if I just now learned her real name?*

Worst-case scenarios filled my head. She was being followed or mugged; she'd been sick—was it serious? My fingers opened and closed, trying to figure out what to do as I sprang to my feet.

**Wes:** Are you ok?

**Wes:** Are you hurt?

Emotion was rising in a way I hadn't felt in a long time. "Can you access a client's address?"

"It's against our privacy policy," he hedged.

"Fuck the policy. She needs help. Can you access it? Her username is Bmoney34."

"Yeah." Cord slid into my chair, and his fingers flew over my keyboard, pulling up screens on our back end I'd never seen before. With three clicks and a stroke over the keyboard, he pointed to my phone, which buzzed. "Just sent it to you. Do you want me to call an ambulance?"

"I'll let you know," I said, already sprinting for the exit.

She didn't live far from our office, maybe nine blocks. I ran, feet hitting the pavement hard as I flew out the front doors of our building.

I repeated the text in my mind, four letters pinging in my head. *Help.* I checked my phone, hoping to see the bouncing dots of a reply, but the ongoing silence ratcheted up my anxiety.

Her building looked like a hundred others in the city, and the main doors were locked. "Fuck!" I growled, pulling on them anyway. I was moments away from dialing 911, even though I had no idea what was going on or if she was even there.

An older couple approached the door cautiously, giving me a wide berth. "A resident has to let you in, son," the man said.

"A friend is in trouble inside. She texted me 'help' but isn't answering her phone. Britta Colby. She lives in 423D."

The couple eyed me warily.

"Please," I said, frantic. "My name is Wes Lawson, follow me if you want, I'll give you my driver's license or my wallet, please just let me in so I can help her."

The woman touched her husband's arm, reached into her purse, and pulled out a phone. She held it up, and the camera clicked. "Okay, Harold, let him in. I have his picture in case he's some kind of sex pervert."

Harold shuffled forward to punch in the door code. "We'll be waiting in the lobby, okay, son?"

"Thanks," I said as I ran inside. The elevator was paused on floor three, so I hurried toward the door marked for the stairs, taking the concrete steps two at a time. I didn't have to go far when I stopped in my tracks.

On the third-floor landing, a motionless form lay crumpled, and I sprinted the rest of the way to her.

Her skin was clammy, but she was breathing and the pulse in her neck was steady. I touched the side of her face, where dark smudges settled under her eyes and her dark curls framed her face. Taking her palm in mine, I dialed 911, telling the dispatcher the address and where to find her in the stairwell.

"B, can you hear me? It's Wes. Help is on the way." I stroked the back of her hand, willing her to be okay. "Britta, can you hear me?" Saying her real name felt foreign, but I wanted to repeat it. "Britta?"

A crease formed between her eyes, and she squeezed my hand as I finished the call. "What . . . ?" She sounded dazed.

"Don't move. I'm here, Britta. I'm here." I brushed her hair away from her eyes. I'd been in her presence for less than two minutes, and I wanted nothing more than to touch her, pull her into my arms, or to carry her to the fucking hospital, but I settled for leaning close and trying to reassure her. "I think you fell, but I'm here, okay?"

"It's you?"

"It's me. Try not to move. What hurts?"

"Everything." She closed her eyes again before her lashes fluttered open. "Tube Sock?"

I smiled at the damn nickname. "It's me, Bubs."

"You came," she murmured. "I'm so sorry. I was going to ask you for help."

"Of course I came." I glanced at the concrete stairs above us and cringed. "Don't apologize. You did ask me for help. Just try to stay still."

Her chest rose and fell steadily, and my eyes stopped on her soft, full lips. When she met my gaze, her expression a mix of panic and pain, my heart lurched. I brushed my thumb gently down her cheek without thinking, and something like relief colored her expression at my touch.

"It's you," she murmured again, raising a hand to touch my forearm.

The door from the lobby opened, and the paramedics called up to us.

"It's me." I stepped back to give them space, unable to drag my eyes from her.

# 23

BRITTA

Hey, #TeamBritta. Claire here. Britta is sick and won't be posting for a few days. Fear not, she'll return soon! Until then, check out the links below to some of her top posts so far.

**COMMENTS:**

@EmilyJane: Feel better soon, Britta.

@TheOneHRR: Rest up, girl. We need #TeamBritta strong!

@AndreaQSmith3: Take care of yourself. We want you back!

---

*HARSH SOAP AND antiseptic.* Blinking repeatedly to make the dim room come into focus, I shifted and winced, my entire body feeling like it was one big bruise. Curtains hung over a window, dulling the early-morning light that took on hints of orange and purple. Slowly turning my head, I noticed the myriad sensors connected to me.

My head pounded, but I tried to piece together what had happened. A vision of a man leaning over me and holding my hand came to me. It was Wes, but that was ridiculous. I didn't know what Wes looked like.

Still, the memory of the warmth of that hand on mine, and those eyes, felt so real.

"Good morning. I'm Diana." The nurse spoke softly as she walked into the room. "How are you feeling?" She was roughly my age, her blond hair pulled into a thick ponytail.

"What happened?" Fuzzy memories of arriving at the hospital came back to me through the sleepy haze.

"You had a bad fall yesterday. A doctor will be in later this morning to talk with you. You hit your head, so they kept you for observation. You were also quite dehydrated when you arrived." She continued to speak in her gentle voice while checking my vitals. She indicated the bag of fluid connected to my arm through an IV.

"Did I come in alone? I remember someone . . ."

She gave a slight smile. "Your brother was with you, I believe."

"My brother lives in Wisconsin."

She adjusted my pillow and checked my IV site. "He had a tall, dark, and handsome thing going on. Does that sound like your brother?"

"No," I murmured, slowly remembering what had happened, the memories fuzzy, then fading to black. "Is my phone here?"

The nurse searched near my bed and held up a plastic bag. Even in the dimly lit room and through the plastic, the cracked screen was obvious.

"I don't think it survived the fall," she said, but held it out to me to inspect. "Is there someone you'd like us to call?"

I shook my head, pain ricocheting with that small movement. "Did he say if he was coming back?"

"I'm sure your . . . brother will be back when visiting hours begin at nine, if you want to see him. Try to rest."

I thanked her as she closed the door, leaving me to stare at the ceiling. The concentration must have exhausted me, because I woke again with sunlight filling the space. This time, a sweeter smell greeted me, and the table next to me held a large vase filled with yellow tulips and pink peonies. "My favorites," I croaked, my throat dry.

"I know." A rich baritone voice drew my attention to the other side of the bed, where the best-looking man I'd ever seen sat in the uncomfortable hospital chair. His long legs tapered down to well-defined calves that I noticed as he stood. His dark hair was cut short on the sides, and the plain gray T-shirt he wore showed his defined but not bulging biceps. "You told me roses were no good."

"It's you? I mean, it *was* you." I croaked again, meeting his hazel eyes.

"It's me." He gave a half smile, crooked and genuine, and held a cup of water with a straw to my lips.

"How . . . ?" With my throat coated, my voice was clearer, but my thoughts were still jumbled. "Thank you," I murmured, taking the cup for myself.

"I made our head of IT get your name and address when I got your message. I'm hoping you won't sue us for breaching privacy rules."

I kept staring at him. I couldn't believe this was real. "You know my real name?" Under the blanket, my fingernails sunk into my palm, and I waited for something to happen, for him to connect me to *Best Life*.

"Yeah. It's a pretty name. It suits you." He scratched the back of his neck after a long moment of my silence but didn't otherwise react. "I, uh, had to convince your neighbors I wasn't a serial killer. How are you feeling?"

"Looks like everything is still attached," I joked. "I can't believe you found me. I can't believe you're here."

He dipped his chin, voice gone softer. "You were in trouble."

My face heated, and I pulled the thin blanket up with a twinge of pain. "I'm so embarrassed. I'm sorry to put you out like that."

He shook his head, dismissing my words. "Did the doctors talk to you?"

"Not yet."

"I shouldn't have, but I told them I was your brother, so they'd let me know how you were doing. You were really dehydrated, and I told them you'd been exercising a lot. What's going on?" The concern etched on his face ratcheted up my level of shame, and I looked away. "That's not like you, to overdo it."

I chewed on my lower lip and noticed the rough red skin on the side of my hand where I must have scraped it when I fell.

"I just got—er—" I smoothed the blanket down over my chest and stomach, looking for something to do with my hands.

"Britta." My name on his lips felt so oddly intimate. It was quiet, a little gravelly, like he was thinking. "It takes time to reach your goals, but you've been doing great, and this . . . If you're not eating enough or pushing too hard, it's dangerous, even in short bursts like this."

"I know," I mumbled. My current surroundings made that clear.

He reached for my hand, paused, and then his warm palm was covering mine. "Promise me you won't do that again." His expression made me believe he was genuinely worried. "Or promise me you'll get some help."

"It was stupid, I just . . ." *What?* I didn't want to admit I'd kissed someone who, funny thing, didn't think I was pretty enough to be seen with in public.

Before he could respond, the doctor entered after a quick rap on the door. "Ms. Colby, I'm Dr. Flynn. Glad to see you're awake." He was a young guy, early thirties with dark skin and an easy, high-wattage smile. "And you are . . . ?"

"My brother," I answered quickly, flashing Wes a tiny shrug.

"Ah, good to meet you."

"I'll let you talk to the doctor alone." Wes stood, and I worried he'd leave. "I'll be back, okay?" He searched my face, but he withdrew his hand, its impression lingering in my brain.

# 24

WES

"WHAT HAPPENED WITH your client?" Cord and I sat at our regular table at the bar. "You said it was handled, but do we need to bring in legal?"

"I asked Pearl to give them a heads-up, but I think we're fine."

I'd spent the rest of the morning at the hospital with Britta. She never explained why she'd made such a sudden turn, and I hadn't pressed her on it. It was strange to be physically near her. Strange but comfortable. Strange but wonderful. Around noon, she told me her friends were coming to visit, and I bowed out, promising to message her later. I oscillated between shaking her hand and leaning down to kiss her cheek, but that crossed a major line as her coach—not that I hadn't already crumpled the line and thrown it across the room. I just gave a short wave.

Cord waited for me to say more, adopting the casual posture that he always used to wait me out.

"She'd been pushing too hard and ended up falling. Bruised, but otherwise seems to be okay and is getting some help."

"Lucky she had the wherewithal to get on the FitMi app to message you." Cord's pull on his beer was deceptively casual.

"She texted me." I mimicked his casual tone, glancing down at my phone, the screen blank. "We should see about building instant messaging into the FitMi system."

"We're beta testing it in the fall. But you gave her your personal number?" His eyebrows rose, the Cord Matthews equivalent to a dropped jaw.

"We chat a lot. It's easier." I leaned forward, my forearms on the marred and dull surface of the wooden table. "Don't give me shit. I know it's against policy."

"It's just that you were so insistent on the policies for coaches when *you* wrote them. What's different about this girl?"

"Why do you assume something is different about her?"

"I've known you for ten years, and you like rules. When you bend them, it's always for a woman." Cord leaned in, his voice lowered, not that anyone in the bar would care. "Listen, I'm just asking what's up. Are you . . . You're not fucking her, are you? I know you know that's a terrible idea."

"No, I'm not fucking her." I narrowed my eyes. "I just gave her my phone number. I'd never met her in person until I found her unconscious in a stairwell."

Cord held out his palms. "Don't get pissed. I had to ask. I know you get along well with clients, but you've never given them your personal information. What's the deal?"

"I like her. She's . . . cool." She made me laugh, she made me get lost talking about nothing, and she had a great smile. Even battered and disoriented under those flickering lights, she had smiled at me when I found her in the stairwell—this tiny, confused smile—and it floored me. It was the warmth I'd imagined all those times we chatted. All morning at the hospital, I had to keep inventing reasons to look out the window or at the TV to stop from staring at her because I wanted to memorize her features. I liked everything about her, and knowing she had been going through something terrified me more than getting information about a relative stranger should have.

Cord nodded. "And . . . ?"

"And, nothing. When I checked in on her this morning—"

Cord cut me off after finishing his beer. "You went back to the hospital? Take her flowers, too?"

I ignored his sarcasm to avoid telling him the truth. "Was I supposed to leave her there to fend for herself?"

"Uh, yeah. She's a client. You're dead set against coaches even emailing outside of the system, and you hung out with her?"

"It was an extenuating circumstance, and I was friendly with lots of clients when I did this work in person. I never crossed the line any further then, and I wouldn't now." I dragged my thumbnail down the beer label, peeling it back as I convinced myself what I was saying was true. "We've become friends. That's the whole story."

Cord's eyebrows quirked. "Uh-huh. For the record, that's bullshit." He stood to get another round of beers, saying over his shoulder, "And you know it."

I checked my phone.

**Bmoney34:** One of the many downsides to falling down the stairs is that your phone will end up unusable. Hope you don't mind going back to chat.

**WesTheBear:** I'm sure it'll be annoying to be laid up without a phone. How long are you supposed to stay home?

**Bmoney34:** Probably just a few days. Thank you again for the flowers and everything else. I still can't believe you were right next to me. So strange after all this time. I hope that didn't mean too much red tape for you with work.

I started to reply. You don't have to thank me. Where else would I be when my favorite person was in trouble? Cord eyed me from the bar, his knowing smirk returning, and I hit the backspace key.

**WesTheBear:** You don't have to thank me . . . where else would I be when my favorite client was in trouble? Do you have someone with you? How do you feel?

I pulled my thumbs back. I was asking too many questions.

"I'm not even going to ask why you have Chat App open," Cord said, falling into his chair and handing me a bottle. "Especially since you only have one client."

I tipped my chin and set the phone down. "Fuck off," I said, returning his smile and sipping my beer. "And it's not like you aren't flirting with an ethical line. You've been half in love with Pearl since she started."

"Since *before* she started. We rode the elevator together before her interview." Cord leaned back in his chair. "I know of what I speak, and how much it sucks to know you absolutely *cannot* act on anything you feel. I'm serious, man. It can be sexual harassment."

I nodded. He was right. "I know."

My phone buzzed on the counter, and Cord nodded his head at it. "You should reply to that. I need to hit the head anyway."

**Bmoney34:** I finally made my friends leave. I feel about how you might expect, but I'm not dizzy anymore.

**Bmoney34:** And before you ask, yes, I promise I will eat something tonight.

**WesTheBear:** Why don't I bring you food, so you don't have to cook?

I set aside my beer and glanced at my blank screen. I reminded myself that what I'd told Cord was true. When I trained people in person, I became friends with some of them. This wasn't that different. Hell, if he were hurt, I'd take him food; same for Pearl or even Mason. *Eh, for Mason, I'd just have food delivered.*

**Bmoney34:** That seems like a huge imposition, and you've already gone so far above and beyond the call of duty. You'll probably drop me as a client and pick up someone easier!

**WesTheBear:** What fun would there be in someone easier?

**Bmoney34:** Ok, but can we meet in my apt and not the stairwell this time?

"You're smiling at your phone. You know that, right?"

I didn't need to look up and see Cord to know he was wearing a shit-eating grin. "Shut up."

# 25

BRITTA

**LIKED BY ONTHECHOPPINGBLOCK AND 1,865 OTHERS**

REPOSTED FROM MARCH 7

Guilty pleasure foods. My coach would tell me that linking food with guilt isn't healthy, and he's right. Still, I know certain foods provide me more nutrition and energy than others, and it's those others I want when I'm down. To listen to my coach, I'll start calling them comfort foods.

I have many, but at the top of the list is pizza. By that, I do not mean the iconic deep-dish Chicago is known for. I like my pizza thin, cut into squares, and heavy with mounds of cheese and sausage. Basically, the exact opposite of the foods I've learned make me feel physically good. There's a lot to unpack there about finding comfort or guilt in food, but right now, I'm going to open the box that just arrived from my favorite local place, stick with comfort, and try to ignore the idea of guilt. What's your favorite comfort food?

LAUNDRY AND NOTES were strewn over every surface of my apartment. Camped on my couch since getting home, I hadn't had the energy to clean. My laptop screen glowed with Wes's last message. *I'll be there in five minutes.*

*Shit, shit, shit!*

It wasn't as if he hadn't already seen me at my worst—lying unconscious under fluorescent lighting had taken care of that.

The buzzer sounded, and I glanced at my yoga pants and old college sweatshirt with frayed edges. My hair was piled in a messy bun, and there was nothing even close to makeup on my face. I'd fantasized about meeting Wes in person, but in my head, I always looked a little more chic woman about town and a little less hungover freshman. I smoothed my hands down over the yoga pants and hobbled toward the door.

I took a deep breath, nerves creeping up my spine. I hoped he didn't notice how my breath caught at his smile when I opened the door. *Damn. It's gonna take time to get used to seeing him in person.*

"Hi," I said before saying the next thing I could think of. "Uh, you've never seen me standing up." *Palm to head.*

"You're right." He held a pizza box and a white plastic bag, the contents of which smelled amazing. "Vertical suits you."

I laughed. "Ugh, oh, God. It hurts to laugh."

His grin spread, slowly revealing a dimple in his cheek. "I'll try not to be funny." He set the bag on the counter and unpacked the contents, arranging containers of breadsticks and dipping sauces. "How are you feeling?"

"Hungry." I tried to get plates from my cupboard, and a small whimper escaped my lips when I raised my arms.

"Hey," his deep voice rumbled behind me. "Let me do that."

He stretched over my head to get the dishes, which meant the hard planes of his chest and abs momentarily pressed against my back. He was warm—*why are men always warm?* He smelled good, too, not like cologne, just natural and clean. A pulse of excitement ran through me with his body against mine. The contact lasted only a moment before he pulled back and set one dish on the counter.

"I remembered what you said about liking pizza on your registration." He motioned to the takeout boxes, and my mouth watered.

I looked at the solitary dish. "Are you going to stay, or . . . ?"

He shrugged. "Nah. I just wanted to bring you dinner, and I'll leave you alone. Sausage is their best, but I got half plain in case you don't like it."

My stomach sank. "Oh, I'll wait. It's fine."

"You said you're hungry, right?"

"It's okay." My face heated, and I hoped the bruises and scrapes hid my blush. Unfortunately, they didn't hide my stomach growling.

He assessed my doubtful expression, and I had the strangest sense that he was seeing into my head. "I'll join you, then."

I attempted the math before giving up. "Isn't this, like . . . a million calories?"

"Probably just a few thousand."

"Is this allowed?"

"I've never told you any food was off-limits." He reached up to grab a second plate and opened the box before returning to my skeptical expression. "Need me to put it in writing?"

The aroma made my head spin. "Yes. This feels like a trap."

He grabbed a pen from my countertop and started jotting a note on a receipt. He handed it to me, our fingers brushing for just a beat. He had messy handwriting, heavy, bold strokes filling the paper. *This is not a trap. Wes.* When I looked up, he flashed me a cute, crooked smile. "I'm hungry, too. Now, can we eat?"

We sat on the couch, and I made an involuntary grunt of pain as I fell into the cushion and my cheeks heated again. "Sorry," I mumbled, face surely crimson.

He let out a long, dramatic old man groan as he settled at the other end of the couch. He grinned when I let out a choked giggle. "What? I thought that's what we were doing."

He had no right to be that good-looking and this nice, but here he was, and I was glad he'd come over.

"Thank you," I said before taking my first bite. "For dinner, and the flowers, and . . . everything. You must think I'm such a pain."

"No," he answered after swallowing. "I think you're committed and trying hard." His eyes shifted to his plate, then back to my untouched food. "And I think something made you doubt yourself and think you're not making enough progress."

Now it was my turn to shift my gaze to my plate full of my absolute favorite. My mouth watered and my stomach rumbled. I was hungry, so hungry that I wanted to just tip the plate to my mouth and gulp it down, no concerns about cheese spilling down my shirt. I remembered how I'd felt on this couch when Ben walked out, and I paused.

"What's wrong?"

I looked down at my plate and pushed things around with my fork. "Nothing."

"Hey." Wes gently took the plate from my hands and set it on the coffee table next to his own. "I don't care if you eat the food I brought. I just thought it might be good to hit reset, to have a meal you love as you start healing, but I can get you something else." His voice was so earnest, his hazel eyes searching my own. His hands closed around mine, almost like he was protecting me. "Maybe bringing food was the wrong thing, period. I don't want you to feel worse." Wes spoke faster, like he needed to get too many thoughts out. "Is this something you've done before? There's help you can get—disordered eating and overexercise are nothing to take lightly."

My face heated. "No, I haven't done it before. It's just hard to . . ." I started the sentence not knowing how I would finish it. His expression was calm, patient, and he continued looking at me. I didn't know what to do with the attention other than tell him the truth. "There's this guy. We kind of . . . hooked up, or we were going to."

His eyebrows rose, and realization or understanding swept over his face, along with something else. It wasn't judgment, but a muscle in his jaw ticked. "The guy from the other night? The one you were cooking for?"

"I had a crush on him for years, he'd been a little flirty but told me he was down for friends with benefits, and that I wasn't . . . up to his standards."

Wes's features darkened. "The fuck?"

On instinct, I rushed to Ben's defense. "I mean—he didn't say that exactly, but he's got a public persona, and I . . . I'm not the kind of woman he needs to be seen with. I get it . . . I mean, it's bullshit, but the pressure to keep a certain way when you're in the public eye, I know that's real." I swallowed thickly. "I wanted to feel I was worth—"

"Stop it." His hard tone took me aback. "He sounds like an asshole."

My immediate reaction was to come to Ben's defense again and explain why it was an issue with me and not him, but Wes looked so unyielding, and his forceful response took me by surprise.

"I know. I'm being stupid," I mumbled.

"You're not. I'm sorry." He handed me my plate, and I missed the warmth of his hands on mine. His expression was pensive, as if he were wrestling with something before opening his mouth to speak again. "I didn't mean to snap at you. That's my stuff. My little sister struggled with self-worth. She stopped eating, and it made all her other problems worse. I'd hate to see that happen to you." Wes's neck colored.

"Is she okay now?"

Wes glanced away. "We don't talk that much anymore."

I wanted to wrap him in my arms, but I clutched the plate instead.

"You're better than easy fixes, Britta. You don't need fixing at all. You're making changes, but not because you were broken to begin with. Please promise me you won't let this guy, or any guy, make you question yourself again. Anyone who makes you feel you're not good enough isn't worth the breath it takes to tell them to go to hell."

I nodded, blinking back tears and hating that something so stupid could make me question myself. Finally, I took a slow bite, the flavor filling my mouth in a way that woke up my body.

The tension in his face dissipated. "Good, right?"

I took another bite, and a low moan escaped my lips. "Yeah." I nodded with a slow smile. "Hey, Wes?"

"Yeah?"

In the aftermath of my fall and the hospital, I hadn't put much thought into what it meant for him to be here.

"You being here . . . This isn't part of the coaching, is it?"

He paused before answering. "No." It sounded like he was admitting something. "I wanted to make sure you were okay, but coaches aren't supposed to meet their clients in person, so . . . this is kind of breaking the rules. Do you want me to leave? I should."

I shook my head, thinking of my own rules. "No. It's nice to have the company." Meeting his eyes, which looked almost green in the light of my living room, I added, "And I'm sorry about your sister. You must miss her."

He nodded, and we chewed together in silence. I was looking so intently at his square jaw that his voice caught me off guard. "Do you really want to jump out of a plane?"

"What?"

"On your application, you said you wanted to skydive."

"You really committed that to memory, huh?" I laughed, vaguely remembering typing that when I put in the application, wine making my fingers a little flirty. "I've always wanted to, but there's a weight limit, so I never tried."

"We should look into it and see what options you have," he said, setting down his plate and taking a drink of ice water. "After you feel good about your *other* goal, of course."

"My other goal?" I matched his movements, wincing when I leaned forward to set down my plate, and realization swept across me. *I want to look and feel good naked.* "Oh," I said, risking a glance at his face. "You remember that, too, huh?"

Wes's eyebrows lifted. "It was . . . memorable."

"Well, that's still number one." I motioned up and down my body with a flourish, and his gaze followed my hands. I dropped them back to the front pocket of my hoodie. "But, after that, yes. Out the plane I go."

"You could jump naked. Two birds and all. I'd love to see that."

My mouth fell open.

"I didn't . . ." He let out a choked laugh. "Shit. I didn't mean that how it sounded."

A part of me wished he'd meant the double entendre, and, overcome with lust, he'd lunge across the couch and take me. Of course, that would mean me crying out in pain, since I was covered in bruises.

He leaned forward. "Once you're healed up, want to try biking or swimming? Both are good cardio, and swimming is good for toning muscles, too. I mean, if you want to stick with FitMi. If you would rather step away, I can make sure you get your money back."

How could I have been so shortsighted? I'd come close to losing this opportunity and handing the position to Claire. I'd risked a lot. "I've always wanted to run. I guess I was never brave enough to start."

"Okay, we'll run, then." He pushed up from the couch and took both of our plates to the kitchen.

"We?"

He rinsed them quickly and spoke over his shoulder. "I'm still your coach."

"Yeah, my online coach." I motioned with a pointed finger. "You're supposed to be digital."

"Who'd call the paramedics if you tripped and fell?"

"Too soon."

"Sorry." His eyes were bright, and I could almost see the wheels of a training program spinning in his head as he glanced at his watch. "I better get going. Running will be good, though."

*What did I get myself into?* I bit my lower lip but was already thinking of how this might play out for Body FTW. "I haven't run since high school gym class, and it didn't go great then."

"It will be great now." He held out a fist and I bumped it, enjoying the warmth of his fingers. "I've got you, B."

# 26

WES

"ARE YOU LISTENING to me?"

"I heard you, Mom."

"I'm going out." She pushed away her uneaten meal, then crossed her arms. I thought she'd be happy about the takeout from Lem's, but she hadn't touched it. The late-April air blew through the open window, bringing in sounds of the neighborhood—people talking and laughing, music blaring from somewhere, and traffic.

"You can't. Not yet." I nudged the food back toward her. "If you break the rules, you're going to jail. It was this or rehab, and you refused to go to rehab."

"I'm caged like an animal." She pushed her hair back from her face. "You must hate me to make me do this." Her leg shook under the table. "Both my damn kids hate me. At least in jail, I could talk to people."

"I don't hate you." I reached for her tapping fingers. When Libby and I were kids, we would hold her hands and it would calm her down. I had only brushed hers when she jerked back.

She frantically ran her fingers through her hair, leaving it tousled and fraying out of her ponytail. "Was I that bad of a mom?"

"C'mon," I started, trying to stay calm.

"I did the best I could with you two." She paced, twitchy and pulling at her hair. "No one helped me. The teachers you two loved so damn much weren't feeding you."

Mine had. I'd find a gym bag filled with food in my locker every Friday, which would get Libby and me through the weekend. My football coach never said anything, never made a big deal about it, but I knew it was him, and I never forgot that.

Mom jabbed a finger at my chest. "I tried. I tried my best. Your dads were never there, but I stuck around. That's something, right? Why're you doing this to me?" She walked toward her bedroom.

My dad's name was Chris, and she named me after him. He was tall, drove a green truck, and liked tequila. Everything I knew about him could fit on a Post-it note. He took off long before I could form any memories.

I reached her in two strides, pressing my hands to her upper arms. Her near-vibrating state worried me. She was ready to jump out of her own skin. "It's okay, Mom."

She collapsed, sobbing against my chest. "Libby wouldn't do this."

I stared at the wall over her head, clenching my jaw.

At one point, Libby would have helped, but she probably would have told me to let Mom live her life and to stop trying to fix everything. Sometimes I wondered if she was right. If I let Mom do her thing without me trying to step in, maybe I'd be happier. Maybe Mom would, too.

I patted her back and let her heave wet sobs against me.

She pulled away and fell to her mattress, clutching her pillow to her chest. "Go away." She didn't look at me as she curled on her bed. "I don't want you here."

"Mom . . ."

She was crying again, sobbing while she yelled and rolled to face the wall. "I want my little girl, but I'm stuck with you, and you take everything away from me. You have since the day you were born."

I stood motionless in the small space, and I was thrown back to being the six-year-old trying to wake her so I could go to school, fighting back frustrated tears because I didn't want to get in trouble for being late again but knowing she'd yell at me for waking her. I dropped my hands to my sides and twisted my mouth to stop the emotion rising in my face. "I love you, Mom."

"Just go," she said from behind her pillow.

My feet landing on the concrete echoed around me in a soothing, pounding rhythm when I left the house. I stalked to my car, muttering, "Fuck, fuck, fuck!" I wanted to punch a wall or break something, anything to take the emotion pooling in my chest and let it out, to forget it, because it shouldn't affect me anymore. "Damn it!" I slammed my palm against the roof of my car, then leaned against the cold metal.

I fell into the seat and peeled out. Instead of going home, I kept driving until the suburbs were in the rear view and I was surrounded by rural stillness. The loud music and high speeds didn't drown out my thoughts. I pulled over on the side of a gravel road and cut the engine, the still night outside a shocking juxtaposition to the music.

My phone buzzed twice, and I considered ignoring it, but I looked on the off chance it might be Libby.

**Jake:** You free Friday? Naya wants to harass you about bringing a date to the wedding.

**Britta:** Sorry to bother you while you're out. We never set a specific time for tomorrow.

My shoulders relaxed, and I sent a thumbs-up to Jake. Naya's not cooking, is she?

**Britta:** Is 6:30 too early? I know you might be out late tonight.

**Wes:** Works for me. Why do you think I'll be out late?

**Britta:** Aren't you out on a date?

I laughed, the sound reverberating off the interior of my car.

**Wes:** Why do you always assume I'm on a date?

**Wes:** And you think I would text you if I was?

**Britta:** I just assumed when you said you had plans.

**Wes:** No date.

**Britta:** And you're not cheating on me with another client? I like to think of myself as your one and only.

**Wes:** No other client's gonna do.

An old Whitney Houston song came on the radio. I remembered my mom laughing, pulling me and Libby to dance with her, twirling around our cramped living room.

**Wes:** I'm saving all my lectures for you.

**Britta:** Tube Sock, are you referencing a song from thirty years ago?

**Wes:** Don't tell anyone.

**Britta:** It's one of my favorites to sing in the shower. A perfect love song.

**Wes:** I think it's about adultery.

**Britta:** But aside from that. Romantic.

**Wes:** You're a romantic, huh?

**Britta:** A little.

I flashed to Britta's face when she noticed the flowers in the hospital. The shock and appreciation, her open expression, had melted me. I imagined her giving me that look again while touching me, her body pressed to mine, and it made me want to have flowers delivered to her daily.

*Client. Client. Client. Change of subject.*

**Wes:** Are you excited to run tomorrow?

**Britta:** Will you be cranky if I chicken out and bail on you?

**Wes:** Yes.

**Britta:** How cranky?

**Wes:** Well, tomorrow is my birthday, so it would be a crappy way to start the day.

I never made a big deal about my birthday. I didn't put it on social media, but I wanted her to know. Maybe it was my mom forgetting or being worried about Libby, or I was just pathetic. I rested my head on the steering wheel. *Pathetic sounds right.*

**Britta:** Really? Okay, in that case I'll be there. I'm just warning you it will not be cute.

She'd struggle at first. Everyone did, but I suspected she'd light up when she accomplished something. And then she'd smile at me again.

**Wes:** Cute is never required at the gym. I'll see you at 6:30 tomorrow.

My engine roared back to life, and I pulled away, heading to the city with "Saving All My Love for You" stuck in my head.

# 27

BRITTA

**BESTLIFEBRITTA 3H AGO**

Some of you are already gym rats. Some of you, like me, have one thing you do, like a dance or spin class, but you leave the rest alone. This post is for others, the readers who are intimidated by the gym or just haven't gone in a while, if ever. Here are the top pieces of advice I can share for surviving.

1. Start where you're comfortable—walking is easy enough, and no one will think it's weird if you're walking on a treadmill at a low speed if you need to start there. Side note: You can also spy on all the other people to see what they do.

**SEEN BY 2,237**

**BESTLIFEBRITTA 3H AGO**

Note: My coach would say not to compare yourself to others, and to ask for help from the staff. That said . . .

2. Find someone who you think will be slower than you—
   competing and beating someone who doesn't know you're
   racing is still a thrill. Does this make you judgmental? A
   slightly bad person? Absolutely. It works, though.

3. Don't stress about what you look like. For starters, no one
   is paying attention to you, and second, if someone looks
   cute while they're working out, they're doing it wrong.

4. Celebrate! Did you push yourself as hard as possible? Reach
   a new goal? Woot! Did you spend ten minutes walking on a
   treadmill after five years of no exercise? Block out negative
   self-talk? Woot! You did it! Pat yourself on the back!

BONUS ITEM: This is truly the most important. Go back tomorrow,
or the next day, or the day after that.

---

THE GYM SMELLED like soap and sweat. I glanced toward the entrance, bounced on my heels, and tugged my T-shirt down. The ladies in my hip-hop dance class didn't care that my panty lines were visible, but now Wes would see them while I attempted to run. Ben's comments still swam in my head, threatening my tenuous equilibrium, and I pushed them aside. *He was a bad kisser. Today, I don't care what bad kissers think.*

The cold air swept into the lobby when Wes pushed through the door, flashing a wide smile. "Sorry I'm late," he said, rubbing his hands together from the cold.

"At least you could be sure I wouldn't . . . run off."

"You're funny in the mornings."

The fabric of his shirt stretched across his chest, and I wanted to drag my palm across it to feel the hard muscle beneath. "Hey," I said, reaching into my bag to busy my hands. I pulled out the protein bar to which I'd taped a birthday candle and held it out to him. "Happy birthday."

He stared at it, a slow grin spreading across his face, but his eyes held an odd expression—surprise mixed with something I couldn't place.

"For me?"

"I would have made you a cake, but I thought you might be more likely to eat this."

He ran one of his fingertips up the length of the candle before taking it from me, our hands brushing. "This is so . . ." His mouth formed an adorable grin he failed at hiding. "Thank you. This is awesome." The smile widened as he laughed. "You ready?" He tipped his head toward the large room.

Five people were on the elliptical machines and the treadmills, while a few others lifted weights around the perimeter and the thump of heavy bass bled through the walls from another room where an exercise class had started. He led me through stretches, and I tried to point my back toward the wall. As I always did, I struggled to get my leg up behind me to stretch my quads, stumbling on the third attempt. *I should make a video compilation of my trying this.* I could see it in my head, and I smiled.

"Here," he said, all business with his deep voice as he stepped behind me.

*Don't look at my ass. Don't look at my ass.*

He steadied one hand against my shoulder and guided my leg. Even through my yoga pants, I felt his heat. Our hands skimmed against each other, but he let his fall away, keeping a palm near my shoulder to help me maintain my balance.

"Thanks," I said, hoping he hadn't noticed my reaction.

"No problem. You can always use a chair when doing that one, especially if you lose your balance."

"Are you calling me clumsy, Tube Sock?"

"Never." He winked and patted the bar on the treadmill. "You ready?"

I stepped up on the machine, intimidated by the wide display with flashing lights and buttons and space for me to enter my weight. *Et tu, treadmill?*

Wes tapped a group of buttons, and the belt hummed to life. He walked me through the settings and let me know some safety practices, including attaching the little plastic clip to my shirt in case I lost control and needed to stop.

"You wouldn't catch me if I went flying?" I stepped onto the belt, moving at a snail's pace. I opened my mouth to say something else, but a woman in a sports bra took the machine in front of us and started jogging. The sounds of her feet hitting the belt over the sound of my sneakers ambling along made me stifle my next joke.

"I'd catch you," Wes said, drawing my attention back to him, and I certainly wasn't imagining touching the dimple in his cheek. "Time to speed up. Tell me how you're feeling, though. Once you're warmed up, we'll switch from walking to light jogging for a short interval."

I nodded, steeling myself. The room was surrounded by mirrors, so if this running experiment went bad, I'd have a 360-degree view of it. Wes stood next to my machine, and I glanced down and watched as his long fingers moved across the display, resting on the up button.

"Ready?"

"Yes," I said, catching another glance at the woman ahead of me, who was running full speed now, earbuds plugged in, laser focused on the news program. Wes tapped the button, and the belt moved faster. "Don't worry about what anyone else is doing."

*I got this.* I smiled at Wes when he adjusted the speed and I could keep up, just breathing harder.

His expression lightened at my smile. It was cute, almost like he'd been waiting for it.

After a few minutes, he raised his eyebrows. "Good work. Jogging now. Nothing too intense."

"Easy for you to say," I mumbled.

"Oh, and here." He handed me a pair of new earbuds from his pocket after unwinding the plastic band holding them together. "I grabbed these on the way over. Wasn't sure you'd bring your own." He plugged them into his phone and motioned for me to put them in. "Running is better with music."

Once I had them secured, he hit another button on the machine.

*Here goes nothing.* I began a clumsy, lumbering jog and stared at the display, because I did not want to get a glimpse of myself in the mirror, especially with Betty McMarathon in the foreground.

Wes fiddled with his phone and looked up, his eyes traveling over my arms and down my legs.

*What is he noticing? Oh, God. Is the sound of my feet hitting the belt louder than everyone else's?* My face heated and my breath came fast, despite this only being a light jog. *Such a bad idea. I'm going to resign.* My head twisted with anxiety until light piano music came through the headphones, and I raised an eyebrow at Wes, who'd set his phone in the cutout on the display.

He shrugged as Whitney Houston's voice flowed through the headphones, crooning about stolen moments. I laughed, despite being short of breath. He mouthed the lyrics and then held up two fingers. *Two minutes.* I glanced at the timer on the machine. I'd been jogging for thirty whole seconds. *Don't let me down, Whitney.*

After five intervals of two-minute jogs, I was red-faced and sweaty. My chest heaved, and even the start of "I'm Your Baby Tonight" was not enough to give me a second wind. I huffed and pawed at my water bottle.

"You did good," Wes encouraged.

"I hate you," I wheezed.

His laugh was low and hearty, even amid the noise and clatter of the gym. "Back on the belt for cooldown, and then we'll try some weights."

I tried to take a few deep breaths, but a stitch in my side made me press a hand to my body as I walked. "I think I'm dying."

"You're not." Wes leaned against the machine, then offered me an easy smile.

"I am. And I'm leaving this world hating you."

"Even though I made you a sick Whitney Houston workout mix?"

I chuckled despite my body insisting I curl up on the floor. "Do you think that phrase has ever been uttered before? *Sick Whitney Houston workout mix.*"

"She was a great artist. Addiction's a bitch." Something sad crossed his face for a moment, and then he shook his head, almost imperceptibly. "Anyway, running is easier with music to distract you."

When the belt slowed to a stop a minute later, I swayed. Though I was on solid ground, I had the sensation of still moving, but Wes's hand was there to steady me.

"I promised I'd catch you."

# 28

WES

WHEN WE SHARED Kelsey's proposal with Mason, he nearly dropped his phone, something I never thought I'd live to see. "She wants to merge?"

"That's what she said." I settled into the chair next to him in Cord's office. I'd had almost a month to roll Kelsey's suggestion around in my head, and I hadn't come any closer to knowing what to do.

Mason slapped his palm to the desk, his expression shifting to gleeful. "We have them on the ropes!"

"She suggested she come on as COO." *And she all but dry humped me while suggesting it.*

Cord's brows flicked up and he looked down. Not-so-subtle code for *I already told you this was a bad idea.*

"She's leading a failing company. Why would she think that would happen?" Mason sat back in his chair and rolled his eyes. "Why not just wait them out?" Mason ticked his fingers. "We have the superior platform, we have the bigger market share, and they're in trouble. We have nothing to gain from merging." Mason cocked his head. "One upside is that you could train their existing coaches—that would help with our infrastructure issues."

We'd had this argument before. "Their coaches aren't qualified—you just ran an entire campaign based on that."

"That doesn't mean I believe everyone we hire has to have a degree in this stuff." Mason adjusted his tie, his watch catching the light and shining in my eye.

Cord finally spoke up, cutting off our debate. "We'll look into it. Is there anything else?"

Mason sighed, pulling his tablet from its position on the desk. "*Best Life*'s Body FTW has been like Internet gold."

"Body FTW?" Cord and I asked at the same time.

"The name of the blog and social media project they set up. The chick reviewing our app and the one who's reviewing HottrYou. It started out as them just talking about what they were doing and the apps, but now it's become a thing. It's all over social media."

Cord and I stared at him blankly.

"You know you run this company, right?"

We shot him matching deadpan stares, and he tightened his jaw for a moment before evening out his tone. Mason held up his tablet to show us the home page. "They want readers to follow the two writers on their *journey* or some shit. We've talked about this. Anyway, huge for us."

Mason kept talking, but I glanced at my phone and thought of Britta and her pretty face, red from the exertion of running but filled with pride, that look of accomplishment that painted her expression. When I'd started the Whitney Houston song for her, I wanted to bottle up how her expression made me feel, like I'd given her the moon and not a Spotify playlist.

"So, what do you think?" Mason's voice cut into my thoughts.

"Sorry. What?" My phone buzzed in my pocket, and I hoped it was Britta. *C'mon, man. Get it together.*

Mason had spoken while scrolling, and I was glad he hadn't seen my face. Cord eyed me curiously, though.

Mason shot us the look he often adopted when we were failing him as CEOs. The blank why-do-I-have-to-explain-this-to-you smirk that always made me vaguely ashamed and then annoyed. "So, you haven't read it at all? You should—it's driving a lot of traffic to us."

"I'll glance at it," Cord said.

"I trust you and your team are all over the . . . Body FTW." Just saying the name made me cringe. Who would name it that? "If we're all set with that, can you see what kind of coverage we could get for this high school program?"

"On it." Mason gathered his things and headed into the hallway. Before the door closed behind him, we heard him call out, "Pearl! Good morning!" and Cord's eyes narrowed.

"Happy birthday, by the way. Want to get lunch?"

"Thanks." I glanced again at the protein bar with the silly candle taped to it. I hadn't opened it yet, liking how it looked on my desk. "Yeah, sure."

"What's really going on with Kelsey?" Cord thumbed at the file of information Mason had left on his desk, filled with projections and engagement demographics. "Got the sense there was something you weren't saying. You looked like you were holding back a Hulk-smash kind of reaction when you told us what she said."

"She . . ." I paused and looked around. I had done nothing wrong, but I still didn't want Mason or anyone else to know. "She came on to me when she brought up the business proposal."

"Seriously?"

"She implied we should get back together in addition to merging."

"You haven't been on speaking terms for years. What the hell happened when you guys had lunch?" Cord had been privy to everything between me and Kelsey—becoming friends, dating, hooking up, and he was one of the few people to know I'd planned to propose to her. He'd seen the breakup and all the fallout. "You didn't sleep with her, did you? I've never had to ask you this about so many women in such a short time."

I glowered at him.

"Can we get back to her wanting to go into business with us?"

Cord shrugged and dropped his chin into his hands. "I dunno. She's smart, but she's . . ."

"Kelsey," I finished. My phone buzzed in my pocket, and I pulled it out. I had two missed texts—the first made me crack a smile; the second made my fingers twitch.

> **Britta:** I hurt. I'm broken. I will never run again. *finishes complaining* How is your day?

> **Kelsey:** Haven't heard from you. Let's talk more about my suggestions over dinner or at my place.

I dismissed Britta's message and handed my phone across the desk. Cord's expression soured as he read the text. "Gonna go?"

"I should tell her I'm sending you instead."

"I'd rather stick my dick in a pit of snakes."

My phone buzzed in Cord's hand, and I leaned forward to grab it but wasn't fast enough. "Ooh, who is Britta?"

"Are you twelve? Give me my phone back."

"*BTW, I wasn't kidding. I am sore from this morning. You broke me.*" Cord read the text in a high voice and then smirked. "Damn. No wonder you're not taking Kelsey up on her offer to hook up."

"Shut up. It's my client. I worked out with her this morning."

His smirk faded. "Wait, the woman from the hospital? You're still seeing her?"

"I'm not *seeing* her." I grabbed my phone from his hand. "We're working out in person. She knows it's separate from the FitMi program." I watched my friend's reaction closely and reminded myself to specify with her it wasn't part of the program. "It's not a big deal."

"It actually is. I trust you, man, but are you sure it's just working out? You seem . . . different. Better, really, and I gotta believe that has something to do with her."

"It's just the gym, and yeah, I do feel better. You were right about picking up a couple clients." My phone buzzed again on the desk between us, and we both glanced down. "Working on this project with the school, the thing for the kids, too."

"You'll tell me if there's something I need to know about the woman, though?" The crease in his brow gave away his skepticism, but he dropped it when I nodded. "Okay. You gonna respond to Kelsey?"

"What the hell do I say?"

"You know I hate to admit Mason is right, but he might have a point about merging."

My phone buzzed again, though it was facedown on the desk.

"As for getting back together?" he said, looking at the pinging notification on his computer desktop. "Fuck. I gotta take care of this. I don't know, man. Leave it alone. Maybe just . . . don't respond."

I sat back in my chair for a minute and stared at the messages before typing out a reply. If I were smart, I'd ignore both women. Kelsey and I had a history. We understood each other on some level, and Britta was . . . I wasn't sure what Britta was—her smile left me confident I could do anything, but she was a client. I glanced at the protein bar she'd given me, sitting on my desk. When she'd pulled it out, an unexpected wave of emotion had hit me. When I was a kid, there wasn't money to really celebrate birthdays, and Mom usually didn't remember anyway. I'd been fingering the candle all day, unsure why it meant so much and not wanting to open it yet.

The office was quiet save for Cord's furious tapping and swearing under his breath. That was familiar territory. I glanced down at my phone and tapped out a message.

**Wes:** Want to meet up tonight?

# 29

## BRITTA

"Hey, everyone! I've spent a lot of time telling you about the FitMi app—the features, the challenges, and the coaching. Today, I'll tell you about me. When I signed up for the app, I was nervous. I downed half a bottle of wine and stood in front of my mirror half-naked. I'd thought I'd stand there and find all my flaws. Undoubtedly, I would have parroted back every outdated, problematic message I've ever received about my body. Why do we do that to ourselves? Instead, though, I looked at my body and found things I loved—my shoulders, my butt, my thighs. I have cute feet, but that used to be one of the few things about my body I liked. When I stood in front of that mirror, I saw a whole person who was gorgeous and *THEN* I signed up for FitMi. I'm sharing all that today because we don't talk about that option enough. You can love your body as is, no matter your size and shape, and you can still want to be in the gym or eating kale (though . . . why?) or doing other things that make you feel good. What makes you feel good, readers?"

I STRETCHED OUT on the floor of my apartment. After that morning, it felt like an eighteen-wheeler had taken me out, and I'd gotten as far as putting on workout clothes before I gave up on going to the class. "Oof," I whimpered. "I hurt." I psyched myself up to sit but fell back. I glanced at the clock on the wall until my phone buzzed next to me.

**Wes:** Ready?

**Britta:** I am on the floor.

**Wes:** We have to stop meeting like this.

**Britta:** I've told you you're not funny. Come on up.

I didn't want to still be lying there when Wes arrived, so I hoisted myself up, a tight heat on the back of my thighs. I flipped the lock and cracked the door.

Catching my reflection in the mirror, I regretted not taking a before picture like Wes suggested. I tried to remember if my arms and chest had looked like this back in February, and I flexed my calf muscle, willing myself to remember the thousands of times I'd looked at my own legs. I pressed my palms to my breasts and squeezed. I thought they felt smaller in my hands, but I clearly hadn't spent as much time groping myself as I should have.

"Oh!" A gravelly voice filled with surprise sounded behind me.

I yelped, whipping around.

Wes stood in front of me, his wide eyes falling to my hands and pausing there.

"You scared me." I caught my breath, cheeks warming as his gaze paused where my hands still clutched my boobs. "Oh, God." I dropped my arms to my sides. "Sorry."

"I didn't mean to scare you. I knocked, but the door was open." He held up his hands, palms toward me as his gaze returned to my face. "Um . . . ?" He scrubbed his hand over the back of his neck, not saying anything, though his cheeks had colored.

*Wes blushes!*

"I was trying to see if I'd changed here." I motioned to my chest. "I can't remember what I looked like before. I was curious and you walked in and . . . that's the story of me groping myself."

His lips tipped up in a lopsided smile. "I'll knock louder next time in case you're inspecting anything . . ." His gaze flicked down my body. "Else."

I let my head fall into my hands and winced, a little from the sore muscles but also in embarrassment.

He noticed my wince and took a step toward me. "Sore?"

"Thirty minutes, mostly walking on a treadmill and lifting small weights for a few minutes, and I can hardly move. I thought I was more prepared."

He motioned to the couch. "Here." Wes sat next to me, the warmth from his body making goose bumps rise on my bare arms. "You're just not used to it yet." He dropped his large hands to my shoulders, angling me away from him. "Is this okay?" He paused, and I nodded, afraid to speak for fear of what would come out. I let my eyes fall closed with his palms on my skin as he unhurriedly kneaded. Facing away from him and with my eyes closed, it was easy to imagine this was more than it was.

His voice rumbled behind me, breath grazing my neck. "You used muscles you're not used to pushing." He rolled his thumbs in small circles at my shoulder blades, and his fingers worked the muscles on either side of my neck. "I should have given you some other stretches to do."

"That feels really good." A moan escaped my lips. "Sorry." *Awkward.*

"It's okay." The husky quality of his voice sent my imagination spinning with fantasies of his hands elsewhere. "What's with all those?" He pointed to my bookshelf where twenty notebooks were stacked.

"I write sometimes." I'd jot down story ideas and poems or just sentences and descriptions. I'd been doing it since college, when I thought my writing career would go a little differently.

"Really? What do you write?" His thumbs moved across my shoulders and against my neck with a steady, even pressure.

"Oh, just this and that." My face flushed, and it had nothing to do with the massage, because this was getting dangerously close to me having to lie more than I already had about my job. "Thank you," I said as I pulled away, my creaking body protesting. "You're good at that." I faced him, backing into the corner on my couch. With a wry smile, I joked, "Foot rub next, right?"

He shrugged and pulled my leg toward him without waiting for me to answer.

"Wes! I was kidding!"

He pulled off my sneaker, revealing my clean white sock, my foot firmly in his hand. "I don't mind."

I held up my palms. "I'm not going to fight you. Have you always wanted to do this?"

"Be a masseur?" he said with a cheeky grin and a wink. He rolled his thumb over my arch. It felt amazing. I'd leave him a five-star review on Yelp. "I'll admit. It's not what I set out to do."

"What did you want to be when you were a kid?"

He was looking at my socked foot, so I had a moment to admire his broad shoulders in his T-shirt. His jaw, covered in stubble, was just enough to scratch if it was against my skin. God, was I a sucker for a stubbled jaw. *Stop it.*

"I wanted to be a teacher," he said.

"Yeah?"

"I liked school." He wrapped his warm hand around my entire foot and squeezed with a slow, steady pressure.

I laughed, remembering how excited teachers had been to see me on their rosters after having my sister. How bamboozled they must have felt once the year began. "English and writing classes were okay, but everything else was just filler."

"Home for me was . . . chaotic, and school was always kind of predictable," he said, looking back to my foot. "I liked that."

He switched to my other foot, and I watched him peel my shoe off, like he was undressing me. *Guess I'm glad the only working out I did in them was getting up off the floor.*

My breath caught. "What changed? Or are you also an undercover preschool teacher?"

He cocked an eyebrow and met my gaze. "Undercover preschool teacher?"

"Like, you sneak in under the radar past the ogling parents and then sneak out unseen."

He laughed, the wonderfully deep sound that sent small bolts through me.

"Thirsty parents would be all over you."

"You think so, huh?"

"For sure. You'd be a TILF."

"TILF?"

"Like MILF, but a teacher instead of a mom." I was rewarded with another of his laughs.

"I didn't know you had a dirty side."

"This whole thing could be a great book idea." Or maybe just a fantasy, because I'd want him, too, especially if he kept touching me in that achingly slow and deliberate way. I wondered if Wes did other things like he gave massages, because he was firm without being aggressive, knew just where to stroke, and just kept going.

"Well, I guess we'll never know." He returned to running his thumb along my arch. "I started playing football in middle school and ended up getting a scholarship based on that. Then . . . life." He didn't elaborate, but a visible flash of sadness crossed his face. Maybe it wasn't sadness so much as longing. It made me want to write something about passion and career paths and where the two sometimes diverged.

"You should be out celebrating your birthday tonight with friends. Unless . . . I promise I'm okay, Wes. I talked to someone, and you don't have to worry about me hurting myself again."

He looked sheepish and set my foot down after one last undulating squeeze. "I wasn't worried." He glanced around my apartment and scratched his jaw. "I just wanted to see you. Maybe hang out. I was thinking we're kind of friends, right?"

"We are," I said. Something about this sturdy, solid man looking unsure made my stomach flutter. It was okay to hang out with friends. It wasn't completely okay to hang out with sources, but he wasn't exactly a source. I searched his face. "So, we do this here," I said motioning vaguely around us. "And then we do the coaching on the app. It will be kind of strange, but we won't talk about your job." I bit my cheek, because then I wouldn't talk about my job, either.

"Is that . . . okay?" He looked like he was used to people turning him down. I had a hard time imagining that happened often. "It's okay to tell me I'm out of line. We can go back to online only."

"No, stay. As long as you keep massaging me." I adopted a playful smile.

I was met with the briefest of flashes in his eyes before he shifted to match my expression. "I can do that."

"That's what I pay for, right?" *Silence.* For a writer, I had a keen ability to say exactly the wrong thing at the wrong time.

The mood in the room had shifted, leaving me wondering if I had imagined the flirty vibe to begin with.

Wes straightened and cleared his throat, leaning against the arm of the couch. "So, what happened with that guy? Kick him to the curb?"

"We weren't really together," I said, pulling my legs under me. I'd texted Ben to tell him I was in the hospital, and he'd replied with a doctor emoji.

Wes contemplated my response for a minute. "You're not seeing him anymore, though?"

I shrugged noncommittally. "No."

"Good. He sounds like a dick. You deserve better."

I snorted. "That's an understatement."

"I'm glad you agree," he said, shoving his hand in his pocket, which had his sleeve riding up to reveal impressive, tanned biceps. "Anyone else on deck?"

"No. My parents will try to set me up with someone back home, and I'm sure my friends here will, too. What about you?"

He shook his head without elaborating, and another moment of silence hung between us, but his tone was light when he spoke again. "You're close with your family?"

"Yes. I have an older brother, and my sister has three boys, plus a ton of cousins, so everything is always loud and kind of sticky."

"That sounds fun." His voice returned to the timbre I was getting used to.

"It is." I wrapped my arms around my legs, pulling them to my chest, the movement stretching me in a way that felt good and awful at the same time.

"Do they know you're doing the program? Are they supportive?"

I laughed, picturing my parents. "Oh yeah. They're kind of aggressively supportive about everything. I come from a big family of literal and figurative cheerleaders, especially about relationships. My mom will be back at full speed trying to set me up with someone from her church, or my high school boyfriend, Calvin."

"Not so into that idea?"

"No, but she's relentless."

He stretched his arms over his head, his T-shirt rising an inch or two over his abs. "Relentless about Calvin or relationships in general?"

*Holy six-pack, Batman!*

I jerked my chin up, hoping he hadn't seen me looking at his stomach. "Um, yeah." I laughed.

He raised an eyebrow, waiting for me to finish.

"Sorry. Yeah, my parents met at a poetry reading in college. Like, my dad was reading a sonnet and their eyes met. My sister married her prom date. My brother and his husband met at the Eiffel Tower while both were vacationing in Paris. They're very invested in me having a love story, too." I loved all their stories, but it made me feel like a disappointment that I didn't have my own yet. "Anyway. When I go home alone, they pounce. It's like walking into this onslaught of love."

Wes nodded, thoughtful. "Maybe you should bring a buffer home, someone to protect you and change the subject."

"Yeah, right?" I laughed and stood with a groan. "You want a beer or some water?"

"Water," he said. "And I'm serious."

When my back was turned, I smiled to myself. I watched the water flow into the glass and let myself remember the feel of his hands.

"So, you really wrote all this?" He motioned to the shelf.

"Yep. You can snoop if you want." I turned back to the faucet, a little excited for him to see my writing. Those notebooks were filled with a lot of random writing, but it was disconnected from journalism and *Best Life* and it was safe. I smiled and glanced over my shoulder, a little giddy at the prospect of him in my place, peeking into my head.

Wes was staring at a page of a red notebook intently.

"Find something good? I don't even remember what's in half of them."

He closed it with a snap, the sound startling me. "Yeah, I mean, from what I saw, you're a good writer." He turned to place it back on the shelf quickly. *Weird.*

"C'mon," I said, handing him a glass of ice water and lowering myself to the couch.

He glanced away from my face when I handed him the water, expression like he was shaking off whatever he'd read in the notebook. "So, buffer?"

"Who would want to drive to rural Illinois to be my buffer?"

"I don't know. A friend?" He lifted the glass. "I would do it. I mean, if you needed me."

I tipped my glass to my lips. "If you showed up, they'd think I'd paid an escort or something."

"Why?"

"Look at you! Anyway, what would my friend get out of this ruse?"

He smiled and waggled his eyebrows. "You'd owe them a favor."

"I'm not sleeping with someone because they protect me from being set up with Calvin." *Except I would totally sleep with you.*

"I didn't say a sexual favor." He tossed a pillow at me.

He was about to say something else, but his phone buzzed, and he pulled it from his pocket. Frowning at the screen, he peeled himself up from the couch. He nodded toward the balcony, and I motioned for him to go ahead.

"Hi," he said, answering the phone and stepping onto the balcony. "Kelsey . . ." The door closing blocked out the rest of his conversation.

*Kelsey.* I thumbed through my timeline while I waited, pretending I didn't care who Kelsey was. I glanced at the insight numbers. Claire's post from earlier that day had higher engagement than anything else *Best Life* had posted, including my latest piece. Claire had been kind lately, and I didn't hate that her numbers were so good. Rather, I really didn't *want* to hate that her numbers were so good.

Wes speaking into his phone pulled me out of my pettiness as he slid the door closed behind him. "Okay. I'll see you tomorrow night." His eyes widened and his face reddened.

She was saying something sexy to Wes, and I felt like a jerk listening, but I couldn't help myself. Was she saying she loved him or describing the things she wanted to do to him?

"Um, okay. We'll see." He tapped the screen and shoved it back in his pocket. "Sorry about that."

"No problem," I said, setting my phone aside. My plan was to play it cool, but I was curious. "Another client?"

"My ex," he said with a sigh, finishing the water in his glass. "Do you mind if I grab that beer after all?"

"Sure, let me." I groaned and pulled myself up, surprised when Wes's hands closed around mine to help me up.

"It won't always feel like that. I promise."

He meant after working out, but as he helped me up, our bodies were close. *I don't mind if it always feels like this.* While I grabbed a beer, one of the craft microbrews left from those I'd stocked for Ben, I couldn't leave well enough alone.

I tried to adjust my voice so it seemed like I was a normal level of curious and not a jealous weirdo. "So, you're going out with your ex tomorrow?" I handed him the opener, and our hands grazed again, that same rush traveling up my arm.

He took a pull from the bottle. "Looks that way."

I flashed back to his face reddening when he spoke with her, and tried to picture the woman Wes would date. I came up with petite, blond, and the owner of killer abs.

Wes shifted back to our earlier conversation. "When do you need me to keep your mom from marrying you off to Calvin?"

"You're nuts," I said with a laugh, refilling my water glass. "They'd think I was dating anyone I brought home."

"And that person might have to fight Calvin for your attention. Think I could take him?"

My laugh came out as a bark, and I almost sprayed water on him. "He's a nice guy, but if memory serves, he's allergic to everything, *very* into birds, and sweats a lot. I'm guessing you could take him with this whole thing you've got going on." I gestured to his arms and hoped he didn't notice how my gaze tripped again on his defined chest.

He shrugged, adopting a cocky grin. "To be fair, you can't control allergies, birds are kind of cool, and I sweat a lot, too."

"Well, my mom would like you if you ever showed up."

Wes leaned against my fridge and sipped his beer, a smile playing on his lips. "Good to know."

# 30

WES

MY FEET POUNDED against the pavement as I shifted into a sprint along the mostly empty sidewalk. Getting a run in before meeting Britta at the gym seemed like a good idea to get my mind off the restless energy I'd felt since leaving her place. My head and my dick had been at odds since I flipped through that notebook of hers. She'd been right; it was a lot of doodles and random sentences or phrases, but I'd stopped on a mostly blank page with three lines. It was a haiku, but that wasn't what made me pause. The words were seared into my head.

*On a precipice*
*My fingers, like your soft tongue*
*Edging me closer.*

As soon as I read them, I imagined her thick thighs spread wide and her hand sliding low. I imagined how her eager fingers would move, then how I'd gently push them aside to make room for my own. When she'd spoken, I had to push away the fog of the fantasy, and it felt like I'd been caught watching her. I couldn't shake the image, and part of me didn't want to.

My breaths came fast and my chest pounded as I neared the gym and willed the poem out of my head, slowing to cool down.

"Good morning," she chimed from the sidewalk in front of the gym. "Looks like you got an early start."

I wiped at my face with my shirt. "Cheaper than the train."

That earned me a laugh, and we headed inside. After warming up on the treadmill, we started with something easy, working on form while she did curls with eight-pound dumbbells. "Are you sure this won't make me bulk up? I mean, it looks good on you, but I don't think I can pull it off." She spoke into the mirror as she concentrated on counting, pacing, and breathing.

I shoved my hands in my pockets to stop myself from reaching to guide her arm. She didn't need it. I just wanted an excuse to touch her. Flexing my biceps in the mirror, I said, "You could pull it off."

She rolled her eyes, a smile on her lips. "You know what I mean."

"Weight lifting will not make you bulk up unless you want to bulk up. The level you're lifting now will help tone muscles and burn calories. It's a good balance to cardio." I admired the curve of her arms, the skin dotted with freckles.

"Will you teach me how to use all these machines?" She took a break when she finished a set, and motioned around the gym, her expression earnest and a sheen of sweat covering her forehead. "I don't want to look stupid getting on and sitting backward or something."

Her brown eyes were playful, and I looked away, searching for something to take my mind off the way they kind of sparkled and how it made me feel. I was glad she'd asked. It reminded me my primary role here was as her coach and not to edge her close to anything. "Sure. By the time we're done, you'll know everything about them."

"If it's easier, you can point me to a good website, or I can watch You-Tube videos or something." She turned again to the mirror to curl the dumbbell to her chest. "How, um, would that work with normal coaching?"

I scratched the back of my neck. "We have detailed videos about using different weight machines. And I'd have you watch a few before trying them out." She met my eyes in the mirror, looking like she was memorizing what I said. "Then after, we'd talk about how it went or if anything was sore." My hand hovered over her shoulder. I'd caught myself before, and I pulled my hand back, crouching next to her instead, following the line of her arm as she finished the last few reps. "I'd ask you how your body felt."

My statement hung in the air, and I scanned the words, realizing how suggestive they sounded. I coughed. "Anyway, that's what it would be online."

"Good to know." She paused, resting between sets. In the mirror, her expression looked relieved. She'd asked me the difference between what we were doing and the normal process a few times. I'd gone so far as to ask if she wanted to be assigned to someone else, but she always refused. "Will you get in trouble for spending so much time with me?"

"No."

She looked at me with one eyebrow raised in the mirror, waiting for more, her facial muscles tightening as she controlled the pull and release of the weight during the next reps, focused and intent. She still thought I was one of the regular coaches. There wasn't really a reason not to tell her, unless it made her treat me differently. I decided I would wait. I didn't want to upset this balance we'd found.

"Keep control here." I guided her arm, my fingers brushing above her elbow and dragging down an inch or two. Her skin was soft, and her breath stuttered when I touched her.

*Shit.*

I coughed into my hand again, looking away. "We're going to jump into an ab workout. Ready?" I pointed to the mat nearby, but when I looked up, she'd drawn her lips to one side.

"I hate sit-ups and stuff. I'm so bad at it."

"I don't believe that."

"Ugh, Wes. Can't I just run up and down the stairs?"

"You want to run stairs?"

"Well, no, but . . . do I have to?" She raised her eyebrows the same way she had when I'd pushed her to go longer or faster on the treadmill.

"Yes. Now, c'mon." I helped her onto her back to begin crunches, showing her how to move her body. My hand hovered over her and I swallowed, cognizant of how much what I was about to say connected to her poem. "Do you mind if I touch you to show you where you want to feel it?"

"I don't mind." Britta rested on her elbows as I settled my fingertips on her abdomen. I could have moved my fingers, pulled them away once she had the idea and then talked her through it, but I didn't. Instead, I pressed lower, letting my fingers splay over her belly, feeling her tense. "Right here," I said, my voice huskier than I planned when I met her eyes. "When you do the crunch, you'll contract your muscles here."

She nodded, cheeks reddening.

I slid my hand away, swallowing what felt like a plum. I cared about Britta, about helping her reach her goals, and she was my friend. Even if I lay awake thinking about the sound of her breath hitching, I was getting too close to crossing unprofessional lines.

"Great," I said, scooting back and beginning to count out loud. Sitting back on my heels, I tried to watch her body not too closely like a guy who wanted her, but as a professional teaching her to do crunches. "Awesome," I cheered for her when she collapsed to the floor. "Knew you could do it."

"I hate you," she panted, staring up at the ceiling.

"You'll thank me someday."

"Not today."

"I'm patient." I walked her through several other exercises, working obliques, doing planks to strengthen her core, and trying a Pilates move where she held her legs off the ground for intervals of ten seconds. Somewhere in the middle, she stopped telling me she hated me, and I wondered if she was enjoying it. She still got excited when she pushed herself a little further or did a few more reps than she thought she could. It reminded me why I loved doing this; that sense of accomplishment was contagious.

"Whew!" She exhaled loudly after the last set of bicycle kicks. "I'm spent." She lay on her back, breathless.

"Let's stretch," I said, hurriedly reaching a hand to help her up again. In the sterile, muted colors of the gym, she was full of color and life, and the moment her hand was in mine, things felt right.

A battle raged among my self-control, my desire to be professional, and my pulsing need to be closer to her. Self-control was losing as I considered just blurting out . . . what? That I liked her? Wanted her? That I was ending our professional relationship because I planned to ask her on a date and hold her hand? I brushed a tendril of hair away from her neck, and her eyelids lowered. "Britt—"

At the sound of my phone, I jumped, digging in my pocket to retrieve it. The only calls that rang instead of vibrating were from my mom, the lawyer, and Libby, if she were ever to call.

"Mary, is everything okay?" My pulse sped at the lawyer's voice on the other end of the call.

Britta's expression was filled with concern, no doubt reading the worry on my face.

"Yes and no. Your mother is fine as far as I know, but she just fired me. I thought you'd want to know."

"Can she do that?"

"She can. We haven't made progress yet with the petition to seek guardianship, and she is a legally competent adult."

Britta tilted her head, but I didn't need to share this with her or anyone else, so I held up a hand indicating I'd take the call in the hallway.

"Her choices are her own, though I reminded her that firing me would not change the terms of her electronic monitoring."

I closed my eyes and pinched the bridge of my nose, leaning against the wall in the empty hallway. It smelled of stale sweat, and the echo of a spin class instructor's cheers rang around me. I wanted to be shocked, but I didn't have that in me, either. "Thank you, Mary."

"We'll talk soon, Wes."

I tapped out a quick text to Kelsey.

**Wes:** Need to cancel tonight. Thing with my mom.

**Kelsey:** That sucks. Talk to you later.

"Everything . . . okay?" Britta's voice behind me was tentative, and she took a cautious step forward.

"Sorry." I dropped my phone into my pocket. "We can get back to your session."

"You look like someone just sucker punched you. What's wrong?" She took another step closer, concern and a new take-charge attitude coloring her face. We were alone in the hallway, quiet save the exhortations from the spin instructor.

"It's just a family thing," I said, attempting to fix my expression. "My mom has some issues. I wouldn't normally abandon you like that while we were training."

"Do you need to go?"

I didn't want to go, or deal with any of Mom's bullshit. I wanted Britta to give me a hug, and not the sexual embrace I'd been imagining when I helped her with crunches, but an honest-to-God hug. I hated that feeling, like I needed someone to take care of me, even though I knew deep down Britta would. *She's probably a good hugger.* "I've got time. Let's finish." The gym was something I knew how to do.

Britta gave me another of her skeptical looks, that familiar crease forming between her brows. "Are you sure? Do you want to talk about it?"

"I'm sure." I motioned back to the weight room, careful not to let our arms brush. "Let's try a few of the machines."

# 31

One of the first things I told my coach was that I didn't want to do yoga. I know so many of you love it, but I never saw the appeal. That is to say, I never did until I found the YouTube channel of a woman who looks like me leading yoga instruction. I saw this beautiful, fat Black woman and thought, "Maybe me, too." Guess what, readers? I love it! Representation is so important in all aspects, but three cheers for fat representation in fitness. We're out here doing it, friends. Having someone I thought I could trust show me the ropes meant everything to me giving yoga a try. What pushed you to try something new?

A HAZE HUNG over the park, and the slick grass was still the dingy brown of winter. I'd arrived early, wanting to give myself extra time to stretch, and make sure my laces were tied well. I'd lived here for years but never paid close attention to the runners in the park.

I was so focused on observing the other people, the familiar voice saying "Good morning!" made me jump, much to Wes's amusement.

I clutched at my chest. "Where did you come from?"

"You weren't paying attention. Too busy checking out those guys?" Wes pointed to two men in their seventies wearing velour tracksuits and bucket hats power walking the perimeter of the park.

I swatted at him, the back of my hand making contact with his chiseled midsection. "Shut up. I wanted to learn the rules."

He feigned injury, clutching his stomach, and backed away. "Rules?"

"You know. How everything works. I don't want to look like a doofus." I was planning a before-and-after post for my first run, and I'd taken the before video earlier in the day, already nervous about what I was getting into.

He stretched while giving me a crooked smile. "You think I'd let you look like a doofus?"

I loved that smile, kind of silly and sexy at the same time. It was also evidence that he wasn't perfect, a reminder I sometimes needed.

"I'll show you the ropes," he said, patting my shoulder and scanning the park. The warmth of his hand lingered, even though he'd only given me a reassuring pat. "Ready?"

I nodded. I was up to running for nine minutes at a time on the treadmill, which I was proud of. Wes said running outside was different, and it might be easier for me, because I got so focused on the digital readout. We started off at a slow jog, and I sucked in the fresh air. It *was* different to move forward—to make progress. Wes set his watch for eleven minutes, and it felt doable.

"Don't forget to keep breathing," he reminded me. We weren't going fast, but I didn't want to jinx myself by using up any breath to respond.

Wes shot me a suggestive look when we passed the velour tracksuit pair. Despite my plan to not use breath for anything but running, I let out a bark of laughter at his playful expression.

My coach wore a long-sleeve shirt that hugged his body. It was bright blue, which looked great against his skin and showed his well-developed chest. Since we'd been meeting in person, I'd started writing less and less about FitMi and more about my personal experiences. Claire had, too, and no one seemed to mind. I figured I'd be writing about that whether or not my coaching was in person. Another glance at Wes, where I saw the hazy sunlight was making his skin appear even warmer, made me question if that was true.

Each time we passed someone, I tensed. The gym was a safe place—they knew us there. Out in the park, though, what would people think? *Are they laughing at my slow pace or wondering what this hot guy is doing with me?* I glanced from left to right, hating that insecurity trickled in even when, logically, I knew better. There was something about being out in the open, being vulnerable to criticism, that still distracted me.

"Try to look ahead instead of at other people," he instructed, interrupting my thoughts, as we neared minute ten.

"Thirty more seconds?" I huffed, pumping my arms and looking down at my watch.

"Let's go a little longer."

"What?" I panted, giving him an incredulous stare. "I can't."

"You can. You're overthinking it," he said, not at all winded from our little jaunt. "Even with a hundred other runners, this is just you. Focus on how your feet hit the pavement." His voice lowered, like what he was telling me was a special secret. "Look straight ahead and focus. No one else matters."

"I don't think—" Despite his instruction, I glanced his way, and my words paused when I saw him.

"You trust me, right?" He motioned ahead. "I'll tell you when we can slow to a walk."

"You're going to"—I sucked in a quick breath—"kill me!"

"C'mon. You got this."

When we'd started out on this run, I'd been a compact race car with careful movements and precise German engineering. After the interminable minutes of running by his side, I felt like an aged dump truck lumbering along the interstate. Sweat ran down my back, between my breasts, and in sheets across my forehead.

"Almost?" I huffed. I had no sense of how much time had passed, and it killed me to not glance at my watch. I tried to count the trees we passed, but it was no use. Had I run for another ten minutes, or had it only been thirty seconds?

"Just a little farther. You feel like you can't, but you're strong. You can." Wes's playful voice was gone. He was in coaching mode, using his encouraging, take-charge tone, the one that made me follow his direction in the gym and that filled many fantasies when I was alone in bed. "One more minute, okay, Britta?"

"I hate you," I panted, willing my tired legs forward.

He pushed the sleeves of his shirt up, revealing his forearms. I wasn't too focused on the run to pay attention to the smattering of hair or how his tan skin showcased the outline of veins visible on the firm muscle. "Dig deep."

The trees in the distance felt like goalposts, and my shoes hit the pavement with heavy, desperate steps.

"Thirty more seconds, c'mon, Britta. Let's finish strong." He sped up, and I groaned, trying to keep up. "Ten seconds." We weren't jogging anymore, we were running, the score in my head swelling to a dramatic crescendo.

When he said "time" and we slowed to a walk, I bent in half to press my hands to my thighs, gulping air. "How . . . long?"

He didn't answer, so I looked up, curious about his smug grin. "What? Twelve? Fifteen?"

"Twenty-one."

"Seriously?" I wheezed. "Really?"

He nodded, the smug grin giving way to a real smile, the one that revealed his dimple.

*I ran for over twenty minutes.* I couldn't believe it, and my exhaustion immediately morphed into feeling like I'd grown ten feet taller. "I used to get winded walking up three flights of stairs!" I wanted to post about it on Instagram and call my dad and email the high school gym teacher who gave me a D. Instead, I lunged at Wes, wrapping my arms tight around his neck. My limbs were extensions of this coiled energy.

It took a second—a long second where I wished I could rewind time—but just as I was about to step back, his defined arms fell around me. His low, rumbling voice made the hairs on the back of my neck stand on end. "I knew you could do it." His lips were close to my ear. "I'm proud of you."

I pulled back, but Wes didn't let me go immediately. His hands inched down my back, and our eyes met. His hazel to my brown, and I silenced the silly idea he was about to kiss me, but, damn, it felt like that with his hands on me and his intense stare pushing the rest of the world aside.

"On your left!" A cyclist flew past, and Wes jerked his hands away, sidestepping the bike and then avoiding my gaze. "C'mon. We'll walk for five or six minutes and then go again."

I realized I'd hugged him while soaked with sweat. Still, my stomach fluttered with the memory of his whispered words in my ear, and I wasn't embarrassed, because he'd seen me sweaty more times than he'd seen me in makeup. He'd actually never seen me in makeup or dressed nicely. There was something a little freeing in that.

As we started walking again, my body protested, but my mind did celebratory high kicks. "I don't actually hate you," I said as my breath returned. I hoped to break the tension I felt after that hug.

"I know." A crease had formed between his brows. He didn't meet my eyes this time but stared straight ahead, and awkwardness continued to creep up between us.

Finally, he shook his head slightly and held out his hand. "Give me your watch. Then you won't be tempted to focus on it." He tapped the face of my watch with his index finger. "Just try it."

I slid the band over my wrist and handed it to him, embarrassed that it was damp from exertion, but he dropped it in his pocket without comment. "Now, would it help motivate you if we were running toward those old guys? We can circle back and see if they're single." He cracked a laugh and moved into a jog, pulling me along.

"You are such a jerk!" I called out. "I take it all back. I hate you again."

We jogged side by side for a few minutes, though this stretch was a little easier. I was already crafting the post in my head, and I tried to re-member all the things he'd taught me, holding my arms in the right way and keeping my breathing steady, not worrying about making my strides too big. Periodically, I'd glance at Wes and catch him watching me, and my already rosy cheeks flushed further. It was during one of those mo-ments of eye contact that a woman's voice behind us cut into my thoughts.

"Wes," she said, slowing her run to a jog on the other side of him. I wasn't quite to dump truck mode yet, but it didn't matter—the woman coming up on his side was moving like a Porsche in skintight Lycra and a sports bra that hugged her frame. "Thought that was you."

"Hey," he said, without much enthusiasm.

I swallowed and turned back to face the fence line ahead.

"How're things? Shame you had to cancel our plans the other night," she said.

Wes didn't really respond but nodded with a *hm* sound. "Little far-ther, Britta," he said, glancing at his watch. "Kelsey, we're working out. Can I catch up with you later?"

*Kelsey.*

Her cheerful expression fell. "Sure. I have a few more miles to go anyway." She glanced around Wes, taking me in with an appraising look. She waved and sped up, calling over her shoulder, "Text me!"

I waited for him to say something, but he just encouraged me to keep going for another few minutes, picking up the pace. "Lengthen your stride . . . good. And remember to land on your mid foot, not your heel." His tone was positive but professional, and our joking seemed to be over. "Lower your hands . . . yep. Just like that."

I shifted from watching the fence line to watching the woman's pony-tail bob out of sight.

# 32

## WES

JAKE'S SHOT BOUNCED off the rim, and I cut left to retrieve it, ran to the other end of the court, and sank the winning shot. The ball whooshed through the net. It was one of the best sounds in the world, the ball going straight through. It almost competed with the sound of Britta's little sigh when we'd hugged in the park, the slow intake of breath when I touched her. Almost. I'd tried time and time again to ignore the memory of that sound and the way it sent heat up my spine.

"That's game!" Aaron clapped, and the other guys on the court joked with one another as we walked toward the benches. "Nice shot, Wes."

"So close," Jake muttered.

Aaron laughed and checked his phone. "Your definition of 'close' is creative. We were already up by like thirty points."

Two of the other guys near us laughed, one of them clapping Jake on the shoulder before leaving the group. Jake continued, "We were just warming up."

I fell onto the bench and took a gulp of water from my bottle. The next game had already started, the calls for the ball and playful jabs from the other group surrounding us again. "You're right. The streak was imminent. You'll get it next time."

"Don't coddle him, Wes. He has the money and gets to have that pretty face. We can remind him he sucks at basketball."

Jake laughed and stretched his arms over his chest. "Wes has a pretty face, too."

"Shit. I guess I'm the funny one." Aaron checked his phone again and tapped out a text before tucking it in his pocket. "Hey, my better half just gifted me with the option to stay out."

"I might suck at ball, but at least I'm not on a leash." Jake playfully jabbed Aaron in the arm. The three of us walked toward the exit, waving to the other guys. "Do you need to ask permission to stay out late?"

Aaron rolled his eyes. "You know my wife and you know our kids. Do you know the shit I'd be in if I left her alone to do all the bedtime stuff herself with no notice?" We walked toward the parking lot, the evening air cool but not cold. It was a relief to not have to wear a coat anymore.

"You're right," Jake said. "She'd eviscerate you."

"Exactly. I can't believe you're not letting Naya know."

Jake's laugh filled the space between us. "She's out of town. Otherwise I would. I'm just as whipped as you." He clicked the key fob and his trunk opened. They must have driven together, because Aaron threw his stuff in the back as well and motioned to the bar a couple blocks in the distance. "You up for a beer? You're the lucky untethered one."

I'd actually never seen two guys more enamored with or happy to be tethered to their partners. They were lucky. "Sure, why not?" Funny thing was, I'd had a moment where I considered texting Britta to let her know I wouldn't be able to chat until later. It wasn't a date or even anything planned, but we talked most nights. I'd ask her how her evening workout had gone, and we'd slowly fall into some random topic. I looked forward to it.

The sports bar wasn't crowded, and we took a high-top table near the back where we could see the baseball game on TV. Jake poured beer from the pitcher we'd ordered. "How's that program you're working on together?"

"This guy came through," Aaron said, handing me a glass. "The kids are going to love it."

I shrugged. "It's been cool." I'd hired a student of Naya's to help develop the curriculum in concert with the school. We weren't even working with the kids yet and I loved it. It was like the feeling of coaching someone new when things clicked for them that first time. Between working on it and spending time with Britta, I almost felt like a new person compared to a few months earlier. Even dealing with my mom was—not easier, but I could manage it better. I still worried about Libby, but the panic I'd gotten used to felt more manageable, too. "Did I ever tell you I used to want to be a teacher?"

Jake leaned forward. "What made you change your mind?"

"The teaching program was hard to balance with football, and I needed the scholarship." My exercise science degree had served me well so far, but working with this program, designing things for kids, it made me wonder if I'd made the right choice all those years before.

"Too bad," Aaron said. "You would have been good at it."

Britta had said the same thing before diving into her TILF description. Just then my phone buzzed in my pocket, and I pulled it out to check the screen.

**Britta:** Did you win?

I unlocked my phone, but Jake spoke before I could decide on an emoji response.

"Aaron, are we sure Wes is untethered?"

I looked up, and the two of them were smirking, enjoying their bit as fake commentators.

"Jake, from the look on his face when he got that text, I'd say the signs point to tethered."

I shoved the phone back in my pocket and waved them off. "She's a client."

"Funny. None of my clients make me smile like that," Jake joked. "Well, I guess Naya did."

I cocked an eyebrow. "Naya was a client?"

He took a drink from his glass before continuing. "Kind of. When Nay and I met, I was consulting for her university. The whole time, when we were first together, my company was making recommendations about her department being cut. That would have been a little before you started hanging out with us."

"What happened?"

Jake shrugged. "We got through it, but it kind of sucked."

Aaron groaned. "That was a mess."

"How'd you get past it?"

Jake laughed. "We all have ethical codes, but between doing something professionally dicey and taking the risk to be with her?" He took a sip from his glass. "No contest."

---

WE FINISHED MOST of our pitcher and talked for a while before heading home. Aaron's comment that I would have been a good teacher stuck with me, and I decided not to check the growing number of FitMi emails in my inbox. Jake's story about how he met Naya and about risk . . . that stuck with me, too.

I had a message waiting from Britta, and I made myself wait to respond. In the park the weekend before, I'd wanted to kiss her. My body and mind were there, and I was seconds away from lowering my mouth to hers. She'd tipped her face up, and I'd sworn it was a perfect moment.

But then that cyclist passed by and I'd realized where we were, and *who* we were, and that stopped me. Add to that Kelsey running into us, and there was too much risk involved. So, I'd waited to respond, not giving in to the urge to look as soon as I picked up my phone. Now, fresh from the shower and sitting on my bed, I unlocked the device.

**Britta:** Did you win?

**Wes:** 🏆

**Wes:** You know it. How was your workout?

**Britta:** Helen kicked my butt as always. You should hire her.

**Wes:** Give her my info.

**Britta:** I'm not supposed to have your info, remember? ☺ I swear, I'm going to get you fired.

I leaned against the headboard, the wood cool on my bare back, my thumbs hovering over the screen keyboard. "Just have her contact FitMi" was easy advice, especially since Britta didn't know my role at the company, but maybe this was my chance to come clean. I scratched at the stubble on my jaw before typing a reply, but she added another message first.

**Britta:** Can I ask you a personal question?

**Wes:** Sure.

**Britta:** It's really personal, so you don't have to answer.

**Wes:** Hit me.

The dots bounced and then stopped, her message hanging. My comfortable bedroom was now too warm, and I stared at my phone with an intensity that would have been embarrassing if anyone else was in the room.

**Wes:** Everything ok?

When she finally responded after another two minutes, what she said threw me.

**Britta:** Have you ever wanted someone you knew you shouldn't?

Her question was so spot-on, I worried she'd seen through me at the park. Maybe she'd known exactly why I pulled back.

**Wes:** What do you mean?

**Britta:** Have you ever wanted to be with someone, like, romantically, but it would be inappropriate? Like, someone off-limits.

My heart rate sped, and I both wanted and didn't want her to be talking about me. The possibility taunted me like a spark in the distance. If I'd spent a moment longer weighing out potential consequences, I wouldn't have answered so openly.

**Wes:** Yes. Have you?

**Britta:** This is probably too weird to talk about, too personal. I don't know why I asked. I just talk to you about everything.

**Wes:** Are you interested in someone you shouldn't be?

**Britta:** Yeah.

**Wes:** Just physically or more?

**Britta:** Both. All. I'm interested in everything.

**Britta:** It's hard to describe. I absolutely can't have him, and I can't stop imagining what if.

*What if.* I swallowed, anxiety, arousal, and hope battling inside me. I wanted her to be talking about me. So many of my what-ifs were about kissing her, and bringing her home, and memorizing her body when I woke with our limbs tangled. My thumb hovered over the call icon, and I suddenly wanted to hear her voice more than anything. This felt like that moment in the park, but there was no one around to stop us, and the risk felt worth it.

A FitMi notification flashed across the screen, an automated note to check my client's weekly summary, the simple white box an ice-water reminder why nothing had changed since the park. I pulled my thumb away from the screen. I had to be sure first.

**Wes:** Do you think he feels the same?

**Britta:** There are moments where I think maybe.

**Britta:** You know that feeling when you're certain someone wants you? Like there's this electricity? It's like that, but then nothing happens.

I dropped my head back against the headboard, frustrated. *Electricity . . . but then nothing happens.* I should have kissed her. The moment was there, and I got in my own head.

**Britta:** Being together would break some serious rules.

**Wes:** Someone who really wants to be with you would be willing to move mountains, let alone break rules.

My body was on edge, muscles tensed and eyes trained on the screen. She'd cut through all my bullshit in a few texts like Britta always did. She knew exactly what was going on in my head. I'd typed, I'll do whatever I have to to be with you, but before I hit send, her next reply popped up.

**Britta:** It could impact my job. It could get me fired.

*She has electricity with someone else.* I reread the response to be sure, because she wasn't talking about me. It should have scared me that I'd wanted Britta in that moment more than I cared about my company, but it didn't, and I'd been about to confess some shit to her that would have ruined everything.

**Wes:** Someone you work with?

**Britta:** Kind of.

I slumped against the bed, all that tension falling away at once, leaving this sinking disappointment in its place.

**Wes:** What do you think you should do?

**Britta:** There's what I want to do and what I should do. But probably look out for my career, right? I mean, a guy isn't a sure thing, and the place I work is really great . . .

**Wes:** That difference between "want" and "should" can be big. "Should" is probably the safer option, though.

The room felt too confined, and I walked toward my dresser, pulling on shorts.

**Wes:** If he doesn't get how incredible you are, maybe he's not worth the risk, anyway.

**Britta:** Maybe so.

I tossed the phone onto the bed and scrubbed my hands over my face. I yanked a T-shirt from my drawer and pulled it over my head. *Damn it.* Tossing the towel into my hamper with more force than needed, I glanced at the message waiting on my phone.

**Britta:** Thanks, Wes. I'm glad I have you.

**Wes:** You have me, B.

**Wes:** And I hope you get your what-if.

# 33

BRITTA

"I have to admit something to you all. I wasn't sick last month—well, I was, but it was my doing.

"Truth is, I got my heart a little broken, and I decided if I was stronger, if I pushed harder, no one could make me feel worthless again. Have you been there before? I hope not. I'm embarrassed I was.

"I exercised too much, I ate too little, and I stopped checking in with my body. I did push myself, but I pushed too far and ended up in the hospital.

"I'd love to tell you I left there having reaffirmed that I would never again worry what someone else thinks of me. I didn't. It's a process, but I'm working on it. I wasn't even sure I should share this failure—even as I hit 'post,' I'm worried you'll be disappointed. I'm disappointed in myself, but I promised to be honest. That was a dark moment, and it still hurts—emotionally and physically. It showed me how easy it was to fall into dangerous ways of thinking, of devaluing myself, and how maybe I was doing it in other, smaller ways. I was lucky—I got help early, and I'm trying again. I'm doing it in a way that's right for me, and I'm getting stronger every day. I hope you are, too! Check out the links below for information on resources for disordered eating and exercise . . . Take care of yourself and take care of each other!"

---

I'D SHOWN MARICELA my Falling and Failing post before I released it on social media, nervous to gauge her reaction. She'd loved it and settled her hand on top of mine, eyes wet with tears, as she told me what she loved about me telling such a difficult story. She'd even asked me to expand on it to write a piece for the next print issue of *Best Life*. I was floored, and I came back to my text exchange with Wes the night before.

I'd left out him coming to my rescue. I'd left out him telling me about his sister and checking on me. It felt incomplete without the Wes pieces, and guilt tapped me from multiple angles. I was putting this deeply personal and painful thing in the world, and leaving him out made me almost desperate to connect with him.

Desperation was the only possible rationale for me asking him that question, but I'd been drafting my post at the time and felt so close to coming clean about my job and why I'd joined FitMi. I wondered if he'd seen through me and knew I was talking about him until he nudged me back to thinking about my job, and either way, that was probably for the best.

---

"I'M IMPRESSED WITH your work so far." Maricela fingered the tablet in front of her containing the report on Body FTW.

"Thank you," Claire and I chimed in unison in response to Maricela's compliment. We exchanged a look that, if not friendly, was not hostile. Even though readers didn't know we were competing, it was ever present between us. But in the month or two prior, the ice between us had thawed, and she'd even texted to check on me after my fall to ask if I needed anything.

We'd had strong readership—#TeamBritta and #TeamClaire social media were trending regularly. I'd shared my goals: to get active, look and feel good naked, and jump out of a plane. Claire left her goal as being beach ready, but the duality of our struggles and triumphs seemed to reach a wide segment of our audience. I'd hoped audiences wouldn't relate to Claire as easily with her already lithe body, but she wrote so honestly, I couldn't even be salty about her getting the attention from readers that she was. *Okay, maybe just a little salty.*

"A health spa nearby has taken an interest and wants to invite you both to join them for a couple days in hopes you can write about self-care. I think it's a marvelous idea if you're up for it."

We both nodded and even exchanged a small smile. Assistants didn't get sent to health spas, so this felt like one step closer to being on the writing staff.

"I want to talk about next steps. Is there an opportunity to up the stakes?" Natalie tapped at her screen.

"Do we need to add stakes?" I cast a sideways glance at Claire, but her expression was unreadable.

"From a marketing standpoint, it will be good to have a hook to keep people interested. As is, there's no finish line."

We fell into silence, the four of us looking in different directions, each lost in thought. I'd liked the project as it was—telling stories, sharing triumphs and failures—but I saw their point. The last thing we wanted to do was leave people bored. I repeated Natalie's words in my head, seeking a good idea. *Raise the stakes. Keep them interested. Finish line.*

"What about a race?" The three other women turned their attention to me. "A 5K or something. It would fit with what we've been doing, we could each talk about training, and there's a literal finish line."

I expected a derisively arched brow from Claire, but her expression remained impassive.

"Do either of you run, now?" Maricela asked.

"I don't," Claire said.

"I don't, either," I said, sitting straighter. "Well, I just started." I imagined Wes's smile when I told him I was going to sign up for a race. He'd be proud of me, and that thought was motivating. "The narrative could evolve. We'd be moving past the apps toward something else."

"I don't want to make this about one of you winning or losing," Maricela said thoughtfully.

Claire and I shot each other a meaningful look, knowing damn well we were competing, and probably one of us would win the position and the other would lose. We didn't comment on that, though, turning back to Maricela.

"I don't think one of us would have to win or lose. We could frame it as competing against our own doubts," Claire said.

"Against our own roadblocks," I added. "Plus, those races are usually big, with lots of runners. Maybe there's a community aspect to it, too."

Maricela smiled widely. "I like this."

Natalie plucked at her keyboard, tapping and swiping furiously. "Me, too. Okay, you two are using FitMi and HottrYou. I'll reach out to see if they'll jointly sponsor a 10K to keep them connected. That way readers can follow your story, but maybe get involved themselves."

Claire and I exchanged a look. "Or a 5K?" Natalie didn't register my question and turned to Maricela, and I took the moment to address Claire. "You're okay with this?"

"Yeah. It's a good idea," she whispered. I knew a little part of her was pained to give me the compliment. That's what I would have felt. "We could involve other writers to talk about running fashion, technology in the races, strategies for motivation. I could see a lot of collaborative opportunities."

"I don't know if my coach will be proud or confused," I joked, though I knew which was right.

"Honestly, I'll be glad to have something else to focus on away from the platforms. HottrYou coaching isn't all that impressive or interesting. Your guy is really good?"

*My guy ... if only.* As a coach, he was resourceful and knowledgeable, and I'd really seen that since day one. When we first started hanging out, I had a hard time thinking about any of that without letting my mind wander to his intense eyes, easy smile, and broad chest. Now, though . . . I knew the way it felt when he teased me to make me laugh, or how he always offered to help with dishes when we ate at my place. The way he listened so intently was inexplicably linked with everything else. In hundreds of tiny ways, I kept seeing how good a guy he really was.

Claire eyed me strangely.

"He's very attentive."

"The app itself is great, and my coach responds with a few sentences once or twice a week when I check in. But it's all stuff I could have googled." Claire glanced back at her phone, her lips pursed, and I got the sense there was something else she wanted to say.

Maricela brought us all back to the project, so I didn't have time to find out what else Claire was considering. "I like this plan. Natalie will work with you to iron out the details."

"Guess you two need to get to work!" Natalie chirped.

# 34

## WES

"ONE MORE SPRINT. One minute as hard as you can. You got this, Britt."

Her cheeks reddened as she approached the end of a high-intensity interval on the elliptical machine. She panted. "I can't."

"There's no 'can't' in my gym. You ready?"

She fixed me with a look that would melt ice, shaking her head, but ticked up her speed, her breath coming fast. "Hate you," she panted.

*How has "I hate you" become my favorite thing to hear?* I had fantasies I wasn't proud of that included her moaning that.

No one looks good if they're putting in a lot of effort on an elliptical machine—it's intense—but I couldn't stop staring at Britta. I was so damn proud of her. She'd tell me she hated me again along the way but give me the biggest, most joyful smile when she finished. No one had ever smiled at me in that way, like I was the highest point in her day. We trained a few mornings a week and were now running four or five days a week. It had felt natural when we started hanging out in the evenings, too, sitting on the couch and watching TV with the citrus smell of her hair filling my nostrils. She still used the app and logged her progress, but I was kidding myself if I thought this time spent together, even in the gym, was just an extension of coaching. Every day I thought about bringing it up, of severing the FitMi connection with her, but then we'd end up at the gym or on the trail. She'd tell me she hated me and then hit a personal best, and I liked being part of her personal bests.

Around us, the whir of machines and the clank of weights was a symphony. "Great job. Thirty more seconds." I always knew what needed to happen at the gym. Not so much with my mom and her mood swings, or in the office, or even with what was going on in my head and my heart about Britta. In the gym, though, I knew what to do.

Her breath came fast, her ponytail whipping behind her.

"Ten seconds. You got this. Push, Britt." She didn't tell me she hated me, but that was only because she didn't have enough breath. I read it on her face, but she tapped a reserve of energy and dug in, her speed jumping a notch. Her chest heaved under her sports bra. *Okay, a few things look good on an elliptical.* "Three . . . two . . . one. Back down to fifty percent for thirty seconds, then we'll cool down. That was awesome, Britt."

She slowed, catching her breath while still moving at a good clip on the machine. She huffed, grabbing for her water.

"Nice work," I said, adjusting the speed.

There it was. Her quick, breathless smile.

None of the distractions in the gym—the smells of sweat and cleanser, the techno music from the aerobics classes down the hall, or the macho jostling for dominance from the weight lifters—could pull my attention from her.

But the shared moment was interrupted by the machine beeping. I glanced anywhere but at her as I tried to regain my composure.

"Wes!" Four strong arms wrapped around me, and I stumbled backward at the impact of the group hug from Felicia and Naya.

"Whoa," I said, stepping back. Felicia had enrolled in one of the first classes I led after graduating, and she'd bring Naya along sometimes. They were the friends I'd first thought of when Britta and I talked about coaching friends. This had been different for a long time, though. "What are you doing here? Don't they have gyms in the suburbs?"

"My friend Jill started teaching a spin class, and I promised we'd come check it out." Naya turned to Britta, who was finishing up on the elliptical. "Is he making you do interval training? I hated when he made us do that."

Britta stepped off the machine. "It's the worst."

"You owe me an RSVP." Naya raised her fists and playfully punched me the way I'd taught her and Felicia to box. Her engagement ring glinted under the light. The thing probably counted as weight lifting.

Felicia punched my arm. "Of course you're coming, Wes."

"Two against one. Not fair," I said, deflecting their jabs. "I'll be there. Sorry, I'll mail it tomorrow."

"And you're—" Felicia tried to hit me again, but I blocked her. "Bringing a date?"

I ignored her question. "You're rusty."

"My teacher abandoned me to start a—"

I cut her off, realizing she was about to out me and I wasn't sure how to manage the fallout. "Yeah, yeah. Excuses. I'll let you know, Naya. We're in the middle of working out, though. Catch you later?"

They took the hint and left after quick hugs and wishes of good luck to Britta.

"They seem cool," Britta commented as she settled into the seat of the chest press machine and I adjusted the weight.

"They are. Naya's getting married next month."

"I pieced that together," she said with a grin, resting her arms on the bars and pushing forward with measured speed. "Excited?"

"Sure, I guess." I held up a hand and circumvented her question. "Pause when your arms get to about ninety degrees." I reached forward, my hands falling on her shoulders to help her adjust her position. The touch was innocent and quick, something I'd done for clients—for her, even—hundreds of times, but as she looked up at me through her thick lashes, I had a flash of what it would be like to be on top of her and have her look at me like that, and I pulled back too quickly. "There you go. Start up again."

Her cheeks colored, and she continued her reps. "So, who will you take to the wedding?"

"I don't know," I answered, looking around the gym. "I'm not really seeing anyone. I just didn't want Felicia trying to set me up."

Britta let the bars return to the resting position between sets. "The woman at the front desk always flirts with you. Maybe you should ask her."

I crouched next to her and fiddled with the weight settings. I'd never really noticed the woman at the counter was being anything other than nice to me. Usually, I was distracted, waiting for Britta to come through the front doors. "I might just go alone. I normally wouldn't go at all—I don't like weddings."

Britta paused with her palms on the handles. "Really? Why?" Her thumbs fiddled with the adjuster, not pressing it down, just moving back and forth, and I dragged my eyes away. Britta laughed. "You get annoyed you can't wear sweats, huh?"

"I do own other clothes." I motioned to my outfit. "I clean up nice."

"I don't believe it." Britta pushed the handles forward, beginning her next set with an exhale. "Send me a selfie before you leave for the ceremony. I want proof."

Her arms extended and retracted twice more, and I watched her face, the way her mouth shifted slightly with each breath as she counted. Her hair was pulled back, and I realized I'd never seen it down. In the middle of the gym, I was imagining running my fingers through Britta's hair.

I flicked my eyes away. "You could go with me and see for yourself."

"Me?" She breathed harder, nearing the end of the set, and a drop of sweat ran down the side of her face.

"You know, to make sure I don't wear sneakers." I could have picked that moment and asked her on an actual date, but I chickened out. Making her feel uncomfortable in the gym was the last thing I wanted to do. "And a wedding is probably more fun with a friend."

"You sure you don't want to see if you can find a real date?" Her tone was playful, but she assumed she was a last resort, which was so many miles from the truth it was laughable.

"I'm just saying it will be your only opportunity to see me in a suit."

"Well, if this will be my only opportunity, I guess I have to say yes." She smiled up at me, brown eyes sparkling, and I was struck by the urge to lean down and kiss her. "I'll be in heels, though, so don't even think about springing a surprise wind sprint on me."

"I wouldn't dream of it." I rested my hands near hers on the bars, not touching them, and tried to keep my smile a normal width. "You got one more set in you?"

She nodded and I stepped back, watching her inhale and exhale slowly with the next reps. It seemed like a weight had been lifted from my chest. The wedding was a few weeks away, and I could figure out a way to say what I wanted before that. We could talk about things, and I could end our coach/client relationship. I could do it right and still have a chance with Britta.

"Oh, by the way. I took your advice."

"Is this when you admit you were wrong about yoga?"

"Maybe." She laughed and wiped her brow before reaching for her water bottle. "I invited someone to come home with me when I visit my family in a couple weeks. He'll be a great buffer to keep their match-making schemes at bay."

# 35

BRITTA

Warning: This post will contain exclamation points.

I've never flat-out hated shopping for clothes, but finding cute stuff in my size can be a challenge in a lot of stores. Someone somewhere decided fat women love floral prints and long, flowing tunics. Some people can rock this look. I am not one of them. My kingdom for a flattering, flirty, youthful ensemble in my size in a store without an empire waist. Here's where the exclamation points come in: I bought a cute dress yesterday . . . with a natural waistline . . . in a store . . . that I love!!!!!!!! Linking to the store and designer below!

RJ HELD UP a pink cocktail dress with a plunging neckline. "How about this?" The color wasn't just bright, it was neon, like back in the nineties electric.

I shook my head. "Maybe something a little more understated." I returned to the rack, pushing dress after dress aside.

"Whose wedding is this, again?" RJ asked from around two manne-quins in coordinating yellow rompers.

"Friend of a friend," I said vaguely, glad she couldn't see my face. Though it wasn't exactly a lie, RJ had a way of lawyering the truth out of me, and I didn't want her convincing me this was a bad idea. "I'm going with him as a favor. You know how it is."

"I thought straight men didn't mind being single at weddings—don't they usually think they can hook up with a bridesmaid or something?"

I smiled, remembering Wes talking about it. I couldn't imagine him being the kind of guy to hit on the wedding party. I had a hard time picturing him hitting on anyone, really—he was always so nice. "I guess some people would rather have a date. Plus, you know I love weddings."

"You do. It's sort of gross." Anti-romance RJ held up another dress, this one high necked with capped sleeves.

I scrunched my nose. Between the cap sleeves, the empire waist, and the complete lack of cleavage, the dress looked like it was solidly in mother-of-the-bride territory. "Uh, maybe something younger."

"So, he's just a friend? Nothing going on there?" RJ's tone was casual, but she was fishing.

"Just a friend," I said, holding up a green wrap dress for her review and hoping she had no more follow-up questions. I had the what-ifs in my head, and that was enough. "What do you think of this?"

"Not bad," she said after a quick perusal of the garment. "Also, were you going to tell me that Del gets to go with you to Casa de Colby? I'm jealous. Your family is the best."

RJ had been home with me a ton of times in college and beyond. I knew she'd considered going to visit my parents without me getting in the way, so she could keep all my mom's cooking to herself.

"I invited you—you'll still be in North Carolina."

"Stupid job interview," she muttered. "Will you bring me home some of Danielle's brownies?"

I laughed and returned to the rack. "I guarantee my mom will have a container of them waiting for you."

"So, is Del pretending to be your boyfriend or something?"

"No," I said, inspecting a red dress with a flouncy skirt. "Nothing like that. Just a buffer to stop my family from going on full tactical find-Britta-love mode."

RJ laughed. "I won't be there to drag them into a college football argument."

"Exactly. Having someone there with me means it's easier to sidestep things, plus there's someone who can change the subject when my love life comes up."

"You know Del is likely to do that by jumping into a lecture about women of color in agriculture and the nexus of sustainable farming and anti-racism, right?"

"Why do you think he's the perfect choice?" Our eyes met, and we both cracked up, drawing the attention of the other patrons.

I dragged my gaze back to the red dress and slid a finger along the fabric. It would cling a bit, and the color was bold and bright, but I couldn't take my eyes off it. Not for the wedding, but maybe I'd have a few dates in the future. Real dates where I'd want to look sexy and eye-catching and it wouldn't be an ethical quagmire to let my date take it off me. I held it up and turned to RJ, who did the same but with a black dress.

My breath caught. It was stunning, with a dipping neckline and a smattering of black beads along the hem. "Oh, I love that," I said at the same time as her. I imagined the lights catching on the beads, tempting Wes to look at me. Sometimes on chat he said things that sounded flirty, and now and then when we hung out, he'd touch me or smile at me in a way that made me think *what if*, but normally, he was completely professional. "They're both so sexy. Too sexy for a wedding with a friend?" I slid a fingertip along the line of beads at the neckline. "I mean, it's not like I need to impress him."

"Who cares about him? You'll be sexy for you in either of these," RJ said, motioning to the dressing room. "And if this friend is interested in women, I suspect he'll be impressed."

# 36

## WES

I TOSSED MY keys and phone on the counter and filled a glass with water. Saturday morning basketball was unexpectedly busy, since Aaron had had to bring his kids and I'd spent the morning teaching nine-year-old Emily to dribble circles around her dad and to score on Jake. I smiled to myself. I hadn't enjoyed the game as much as I had this morning in a long time. My phone buzzed on the counter.

> **Britta:** Want to see a movie later?
>
> **Wes:** Aren't you going home this weekend?
>
> **Britta:** Something came up with Del's research, and I don't have a car. Looks like I'm staying in town.

She'd talked about it all week and told me all about her nieces and nephews and how much she couldn't wait to see her family. She hadn't told me much about Del other than that she'd known him a long time. I hadn't been able to suss out whether he was the guy she kind of worked with who she liked, or if he was something else. Without any other information, I didn't like the guy.

**Wes:** That's too bad. Are you ok?

**Britta:** Sure. Bummer, but I'll see them all in a couple months.
Movie, though?

I glanced at my keys and the clock on the microwave before tapping
out a message.

**Wes:** I don't have anything going on today. I can drive you.

---

"ARE YOU SURE you won't let me pay for gas? I can't thank you
enough for doing this." Britta faced me and offered for the fifth time. The
farmland and open sky stretched for miles, a blur of green and blue as we
cruised down I-80. "I owe you big-time. Seriously, Wes. Anything you
need and I'm yours."

I waved her off, because "I'm yours" meant a whole lot, and I hadn't
put my plan to tell her how I felt into action. That was back on hold until
I knew what was up with her and the guy she worked with. My plan was
to tell her when she got back from visiting her family. Mom was doing
better and almost finished with her house arrest, and I was enjoying work
instead of looking for distractions. I glanced at Britta, and that feeling I
was getting used to, that it's-going-to-be-fine feeling, washed over me. "I
don't mind. I like driving, and I don't get to do it that often. You sure your
family can give you a ride back?" My hand itched to reach across the
center console for Britta's. Since I'd decided to do something, to ask her
to the wedding, I'd been impatient to spend more time with her. "Will it
be okay without your buffer?"

She nodded and laughed. "Yes. And, they're not *that* bad." She glanced
out the window.

I nodded.

"And I'll hop out of the car before they can pounce on you, I promise.

My mom is like a dog with a bone when there are new people to feed. You'd be stuck there for hours."

"Ah, but what if Calvin is there?"

"Just shield me. I haven't seen him since high school, and he's a nice guy, but . . . no. His family usually comes to these things, so hopefully he's not in town." Her laugh filled the space, and I relaxed in my seat, contented. I liked hearing her laugh in my car. I liked hearing her laugh anywhere.

"What if he turns out to be wealthy?"

She rolled her eyes, which buoyed me. "I'm sure my mom would have mentioned it, but I don't care."

At this point, I didn't think it would make a difference to her that I owned FitMi. We were only ten minutes from our destination, so it definitely wasn't the time for confessions, but I would tell her about my role in the company when she got home. That way the air would be clear. In the moment, though, I returned to Calvin. "What if he's really good-looking, too, though?"

"Really good-looking *and* wealthy?" She paused. "Well, then you probably need to get back to the city immediately. Relieved of duty, sir."

"I see how it is." I loved when she returned my teasing. Kelsey would get annoyed with playful banter and refuse to respond until I was serious again. The more time I spent with Britta, the harder it was to remember why I'd stayed with Kelsey for so long.

"You know you're my favorite." Her fingertips brushed my knee, and it sent a jolt straight to my groin. Her hand fell away, and I shifted in my seat. If she kept her hand there, I might be sporting a semi when I pulled up to her parents' house.

Britta touched me like she'd been touching people her whole life, like she didn't know how important it made me feel.

I let my thoughts fall away from her hand, and Britta directed me off the interstate and through the small town. She pointed out the intersection that used to hold the town's only stoplight before the second was installed, as well as the library where she'd first checked out Stephen King novels she had to hide from her parents. It was fun seeing this side of her, learning her history. She motioned for me to turn down a gravel road. "The house is up ahead."

"Holy shit," I muttered under my breath. We came to a stop, and I cast a quick glance through the windshield as we approached—the trees were like a canopy above us, boxing us in, but the sky and land seemed to go on forever around us. "This is where you grew up?"

"What are you looking for?" Britta's tone was playful as she followed my gaze into the trees.

"I grew up in the city, remember? It's so . . . open out here. Aren't there other houses?"

"Not for several miles. Are you scared of being in the country?"

"No. It's just . . . quiet." With the windows down, the only sounds were my tires crunching over gravel and the wind around us.

"It won't be quiet once we get near my family." Britta settled her hand over mine. "When you slow down to let me roll out, I'll keep you safe. I promise."

She'd said we were going to her parents' house, but a more fitting word would have been estate. We crested the hill, and the large house and expanse of land met us at the end of the gravel road, where the concrete took over. We were surrounded by trees and shrubs, and the path leading up to the house was lined with yellow and red flowers. The lawn ahead was manicured and a shade of green I'd thought only existed on TV. Several cars filled the driveway already, and kids zipped back and forth across an open green space.

"Wow," I said, pulling to a stop. Three men stood around a firepit in the back of the house, arranging wood, and a huddle of people was at a table focused on a card game. It looked like a family on a sitcom. "This place is really nice."

She nodded and opened the car door. "It is. My mom's grandma left it to her. They sold most of the farmland a long time ago, but this is where I grew up." She motioned to the house.

"Wow," I repeated under my breath, grabbing her bag from the trunk and eyeing the lush surroundings. I had money now, but I had never grown out of feeling like an interloper who might muddy the carpet, even while we were still outside.

"Thanks again for driving me." She looked up at me, sunlight warming her face. "Do you want some water or food or something before you head back?"

Before I could respond, the front door flew open and two kids sprinted down the steps, a blur of brown hair and bright colors. "Aunt Britta's here!" they screamed before tackling her to the ground in two bear hugs. She laughed as one more small body leaped onto the pile.

"Give her a minute to breathe." A voice similar to Britta's but deeper rang out from the top of the steps. The older woman wore jeans and a plain gray T-shirt. "Kids!" she said more firmly, pulling the littlest one up while the other two peeled themselves away.

Britta huffed, blowing wayward curls from her face with a gleeful smile as she tried to return to a post-tackle upright state. When I offered my hand, our eyes met for a second. Something electric passed between us as she gripped my palm and regained her balance. "Thanks."

"Now, my turn!" Her mom scooted past the kids and wrapped Britta in a hug with just as much enthusiasm, minus the tackling. "Honey, you look so good. You're glowing!" Gripping Britta's arms, her mom looked her up and down, and Britta's cheeks colored.

"And you must be Del. I'm Danielle, Britta's mom. Welcome!" She turned with her hand held out. "We've heard so much about you."

*Nope. Not jealous at all of Del.*

"Mom, Del actually got held up with work. This is my . . ."

I hung on her pause, curious what she'd say. She finished it with, "This is Wes. He was nice enough to drive me out when Del had to cancel because of a thing at work."

I held out my hand. Her mom didn't register any recognition when Britta said my name. That hurt more than it should. "Nice to meet you."

A young boy in a bright orange T-shirt with a football tucked under his arm pulled on my shirt. "You're big."

"Um, yep." I crouched down. "What's your name?"

"I'm Jon. Are you Aunt Britta's boyfriend?"

"Hi, Jon." I sidestepped his actual question. "That's a cool football. Do you play?"

"Not yet. Do you know how?"

"I do." It was apparently my day to teach sports to kids, and Aaron's comment that I would have been a good teacher came back to me.

"Can you show me how to throw a spiral pass? My friend Carter knows. Carter's dad taught him, but Mom says my dad can't because he's useless with sports."

Britta's *he's not wrong* expression made me laugh, and she ruffled the boy's hair. "Wes has to go soon, so he won't have time to play with you."

"Oh no!" Britta's mom interjected. "Don't go yet. Stay for lunch at least. You drove all this way. You have to at least let us feed you." Britta's mom didn't really ask me to stay so much as decree it.

"Mom," Britta started, holding up a hand. "Wes has to—"

"A plate of food. It's the least we can do to thank you for bringing our girl to us." Danielle shushed her daughter and patted my arm. "We insist."

Britta mouthed "Sorry," but I shrugged and nodded.

Jon pulled on my arm again. "So, can you teach me?"

"Sure, buddy. Can I help your aunt get settled first?"

"Okay!" Jon yelled the response and then sprinted toward the other kids playing tag.

"Winning points already," Britta said under her breath as I stood. "I guess you're going to get to meet everyone."

I leaned in so my lips almost brushed her ear, her mom momentarily distracted by one of the other kids. "I don't think I'd want to cross your mom."

Britta giggled, and I wanted to slip my arm around her and pull her closer against me.

Her mom spoke over the low roar of the kids. "Drop off your stuff in the blue room. That's where I was going to put you and Del." The blue room implied they had so many rooms that a coding system was needed. I'd shared a room with Libby until I was sixteen and then moved to our couch when we had a couch. I'd caught something else—she'd only said one room.

"Were you planning that Del and I would share a bed?"

"Oh, come on, now," her mom said with a playful shove to Britta's shoulder. "I'm not that old-fashioned. I don't care if you share a bed with your boyfriend."

"Mom! I told you we're just *friends*."

Her mom looked apologetic and bit her lower lip, like Britta did when she was embarrassed. She also eyed me, clearly trying to figure out my deal. I would have liked to know, too. "I thought that was code, like that Netflix and chill thing. You kids never tell me what you really mean."

I could have kissed her mom for revealing Del was just a friend.

"Britta's friend! Hurry so we can play!"

Britta's mother turned to scold Jon for being rude, and Britta tilted up her head. "It looks like you're a wanted man."

Her mouth was tipped up in a grin, brown eyes dancing in a way that made me want to kiss her, a craving I was getting more and more used to and finding harder and harder to resist. "I guess so," I said as her mom turned back to us.

"Well, you better go put your stuff down before Jon tackles you and drags you out himself." She shooed us toward the stairs but called over her shoulder. "And stop side-eyeing me, Britta Christine. You friend isn't here anyway, so the bed doesn't matter."

A chorus of yelling bled through the nearby window from the group outside. "Spades," Britta said. "We're a little competitive."

"That's kind of cool." All around me, her family was loud and laughing. Britta's mom had returned to the porch with another older woman, both holding iced tea glasses. "Everyone seems so . . . relaxed."

"We're close. Most of my mom's family lives nearby, but my dad's family usually only visits once or twice a year."

My attention was torn as we made our way up the brightly lit staircase to a long hallway dotted with family photos. I tried to take them in and was also admiring Britta's ass as she climbed in front of me.

"Ugh, I hate that she has the old photos up," Britta said, motioning to portraits filled with big curls and the same smile. Britta as a smiling toddler in a bikini, sticking her belly out. Britta wearing braces and sporting a crooked smile, maybe from middle school. Britta in a bright orange dress standing next to a bride. She pointed to that one. "My sister's wedding. No one who really loves her sister picks dresses that color."

"I don't know; it kind of suits you." I knew nothing about fashion but knew that dress was ugly and fit Britta's body poorly, but I hadn't noticed that initially. I'd been drawn to her smile. "And it's nice that your mom hangs on to so many memories." Several years earlier, in the back of a drawer, I'd found a few Polaroids of Libby and me. I'd relocated them to my own nightstand. After so many months of silence, Libby had finally responded a few weeks earlier—just with an emoji and "I'm fine," but it was something.

Britta motioned to the wall. "It's nice, but it's like a reminder of every awkward stage of my life every time I walk down this hall." She pointed to, admittedly, a bad photo. Britta was maybe thirteen or fourteen, and her hair stuck out in all directions, large pimples dotting the tip of her nose and both cheeks in a connect-the-dots effect.

"Oh, wow," I said with a laugh. "Your glasses . . ."

"Right? Lime green and the size of my entire face. I didn't even need them; I just thought the frames looked cool." She shook her head at the photo. "What if I was bringing an actual boyfriend home? Who would want me with this haunting image so nearby?"

"I'm sure he'd still want you." *How could he not?*

"C'mon. Jon is probably lurking on the stairs to grab you." She nodded her head into the door she opened, and we walked into a large bedroom with pale blue walls. An armchair sat next to a window that overlooked the front yard, and the room had its own adjacent bathroom. This room was bigger than most of the apartments I'd grown up in.

"Welcome to the blue room," she said with a grand gesture at the pale-colored walls. She paused as her gesture returned to the bed, a king-sized mattress in white linens. Her face twisted. "I can't believe my mom thought I was dating Del. I mean, I asked him to be my buffer because he never cares what other people think, but sleeping with him?" She made a face.

"So, just a friend, then? I was kind of wondering if he was the guy you were talking about having a thing for. The one you work with."

Britta glanced away and toyed with her suitcase. "Uh, no. Not him. I've known Del since college. Don't you think you'd know if I was dating someone? I spend all my free time with you."

"I guess so. I was just curious." I cleared my throat and took a step back when she looked up at me with those big eyes. "I haven't seen much need for buffering yet. Your family seems kind of awesome."

"Have no doubt, my mom is downstairs scheming." She sat on the edge of the bed. "If I actually brought a boyfriend home, she'd immediately start planning a wedding."

I was fairly certain my eagerness could be read from space, so I turned, inspecting some artwork on the wall. "You've never brought a boyfriend home?"

"Never felt right. They all ended up wanting to change me in some way. To be different physically, professionally, personality-wise. Never seemed worth the hassle to introduce them to my family."

I ignored the painting and faced her again. "No one who deserves you would want you to be any different."

"I know, Coach." Her wry smile stirred the now-familiar feelings in my chest. "But thank you."

I shrugged, like I hadn't just been a millisecond from telling her she was perfect. The welcoming scent of her—the citrusy hair and something else that always seemed sweet—it was too much. I stepped back again and looked out the window, taking in the expanse of the yard filled with people. "So, what do I need to know?"

LUCKILY, I HAD gym shoes in the back of my car. Jon didn't let me off the hook with throwing the ball, and I'd been drafted into the kids' football game. As I closed the trunk, I heard Britta's family in the back of the house—kids squealing, adults laughing, and the low hum of people having a good time. The entire scene was something from a movie—red-checked tablecloths under mountains of food, the Spades tournament in full swing, and everyone happy—it was weird, but there I was in the middle of it. A car pulling in behind mine shook me from my observation, and a guy dressed casually in jeans and a T-shirt stepped out.

"Hey," he said with a wave, which I returned as he neared. "Always a party at the Colby place, right?" He pointed to the side of the house where Britta's family was scattered. He seemed familiar with the place.

"Yeah," I said, noncommittal.

The guy laughed, seemingly unperturbed by my tone. "Seems like if there's something going on in this town, it's here."

I nodded.

He reached his hand out. "I'm Calvin. My parents are their closest neighbors."

I nearly stumbled and glanced around, as if Britta would be nearby giving me a nod. Apparently, I was chatting with the opposition. He wasn't what I was expecting—from Britta's description, I'd envisioned a mash-up of the main characters from *The Big Bang Theory*, but he was a good-looking guy.

*Would Britta be into this guy?* An unexpected uneasiness settled in my gut.

"Wes." I shook his hand, gripping a little tighter than I needed to. "I'm here with Britta."

His eyebrows rose. "Oh," he said, surprise coloring his face. "I, uh, didn't know she was seeing someone."

I let his statement hang in the air, answering with only a flat expression.

He adjusted his glasses. "You guys been together long?"

"We met a few months ago." I tried to keep my answers vague as a moment of doubt crept in, wondering if Britta actually wanted me to do this. He was sizing me up, and I stood a little straighter. *In for a penny* . . .

"We, uh, dated in high school." He let out a nervous laugh. "I was hoping to catch up with her again."

We neared the house, and Jon, Britta's nephew, ran toward us, clutching the football. "Britta's friend! Can you throw me the ball? My brother doesn't think I can catch it, but I told him I could 'cause you taught me." The kid's face was red, hair matted to his forehead with sweat, and his smile, missing two teeth, was wide. He tossed the ball to me, and I told him to go long, motioning toward the expansive tract of land behind the house.

Calvin and I watched the kid run back to the stretch of grass near Britta and two other women. He cleared his throat. "This is a little awkward, but I've known Britta a long time. I still care about her, so if you hurt her—"

Jon reached a stopping point, and I threw what was arguably a perfect spiral pass. I was posturing for the guy beside me and the woman watching us, but I couldn't help myself.

I turned to Calvin and raised an eyebrow. "You'll hurt me?"

He laughed again, a genuine one this time, and his features relaxed. "Probably not, but I'd try. She's a cool girl. A really cool girl, and always has been. So, just know I'll be waiting in the wings."

I glanced at the woman in question laughing at something Jon told her after catching the ball. Britta's smile brightened, and she looked at me, a happy, curious expression on her face, probably wondering what we were talking about.

I felt bad for Calvin. He seemed like a nice guy, but I didn't feel bad enough to step aside. "Sorry, man. I think you'll be waiting awhile."

I jogged toward Britta, catching a decent pass from Jon as I neared. She looked up at me skeptically, and I shrugged, leaning in to brush my lips against her ear, my arm snaking around her waist.

She stiffened against me, surely surprised by my sudden PDA. *I'm doing what she asked and being a buffer, right?* That was my excuse for pulling her to me and enjoying the way her curves aligned against my body as she relaxed. *It's allowed. We're pretending.* "It's possible Calvin thinks we're dating." *Because I basically told him we're dating.* "How do you want to play this?"

Her expression shifted in recognition as our eyes met. She wrapped her own arm around me. "You are a lifesaver," she said in a low voice only I could hear, keeping her body pressed to mine, and I thanked God for Calvin.

## 37

### BRITTA

When I signed up for FitMi, I mostly did what my coach told me, and I had success. I planned to be more active and assumed I'd build some muscle, but I don't think I really cared—I don't think I really *wanted* it—until recently, when I admitted how much I love seeing what I can do, the goals I'm capable of reaching. You know that kind of wanting where you can see what you desire in front of you and can almost touch it? Where you just know the air will taste a little sweeter once you get it, and it feels like maybe, just maybe, there's a chance it's possible? The wanting. Wow. It gets you.

"YOU'RE SURE YOUR aunt Delia won't corner me for a rematch?" Wes's smile put me at ease before he slipped out of the room and walked down the hall toward the restroom.

He'd been a perfect buffer the whole day. It was a miracle they hadn't brought up the *Best Life* posts. My aunt asked about it once when Wes was mercifully distracted, and I told her I was hoping to forget about work for the weekend. I hated lying, but I didn't want to complicate the situation even more than it already was. Whenever Calvin and his family were nearby, Wes stood closer and made a point of touching me. I knew it was for show, that he was doing what I had asked, but it was still nice to feel like part of a couple.

The football game had turned into lunch had turned into games, and by the time it was nearing dinner, my mom insisted Wes stay overnight, that it was too late to drive back anyway. I saw through her thinly veiled ruse, and I was sure Wes did, too, but after some coaxing, he agreed.

My mom's words, whispered as Wes helped my dad grill burgers, played in my head. *I know you said you're just friends, but he's perfect for you, and that boy likes you.* He was only pretending, I knew that, and it wasn't perfect—or rather, I wasn't perfect for him. I'd been lying to him about my real job for months, and I didn't know how I was going to tell him the truth at this point. When he fell into comfortable trash talk with my family during a Spades tournament, it was hard to remember that.

I'd pulled on a tank top and flannel sleep shorts with yellow ducks while waiting for Wes to return. The evening temperature was ideal for an open window—not too humid or hot, with a nice breeze blowing through the trees. The cozy ambience, with only the bedside light and the chirps of crickets and the din of cicadas drifting in from outside, soothed me.

My breath caught in my throat when Wes stepped inside and closed the door behind him. "No Aunt Delia?"

He smiled, tossing his jeans and T-shirt on his gym bag and kicking off his shoes. "I saw her coming, so I hid," he said, plopping down on the mattress. "She's relentless."

"No one ever beats her and my uncle. You're a legend in my family now." I shifted my gaze to his face, but it wandered back to admire his body in what I hoped was a subtle sweep.

"Well, I had a good teammate." His basketball shorts rested low on his hips, and a tight white T-shirt clung to the expanse of his chest and ridged abs. He caught me staring, and my face felt hot.

When my mom insisted he stay the night, she'd brought a sleeping bag and extra pillows, but winked and whispered that the bed might be more comfortable. I'd been grossed out at my mom choreographing a hookup for me, but watching him crouch and arrange the pillows, I thought the same. "We could share the bed," I said. "You're going to be uncomfortable on the floor."

"I'll be fine down here." He fluffed the pillows and unrolled the sleeping bag. It was comically small, making me wonder if my mom had brought up a child-sized one.

"Come up here." I patted the bed, and he hesitated. "I won't be able to sleep if I know you're on the floor."

He pushed back the too-small sleeping bag and stood. "Are you sure?"

"Positive." That was an understatement. Except sharing a bed with someone I found so irresistible was probably the worst idea of my life.

"I'll try not to snore." He had a dimple in his right cheek that showed up when he smiled like that, and I fantasized about running my fingertip from that divot up to slide through his hair, the curls visible with it grown out. His words pulled me from my fantasy as we both took the far edges of the mattress. "Everything okay?"

"Sure." I turned the bedside lamp off and flipped to my side. The moonlight filtered in from the open window, and I took in his profile as he lay on his back. "Thank you for doing this, for putting up with the entire Colby crew."

"It's been fun. Your family is awesome." He propped his head on his elbow, body angled toward me. "And besides, you're an easy fake girlfriend to love."

My breath stuttered at his words. "Whoa, cowboy. Love? You're moving a little fast, aren't you? We've been fake dating for less than six hours."

"When you pretend to know, you know." His low chuckle shook the mattress enough to put my body on a delicious edge. "And after defeating your aunt, I'm feeling confident."

"Fair. And, I'll admit, the pretend sex *is* good—"

"Good? C'mon, girl. I rock your imaginary world."

I nodded, warmth curling in me at the thought. "Fake nirvana and waking the invisible neighbors, every night." The trees swaying in the breeze and the gentle chirping of crickets outside offered background noise as we lay together in a brief silence. "I don't want to be that girl who needs to ask, but it's not just physical, is it? I mean, you have real fake feelings for me, too?"

His gaze met mine, and he adopted a gravelly, sexy rumble that left a very real ache between my thighs. "Oh, baby," he groaned, inching closer to stroke the side of my face. "I don't know what to do with all the real fake feelings I have for you." His thumb grazed under my lip, and he looked at my mouth for a split second. "It's all I think about."

My body was a pot of water one instant from boiling over with his hand still against my cheek, our bodies so close that his body heat would have warmed me, if I wasn't already flushing from the idea of ripping his clothes off. In the dark, his hazel eyes were shadowed, but I felt like he could see me, really see me. Neither of us moved, and the eye contact seemed endless.

Eventually, he pulled his hand away, breaking our stare. "I mean, pretend to think about."

We returned to silence, now less than a foot apart. I followed the line of his arm, tracing the muscles with my eyes.

"I'm sorry," he said, cutting into my thoughts.

"Why?"

"You got quiet. I took the joke too far."

"Not at all." *Please touch me again.* "This is weird, though, right?"

"Talking about our pretend sex life?"

"Yeah." I smiled, despite my sexual frustration. "Unless you do this with all of your clients?"

"It's more fun with you than the last guy." His voice was back to normal, the smile evident in his words. "And you smell better."

I punched him in the arm, and he feigned injury.

He added in a more serious tone, "You're not just a client. I hope that's clear. I . . ."

His fingers twitched, and I hoped he might touch me again, pull me to him, kiss me, but he kept his hand where it was, and he didn't finish his sentence. That was the moment to tell him about the *Best Life* assignment and come clean, but I let his statement hang there too long, scared about what telling the truth would mean, how it would change things between us.

"For the record, you're actually kind of great, Wes."

The silence between us returned, filled with the things said and unsaid. The heat from his body and mine formed a cozy cocoon. After a moment of my admission hanging in the air, I glanced over, seeing his arm curled under his head and his eyes pointed to the ceiling.

"You're pretty great, too, Britt."

## 38

WES

THE SUN SHINING through the window pulled me from a pleasant dream I couldn't grasp the ends of, except for the memory of Britta's smooth skin and how good she smelled. A light breeze moved through the room as the distant sounds of rustling leaves and chirping birds brought the morning into a slow focus. My eyes closed again as I took in the warmth surrounding me, before my eyelids flew open because her sweet smell and warm skin hadn't been part of the dream. Britta's soft breasts and stomach pressed against me, one leg hitched on mine and her arm draped across my midsection. Her head rested on my chest, hair coming loose from the scarf she'd used to wrap it, and I had an immediate sense of rightness with my arm settled around her.

I stroked my fingers over the soft skin of her back. It was a half-hearted attempt to wake her; I was sure she'd shift away at any moment, pulling her soft curves and body heat away from me.

Britta released a soft moan in her sleep, her breath warming my chest through my shirt as she shifted, not away but against me, her hand sliding lower on my stomach, fingertip just under the waistband of my shorts. The sensation was like being struck by a bolt of lightning and craving another.

My dick, hard as a rock, ached for her fingers, her body to move just a little more. I stared at the ceiling, mind racing with thoughts and decisions. *She's still a client and my friend; this is wrong.*

Britta stirred again, her finger curling under the hem of my T-shirt. *I should move away from her before I can't.*

"Britta," I whispered, a hint of desperation in my voice as I nudged her hand away from my shorts. I meant to rouse her enough to slip out of bed, maybe to take a walk down the hall toward a hopefully cold shower. Instead, I dragged my fingertips over the nape of her neck, not wanting to startle her. I stroked my thumb back and forth, repeating her name in a whisper. I wished I could reach her shoulder from this angle so I could kiss her there and wake her up, use that as a proxy for verbally admitting everything I felt.

We'd joked about our fake sex life, but I'd lain awake imagining being with her. My thoughts weren't all pure, but I'd wondered if it might be okay to hope for something real with her, to imagine being her partner for Spades, and the guy who got to hold her hand for no reason, not just when Calvin was nearby.

She stirred again, her breath coming faster as she realized her surroundings. She looked at me, then down at how our bodies were aligned. Her cheeks reddened, and she was obviously embarrassed. "I'm sorry, I—"

"It's okay." Our eyes met, and her plump lips parted. I'd stared at those lips so many times, imagining how she'd taste, and how she'd sound murmuring my name. My free hand dropped to hers, the weight pressing her palm to the exposed skin of my stomach. I couldn't stand the idea of missing her touch again, and I searched her wide brown eyes. "Don't apologize."

I worked my fingers under the scarf and into her hair, feeling how soft and thick her curls were, and leaned my face closer to hers, so our breaths mingled. I kept my movements slow, wanting her to have time to push me away, for one of us to remember this was a bad idea. We didn't, and our lips hovered close. "Britta," I said, aware of every point where our bodies connected and the way her irises darkened. "Can I kiss you?"

She tipped her chin, and when our mouths met, I took her lower lip between mine and sucked, slowly, patiently, willing myself to savor this. It wasn't a tentative kiss, though. It was what I'd been craving for months, and I breathed her in.

She arched against me, whimpering my name, and I was lost, gone at the idea she'd been craving this, too.

"Britta," I said into her skin, kissing her neck and loving the way her nails grazed my scalp. Her body was eager, and she pressed her hips to me, searching.

"We shouldn't, but—" She panted, grabbing my hand and pushing it up to cup her perfect full breast over the thin fabric of her tank.

*My God.* I massaged, taking as much in my palm as I could before gliding my thumb over the peaked tip of her nipple. She shuddered under me, and I did it again, wanting to bury my face under her shirt, seeing if she shuddered like that when I glided my tongue over the sensitive spots.

"You're my coach." She let out the words between kisses. "And I'm . . . I'm . . ."

"Do you want me to stop?" I pulled my lips from hers, stilling my hands and looking down at her beautiful, open mouth, her wide eyes. I didn't give a damn about being her coach, not after kissing her, and not after having her like this, but the last thing I wanted was her feeling uncomfortable.

She shook her head, pulled her lower lip between her teeth, and searched my face, eyes bouncing between mine for interminable seconds. "Don't stop." Britta shifted her thigh to my hip, opening herself to me, and I dragged my palm from the luscious weight of her breast down to knead her ass as she pleaded, "Don't stop."

I rolled her to her back and settled between her legs, pressing myself against her heat. She let out a small, strangled cry against my shoulder when I ground my length against her. I couldn't decide where to touch, where to taste her—I wanted to be everywhere, and she was still letting out muted whimpers and moans that sent me into overdrive. I wanted to tell her I was crazy about her, that she was always on my mind, that the thought of her with someone else drove me nuts. Britta's kiss was like her smile—it made me feel invincible, and I dipped my head for another.

"Wes! Are you up? Wes! Hey!" A bang against the door, and Jon's small voice called from the other side. "It's morning! We can play football again!"

I sucked in a ragged breath and locked eyes with Britta, who pressed her lips together to stifle a laugh. "Okay, buddy," I called out. "Um, give me . . . a little time."

"Grown-ups are so slow!" Jon yelled, his feet pounding on the hardwood floors.

"Fuck," I whispered, rolling to my back, pulling Britta with me, her head again resting on my chest.

"You kissed me." She scratched her nails over my stomach, making me inhale sharply. When she lifted her head to meet my eyes, her cheeks were flushed.

I rubbed my thumb over the back of her neck. "I think you kissed me first."

"This is complicated." She slid her palm up my chest, her gaze following its path until she cupped my neck. "There are probably things we should talk about."

This hadn't been my plan, but it was happening, complication be damned. "Definitely complicated, but . . ." I stroked the side of her pinky finger up and down. "But worth it." I wanted more than just that moment and more than stolen hurried kisses. I wanted to tell her I wasn't pretending, that what I felt for her was bigger and deeper than what I'd ever felt for anyone else. When I opened my mouth to say it, my phone vibrated on the dresser where I'd tossed it the night before, making us both jump.

It buzzed again and we giggled. Britta's lips brushed against my shoulder, and I pulled her closer. The vibration stopped, and I slid my finger along her cheek, brushing strands of hair away.

It wasn't lost on me that it was the first time I hadn't tensed at a call.

I felt okay letting it go when I had Britta in my arms. I was okay with not being in control of things. "Sorry. Go ahead. What happens next can be anything you want, Bubs. It can be nothing at all, or . . ." I traced my fingers down her neck, enamored with getting to touch her in that warm bed with the breeze blowing in. I felt like I was where I was meant to be. "I . . . Britta, I think I'm fall—"

"Wes, wait." Britta bit her lower lip and pulled back, meeting my gaze. "I need to tell you something before we . . . before anything else. It's important."

I didn't know what her expression meant, and my mind jumped to the worst possibilities, that she didn't want this, that she immediately regretted this. I loosened my grip, giving her plenty of room to move away, but she didn't. "What is it?"

She slid her palm across my chest, but she didn't pull away. "I didn't tell you sooner because . . . well, it will ruin this," she whispered, dragging her gaze from mine.

I let out a slow breath. "No." I nudged her chin up. "There's nothing you could say that would. Nothing, okay?" My phone buzzed again, the sound filling the space, but Britta had smiled, and I could block it out. "Hold on. I'll silence it."

I fumbled for the phone with one hand and pulled away from her to reach it. The name on the caller ID flashed, and I answered immediately.

"Hello?" My voice was thick and raspy, and I repeated myself. The voice on the other end of the line was enough to drain all the blood from my face.

# 39

## BRITTA

WE WERE ALMOST to the hospital. Wes's face contorted every now and again, as if a bad memory were playing on a loop and he was biting it back. He'd told me I didn't need to come with him, but after the phone call, he was ashen. My unflappable coach seemed shell-shocked.

"Do you want me to order a ride to take you home?" As we exited the interstate, his voice startled me.

"I'll stay with you."

"I'm not sure how long this will take or what's going on." He glanced at me, worry etched in the lines of his face, one hand scrubbing the back of his neck.

"That's okay." The day before, I wouldn't have thought twice about touching his shoulder or taking his hand, but what were the rules after that kiss?

We pulled into the parking deck, but he didn't move, his hands gripping the steering wheel as he stared forward. "It's just that she's . . ." He drummed his fingers on the steering wheel. "I don't know how she'll be today, and she's . . . It's complicated."

He swallowed, his features set in a firm line.

"Take care of your mom. I can wait. I don't want to abandon you, okay? Is there anything I can do? Do you want me to call your sister for you?"

I touched his forearm, but he flinched away, saying only "No" before stepping out of the car.

It was ten in the morning when we walked into the building. For July, it was cool, a chilled wind blowing around us in the midmorning sun. A receptionist directed us to the sixth floor. The whoosh and whir of the elevator's machinery filled the silence. Wes tapped his hand against the metal, making a hollow clang that reverberated.

"Did they give you any indication of what's happened?"

"She's . . ." He drummed his fingers against his thigh, avoiding my eyes before shoving his hands in his pockets. "She's been an addict my whole life. Booze, oxy, heroin. She was getting clean, though. I thought she was, anyway. She hasn't been using."

My heart broke at his defeated tone. He was always so positive and playful, and I wondered if he felt like he had to be, if this had been weighing him down. There was a lot he'd never told me.

"She's been on house arrest. She'd been doing okay, but she left sometime last night, walked out and got fucked-up. They found her early this morning."

"Wes," I said, although I didn't know how to finish the sentence. It didn't matter. The doors opened, and he squared his shoulders before walking out. I followed him toward the reception desk, thinking for the first time that coming with him might have been a mistake and that there was a lot about Wes I didn't know.

"Shelly Lawson?"

"I believe the doctors want to speak with you first," the woman behind the counter said.

"I'll just find a place to wait," I began, looking for a waiting area on the floor, but a middle-aged woman in a white coat approached us before we stepped away from the desk. She had the practiced, even expression of someone used to delivering bad news in a caring way.

"Mr. Lawson? I'm Dr. Stevens. Could we talk for a few minutes?"

Wes stiffened. "Is it bad?"

I caught the shake of his hand at his side, and this time he didn't flinch when I moved my hand to his.

The doctor's expression didn't change. "Let's step into the meeting room."

"Okay." His strong, straight shoulders slumped, and I followed him into the small room, our hands still joined.

"So, it's bad? Did she overdose? Is she . . . is she dead?" His voice was low and choked, like he needed to clear his throat but couldn't. He looked at his phone then, staring at the blank screen, and I wasn't sure why.

"She's alive. She was unresponsive on arrival but is resting now. She had a large amount of oxycodone in her system. The immediate intervention was as effective as possible; however, her heartbeat is irregular, and she was having trouble breathing, so we've admitted her." Pulling a tablet from her lab coat, the doctor navigated to the screens she wanted. "She has a history of drug and alcohol abuse?"

Wes nodded, and the doctor folded her arms on the table in an authoritative but not unkind way. "It is likely that the shortness of breath, the slowed heart rate, and other symptoms such as forgetfulness may not markedly improve. It seems they've been occurring for a while, but if your mother continues this level of substance abuse, she will likely die, and sooner rather than later."

Wes nodded twice, wordless, jaw clenched. He held the phone so tightly, I thought it might break.

"We'll encourage her to participate in rehab and seek help." The doctor gave him a moment to process the information before continuing. "I imagine you already know addiction is challenging to tackle."

He dropped my hand and ran his fingers through his hair again, words choked. "Yeah, I know. What do I . . . what should I do?"

The doctor assured him they would run more tests, then meet with him to discuss options. "I wanted you to know before you saw her. She's been asking for you and Libby." The doctor cut her gaze to me.

"Libby is my sister," he said, his voice hollow, not looking at me. "She won't be coming."

"Ah. Well, know she may not be fully herself yet as the drugs wear off."

I ignored how much it stung to see him putting walls up around himself as she gave him more information and offered to take us to the room.

Wes walked stiffly, one hand shoved in the pocket of his jeans, the other fisted at his side. This hospital was nice, but his mom's room seemed drab, no sunlight. A frail-looking woman with thin blond hair lay in the bed. She was conscious, but her eyelids were hooded.

"I'll leave you alone." The doctor stepped out into the hall, and we hung back.

The tension rolled off Wes in waves, his knuckles white from the way he'd clenched his fist. I grazed my fingertips along the back of his hand—he still hadn't looked at me. "Do you want me to leave you alone with her? I could call someone?" I thought he might grab my hand again, link his fingers with mine, and let me offer some comfort, but he just shook his head.

"You can stay if you want. The only person I need to call is her lawyer."

"Baby." Wes's mom turned and her face lit up, a sleepy smile crossing her chapped lips. "You came to see me."

He stepped closer, his voice thick. "How're you feeling?"

She reached a bony finger to touch his hand. "You haven't visited me."

The muscle in his jaw ticked, and he took her hand carefully, as if it might break. "I know. I'm here now, though." He sank to the side of her bed and was fighting back what looked like despair and anger, trying hard to keep his shell in place as he stroked her tiny hand.

"So grown-up, like a man. Where's your sister?"

His features tensed, but his voice remained steady. "She's not here."

The woman's face fell, and she glanced in my direction. "Is this your girlfriend, Chris?" She motioned me over, not quite focusing on my face.

*Chris?*

"Hi," I said. "I'm Britta." I held out my hand, and she weakly gripped my fingertips.

I cut my eyes to Wes, wondering why she'd called him the wrong name. He got his hazel eyes from her—they were the same gold-flecked shade. "I'm Wes's . . . his . . ." I paused, making eye contact with Wes across the bed.

His face was unreadable, dazed, but he interrupted my floundering. "Client."

That hit me like a bucket of ice water.

"Sure, she is." Her face cracked into a sleepy, mischievous smile. "You've got big tits. He likes that."

"Jesus, Mom," he muttered, rubbing the spot between his brows.

His mom's light, conversational tone, like we were old friends, threw me, even though the doctor had warned she might lack a filter. My eyes shot to Wes's reddened face. He didn't smile back.

"What? A lot of boys do." Her eyes crinkled at the corners, and she looked me over. "You're pretty," she said, taking in my face. "I used to be pretty." Sadness filled her voice. Her brow creased, and she touched her hair, pulling on the strands. "I must look bad."

"Mom, don't worry about it," Wes said, trying to catch her hand.

"No, no. Look at me. It's bad, isn't it?" She grew agitated, pulling away from Wes's attempts and trying to finger comb her tangled hair.

"It's just a little messy," I said, trying to calm her. I laid a hand on her forearm, guiding her arm down. "Would you like us to comb it for you?" The offer softened her features, and she slowed her clawing.

"Libby liked to comb my hair when she was small." She took on a faraway expression. "Would you?"

I glanced at Wes, who focused on the wall. I peeked into the bathroom, where there was a small toiletry kit provided by the hospital, and found a comb. I perched by the side of the bed and ran my fingers over her head. She closed her eyes, and I met Wes's gaze.

"You don't have to."

"I don't mind." I worked the comb through her hair gently.

His mom's voice was calmer now. "Do you know Libby?"

"No, Mom."

She returned to looking at me, ignoring Wes.

"Oh," she said, her face twisting, then shifting again, realization blooming across her features and her tone flattening. "She left."

"Yeah. A long fucking time ago," he muttered, fists balled at his sides again.

"I know that," she said, voice sharpening and hands twitching again. "I remember." She picked at the blanket around her waist, pulling at unseen threads. "She ran away, and you were gone. You weren't there to stop her."

Wes's entire body tensed. My eyes shot to his again, but his face was a mask—it was pain and shame and hurt all frozen in place. His voice was barely audible when he choked out a response. "I know."

*My God.*

"She was such a good girl," his mom said, glancing away from her son. Her tone was different; it was sweeter, wistful. "The best thing I ever did. She was going to be a famous singer. Who knows what she's doing now."

His frozen expression hadn't changed, lips pressed together, eyes focused on the wall.

"Chris is still here, though." Her voice was dreamy. "He's a good boy."

Wes ran a hand through his hair again, his muscles taut.

"He's a good man," I said, continuing to brush her hair. I got the sense he needed to hear that, like no one had bothered to tell him, but he stepped away from the bed and walked to the window, and I doubted he was listening.

"Yes," she said, eyelids drooping. I stroked her hair as I combed, hoping that might calm her. She smiled again, looking at Wes. "I'm glad you're here, Chris." Her eyes closed, and her features softened into sleep, her frail body sinking into the pillows.

Wes stood at the window, his back to me. "Thank you," he said without looking at me, his voice thick, affected. "For doing that. For talking to her."

"Sure," I said, keeping my voice low to not disturb her when it looked like she was asleep. I took the few steps toward Wes, feeling awkward and unsteady.

"She calls you Chris?" At first, I'd thought she was just confused, but he hadn't seemed to react to her using that name. It was familiar, but I couldn't place it.

He nodded. "Wesley is my middle name. No one calls me Chris but her and Libby."

I had a hundred questions but slid my hand to his back, my palm moving over the cotton of his T-shirt, his tensed muscles bunched under the fabric. "Wes, are you okay?"

His gaze was locked on the sky, his tone flat. "Yep."

I didn't know what he wanted, if touching him was the right thing. He said nothing, didn't hang his head or appear to be crying, but his body was held so tightly in place, it might break at any moment. *Screw it.* I wrapped my arms around his waist, pulling him back against me, tentatively at first and then more firmly, my cheek pressed between his shoulder blades. I didn't have any words, so I listened to his breathing and the thudding of his heart.

"She's right," he said, not looking away from the window. "I wanted to get away from my life and her, and I wasn't there when Lib needed me. I was always the person she could count on, and I wasn't there. What does that say about me?"

Tightening my hold, I wished I had the leverage to pull him into a real hug. I wasn't even sure he knew I was touching him. "You were trying to live your life."

He laced his long fingers together behind his neck, dipping his chin to his chest, the muscles across his shoulders straining as stress radiated off him. "When I came home, it was too late. She and Mom were fighting worse than they ever had. She wasn't eating or taking care of herself. Something snapped and she ran away. The first time I heard from her, she was in Florida, then she bounced around Texas. The last time she gave me a location, it was Phoenix, but that was over a year ago." His voice, quiet in the dim room, edged toward cracking, and I pressed my face into his back.

"It's not your fault she left."

His words kept coming, like water pouring from a faucet. I didn't know if I should try to shut off the valve or catch the deluge.

"I tried to get Libby to stay with me, to get away from that house and the drugs and the guys Mom brought home, so I could help, and she shut me out. The last thing she ever said was *leave me alone*. And I did. I left her alone to deal with it, and I went back to school because I wanted to—because I wanted to put myself first for once. I figured I'd let her cool off and try again—that maybe one time I wouldn't step in, but let the two of them work it out, but then she was gone."

My tears left wet spots on the back of his shirt. With the low, hopeless tone in his voice, I had no idea what to say, so I just kept holding on to him.

The ambient hospital sounds outside the closed door provided a muffled backdrop to our conversation, reminding me things existed outside of the room. "What can I do, Wes?"

He pressed my hands harder against him, the beat of his heart consistent under my palm. I wondered in that moment if that was his way of telling me he'd let me be the one to hold him.

"I shouldn't have brought you here." His voice was rough. "And I shouldn't have kissed you. I'm your coach, and that's all I should be. I don't . . ." He paused, but I heard his slow intake of breath. "This morning shouldn't have happened. It was a mistake."

Shaking my head against his back, I racked my brain for what to say to change his mind. I tried to gather up the shards of memory that fell around the word "mistake." I didn't have the chance, as the doctor returned to the room. "Mr. Lawson?"

He gripped my hands for another moment, then let them go, pulling away before turning to the doctor, leaving me facing the open window, the gray sky beyond it.

# 40

WES

I CANCELED THE morning run with Britta for the third time that week. I'd put off preparing for a big meeting and stayed at work late the night before, but needing to catch up on work wasn't the only reason behind the decision. I didn't know how to face her—not after that kiss, and not after that embarrassing breakdown at the hospital.

I couldn't forget the combination of Britta's lips, her supple body pressed to mine, and that little sound of surprise she made when we connected on the bed. All of it had been playing on a loop that left me uneasy and feeling guilty, because I'd never wanted to be that guy who took advantage. I'd spent my whole life trying not to be that guy, and being with her made me feel so good, I hadn't cared that hooking up with her coach might derail her plans. I'd been ready to risk that because of what I wanted. Being around my mom and her talking about Libby just hammered that home.

I'd texted Libby to let her know Mom was in the hospital, and I couldn't believe it when the dots bounced indicating a response, and I'd held my breath.

**Libby:** Is she going to make it?

**Wes:** Yeah. For now. I can't believe you answered. Are you okay? Where are you? Do you need me to send money? Can I see you?

She hadn't written back. I'd spent the last few days in a weird place of complete relief she was alive and loss at her not saying anything else after I came on too strong. I shoved the phone back in my pocket.

When I stepped off the elevator, I spotted Cord perched on Pearl's desk, both of them laughing. The sound grated on me, and I shifted my jaw back and forth.

Pearl straightened and smiled, but I didn't meet her gaze and just focused on the door ahead of me. "Good morning, Wes. I came in early and arranged for your—"

Pearl was so much better than this job. She was better suited to be in charge than me, that was for damn sure, and suddenly, I knew seeing her would just be something else to feel guilty about. "Thanks," I said in a rushed tone without looking up. I closed the door to my office behind me, but I was alone for only a moment.

Cord stormed in. "What the hell was that?"

"What?"

"Why were you such a dick to Pearl? She got in early today to get everything ready for our meeting. Since you forgot about that shit until the last goddamned minute."

"I'll apologize later." I tossed my messenger bag by my desk and shook the mouse, then banged it against the desk to wake up the machine.

Cord crossed his arms over his chest. "Apologize now."

"I said I'll do it later. Step the fuck off." I banged the mouse and the screen lit up.

"You've been a moody, short-tempered, unreliable prick all week. What the hell is wrong with you?"

"Are you suddenly her knight in shining armor or something? Pearl's fine."

"That woman is one of the few people in the world who give a damn about you. And maybe you've forgotten, but you run this fucking company.

People depend on us. I don't know if you're bored or you need a different distraction or whatever, but you need to figure it out. No one twisted your arm to be here, so stop acting like it's a goddamned chore to do your job, and grow up." Cord took a step toward me and we squared off.

"Fuck you. I don't need a lecture." I held my fists balled at my sides.

His nostrils flared as we faced each other, voices raised. We were posturing like two people about to brawl.

*What am I doing?*

"Damn it," I muttered. I sunk into my chair and pressed my fingertips to my forehead, the dull ache stretching into a throbbing pain. "I'm sorry. Maybe I need the lecture. Everything is fucked right now. Mom overdosed. She's getting worse. Libby is MIA again."

"Shit, man." Cord blew out a long breath before crossing the room and sitting on the other side of the desk. "I didn't know."

I took in the exposed ductwork in the ceiling before meeting his eyes. "You're right. I've been a dick, and I'll apologize to Pearl. I've just been . . . it's been rough. I'm sorry."

"You want to talk about it?"

"Nah. I'll get it together."

Cord studied my face. "For the record, I'm one of the other people who give a damn. You don't always have to keep this stuff to yourself."

I grunted with a nod. My head pounded. I considered telling him everything about Britta. Part of me was still hoping I could rewind to the moment before I felt anything, and it wouldn't matter. *She's a client. She's just a client.* It wasn't working. "I'm sorry, man. I'll make it up to Pearl. Is there something going on with you two?"

Cord shrugged, but the corner of his mouth twitched. "We're just friends." He glanced at his watch and grimaced. "Want to meet up in thirty to go over things ahead of time?"

"Yeah. I'll see you in the conference room."

I glanced at my phone.

**Wes:** What flowers say, "I'm sorry for being an asshole?"

**Britta:** Depends. Who are they for and what did you do?

**Wes:** Someone I rely on for pretty much everything at work, and I've been a jerk.

**Britta:** I'd go tulips. And maybe cash. Perhaps a puppy?

**Wes:** On it. How was your run this morning?

**Britta:** Did almost four miles.

**Wes:** That's great. I'm sorry I canceled on you.

The dots bounced, but she didn't respond. I could picture her, biting her lower lip and second-guessing what she wanted to say. *God, I fucked everything up.*

**Wes:** Should I send you tulips and a puppy, too?

It was the first honest thing I'd said to her since the hospital, and the muscles in my neck relaxed as soon as I sent it. I missed more than talking to her—I missed the smell of her hair and how her voice turned up when she told me she hated me—but I didn't get to say those things, not after everything that happened in the hospital. I didn't want to mess with her head any more than I already had.

**Britta:** Just the cash would be fine.

**Britta:** But seriously, I'm here when you need a friend.

Reading "friend" was a stab to the gut, but she was playing by my rules. I just needed to keep what I was feeling in check.

**Wes:** Gym tomorrow morning at 6:30?

**Britta:** Sorry. I can't tomorrow.

# 41

## BRITTA

**LIKED BY NATCANDOIT AND 8,923 OTHERS**

I took a long time to work up the courage to try the weight bench. I watched the how-to videos on the FitMi app and asked my coach, but I was still nervous when it came time to add weight to the bar and stretch out on my back—what if people laughed at how little I added? What if I looked silly? On top of all that, I had an irrational fear I'd fart while lifting and everyone would stop and stare. I think this whole journey is like that—watching from the sidelines and learning, and then feeling uncomfortable when you try something new. What made it easier was having my spotter there—someone to catch the weight if it came to that. I think we should have spotters on hand more often in life. Here's a photo of @BestLifeClaire and me on our way to a weekend retreat. If you're using FitMi coaching, you have a built-in spotter, but who else is supporting you?

AFTER ALMOST TWO hours in the car, Claire and I stepped out in front of the Meadows of Venus Resort and Spa. Beyond the pristine brick facade of the building, sunlight glittered off the ripples in the lake, and I inhaled the clean air.

While Claire checked us in at the front desk, I pulled my phone from my pocket, hoping for a message from Wes. Even though things were awkward, not seeing him felt worse, so I figured I'd bite the bullet and pretend it never happened, and maybe we'd get back to normal. I'd done that with Ben, and we just stopped talking. I hoped this would work out better.

**Britta:** We made it. I will never get tired of how fresh air smells.

**Wes:** How does it smell?

**Britta:** Fresh.

**Wes:** You should research adjectives. Did you pack your running shoes?

**Britta:** Yeah, I'm going before dinner tonight. I'm not used to running without you barking at me.

**Wes:** You might grow to like it.

*I doubt it.* I tucked my phone back in my pocket and felt guilty about lying to him about my role with *Best Life*. Maybe it was best that nothing romantic would happen—I needed the writing job to move forward with my career, and I was probably already too close to my coach, even without the kiss. *That kiss.* The feel of his hands on me. The promise of more when he pressed his body to mine.

"We're all checked in," Claire said, handing me my key and interrupting my thoughts.

"Thanks." We walked toward the elevator, and Claire pulled two manila folders from her oversize bag. "We can take advantage of the treatments, and there's just a few things we'll do together, including floating meditation."

"Floating meditation?"

"I guess they give us wine and we float on rafts in this cordoned-off part of the lake."

"Like a lazy river? Did you do that in college? Grab a cooler of beer and an inner tube?"

Ours eyes met, and her face cracked into a smile. "A very expensive lazy river, I guess. Natalie requested we write about it. I guess it's one of their selling points." We shared a chuckle as the elevator doors closed.

I HAD A spacious room with a view of the lake from the balcony. The sky became a deep azure as the afternoon wore on. I lost the battle to be cool and turned to snap a selfie, angling the camera from above my head to catch my face surrounded by sunlight and nature. I looked pretty in the photo, not that it mattered.

> **Britta:** I still don't have a good adjective for how it smells, but isn't this view amazing? Do you wish you were here?

I didn't expect the bouncing dots of his reply so quickly.

> **Wes:** More than you know.

> **Britta:** Do you have fun plans for the weekend?

> **Britta:** Hot date?

I hit send before my thumb wandered to the backspace key. He wasn't responding, but I braced myself anyway. *Worst-case scenario: He's on his way to her place now with a bottle of wine, a box of condoms, and an engagement ring.* Wes was my friend and my trainer, and kissing me didn't seem to have meant anything. Maybe he did that with women all the time, and he could take wine, condoms, and rings to all kinds of other women. Still, I hoped he was at home in sweats, alone.

**Wes:** No date.

**Wes:** [audio file]

I hit play on the voice recording, and Wes's voice filled my room.
"Pick up the pace."
"Eyes forward."
"You're doing great."
"One more mile."
"I know you can do it."
"Push."
"I believe in you."
I listened to it twice, my smile widening with each phrase, and pictured his expression when he was waiting for me to laugh at his joke.

**Wes:** So you won't miss me barking at you on your run.

I listened to it one more time, shaking my head and dropping into the chair on my balcony. I scrolled to the latest comments on my Falling and Failing post. I'd been amazed at the initial response, and the comments kept coming.

**@MaryJoMazing:** Thank you for sharing this story. We do these things to ourselves, and for what? I'm so glad you came to your senses quickly, and I hope you're healing.

**@justhaley91:** I read your story and didn't realize I was crying. I've let so many men shape how I feel about myself and what I need to be. Making me think I'm not good enough. Thank you for telling us about your fall—and how you're getting up. I'm trying to be like you, Britta!

**@TheOriginalBL:** I love how real you are. I feel like I know you and you get it.

**@GrzzldJoeTC:** I didn't realize the damage I could be doing until I read the links you shared at the end of the post.

I wanted so badly to text Wes and tell him how good I felt, how much this meant to me, but it felt wrong now. I never thought I was someone who would so easily compromise ethics, but I never planned on Wes. My mind wandered to the events of the weekend before. Wes's grin during Spades and the feel of his back against my face when he was telling me about his sister. His mom calling him Chris . . . My head snapped up, mind at attention. His mom called him Chris, and he said that Wes was his middle name. Her name was Shelly Lawson. I scrolled back through the notes I'd gathered when preparing for the start of Body FTW and found my research on the founders and CEOs of the company: Cord Matthews and Christopher Lawson.

*Holy shit.*

<hr />

AFTER DINNER, CLAIRE and I met on the shore for the grown-up lazy river. My mind was still spinning at the revelation that Wes wasn't just my coach—I'd made out with the CEO of the company I was reviewing. That was setting aside the fact that we'd been moments away from doing much more than making out. He'd been pressed against me, and the memory of his body, the heat and size of him, left a flush traveling up my neck. Knowing how his thick erection felt between my thighs was a lit match on the kindling of my already singed ethics. I balled my fists and tried to put it out of my mind. I had work to do, and thoughts like this were going to get in the way of everything I'd been working toward.

The attendant walked us through the safety information, letting us know a lifeguard was always there, and made sure we were comfortable in the water in the unlikely event we fell in. I'd imagined the rafts like those flat inflatable ones from childhood, but the guides welcomed us both toward the dock, where the rafts floated at the bottom of a small ladder, loaded with cushions and drink holders. "And would you prefer your rafts linked or separate?"

"Linked, please." Claire surprised me with her answer.

I toyed with the hem of my cover-up before handing it to the young attendant, asking her to hang it up. I noticed the feel of the breeze on my chest and added some extra sway to my hips just for my own benefit.

After they launched us, Claire and I lay on our respective rafts for a few minutes as we drifted. I'd been skeptical, but the gentle sway of the water and the stillness of the night was relaxing. Settling against the pillows, I sipped my wine.

"That's cute." Claire's voice startled me as she nodded toward my swimsuit, and I instinctively scanned her comment for sarcasm.

"Thanks. Yours, too." We returned to our silence, which was infiltrated only by the lapping of the water and the distant sounds of cicadas.

Claire took a long drink from her wineglass and settled it back in the holder. "Can I ask you something? Maybe call a cease-fire on our competition for a few minutes?"

I'd just swallowed my wine, or I might have sprayed it in surprise. I glanced over at my colleague, expecting a smirk, but she looked genuine. "Sure. What's up?"

"You can't tell anyone." She lay on her back and spoke into the air before squeezing her eyes shut, her mouth pulling to the side.

"What happens on the lazy river stays on the lazy river and all that."

Claire turned toward me, her head propped on her elbow. I admired her waist as she shifted. I'd been trying hard to stop comparing myself to other women, but it was always so hard with Claire, since we were so competitive in other ways.

She took another drink of wine. "You wrote that piece about your fall and how your coach helped you get back on track, right?"

"Sure." That had been the hardest piece I'd written, but the comments poured in daily from people who identified with what I'd said, who had real struggles with eating disorders or just felt like giving up. Maricela had given the green light to my suggestion to interview experts on eating and exercise disorders and a well-known speaker about fat phobia.

"The not-eating, crash-dieting thing? Well, my coach has *encouraged* that. Not to that extent, but she recently told me a good way to drop a few pounds in a pinch was to fast for a week or two. I did my own research, and even people who recommend fasting don't recommend doing it like that. I mean, I didn't listen, but I'm worried others might, that they might take it further, and it's dangerous advice. I did some digging, and the coaches get bonuses based on the successes of their clients. Like, dollars for pounds lost."

"Wow." I'd known for a long time that the app I was reviewing was better, and not just because Wes worked there. *Or owned it.* What Claire was describing sounded terrifying, and I couldn't help but wonder where I'd be if I were in her shoes, if I had a coach who didn't care if I went down a dangerous path. I grimaced. "What are you going to do?"

Claire looked away from me, and her gaze swept over the water. "What would you do?"

I pictured Wes's face when he talked about his sister and her eating disorder, and my stomach sank. "I don't know . . . but you have to say something. People could get hurt."

Claire plopped back. "I'm working on it. I want a few more people on the record. I'm giving you a heads-up, too, because when I out HottrYou, this project might end."

"Is there any chance it's just your coach? Maybe you got a bad one?"

She shook her head. "I've been meeting other people through their message boards . . . it's common. Two people told me their coach encouraged them to do these wildly unhealthy diets, and one tried to get her to buy some weight loss protein powder he was selling. Others said their coach recommended these intense exercise regimens but didn't give any guidance on doing them safely. I talked to one guy who reported a heart condition early on, and the coach forgot about it when recommending things. The guy had to remind him multiple times."

I didn't have any sort of response, just looked at her trying to piece all this together. I had no idea how, but this needed to come out. A little part of me also knew that if Claire sank the project, I didn't have to admit to my inappropriate relationship with the CEO of FitMi and could figure out how to tell said CEO who I really was.

"Everyone I've talked to assumed it was just them, and it's buried. I want to get it right." Her voice was low, like someone might overhear us. "And I can't wait much longer."

I might come out on top, but that felt like a hollow victory, especially with the secrets I was keeping. "I'm sure we'll figure something out."

Claire's expression lost a touch of softness, and she emptied her glass, shoulders square. "We?"

"I'm not trying to steal your story. I just meant I'll be supportive."

"Oh." She settled back on the raft. "That means a lot. Thanks."

I finished my glass of wine and poured more for us both. If we were having a truce in the middle of a lake, it was better we both get a little soused. My phone buzzed in the plastic holder, but I ignored it.

"Do you remember when you started at *Best Life*?" Claire's question surprised me.

"Sure. You were new then, too." She, Ben, and I had all joined the *Best Life* team at around the same time. I'd been excited for a few minutes to have fellow newbies, until I realized I was drooling over Ben, and Claire didn't like me. Ben didn't stay an assistant for long, though.

Claire sipped her wine, looking out over the lake.

"What made you think of that?"

She looked toward me with a wry smile. "You know, I let Ben convince me you were a threat? He'd throw in comment after comment about how two women of color coming on at the same time, we'd always be compared to each other."

My face warmed, because I remembered him saying something similar. I figured he was looking out for me, that it was a sign he cared. "He told me I really needed to distinguish myself as the voice of color in the room. As if we'd have the same perspective."

"Exactly. But he got under my skin eventually, and I started to see you as the competition."

"I did, too." I'd put a lot of energy into outdoing Claire over the years. "Honestly, I never thought twice about it. Why would he even do that?"

"He's an asshole." Claire sighed, raising her glass to me. "Plus, we were so focused on each other, we never had time to be a threat to him."

My phone buzzed again, and Wes's name and photo flashed on the screen with an incoming text.

"You're right. God, we've been acting like rivals for years."

"Patriarchy. Am I right?" She waved a hand in the air. "I have no idea why you still like him, by the way."

"I mean, he has his flaws, but he's a decent guy."

She arched an eyebrow, finishing her second glass of wine.

"I mean, he's not a serial killer."

Her raised eyebrow twitched. "You might need to raise your bar for 'decent.' Is that him blowing up your phone?" My phone buzzed one more time, and Claire glanced at the screen, her expression surprised and something else I couldn't read.

I lunged for it, but the raft shifted, and I dropped my hands, worried about tipping into the water.

"Who is Wes?"

"Why?"

"Because he texted you a selfie and he's fucking hot."

I expanded the photo preview on the screen. Wes was on his balcony, the city lights spread out behind him. The red FitMi Fitness T-shirt hugged his muscled torso.

**Wes:** The city air smells like city air.

**Wes:** Wish you were here?

"Does he work for the company?" Claire made a grab for my phone, but I pushed it down into my swimsuit.

"He's . . ." I had no idea what to say. I had no excuse to explain who he was and why he'd be wearing a FitMi shirt.

Claire narrowed her eyes and cocked her head to the side. "Wait. Is he your coach?"

Busted. It was a moment of truth that would test the tenuous truce we seemed to be forging. I nodded, mumbling, "Yes." I wasn't brave or drunk enough to tell her the rest of what I'd learned.

"And he's texting flirty selfies at 9 p.m.?"

"It's an inside joke . . . it wasn't flirting."

"Sure," she said, lying back on her pillows. "Looks a lot like flirting to me . . . unless it's more than flirting." Claire's eyes cut to me slowly, a grin spreading across her face. "Are you sleeping with your coach?"

My face heated. "No! We're friends. We work out together."

"In person?"

I nodded.

"FitMi doesn't offer that, do they?"

I shook my head. All of this was wrong on some level, but Wes made it seem like it was fine. I'd been on the cusp of telling him the truth in bed last weekend, but then everything happened with his mom, and he'd made it clear he didn't want to be with me anyway. Claire was the last person I should trust, but under the stars, with the wine and sharing secrets, confessing didn't feel as scary as I thought it might.

"And there's nothing going on?"

"Nothing going on. I mean, once . . ."

"What?"

"Something kind of happened once, but it was a mistake. It meant nothing. Look at him."

"You like him?"

"It doesn't really matter. Nothing's going to happen again." My phone buzzed, and Claire glanced to my right boob, where the device was shoved into the ruched fabric. "Please don't say anything, Claire. It's not impacting what I write about the company. I've stopped focusing on FitMi altogether to make sure I'm not writing something biased."

She looked doubtful. "Setting everything else aside, it's a pretty big deal. And I know you know that . . . but I've read your stuff, and it doesn't sound biased. But if you like him . . . I give you a hard time, Britta, but don't sell yourself short. He's texting you, for starters, and it's not a booty call or a sext. In my experience, guys who look like that don't want to chat unless they like you."

"Even if that were true, he's my coach." *And owns the company. And thinks I was a mistake.* "Please don't say anything. I am making sure nothing gets in the way of my writing."

"I won't say anything. I can beat you fair and square." She shrugged. "And maybe when the story is over, you can start something with him."

I leaned back on my raft and listened to the water lapping against the surface. I wished it were as easy as Claire suggested, because we'd already started and now we'd stopped. "I should probably put him out of my head."

Claire motioned to the water. "Lots of fish in the lake."

# 42

THE NEXT FRIDAY, Britta and I were on mile two, our shoes hitting the pavement in tandem. It was a cool morning for late July, and the angry-looking sky hung low, but being next to Britta again lightened the dark cloud I'd been under.

Her brows pinched, and she kept looking at her watch, or where her watch would have been if I hadn't put it in my pocket. I wasn't sure why she put it on only to hand it to me, but I liked that brief contact with her fingers every time we ran, so I never commented.

"Hey," I said. "You haven't told me you hate me yet today."

"I do," she huffed. Her face was red, but she looked strong, back straight and body relaxed. When we first met again in person after the trip to the hospital, it was as awkward as I expected, but once we started running, we fell into our old patterns. We could go back to how things were. It wasn't going to be so hard.

"One more mile," I said.

Britta groaned, a low, guttural sound, but despite her protests, she kept going, which I liked about her. She powered through. Even when she didn't believe in herself, she believed me. I'd been training people for years. No one had ever made me feel as trusted as Britta did. I, once again, wanted to kick my own ass for screwing it up.

"I don't know if I can do it," she panted a few minutes later.

"You can." I slowed our pace. I'd inadvertently sped up when she groaned. "What about this? If you finish, I will buy you coffee."

"Oh yeah? Plain black coffee, or are we going for fancy?"

I chuckled. "Whatever you want." I mentally ran through my checklist of things to do that day, but I had time. Pearl had moved my meetings to later in the morning ever since Britta and I began training on weekdays. I ignored the big flashing light in my head reading *Warning! Warning!*—I was planning my life around this woman while pretending she was just my friend.

"Well . . . what if we got smoothies instead? I made that recipe you've been trying to talk me into."

"Are you telling me you've changed your opinion on kale?"

"I'll never admit it!" She pulled ahead, surprising me. If I were a better coach, I would first note how her stride was more confident or how her form was excellent as she ran. Instead, I admired her round, full ass in her running shorts, remembering how good she'd felt in my hands. I sprinted to catch up.

We ran another few minutes before the first raindrop hit my lip, then more on my cheek and arm. I glanced at Britta scrunching her nose when fatter drops fell onto her skin.

"Want to grab a Lyft?" I asked, looking around. The sky had turned from overcast to an ominous shade of gray and didn't look like it would be a wait-it-out passing storm. Thunder rumbled nearby. "Or we're close to my place if you want to take shelter there."

"How far?" She shielded her eyes as the rain pelted us.

"Maybe five minutes that way," I yelled, motioning north.

"Let's finish, then!" she called back, pushing water off her face.

We darted between people huddled under umbrellas and scurrying for cover. The rain fell in sheets that soaked us both, my shoes getting soggier with every landing on the flooded sidewalks. Britta's pale pink T-shirt was plastered to the swells of her breasts. Her dark hair, slick with rain, threw off drops of water as she bounced with every step. I longed to take her arm and pull her into an alcove, pressing her slippery body against a wall. I didn't want to remember how her curves felt against me, under me, but I couldn't push it from my head.

As we narrowly avoided an elderly couple huddled under a brightly colored golf umbrella, she flashed me a wide grin. Then I didn't want to pull her into an alcove just to feel her body; I wanted to kiss her and tell her she was perfect. The only options were alleys and crowded bus shelters. *And she's your client.* The reminder was short-lived when Britta shot me another smile, water streaming down her face as we reached my building.

"That was awesome!" She wrung out the edge of her shirt and then her ponytail on the sidewalk under the awning. I watched her movements, trying to shake some water off myself, but it was useless to pretend her hard nipples poking against her sports bra didn't transfix me. The cold didn't stop my dick from twitching.

I held the door. "C'mon, let's get inside. I'll get you a towel."

Britta leaned against the elevator wall, catching her breath from the sprint and stretching as we rode. Pride suffused me—in February, she didn't run. Now we were soaking wet after sprinting down Division Street together. Her shorts clung to the curves of her hips, and I imagined easing them down her thighs, remembering how she'd liked my hands against the skin there.

"I must look like a drowned rat," she said, letting her foot fall back to the ground after stretching her quads.

I bit back the mushy things I wanted to say. "Maybe like a raccoon who fell in a lake."

She swatted at my stomach—and the subtle brush of her hand against me was a maddening sensation. "That's worse!" She tried again, this time with a jab, but I blocked her fist as we exited the elevator.

We'd done a few boxing workouts—she loved it, and I liked play sparring with her. It was another excuse to touch her that was within professional boundaries. "A swimming raccoon is worse than a drowned rat?"

"Yes." She bit her lip and smiled. "I don't know why, but it is."

My gaze tripped on her lips, and she landed a soft punch to my stom-ach. Her expression brightened. "Gotcha!"

"Are you trying to intimidate me?"

"Is it working?" She looked down at her hands, realized she was still touching me, and let them drop.

"You're terrifying," I said, turning to unlock the door. I was inviting trouble, because even after turning away, my body buzzed where she'd touched me.

The open space was dim, and the storm spread out before us through the floor-to-ceiling south-facing windows. Lightning streaked the sky, and it looked more like midnight than eight in the morning. "Wow." She joined me in admiring the view.

I kept the air-conditioning high, and she wrapped her arms around herself.

I ran my hand over my neck to keep from wrapping her in a hug to share our warmth. "You can borrow some dry clothes. Let me get you a towel."

I looked around at anything besides her, because now she planned to strip down in my house, and my libido screamed how unfair it was that I wasn't going to do a damn thing about it. I rummaged through my draw-ers and pulled out a pair of basketball shorts and a T-shirt and handed them to her, pointing her in the direction of the bathroom.

"Thanks!"

After she closed the door, I let out a slow breath. The wedding was the next week, and we hadn't talked about that or what had happened at her parents' house, and I wasn't sure I wanted to face it.

I pulled my phone from my pocket, thankful for the waterproof case. I had a few texts waiting from Cord.

**Cord:** It's torrential outside and the wireless is out. You might want to work from home. Tornado watch nearby.

**Wes:** Shit, I might. Things ok there?

**Cord:** Pearl and I are waiting it out.

**Wes:** Alone?

**Cord:** Shut up. See you later.

The door to the bathroom opened, and Britta stepped into my room. My gray T-shirt covered her curvy body. It was a worn and soft shirt from college—my favorite. Athletes got lots of apparel and swag, so it hadn't been obvious that I couldn't afford to buy other clothes. The fabric hugged her breasts and belly, and I tried—and failed—to not take in an eyeful. I reminded myself to keep things on a professional level.

She padded toward me in her socks, wet clothes in hand. "I like this shirt. Watch out or I might steal it."

I chuckled. "Your right hook is getting better. I don't know if I'd win if you fought me for it. Hey, there are tornado watches. You may want to hold off on leaving."

She looked out the window in my bedroom, where the sky was still dark, the city blurry as rain streaked down the panes of glass. She cut her eyes between me and the storm and pulled her lip between her teeth. "I should probably get home."

I nodded, swallowing my disappointment, because she was right. Nothing good would come from staying here together. I nodded toward the door. "I'll walk you out."

I leaned against my kitchen counter while she put her wet shoes back on next to the door. "So, uh, that wedding is next week. I wasn't sure if you still wanted to go with me, or if you'd rather not. It's okay if it's too . . . weird now."

She seemed to mull it over, biting her bottom lip. "I'll still go with you. As a friend, I mean, if you still want me to. It, uh, doesn't have to be weird." She stood after tying the laces, hands fiddling with the hem of my shirt, her wet clothes on the floor at her feet.

I motioned to the small pile. "I'll get you a bag for those." Opening drawers was a good distraction from this altogether awkward moment. "And you're right. Doesn't have to be weird. Who knows. By next week, maybe you'll have found someone much better to kiss." I stilled, my hand in the drawer. *What am I doing?*

Britta stilled, too, and my apartment buzzed with my dumb decisions and the air conditioner. Finally, she spoke to my back. "We'll see, I guess. I, um, have a date tomorrow."

"You do?" In my head, my swallow was loud and exaggerated, like in a cartoon, and I felt like she'd hit me with a two-by-four. I stood and faced her, hoping she wouldn't be able to read my reaction. "Wow. Who is he?"

"I met him on Tinder. His name is Snakebite, and he told me he runs a hedge fund. We're taking his van to a cabin in the woods."

I almost dropped the plastic bag I'd found for her clothes. "What?"

"Gotcha," she chuckled, and reached for the bag. "He's an accountant I met at work, *Daaad.*" She adopted a whiny teenager voice, shoving her clothes into the bag. "Are you going to demand to meet him before our date and warn him that if he hurts me, you'll hurt him, too?"

*If he hurts you, I'll kill him.* I had no right to demand any information about her date, but damn, it felt like a betrayal. No—like a rejection, even though I was the one who had put a stop to what was going on with us. It had only been a couple weeks since the morning at her parents' house. "I was just curious," I grumbled.

Her tone softened. "He's a nice guy. You'd like him."

"Good for you," I said, reaching to her side to open the door. "I hope it goes well."

After she left, I pulled my phone from my pocket to find a text from Kelsey.

**Kelsey:** I'd still like to talk. Maybe more. Drink tomorrow?

I needed to shake Britta from my system, and even though any other woman in Chicago would have been a better distraction than my ex, I already felt gutted and a little reckless.

**Wes:** Sure.

# 43

It may surprise you to know I read every comment left on these posts, and a few days ago, someone asked how I maintain my confidence while identifying problems with my body. I've been thinking about this. I try not to look at my body as problematic. It's the only body I have, right? That said, I don't think I maintain confidence—I question myself all the time—but I'm getting better at hearing the criticism and dismissing it for what it is. I don't expect to run a marathon tomorrow, just like I don't expect every first kiss to end in a happily ever after. That critic inside my head isn't always tuned in to the possibilities.

THE DRESS I wore was the one I'd bought with RJ, and the bodice hugged my breasts before flaring out into a flirty skirt. Bright red, the color popped against my skin, and when I slipped into a pair of nude pumps, I felt like a supermodel. I snapped a selfie, sending it to RJ, and after a pause, I texted Wes.

**Britta:** Raccoon, my ass! [photo attached]

**Wes:** Wow.

**Wes:** And I never said I didn't like raccoons.

**Wes:** Shouldn't you be out with Norbert?

**Britta:** His name is Donovan, and he's picking me up in ten minutes. What are you up to?

**Wes:** Followed your lead. On a date.

Uneasiness crept in. I'd actually been more excited to send Wes the photo than about the date. We'd mostly gotten back to normal with our routines, running in the mornings and going to the gym, but Wes was more careful of boundaries around me. Guarded. We didn't hang out in the evenings anymore, and now he was out on a date, too. Maybe that was for the best. Maybe we were both moving on.

**Britta:** Stop texting me, then 😊

He didn't respond, and the buzzer sounded.

LATER THAT NIGHT, RJ settled onto the other end of my couch with a glass of wine. "So, what happened? This was the guy from work, right?"

I tucked my legs under me, the gorgeous dress abandoned for shorts and a T-shirt as soon as I got home from dinner. "Yeah, Donovan." I sipped from my glass of the rosé my friend had brought with her.

"And yet, you're sitting with me at . . ." She dramatically looked at her phone. "Nine thirty-eight instead of sitting with him, ideally on his face."

I almost spit out my wine.

RJ shrugged, settling into the couch. "So, what gives?"

The date had been fine. We went to an Italian restaurant and chatted about work. Since he worked at *Best Life*, I could be honest about what I did. I'd catch myself wanting to tell Wes about an idea I had for a story or to share my outrage at some comments someone left. I could do that with Donovan, but my heart wasn't in it.

When he excused himself for the restroom, I checked for a reply from Wes and was disappointed to find none, which was ridiculous. "It was fine. He was nice, cute—if a little boring." Of course, the whole time I was worried because my trainer was on a date, too. *Or already touching her. Or sleeping with her. Or falling in love with her.*

RJ narrowed her eyes. "What are you not telling me?"

My cheeks heated. I hadn't told her about my attraction to Wes, and I wasn't sure why. In part, I didn't want to put my crush into the universe only to have nothing come of it. More than that, I knew RJ would remind me how professionally dicey the situation was, and I didn't want to face that. My best friend was many things, but hopeless romantic was not one of them. She held my gaze.

"Stop lawyering me."

She took a large drink from her wineglass and settled back in her seat, expectant. "Spill it."

I told her everything about working out with him, the shared looks and touches, and the morning in the blue room. I finally circled back to my date.

"Donovan was interesting and sort of funny, but when he held my hand, I felt . . . nothing." He was the perfect antidote to Ben and Wes—smart, unassuming, and cute, but not too hot—and I should have been into him. Unfortunately, I was more interested in what Wes was doing than in the man holding my hand.

When I paused, she gingerly set down her glass. "Let's forget for a moment that you're on friend probation for not telling me this until now." RJ stood, stretching her legs, and walked toward the kitchen, snatching my glass along with hers to refill them.

While I waited, I toggled back to the text exchange with Wes, knowing nothing had come in but looking anyway.

RJ returned with the wine. "Well, I'm here and we have wine. What conversation do you want to have?"

"What if we have no conversations and just drink more?"

She ignored my question. "Obviously, I want to know about the guy—and I know you're checking your messages from him right now—but do you want to talk about him and what it means for work, or work and what it means for him?"

"What's the difference?"

RJ eyed me over her glass before setting it aside. "The difference is which comes first." With me, her intense gaze never lasted long, and she softened. I never wanted to face it in a courtroom, though. "What does he look like, anyway?" She held out her hand. I set my phone in her palm, Wes's photo on the screen, and her eyebrows lifted. "Well, nothing wrong with him. If I keep scrolling, will I get to the nudes?"

I laughed and snatched it back. "Be serious."

"Okay. Okay. He's hot, but if he doesn't want to be with you, he's not worth it, and I can't abide you falling for someone unworthy again." RJ had hated Ben from day one.

"He's not unworthy. He has a lot going on. His mom is sick, and he runs the company," I said.

I was met with another raised eyebrow. "And he doesn't know who you are?"

"I know that's a problem we have to face, and I let things get way out of hand, but hanging out with him is . . . I don't know. It's affirming. He's a good coach and so much fun to be around. I never would have started this running stuff on my own without his encouragement." *Also, he gives great massages and kisses like it's a superpower and his smile warms me up. Plus, I'm sure he'd give my favorite vibrator a run for its money.* "So even though we're back to being just friends, I don't know what to do."

RJ nodded thoughtfully, weighing out the story. "It sounds like this boils down to your job or him. Can you keep both?"

I shook my head. "I don't know how. Also, I can't keep him because I don't have him."

"Okay. So, it's keep the job you have or prioritize the guy you don't."

"Seems like an easy decision when you put it that way."

RJ shrugged and sipped her wine. "To me, it does, but I'll always pick the job over the guy, so I'm biased."

"And he doesn't want to be with me," I reasoned. I glanced at my screen again, where the lack of notifications was impossible to ignore. "Maybe I just need to get back on track and focus on my writing. We're not hanging out outside of the gym at all anymore. It's like this detour never happened and we're just back to the training program."

"No more unworthy men," RJ added, finishing her wine with a firm nod.

"No more," I echoed.

# 44

**Britta:** Stop texting me, then 😊

I scrolled back up to the photo she'd sent and simmered. She was wearing makeup. I'd never seen her dressed up before because we were always working out. The dress hugged her curves like it was custom-made for her, and I traced a fingertip down the line of her body in the photo. She looked amazing, and all of it was for this other guy. I thought back to Calvin saying he supposed he'd missed his shot. I'd done the same.

I had no business staring at this photo when I couldn't date her. I was the one who'd pushed her away . . . and what had possessed me to go out with Kelsey, of all people?

*Because I need to shake Britta out of my system and remind myself nothing can happen with her.*

I tapped out a smart-aleck response to Britta but set my phone down as Kelsey approached the bar.

"Wes," she said, her voice breathy. She leaned in to kiss my cheek, and I inhaled the scent of her perfume. It had been a cheap knockoff back then, but maybe this was the real thing. Either way, the scent brought back hundreds of memories.

She took the seat next to me at the bar and ordered a vodka tonic with lime. She had drunk beer when we were together, extra hoppy IPAs that made my toes curl.

"I was glad you texted." She dragged her hand over my forearm, tracing her fingertips along a vein. When we broke up, I had dreams about feeling her fingertips on me like that, but now it just tickled in a vaguely unpleasant way.

"How have you been?"

"Good. Work is work. Life is fine." She paused, dropping her fingertips to rest on my knee under the bar. She only used this smoky, sexy voice when she wanted something. "Have you given more thought to merging the companies?"

"We're looking into it," I said, taking a swig from my beer.

"And . . . us?" She looked up through mascara-coated eyelashes, her eyebrows in sharp arches. Her hand slid further up my thigh, and a heavy breath escaped my lips. This interaction made me feel like the slimy guy I always promised myself I wouldn't be.

"Still under consideration," I said, keeping my tone neutral.

She straightened her back and sipped her drink. "You know we go well together."

"We used to."

"We could again. Look." She held up her phone and leaned into me, enabling selfie mode. Before, it had always been me trying to get her to be in a photo and not the other way around. The memory struck me as she clicked the button and our image froze on the screen—the moment looked false. My expression was almost wistful, and Kelsey grinned. "We still fit together. I miss being with you, Wes. No one ever got me like you did. Plus, working together, we could move mountains."

I searched her face for some small crack in her demeanor, but she said *I miss you* the same way she'd ordered the drink. Matter-of-factly. "We're different people now."

"We're better," she said, dropping her phone into her purse. "Not scraping by or doing jobs we hate, not at the mercy of our families."

I nodded without comment.

"We were always good in bed." She returned her hand to my arm. "Let's start there." It wasn't a question; it never was with Kelsey. It was always a statement. She slid her fingers over my jaw. Britta had commented in passing that she liked seeing a five-o'clock shadow on men, and I'd forgone shaving quite so regularly. "This is a new look; I like it."

I finished my drink, eyes flicking to my phone sitting on the bar.

"You don't want to talk. That's fine." Her hand fell and she finished her drink. "Want to get out of here?"

I touched her lower back to guide her through the crowd as we walked to the exit. I'd done it hundreds of times, but everything about the intimate gesture felt wrong.

BY THE TIME we stepped into her apartment, the inkling that this was a bad decision was a steady stream of foreboding.

"Wine?" she asked, without stepping into the kitchen.

I shook my head.

"Me, either." She stepped forward, sliding her hands up my forearms and over my biceps. The rush I expected didn't come. Her body against mine was all sharp angles. Everything about it was too sterile, too laced with history. Too not Britta.

Her lips neared mine, but I rested my hands on hers. "Kels, wait. Stop." I pried her hands away and returned them to her side. "I'm not feeling it."

"What do you mean, you're not feeling it?"

"It's not working for me." I would have thought she'd noticed I wasn't into it. "Is it for you?"

"If your dick still works, I'm guessing you'll feel just fine." The breathy voice was gone, and a hundred iterations of that demanding, demeaning tone flashed through my mind, only this time I didn't try to explain it away. Kelsey always lashed out when she felt dismissed, but it didn't mean I needed to take it.

I stepped around her, heading for the door. "I'm going."

"Wait. I'm sorry. That was out of line. I'm just . . . worked up, and you know I don't like talking about feelings. We can slow down."

"No, Kels. This is not going to happen."

"Is there someone else?" She crossed her arms over her chest. "What gives?"

I didn't owe her anything, and I could have lied, but I didn't want to deny what I was feeling anymore. "Yes. There's someone else."

Kelsey looked like I had slapped her, and I regretted my honesty immediately. She acted hard, but life had taught her to be that way, and for the first time, I wondered if this getting-back-together idea was genuine and not just her playing some game. The flash of vulnerability on her face, the hurt, was only there for a moment, though. "Who?"

I ran my hand over the back of my neck. "Does it matter?"

"Unbelievable. Why did you ask me out if there's someone else?" She rested her hands on her hips. "Next thing you know you're going to tell me it's someone cliché like your secretary, or maybe someone your mom brought home, or even the fat girl from the park."

I bristled, anger flaring, and my head snapped up. I balled my fists at my side and met her cold stare.

Her voice was back to icy, resolute, and hard. "Wait . . . seriously? You don't want to fuck me because it might mess things up with . . . *a client?*"

"This was a mistake."

"I guess so. I didn't realize your tastes had changed so much."

"Goodbye, Kelsey." I stepped into her hallway and ordered a car. The gravity of what I'd admitted to Kelsey, of all people, hit me, and my head went in all directions. I didn't know what to do. I headed straight home to shower off the scent of Kelsey's perfume, then to crash, but I could only toss and turn all night. Despite my best efforts to think of anything else, my mind kept wandering to thoughts of Britta and her date every time I glanced at my phone.

## 45

**BRITTA**

I love weddings. It's pathological, really. Trash TV focused on mis-behaving brides? I'm in. The Instagram account for a big-budget wedding planner? I'll scroll for an hour. The best, though, is attend-ing one in person. As a kid, I noticed none of the people in white dresses on TV or in bridal magazines (yes, I was that thirteen-year-old) ever looked like me. They were tall and thin with graceful necks and toned arms. Where were the rolls? Were you not allowed to get married if you had a little flab on your arms? I knew it wasn't true, so I started searching for wedding gowns designed for fat people. At this point I was seventeen, and my parents had the good sense not to ask questions about my growing wedding dress folder. I still have my original research, and I am up-to-date on designers. Should someone propose tomorrow, I would be ready. I thought about all this at the gym this afternoon when I overheard someone lamenting that they had to work out to fit into their dream wedding dress. Best believe I will get married in a dress that fits me rather than being worried about me fitting a dress. Who needs that kind of pressure? Anyway, click through to see a few of my favorite designers helping fat soon-to-be-weds and hopeful fat singles like me know there are a lot of stunning options.

---

USED TO SEEING Wes in workout clothes, I was surprised when I opened the door to greet him before his friends' wedding. The lines of the gray suit brought out his squared shoulders and trim waist, making him appear even sexier than normal—something I hadn't known was possible. I'd been pushing thoughts about how much I wanted to kiss him again out of my head. It wasn't easy to do when he was in track pants and T-shirts. It was impossible to ignore with him in this suit. "Hi," I said, recovering quickly. "Come in."

"You look startled." He stepped into my apartment with an easy smile.

I wanted to stare at him a little longer, to let my eyes roam over his body in the suit, but that wasn't allowed, and I didn't want to make him uncomfortable. He'd made it clear nothing romantic was going to happen between us, and I'd decided the smart move was to leave well enough alone. "I've never seen you dressed up before." I fumbled with my shoe, bending to adjust the strap, and wobbling.

"I told you I clean up nice." Wes steadied me, and heat coursed through my body. I stiffened at the touch, and he pulled his hand away.

"You do." The weight and heat of his palm had seared into my memory. Despite our pretending to be back to normal, I hadn't stopped thinking about the way his body felt pressed tight against mine, and I hadn't stopped replaying his words—that it was a mistake. *Enough. Enough now.* I shook my head and regained my balance, pulling away from him and offering a small smile. "Give me just a minute?"

"Of course," he said, tucking the hand he'd touched to my spine back in his pocket.

In the bathroom, I stared at my reflection. My hair hung loose, and my Spanx slip did everything it advertised. I hadn't planned to wear one under the black cocktail dress but second-guessed the decision at the last minute. I'd made a note to put together a post on why it felt hard to break up with the body shaper. I ran my hand down the fabric and wondered what Wes thought of how I looked, but held that question at bay. Resting my palms on the counter, I leaned forward and released a long breath.

Attending weddings always made me wonder if I'd have one—the big reception, RJ and Kat helping me into my fancy dress, the adoring man I got to call my husband holding me close. I rarely admitted to myself that I wanted it, but I did. Taking a deep breath, I vowed to get my emotions in check and stop these fantasies in my head about Wes. *I will find someone. I'm a lovable person, and kisses that don't lead anywhere don't mean future kisses won't. I just need to get realistic about who I fall for.* I studied my reflection one more time and decided I would call Donovan the next day to see if he wanted to try again, or maybe sign up for online dating. Hell, maybe I could give Calvin a chance—it would make my mom happy. My lingering feelings for Wes were unprofessional and distracting. I nodded at the mirror. *Enough.*

THE MAID OF honor turned to me after wrapping Wes in a hug. "Sorry to maul your date. I'm Felicia." She reached out to shake hands, her voice confident. "Oh," she said. "We met at the gym, right?" She gave Wes a curious smile and turned back to me.

The wedding had been lovely, but the space between Wes and me had felt off all night, like we didn't know how to be near each other. He'd lean in to tell me something as I turned my head to look elsewhere, or we'd start talking at the same time and not know how to recover. It was like we couldn't even figure out how to be friends anymore. As Felicia chatted with him, we stood by the bar with our cocktails, and having her there provided a brief reprieve from the weirdness.

It returned when she was called away.

"She seems fun," I commented as we looked for our table in the reception hall.

"Yeah," he said, glancing around. "Definitely."

I hated this. Even if nothing more would ever happen, we were still friends, and every interaction so far tonight had been awkward. "Quick," I said, trying to wrestle the moment from the silence growing between us. "What is your least favorite wedding tradition?"

"That's a tough one," he said as we sat. He looked a little relieved and leaned forward, surveying the room. "I guess the couple feeding each other cake."

"You're a hater of fun? Or just wasting cake?"

"Think about it, we're all sitting here watching them cut a cake. For starters, why is that a thing? Do married couples often cut cakes together?" He held up his fingers and ticked off his points.

I sighed, one arm perched on the table. "I think it signifies taking care of each other or something. It's playful and romantic."

"It's messy and pointless," he responded, holding my gaze.

"You wouldn't want to publicly rub food on the woman you love?"

"I'd rather do that privately." He winked but then caught himself, and his face shifted back from flirtatious. "What's your wedding red flag? You like everything, huh?"

I took a sip of my drink. "I don't like the 'Chicken Dance,'" I said after thinking about it for a minute.

He cocked his head to the side. "The 'Chicken Dance'?"

I tried to describe it, walking him through the steps, but he still looked confused.

"I don't think I've ever seen it."

"You have," I said.

"Don't think so," he said, brows knit.

I stood, tucking my hands to my chest, and flapped my arms like in the dance. I realized my mistake immediately, because his face cracked into a grin. I stepped forward, and he held up his palms defensively.

"Oh, now I recognize it." He tried to hold in his laugh, but his shoulders shook.

"You're such a jerk." I swatted at his chest, but he dropped his hands to my hips, holding me in place defensively, though it didn't feel defensive.

The way his palms settled on me, I imagined him pulling me into his lap and kissing my neck and his hands running up my thigh and how his stubble would feel against my skin. Goose bumps rose on the back of my neck, and I looked down at Wes, whose own gaze had darkened.

His fingers flexed, and I jerked back when I let myself realize how good it felt. *Enough.*

"Britt," he said, brow furrowed.

I shook my head as a voice boomed from the sound system, interrupting our moment of connection. It was accompanied by a knife tapping a glass, and the room hushed as the groom paused on the stage. Wes gave me another searching look, but I slipped from his grasp and took my seat, facing the couple and avoiding his gaze.

"Thank you," the groom said from the stage. "We're so glad you could be here. It means the world to have everyone we love with us, but the only person I need here today, or any day, is Naya." The room fell into an *aww*, and I caught myself placing my hand to my heart when he turned to her. "You're the strongest, most beautiful, and most amazing woman I've ever known, and I feel lucky every day to spend my life with you."

She swiped a tear from her face.

"I never knew life could be like this. You're the only one I want to conquer fears with, the only one who can match me pun for pun." A rumble of laughter rolled through the room. "And definitely the only one who could teach me to make a free throw." A cheer erupted from across the room, along with a few hoots from other guests, including Wes. The bride laughed with them, and I caught a quick glance of Wes's smile, joining in on the joke, the uncomplicated affection he had for the couple clear on his face.

The bride smiled, her eyes bright, even from our spot far from the stage.

"Simply put, you are my only, my everything, and my forever, and I'll try my best to be the man you deserve every day."

She made a check mark in the air with her finger before they kissed, to the applause and cheers from all their guests.

I dabbed at my face with a napkin. That had felt like a speech from a movie, something fictional, but it was real, right in front of me, and my heart lodged in my throat.

Wes's arm rested on the back of my chair, the tips of his fingers brushing my shoulder. "Don't cry," he whispered into my ear.

I laughed at myself and pushed away from the table. "I don't even know them, but that speech was so moving. Made me think, you know, I'd want someone to say something like that to me." I shook my head. "Sorry, I'm fine," I said, sitting up straighter.

The DJ announced dancing, and the opening beats of the music filled the hall as Felicia and a tall man approached our table. "My husband will not dance with me," she called out over the music. "Will you two?"

Eager to escape the awkwardness between us, I stood. "I'm in. Who can resist 'The Electric Slide'?"

"It's electric." Felicia's smile broadened, and she took my hand, pulling me to the dance floor. I didn't look back at Wes.

*Enough.*

# 46

BRITTA MOVED TO the beat of the song with Felicia, dipping and twisting, and it took monumental effort to shift my focus to Aaron. "How's it going? Work good?"

"All right." He shrugged. "Your PR people called me this week to arrange some magazine article about the company and the mentoring program."

Another check in the positive column for Mason. "I think it's supposed to be kind of a puff piece, but maybe it will get some donations."

Aaron laughed. "Oh yeah. Just a small piece in a national magazine. What's it like being such a god among us mere mortals?" Aaron took a swig from his beer.

"Fuck off," I shot back with a wry smile.

"I'm just giving you shit. I know you love doing the CEO thing."

"It's a good gig," I conceded with another glance to the dance floor. "It's how I met Britta."

"She works for you?"

"Client."

He blew out a slow breath and cut his gaze to the dance floor. "So that's the elusive Ms. Complicated, huh?"

I laughed. "You could say that."

Jake approached the table. "Save me."

"Man of the hour," Aaron exclaimed as Jake joined the table. "You made the rest of us look like slobs with that speech. Thanks for that."

Jake brushed his shoulders with a flourish and took the seat next to Aaron, loosening his tie. "Promise to not ask me about flowers, rings, proposals, or babies."

Aaron placed his hand over his heart. "But I've been dying to hear, in painstaking detail, about these centerpieces."

"They're peonies and ranunculus flowers," I said absently, bringing my attention from the dance floor to the curious looks from my friends.

"I guess if I get that question, I'll send them to you," Jake said with a laugh. "Later, we'll come back to why you know that, but please. Any conversation not related to this wedding."

"Wes here just informed me that his date is the woman he was texting after basketball. The client." Aaron raised his eyebrows suggestively and nodded toward the dance floor.

Jake stretched across the table to clap me on the shoulder. "So, you took the shot, huh?"

I let my gaze wander to Britta again as I sipped my drink. The song had shifted to "It's Tricky" by Run-DMC, and she and Felicia were doing the Running Man along with some others on the dance floor. She was laughing, her face lit up, and a smile curled my lips. I was transfixed, hoping she'd meet my eyes.

"We lose you?" Jake's voice snapped me back. He and Aaron shared a wry look.

"Sorry, got distracted."

Both men laughed. "Clearly."

"Take my shot? Kind of. It's still complicated."

"Still worth it?" Jake glanced from me to Naya, who was smiling kindly to a group of women and then flashed a *help me* expression as she strode toward us.

His question hung in the air as Naya joined us and sat on his lap. "Hello, Wife."

She reached for his glass of Scotch. "Three of your sisters just cornered me with baby name suggestions. You know I can't handle them when they team up."

I looked between her and the glass. "Are you guys expecting?"

"No," Naya exclaimed before taking a sip, at the same time as Jake said, "Not yet." They shared a look that seemed equal parts good humor and I-know-what-you're-thinking. It felt embarrassing to swoon at shit like that, but I was jealous of the easy way they could be together. I glanced at the floor again, where Britta was doing a poor impression of the Hustle with the best man and his husband.

"Dance with me," Naya said, setting down Jake's glass after taking another sip. "I'm a little drunk and in the mood to make a fool of myself."

Jake kissed her cheek before downing the rest of his drink. "Can you believe she didn't dance when I met her?" He stood, twining his fingers with Naya's. "Good luck, Wes," he called over his shoulder as they moved through the crowd. "It's worth it!"

Aaron followed my gaze to where it had landed on Britta hugging her dance partners as the song ended. The men she was with were married, but jealousy still needled me. I wanted to hug her, and as I watched her smile and laugh, all the reasons we couldn't be together felt hollow. The music shifted to "Perfect" by Ed Sheeran, and I appreciated the melodic opening chords.

My friend tapped the table with his glass. "What're you gonna do?"

I threw back my drink. "I guess I'm gonna take another shot."

Britta was on her way off the dance floor, chatting with Felicia, when I reached her.

"Oh, hey," she said, her voice hedging in that way it had been all night, like she was holding something back. She was holding back, and I'd been, too, but I shrugged that away.

I slid my hand up the middle of her back, my middle finger dragging along her spine. "Dance with me?"

She turned, biting her lip. "It's a slow song."

"Dance with me anyway." I took her hand, and Felicia waved with a knowing smile as I led Britta back to the dance floor. She smelled like coconut and something flowery, and she looked up at me with those big eyes—beautiful, perfect eyes.

"I like this song," she commented without breaking our eye contact.

"It's no 'Chicken Dance' . . . "

She pressed her palm to my chest. "I hate you."

I leaned down so our noses were inches apart. "Do you?"

A little breath puffed from her mouth as those full red lips parted slightly. She shook her head. "No."

"Good," I said on an exhale. *Here goes nothing.* I leaned in to her ear, my lips brushing the delicate skin. She shivered at my touch, and that alone was so fucking sexy. "Because I like you."

"I know." She glanced down. "As a friend."

"No, I mean, I like you, like you." *I sound like a thirteen-year-old. Shit, this is not going as planned.* "I don't want to lose you."

"C'mon," she said, meeting my eyes again. "Wes. Don't. I know you're having a hard time with your family and everything, and I won't abandon you. You don't have to pretend you feel something for me to keep me in your life."

I growled at her assessment, frustrated that I'd led her to believe that was true. "That's not what this is."

"It's okay. I get it. You feel guilty about kissing me, but I'm fine. It happened, and I'm not your type, and that's okay. You can keep being my coach. I'll find someone, and—"

"I can't be your coach anymore," I said, holding her tighter, my voice sounding more desperate. "And I don't want you to find someone else." My pulse raced, but I paused, took a deep breath, and then dragged two fingers slowly over her bare shoulder.

She gripped my shoulder and looked up at me with wide eyes, her teeth sunken into that plump lower lip I remembered the taste of.

"You're funny and caring. You're smart and sexy. I don't have words for how good I feel when I'm around you, Britta." My heart was beating like I'd just finished sprinting. "So, I said it before. I like you. I like your smiles. I like your jokes. I like your kisses. I like your heart, and I—"

"But you said—"

I leaned closer to her other ear. "And I want you. I want you in every way a person can want someone. I should have told you at your parents' place, or before you went on a date with that guy, or at the hospital when you took care of my mom, or on any of the random Tuesdays when it felt like my heart would pound out of my chest at the sight of you. It wasn't a mistake to kiss you. I just didn't think I deserved to feel that good. I know everything with my mom and Libby had me kind of messed up, but you're in my head, Britta. In my heart. Hell, you're in my damned bones."

She touched a palm to my cheek and studied my face as the music swirled around us. Her hand slid down to rest on my chest again, and I felt the weight above my heart as her expression shifted to doubtful. "Wes, after last time . . . How do I know you won't regret saying this tomorrow?"

"I've been holding this in for so long." I hated myself for hurting her, and I pulled her to me, needing to feel her and hoping she felt the truth in my touch. "I shouldn't think about you as much as I do or count down the hours until I see you next. I shouldn't want to kiss you again more than taking my next breath, but I do."

She searched my face, but her palm didn't leave my chest. "Wes . . ."

"I don't regret saying it. I never will, but tell me to stop and I'll stop," I rasped. "I know I don't deserve a second chance after pushing you away. I let other stuff get in my head, stuff that isn't as important as you. If it's too late, though, just tell me. It's what I deserve to hear, but, Britta, you're the one for me. I don't want you to be my client. I want you to be my everything, because it feels like you already are."

"Are you sure?"

"Yes." I angled her face to mine, our breaths mingling, bodies tensed. The dance floor shifted as a recent pop song played, but I could only focus on my heart pounding. "It's you. It's been you since that first message, and it will be you until long after the last one."

My lips brushed hers in a soft, slow sweep, and all the disparate parts of me—the hurt, the past, the guilt, the longing—all seemed to snap into place.

# 47

BRITTA

WES PRESSED ME to the wall of his living room after we stumbled through the door, his hands tangling in my hair and strong arms caging me, his body hard everywhere.

I pulled back to take a breath, watching him do the same. "God, Wes."

His finger slid along my collarbone, sending jolts of anticipation through me as he slowed his pace. He drew in a ragged breath. "Your skin is so soft." He dropped his lips to my shoulder, then kissed the path he'd traced moments before.

My breath stuttered, and I had to remind myself to inhale again.

"So sweet," he murmured against my throat before trailing his lips up my neck. His fingers stretched at my back and pulled me to him, my body pliant and ready. His hand, always so warm, trailed lower until it rested on my ass, gripping and massaging through layers of fabric.

"Wes." My voice was somewhere between a whimper and a gasp as my body flushed. His hands were everywhere, and his lips and tongue devoured my throat, lightly nipping and stroking in equal measure. I gripped his shoulders, the rigid line of his erection pushing against my stomach. I wasn't sure I'd ever been touched like this in such a frenzied, wanting way that still felt like us, like love.

Every hard, hot sign pointed to the fact that I turned him on. I couldn't think about anything else when his mouth was on mine, our tongues dancing together. I'd never seen him out of control, and it was hot knowing I did that to him, that I could drive him this wild.

He trailed his lips across my chest, dropping sweet kisses along the skin between the tops of my breasts. "I've dreamed about kissing you here." His thumb ghosted over my nipple, and I released a raspy breath.

He pulled back and looked into my eyes, his palm cupping my jaw. His eyes were dark with arousal. It was Wes. Wes who pushed me to do one more mile, who cooked Thai food with me, who taught my nephew how to throw a spiral. Wes who had put so much into FitMi to make it a good company that helped people be happy. I had to tell him.

I placed my palm over his. "Wes, wait."

He stilled immediately, confusion and concern painting his features.

*Deep breath. Just say it fast.* "I haven't told you, but I work for a magazine and I'm writing about FitMi. I need you to know before we . . ."

"I had no idea that's what you did, that you were writing." His eyes widened, but he didn't budge from my side. "You're the journalist?"

"Well, I'm trying to be. This is my first break, but I'm sorry I didn't tell you before. It's . . ." I trailed off but examined his features while he processed my admission.

"It's okay," he murmured. "I mean, I'm surprised, obviously, but you're getting to write just like you always wanted." I hadn't expected the smile, or for his voice to sound proud. If anything, he'd pressed closer. "Britta, that's amazing."

"You're not mad?"

"I'm actually excited it's you writing about the company. You get what we're trying to do. You get me, and you're doing what you always wanted." His thumb grazed my cheek, but his expression shifted from concerned to contemplative. "There's something I need to tell you, too."

"That you own FitMi?" I rested my palm on his chest, still amazed I could do that, to touch him after so long. I registered his shock as he stiffened, eyes going wide. "I figured it out when your mom called you

Chris at the hospital. Your real name is listed as one of the company's founders."

"You should be an investigative journalist." His eyes fell closed, and he touched his forehead to mine. "I'm sorry I didn't tell you. I missed coaching after having stepped away from it, so I took on a client." He met my eyes. "I planned to find my mojo and go back to running the business, but then I found you. I should have told you sooner; I just didn't want it to change how you acted around me."

Wes dropped a kiss on the tip of my nose before meeting my eyes again. "I am sorry I lied. I should have been up-front with you, and I don't want us to start anything like that. I never want you to doubt what I tell you."

I rested my palms against his chest. "We both messed up. I only want the truth with you."

"We can go slow," he hummed into my neck, and I rolled my head to the side to give him better access to my sensitive skin. "If you want to, I mean. We don't have to jump into anything tonight. If you want to wait until the story is done, I get that. I want us to be for a long time."

We were still fully clothed, standing in the living room of his apartment, but we were bare. Our secrets were out, and even though nothing was solved or figured out, I loved how Wes held me. We were in this together. I arched into him, pulling his face to mine. "I want us, and I don't want slow." The room was quiet except for our heavy breathing.

"Can we talk about work later, then? Because I need to kiss you again." Wes's fingers threaded into my hair. "You're perfect," he said, his voice husky. His lips and tongue were playing over mine, insistent. Wes kissed me like I was the only woman in the world.

"More," I moaned, then added with a smile, "A little further. Dig deep. Keep breathing."

His laugh against my neck somehow intensified the heat and tension that were coursing through me. "Such a demanding coach." His kisses were making the sensitive area along the side of my neck vibrate with need. I'd never known I needed to be kissed there. *This is going to happen.*

"You'll thank me later." I pressed my own hands against the hard plane of his chest, roaming the way I'd wanted to for so long. We stumbled down the hall, pulling his shirt from his pants and tangling with the buttons.

"Pretty sure I'll thank you now." As we made our way into the bedroom, he fumbled with the zipper to my dress. We gave up trying to claw at each other, and he pulled off his shirt, baring his chest. I dragged my fingertips down his abs, stroking the ridges. His muscles rippled under my touch, and I admired the defined cut of his body disappearing into his pants, the fine smattering of hair below his belly button.

He watched my fingers trace over his muscles before pushing my dress down my shoulders, the material falling to the floor. His hands traveled down my body, and back and forth over my ass, then up my spine and sides, fingers searching. He pressed his lips to my neck. "How do I get this off you?"

*My Spanx.* I would never second-guess myself again.

"Oh, God," I muttered, pulling back. "I forgot I was wearing this. Just—um—give me a minute." I stepped back, turning away and attempting to peel it over my hips with even a tiny modicum of grace. I felt like I was uncasing sausage, and I rethought my earlier girl-power stance on this body shaper slip, because as sexy as it made me feel in that dress, taking it off was another story.

Wes stepped forward, his hands sweeping over my hips from behind as he dropped kisses on my shoulder.

"What are you . . . doing?" I huffed, still trying to get the thick fabric over my belly.

"Helping." He stroked the indentations left by the garment on my thighs and took over the pulling. He spoke against my neck, the breath caressing my skin. "Why are you wearing this, anyway?"

"To look hot in my dress," I said with a huff, still pulling and wiggling.

"You look hot in everything you wear. You didn't need this." Wes's lips grazed my neck. "Do you know how much torture it was to hear you say you wanted to look good naked when I was positive you already did?" He helped me pull the shaper over my boobs, where it got stuck for a moment, leaving my arms raised over my head, the shaper clinging to them.

From inside my cocoon of spandex, I worried I might have to cut the thing off and wondered whether it was too early to suggest bringing scissors into the bedroom.

"It's stuck."

"Let me just . . ." We pulled and twisted, and I was laughing again when it slid over my head, probably leaving my hair a wild mess.

"Sorry," I said, tossing the traitorous thing to the floor.

"Don't apologize for less clothing." He met my smile, his hands traversing my bare belly, my back, down my spine to massage my backside, and then up. "You always make me laugh, Britta." He kissed me again, lips exploring as he cupped my breasts, kneading while his kiss kept me planted in place, his thumbs rubbing over my nipples with just the right balance of speed and pressure, mixing it up just enough to keep me anticipating his next stroke.

"That's not my goal when I'm in my underwear, Wes." I unbuckled his belt, and he let me take over, pushing his pants over his muscled thighs to reveal black boxer briefs, the fabric bulging and misshapen.

He followed my movements, gaze flicking between my hand and my chest. "I fell in love with you when you made me laugh," he murmured.

I froze and my eyes flashed to his, the light from the city below giving the room a soft glow. "What?"

"You heard me." He held my gaze, his eyebrows lifting slightly before he pushed his briefs down, his thick erection springing free.

"Did I?" A hundred dirty thoughts flashed in my head because *Oh. My. God.*

He climbed on the bed, pulling me down to the mattress with him. Wes smelled like soap and Scotch, and I inhaled the oddly satisfying combination while sliding my fingers through the smattering of chest hair and tracing the hard muscle of his abdomen. His words still hung in the air, and his lips met my neck again, while he reached behind me to un-snap my bra. Tossing the material aside, he held my breasts reverently, rolling my nipples between his thumb and forefinger. "You're quiet," he said against my skin, before trailing his lips down, dotting tiny kisses in circles around my nipples before taking one into his mouth. His tongue paused, and he let his mouth hover over my sensitive, peaked flesh. "Is this okay?"

A whimper escaped my lips as I nodded. I expected it to feel weird being naked with him, to have him see me—all of me—but it felt like the most natural thing in the world. "You said . . ." I trailed off, lost in the pleasure of his tongue.

He took my other nipple in his mouth, his free hand sliding over my belly and easing my thighs apart.

My head fell back with the wave of sensations from his tongue and fingers, the anticipation as he stroked the insides of my thighs and then the wet fabric between my legs. "Do you want my fingers here?"

When I nodded, he dragged his knuckle back and forth, creating the most delicious friction. I'd dreamed and fantasized about how that fric-tion would feel, but my imagination didn't do him justice.

His tongue whorled around my nipple again, and he slid his fingers inside my panties to stroke my wet folds before pulling the fabric down my thighs. My nipple came away from his lips with a pop, and he took the other into his mouth. I bucked against his hand, shameless. I cried out, squirming, wanting more, wanting everything. I ran my hand roughly through his hair. "You said you . . ."

His fingers were long, but his strokes were gentle. I was aware of every moment and lost in his heat at the same time. Wes's thumb circled my clit before one long finger dipped back into me with aching restraint, again and again.

All thought left me. *This is how I go out. I'm dying. I'm dead.*

Pops of color flashed, and sensations overtook me—he pressed against my walls, his thumb teasing, his mouth on me. I was so ready. My body rose, and heat gathered low in my belly. Still, his words circled me.

"You said," I panted again, meeting his eyes.

"I said," he repeated, sliding a second finger inside me, stretching me and pressing against the tight bundle of nerves. His expression was hooded, the intensity in his eyes flashing when my body reacted to the new sensation. "I fell in love with you."

I cried out, so close to exploding under his touches. I met his fingers with my hips, seeking more, wanting just a little more to push me over the edge.

He thrust his fingers faster, his thumb against my clit and his words in my ear. "I'm in love with you."

I cracked, hearing the echo of his words over and over as my body lit up in hundreds of flashes of bright light.

"Britta, I love you," he repeated into my ear as I came down, body reeling, surrounded by his heat. "There was probably a more romantic time to say that, but I couldn't wait any longer."

# 48

I HADN'T PLANNED to tell her I loved her, and definitely hadn't planned to do it while edging her to orgasm with my fingers, but my plans seemed to matter less and less when I was around her. The entire night had been one surprise after another, and learning she was the one writing the story about the mentoring program was completely unexpected.

When Britta's trembling subsided, she sank into the pillows, her body limp and cheeks flushed. "I knew you'd be good at that," she said in a breathy voice.

I planted gentle kisses on her shoulder and collarbone. "Oh?"

"I've been fantasizing about your touches since the first time you gave me a back rub." She slid her fingers down my chest, slowing over my stomach.

When she wrapped them around my erection, giving an experimental stroke, I closed my eyes against the rush of pleasure. I should have slowed down to consider what it meant that I'd confessed I loved her and she hadn't said it back, but I ached to be inside her and it was all-consuming. I reached for a condom in my nightstand and rolled to my back. "I've been fantasizing about you on top of me."

"You have?"

Dragging my index finger up and down her thigh, I tilted my head to meet her eyes. "I want to see your beautiful body and have my hands free to touch you." I kissed her, our lips coming together slowly and sweetly, but both of us quickly succumbed to the growing heat. "Please let me see you." Stroking her calf, I guided her thigh over my hip. I kissed her, my tongue stroking the seam of her lips.

She nodded and watched me roll on the condom. Britta grinned and slowly shifted her body to mine. I'd never experienced such an overwhelming urge to take in a person all at once, but tried to go slow, to give her time to be comfortable. I guided her hips forward, my dick brushing against her slick heat. "Fuck," I moaned, close to coming from that small touch. She was right there, the head of my cock nudging at her entrance as I held her gaze. "You're so beautiful." I lowered a finger to circle above her clit, pulling a delicious moan from her throat. "I knew that before I ever laid eyes on you."

She whimpered and sank down, bringing me into her body inch by inch, her heat tight around me. She was tentative at first, her eyes meeting mine, and I stilled, letting her lead. Her whimper was the best sound I'd ever heard. I wouldn't last long this time, but *fuck*. I leaned forward to take a perfect hard nipple in my mouth, which made her grind against me faster. She liked when I used my tongue on her, and I was more than happy to oblige.

Britta cried out, pressing her palms against my chest as she found her rhythm and chased her pleasure. The set of her jaw and the look in her eyes made it clear she believed how much I wanted her. I felt it in the roll of her hips when she didn't care, because she wanted me.

"Britt," I panted, heat pooling at the base of my spine, my orgasm building.

She rode me with abandon, rocking and moaning against me, her full, round ass landing against my thighs with a maddening rhythm. She looked free, and I wanted to hold her and never let her go.

Her voice hitched and she tensed, the most amazing expression crossing her face as she dug her fingers into my chest. "I'm coming! I'm coming!" She repeated the words as if I couldn't tell, as if her entire body wasn't erupting, and I gripped her waist harder, my own release barreling through me, as she spasmed around me. The world cut out, and there was nothing but her. She mewed, tiny whimpers as her rocking slowed, and I stared at her, regaining my breath and knowing the rest of me was lost to her.

She slumped onto my body, breathing hard, her heaving chest against mine. "Wes, holy . . . wow. Best workout ever."

I laughed. *God, this woman.* I wrapped my arms around her. "Ready to stretch?"

"I hate you," she said, resting her head against my shoulder, fingers dancing over my chest before she flattened her palm over my heart. "I hate you . . . more than I've ever hated anyone."

Those words filled me—like they were part of me, and she wouldn't pull them back. Even though she hadn't said it, Britta's love felt like it belonged to me, and I wrapped her tighter in my arms.

# 49

BRITTA

I made a discovery this weekend, readers. As we all know, sex can be good cardio, and good sex can . . . well, burn a lot of calories. What I hadn't counted on was the FitMi app already having a pre-made entry for sex on their exercise tracker. I know how many calories you burn is based on the type of activity, length of time, and body type, but still . . . doesn't sex being in the app make you want to exercise a little bit more? I wonder what badge this might lead to . . .

WES STEPPED INTO the bathroom, and I felt an odd sense of loss, lying there alone on the bed. I snatched my phone from my bag on the floor to distract myself from the competing forces of my mind whirring and my body completely relaxed.

**Claire:** Rumor is that Maricela decided who will get the promotion.

**Claire:** I'll buy you a consolation martini on Monday. ☺ 🍸

I stared at the text and took in the feel of Wes's bedding under my naked body, the scent of us lingering in the air. I let my eyes fall shut, relishing how comfortable it felt. If the promotion would be decided soon, I'd have a better idea of where the project was going. I could ask Natalie for help on how to manage the appearance of a potential conflict of interest. I was certain readers would love a happily ever after story.

"What's wrong?" Wes walked toward me, still gloriously naked, so at ease with himself, and I drank in the sight of him, still amazed this was real. What was better, his eyes traveled my body, displaying the same expression I imagined I must have had. I set my phone on his nightstand and enjoyed him looking at me as I followed the lines of his body to his belly button, then down the thin line of hair. *Damn.*

"Absolutely nothing's wrong."

Wes climbed into the bed, wrapping his arm around my waist and pulling me back against his chest. "You sure? You looked concerned," he said, nuzzling my neck and stroking me from my hip up my side and then around my body.

I liked feeling his hands on my stomach, and I smiled. I settled back against him. "Very sure."

"There's so much I don't know about you." His warm, hard chest against my back felt right. "How long have you worked at the magazine?"

It was so freeing to get to talk about this. I couldn't believe he was so unbothered. "Four years. I've wanted to tell you about it."

"I knew you were an excellent writer after I looked through your notebook in your apartment." He dropped kisses on my shoulder, these sweet little pecks that made me want to pause and write an ode to his lips. It was as if someone had opened up a valve in Wes and now all this affection was flowing out of him.

"Oh yeah? My doodles inspired you?"

"You could say that." His breath puffed near my ear, and a trickle of anticipation eased down my body. "I read a haiku you wrote about touching yourself."

"What? No!" I tried to turn to face him, but he held me tight. "I can't believe you read that!"

He nipped at the sensitive skin below my ear. "I committed it to memory. *On a precipice, my fingers, like your soft tongue, edging me closer.*"

My entire body flashed hot. "Well, that's embarrassing."

"Informative," he said into my neck. "I'm very interested in using my tongue to take you to a precipice."

"I can't believe you never told me you read that, or that you wanted to know anything else about me after!"

"I want to know everything. How do you take your fancy coffee?"

I smiled. "How do I *like* my coffee, or how do I pretend to like it since meeting you?"

His laugh rumbled against my shoulder, and he squeezed me to him. "Both."

"Skim milk and two stevia packets," I began, feeling his nod against my skin.

"And how do you really like it?"

I turned in his arms. "Caramel latte with whipped cream and a little chocolate sauce. Maybe a donut on the side."

My breath hitched when his thumbs slid in slow circles over my thigh. "You like when I touch you there?" he murmured against my shoulder.

"I do," I said, as his lips migrated to my ear. "But I was reacting to the memory of the latte."

"A guy's pride can only take so much." He began the slow circles between my waist and hips again, fingers kneading, then venturing to caress my backside. "You can still drink the lattes. Maybe I'll have one, too. I can think of some new cardio I'll be adding to my rotation."

"Always in coach mode, huh?"

He gave me a small smile, eyes still roaming over my features. "It'll be hard to remember I'm not your coach anymore." Wes's hazel eyes were still leveled with mine, his expression hopeful, with small traces of concern at the corners of his eyes like he was waiting for the sky to fall. I traced a fingertip over his cheekbone. The way he nestled his cheek against my hand, the vulnerability in that action, convinced me I'd made the right call to tell him when I had.

"Do you want to talk about work now?"

"Okay." He nodded slowly.

Our naked bodies were pressed together, and the echo of his "I love you" still hung in the air. I swallowed. "I really am sorry I didn't tell you sooner about the magazine," I said, gathering my courage and looking him in the eyes. "I'll . . . I don't know what I'll do, but I'll make it right."

He searched my face, tracing his fingertip down my side. "We'll make it work. I can't imagine many people would care, and maybe you can disclose that you're in a relationship with me."

I hadn't thought about us in those terms yet, and a smile spread across my face, which triggered a smile across his face, and then we were lying there grinning like we were telling jokes and not weighing our ethical missteps.

"If you want to, of course."

"I'll disclose it," I said, unable to stop the smile. "Our relationship."

"It shouldn't be that big a deal, right? I'm excited it's you writing it, but it's not like a hard-hitting exposé or something, is it?"

A small hurt crept in again, because he was right. I wasn't breaking some big scandal, even if it felt big to me. "No, but we should have a plan. Ground rules."

"I can do ground rules."

"Exactly." I rested my palm against his chest, the steady beat of his heart so close to me. "Can we hit pause on deciding anything? I need to think through this and talk to someone at work." I dreaded the conversation I'd need to have with Natalie, but despite my worry, my lips tipped up of their own accord. "I want to do it right."

Wes dipped his chin and brushed his lips against mine. "Okay." His hand settled possessively at my back, and he kissed me again. They were the lazy, unhurried kisses we could share because we had time.

I sighed when our lips parted. Everything was out in the open, we were really doing this, and I felt light. "I can't believe how perfect this feels."

# 50

## WES

AFTER AN EARLY-MORNING run—and post-run shower—with Britta, I walked into the office with a spring in my step and the taste of her kiss on my lips. I finished tapping out my text in the elevator, ignoring the pile of missed calls. It had felt so good to put FitMi away for the weekend, and I wanted it to last a little longer.

> **Wes:** I know we're not talking about work yet, but I'm glad it's you writing about the mentoring program. I haven't been this excited about something (besides you) in a long time.

"Good morning," Pearl said without looking up from her keyboard. The massive bouquet of tulips I'd had delivered filled the space with color. I'd tried to apologize in person, and she told me not to get all sappy on her, then muttered something under her breath about Cord minding his own damn business.

"It is good, isn't it?" The memory of Britta's soap-slicked body and her cries growing louder and more frantic as I took her against the wall made me want to give everyone a raise, pump my fists in the air, and run a victory lap around the city.

"You seem . . . happier," Pearl commented, skeptically walking in to hand me a couple of files and a few messages. "They give you an extra scoop of wheatgrass in your protein drink this morning or something?"

"Just a beautiful morning." I flipped through the messages, pausing on one with *Mason* underlined three times.

"He's been lurking since seven. Said he's been trying your cell and emailing."

I'd turned my phone off on Saturday night, deciding to give up everything but Britta. I'd given myself permission to not worry about missing a call from Libby, or Mom's rehab facility. "He's never in early," I noted, glancing at the other messages. "I need to talk to him anyway, though."

"I am tired of seeing his twitchy little face, so please call him back."

"Do you want me to fire him for you, Pearl? I'm having a great morning. That could only make it better."

She nudged me toward my desk. "Don't bother . . . unless he tries to date another one of my sisters."

Cord popped his head into the office at that moment. "Morning," he said with a smile that widened on Pearl.

She gave him a tight-lipped grin that might have lasted a little longer than normal, but then turned back to me. "You need anything else, Wes?"

"I'm good, thanks, Pearl." She nodded and walked out with another short glance at Cord.

He followed her with his eyes, and I smiled to myself. *No chill*.

Cord dropped into the chair on the other side of my desk. "How was your weekend?"

"Pretty fucking awesome." I needed to at least fill in Cord. "Gotta tell you something, though."

Mason knocked and then stepped inside. "I called you ten times." Even his impatient tone couldn't dull my mood.

"My phone was off. What's up?" I sat back in my chair, expecting Mason to take the seat next to Cord. Instead, he stalked back and forth in tight circles.

"Haven't I asked you to help me help you? I've told you I can't do my job if you keep me in the dark." He was running his hands through his disheveled hair.

I exchanged a look with Cord, who shrugged. "What are you talking about? What's to tell?"

"A reporter, Wes? You loosen up for fifteen damn minutes out of your whole uptight, rule-loving life and it's to bang a reporter who holds the company's reputation in her hands? That's the last thing we need."

Cord asked, "What the hell are you talking about?" at the same time I asked, "How did you know?"

Cord looked to me expectantly, and the two sets of judging eyes on me didn't feel great.

I held up a palm. "It just happened, and I think 'holds the company's reputation in her hands' is a bit much. You said it was a goodwill piece."

Mason laughed, but it was mirthless. "I said the mentor program article was a goodwill piece. Try again." He tossed his tablet and a few printouts on my desk, and Cord and I leaned in to read them. The header read *Best Life*, the site that had a reviewer using the app. I looked up from the tablet.

"Oh, shit," Cord muttered, reading the printed pages.

"Read on," Mason said, pinching the bridge of his nose.

*Body FTW* filled the header, with links to the writers, the blog posts, the apps, and other social media. I scrolled down, and my hands stilled.

*Two* Best Life *staff members are on healthy living journeys using two competing apps that offer coaching. Claire and Britta are getting real about bodies, fitness, wins, losses, and life.*

I reread the lines a few times. When Britta said she worked for a magazine, I thought she'd known about this conflict for a couple weeks, not since February. I clicked the link to learn about the women. Britta's smile. It was the same smile she'd given me that morning when I kissed her during a break in our run. The other photo was of a pretty woman with a slim build.

My stomach dropped. "She's the reviewer for *Best Life*?"

Mason scrolled on his phone and held it out for me to see. It was someone's selfie in the park, but in the background was us after we'd run that first time. We were hugging, but her face was visible, as was the FitMi logo on my shirt. The top comments under the photo were:

**SuperClown:** Isn't that the chick from @BestLife in the background?

**Amandamanda:** It is! I love her. Is that her coach?

**SuperClown:** Looks like he loves her, too *wink*

"Yeah," Mason said when I looked up, derision dripping from his voice. "Keep going."

**AnonymousE7:** I checked out this app because of how passionately you wrote about the dedication of the coaches. I didn't believe an app could connect you with someone as caring as you describe your coach. Now I know why. You should have told readers it's because you're sleeping with him. I'm disgusted with this site, you, and this app. I'm canceling my subscription to both and telling everyone I know to do the same.

I stared at the replies under the main comment—there were many—and instantly my head started to pound. "How did anyone know?"

**TbirdNicole_7836:** Are you serious? I chose #TeamBritta because I like an underdog, but she was screwing the coach the whole time? #TeamClaire #TeamHottrYou

**AugustusGloopLover:** @FitMiFitness has been great for me, but I didn't know sex with the coach was an option. How much extra does that cost?

**AnnieApple:** You should be ashamed of yourself.

**Burt_the_destroyer**: I like my girls with a little extra meat. Want more "exercise"?

**RosieEarl:** I loved this because you seemed so real. I'll never believe another word you write. This is so disappointing.

I couldn't hear anything over the pounding in my ears, and I pushed the tablet back across the desk, looking up to meet Cord's and Mason's expectant faces.

"Well?" Mason said. "It's true? You asked me not to intervene on assigning the coach, so I left well enough alone. Then this morning, when I asked Pearl to look up the coach's information, imagine my surprise when it was *your* fucking name!" Mason's voice rose, and he began pacing again.

"Look, it's not like that," I said. "It's . . . she's special."

"Wes, you hired me to manage how this company is viewed. I don't care if she's the reincarnation of Eleanor Roosevelt with candy cane–flavored nipples, and the cure for the common cold is between her legs. This looks bad." He jammed his thumb into the printout.

"I knew you liked a client, but I didn't know she was the reviewer," Cord said, looking back at the comments.

"She never—" I pulled at my hair. "She told me this weekend she was a journalist, but I thought it was for the mentoring thing . . ." It had seemed so easy. Apparently, too easy. I kicked myself for not asking more questions, for not clarifying where she worked.

"For starters—and I can't believe I need to tell you this—don't sleep with *any* journalists writing about the company. None of them. Writers for newspapers, magazines, and PTA monthly newsletters are officially off your booty call list. Second, I've been sending you posts for months. You read none of them?"

"I fucked up, okay? Just let me think for a minute."

Mason huffed and sat down in the chair next to Cord. "You need to be straight with me. No bullshit. What is going on?"

"I'll tell you, but I need to warn her first," I said, pulling my phone from my pocket to text Britta. "She's going to be completely caught off guard by this."

"Good luck. Natalie called me to see what the hell was going on, because your girl isn't answering her phone or responding to texts, either."

I remembered Britta's phone pinging the night before. We'd been on the bed, things heating up, and she'd set it to do not disturb.

"Believe me when I say she knew as soon as she got within fifty feet of her office. Tell us what's going on so I can get in front of this."

Mason motioned for me to keep going.

Cord said nothing, and his silence was damning.

"We were friends until this weekend."

Mason eyed me skeptically, and Cord raised an eyebrow, his lips twisted to the side.

"I swear," I repeated. "We never slept together before this weekend."

"It doesn't matter. *Best Life* has a huge following, and this is out there on social media already. It's garnered a ton of engagement, and there's . . . a hashtag."

"What do you mean?" Cord pulled out his phone and tapped something into his search engine, and his features contorted as the results populated. "Fuck," he muttered under his breath.

This morning had gone from the best day of my life to me wanting to sink into the floor. I looked at the results on Cord's phone under #MakeBrittaSweat. Post after post shared the comment and memes using her headshot. They nauseated me. "Who are these people and why do they care so much?"

"Because people like a scandal," Mason said. "Are there more pictures of you two?"

"Not *those* kinds of photos."

*Fuck, I need to text Felicia to make sure no one posted anything from the wedding.*

Mason nodded and made notes on the tablet he'd pulled from my desk. "I think we need to deny it, share a link to our nonfraternization policies, and remind the public we hold"—he let out a mirthless laugh—"hold ourselves to a higher ethical standard."

"What about Britta?"

"What about her? Forget her for a few minutes and think about you. Your face is obscured, and other than being identified as a coach, you're not mentioned. If there aren't pictures . . ." Mason was noting something else on his tablet. "This might work."

I interrupted. "There shouldn't be pictures."

"Fine. Then she can deny, too. What else do I need to know? You were together this weekend. Was that the first time meeting in person? Push comes to shove, it was a slow buildup to love while you chatted, blah, blah."

Cord shot me a look across the desk, and I shook my head, my face heating because his disappointed expression made my stomach drop. *She hasn't been lying to me for a few weeks about her job; she's been keeping it a secret for months, knowing who I was.* My stomach roiled. "We've been hanging out for a few months."

Mason's eyes widened. "What the hell were you thinking? Can I remind *you* about our strict nonfraternization policy?"

I slammed my head into my hands. "I know, okay! It just . . . happened, but it wasn't sexual until two days ago. There were extenuating circumstances, and she's special. People would understand."

Mason expelled that dry laugh again. "I think you are unfamiliar with *people*. Let me introduce you," he said, pointing to a printout of comments and the social media stream. "'Extenuating circumstances' sounds like an excuse to get your dick wet and make sure the company got good coverage. No, I think we deny a sexual relationship, and you need to distance yourself from her. You're not celebrities, but you're not nobodies, either, and cameras are everywhere."

Mason took a call then, holding up a finger. "Yes, we're going with that. Put together some language. I'll be there in five." He hung up without pleasantries. "You heard me, right? If there are pictures, this strategy doesn't work. If you've been fucking her for months or weeks or kissing her near a camera, this won't work."

"It was this weekend," I repeated.

I glanced back down at his tablet, new notifications popping up on the #MakeBrittaSweat hashtag.

*Fuck.*

# 51

BRITTA

I WALKED ACROSS the office building's lobby a little slower than normal, my heels clacking against the marble floor. The way the sunlight reflected off the chrome and glass accents gave the space an extra sparkle, but I was also a little sore from the weekend's exertions, particularly the run that morning and the shower afterward. I squeezed my thighs at the memory of Wes on his knees, water spraying his tanned shoulders, and then him standing behind me. A warm feeling settled low in my belly.

We'd spent all Sunday lost in each other. I'd already known Wes was hot and sweet and wonderful, but the way he touched me, kissed me, how his tongue felt on my softest places and how he stroked me so deep, filling me—all of it made goose bumps prickle at even the hint of memory. I smiled to myself, glancing at my phone, where I could see he was typing a message. I'd never plugged it in, and the battery was hanging on by a thread. I saw I had a bunch of missed texts—probably the text thread with RJ, Kat, and Del. I'd missed an episode of our favorite reality TV show and the subsequent commentary and debriefing. I didn't toggle over, not wanting to miss Wes's message with my battery so close to dying.

"Morning, Anthony," I said to the security guard, who tipped back in his chair.

"Got a message they were looking for you upstairs," he said, picking up the phone. "Told me to be on the lookout."

"Thanks," I said. I couldn't think of any reason they'd be looking for me, except that maybe Claire had been right and Maricela had news about the promotion. The way my luck had been going, I had a feeling it was mine. Even if it wasn't, I was going to be fine.

I leaned against the cool metal wall of the elevator, my eager anticipation leading to yet another moment to think about Wes, as if he hadn't been consuming my thoughts all morning.

I read his incoming text, confused. "What mentoring program?"

The doors opened to Natalie's hard stare. "Were you ever going to answer your damn phone?" She hissed, pulling me by the arm from the elevator.

*What the hell?* "I had it on do not disturb. What's going on?"

Natalie looked like someone had deleted her Instagram feed. "Your secret is out and it's *everywhere*."

"What secret?"

"Come with me," she huffed, pulling me into her office. When we were behind a closed door, whatever modicum of restraint she'd been applying cracked. "You're sleeping with your coach?"

"How did you . . . What do you mean?" The last person I wanted knowing details of my sex life was Natalie.

"Who ignores their phone for twelve fucking hours? See for yourself. This was posted this weekend."

Stomach lurching, I pictured many photos we could have been in at the wedding—Wes handing me a drink, Wes kissing me on the dance floor, the two of us climbing into a cab together. We'd been so careless.

Natalie turned the monitor, showing me a social media post. The photo on the screen wasn't from the wedding, though. My arms wrapped around Wes's neck and his at my back. It was in the park after our first run together outside. "Someone posted this photo, and one of their followers recognized you from Body FTW." I scrolled through the comments, my heart pounding.

**KDRuple7:** Did you see this? Someone claiming to be her friend said they're sleeping together!

**AmbreAmbre:** "The coaching for FitMi is incredible." Some might say he leaves you . . . breathless? Kudos, girl. I'd sleep with him if I had the chance, too!

**Harper98Lions:** Looks like Britta was more interested in another body. @FitMiFitness, how many of your other coaches are seducing lonely clients? Damn, this was back in spring! #MakeBrittaSweat

**Lydia.Frank:** Girl, you really are living your @BestLife.

**Jfil48:** That @FitMiFitness coach is fucking hot. Too bad I'm not thicc enough for him!

**SPHunt:** @FitMiFitness just posted a few minutes ago. Anyone want to read their policy on not screwing clients?

**LittleHippoMom:** @FitMiFitness must be struggling if they have to resort to this for clients. Whatever they pay that coach, it's not enough. #MakeBrittaSweat

**GGMikeXX:** @BestLifeBritta, want to do a story on insurance agencies next? I'm just saying I'm available for an "interview."

Shame, anger, frustration, and helplessness rose in me as the replies kept populating. That wasn't even a careless moment—it was a beautiful moment, and I felt violated seeing it on the screen.

I looked up, panic-stricken, to meet Natalie's gaze. "How did they know?"

"What were you thinking, Britta? And how could you not tell me?"

"It . . . it just happened this weekend."

Natalie looked at me like I had two heads, both of which were shoved up my own butt. "So, it's true? You're sleeping with the coach whose company you've been reviewing and promoting for months?"

"Not until this weekend," I clarified. "We were friends before. This picture is innocent." At the time, I'd brushed off the notion that Wes wanted to kiss me, but seeing the photo now, even without seeing his face, I was sure he did.

Natalie stared at me, eyes like steel, and pointed to the screen. "Believe me. It does not look innocent." Finally, she rubbed her temples. "This is a nightmare. Body FTW, which has been tremendously profitable for us, now looks like a sham, and the coach looks like a sleazy dick, which he probably is."

"He's not," I insisted.

"You need to tell me everything so I can advise Maricela on how we're handling this."

I slapped my hand to my mouth. "Oh, God! My post from Saturday . . . it's about sex." My face burned at the memory of happily discovering sex was in the FitMi list of exercises and writing about it.

"I deleted it, but not before thousands of people viewed it." The land-line on her desk rang. "You screwed us here, Britta." Natalie picked up the receiver and spoke without preamble. "Hey . . . she's here." She cut her eyes to me, and I dropped my gaze to stare intently at my hands.

I itched to text Wes. This couldn't bode well for him, and the last thing I wanted was to be another woman who let him down. Over the weekend, we'd been lost in each other physically, but in those still moments, holding each other, he'd opened up. Wes had told me more about his mom and sister, about his ex and what had happened with them. He'd looked so relieved to talk about it, like he was releasing a pressure valve. My stomach sank at the idea of him closing that valve back off.

Natalie's conversation continued. "Who's the coach?"

I swallowed, realizing she didn't know, that Wes's identity wasn't out there yet.

"Mason, your guy's inability to keep his dick in his pants around a client got us into this mess. Give me a name," she said, like I wasn't in the room. "Yes, my reporter didn't keep it in her pants, either. Do you really want to play semantics right now?" She was silent for a moment and cast me sideways glances.

She dropped the ear set into the cradle forcefully. "They're closing ranks. Who is your coach?"

I swallowed. I needed to talk to Wes, to protect him from this. My name was tied to it, but his wasn't. "Just . . . a coach. It doesn't matter."

"Why do I even bother?" she muttered under her breath. "Without a face for him, this is all on you. The public isn't kind, and hashtag Make-BrittaSweat is only the beginning. FitMi wants to deny it, and I'm inclined to agree. But otherwise, you need to play up the he-took-advantage-of-me-when-I-felt-ugly angle or something. You're a good writer, so I'm sure you could spin a convincing tale."

I recoiled, sitting back in my chair with such a start it almost tipped backward. "He *didn't* take advantage of me. I would never say that." *That would destroy him.*

Natalie held up a hand. "We'll cross that bridge when we get there. Is there anything else I need to know?"

I opened my mouth to talk, unsure what else I should tell her, but Natalie was already speaking. Well, not so much speaking as cursing.

"Of-fucking-course." She stared at her monitor.

"What?"

Natalie's eyes were wide. Her voice boomed and bounced off the walls of her office "He's the damn CEO!?" She shook her head at me and picked up the phone without another word. "You didn't think to tell me your guy runs the damn company, Mason? Someone just posted his name and photo, and this shitstorm just got monumentally worse."

I buried my face in my hands, willing this day to start over again, for me to be back in Wes's bed under the warm covers with his lips on me. *This is a complete nightmare.*

"I'll be back." I needed to check in with Wes; we needed a plan. As I hurried to my cubicle, eyes darted to me and then away: a few sympathetic glances, a few curious ones, and a lot that looked judgmental as hell. Slinking to my desk, I dug a charger from my drawer and plugged in the device. I was tapping my foot, waiting for it to boot up, when Claire walked up to my desk. "I heard—"

"How could you?" I hissed at her through gritted teeth. "I told you all of that in confidence and you pull this? Dropping an anonymous comment that we were sleeping together?"

Her features morphed to disgust. "You think *I* did this?"

"No one else knew. You had your chance to make it worse for me and you took it."

Claire stared down at me, gaze cool. "You're unbelievable." She walked away, and I turned in my chair, banging my knee into the desk. My phone screen flashed, and hundreds of notifications popped up. I ignored them all and opened my texting app, where I had a new message waiting from Wes.

**Wes:** Are you okay?

The time stamp was from fifteen minutes earlier.

**Wes:** I didn't realize you wrote for Best Life. You've known the whole time?

**Britta:** When I told you I was a journalist, I thought you knew. I don't know how this happened.

I stared at my phone, hoping he'd say something else while I tried to find the right words. I watched the bouncing dots, but nothing else came through.

Natalie's voice broke into my thoughts as she invaded my cubicle. "My office—we need a closed door."

I wanted to send another text, but my phone was at one percent, and it would die if I unplugged it. I glanced at it one more time before following Natalie back to her office. "This is a mess," she said once the door closed behind us. "FitMi confirmed what you said, that the sexual relationship just started."

"Well, that's good, right?" I bit back the concern about exactly how many people were discussing my sex life at that moment.

Her stare was cool. "No one will believe it."

"But it's the truth."

"The truth is subjective." She pointed at the screen. "Tell me about this photo."

"We ran in the park, and I was excited because I'd gone longer than I ever had." I tried to explain it as best I could, but it sounded paltry. I didn't know how to give that moment—the elation and pride I'd felt—the significance it deserved while still insisting we were just working out together. It had meant so much because Wes was there with me. My voice hitched as I finished the story, my nerves frayed.

Natalie's tone softened. "Britt, I'm coming down hard on you, but people love Body FTW, and they loved you and Claire. This feels like a betrayal." She sighed and reread her notes. "Let me call Mason. We'll figure out something and let it blow over."

I nodded. People only cared about sex scandals if the details trickled down. Without any, interest would dry up.

"And you need to stay away from him."

"What?"

"We can't deny this only to have someone spot you canoodling at the park or buying condoms or something." She must have read my face, and she softened her tone again. "I guarantee his people are telling him the same thing. This is for the best."

She tapped at a few things on her screen and grimaced. "And stay off social media today. Just . . . trust me on that one."

When I returned to my desk, I swiped to dismiss the explosion of notifications on my social media accounts and texts from friends. I ignored all but a few.

**Mom:** Honey, what is going on? How much trouble are you in? People are saying horrible things.

**RJ:** Who do I need to hunt down?

**Kat:** Britta, are you okay? Don't respond to anything—I know it will blow over.

**Del:** Can I borrow your cheese grater? Oh, and there's something going on on social media. Kat and RJ left me like 20 texts about it.

**Wes:** We need to talk.

I replied to the messages from my mom and my friends, telling each I'd check in later.

**Britta:** They said we shouldn't be seen together.

**Wes:** Fine, but I need to talk to you. My place at noon?

I bit the side of my thumbnail, trying not to notice the three interns passing my cubicle in a flurry of whispers and giggles. I wanted to escape back into the cocoon of his arms, to hear him tell me I was beautiful and strong, but I doubted that's what *we need to talk* meant.

**Britta:** Yeah, I can be there.

He didn't reply.

# 52

## WES

WITH MY MOM, with Kelsey, I was always looking out for an agenda, there was always some angle, but I'd never felt that with Britta. Now I questioned everything. We'd been working together for months. I thought back to the jokes and texts, the runs in the park and mornings at the gym . . . the entire time, she'd been writing about the coaching program, and I couldn't shake the thorn that she'd known this could put my business at risk and still lied, presumably for her own benefit with this Body FTW project. I'd lied, too. Everything that had felt so perfect twenty-four hours earlier felt sordid and regrettable now. Another mistake, only this one was entirely public.

I'd stopped scrolling back to the message thread with Libby so often. For years, it had been a habit and ritual, and I found myself doing it again. Checking. Worrying. Willing her to answer.

**Wes:** I hope you're okay.

After a few seconds, I set my phone aside and clicked through the posts. Every word was Britta popping off the page. Even as I seethed at her betrayal, at some asshole making what we had into something that looked dirty and suspicious, and at myself for leaving so many boxes unchecked, I marveled at how she was so raw, so vulnerable, so . . . her in every single post. Titles like "A Few Things to Remember About Spandex," "Crunches Are as Awful Now as in High School P.E.—Here's Why You Should Do Them Anyway," and "Dear Running Shorts: Get Out of My Butt" made me laugh.

Other posts like "The First Boy Who Told Me I Was a Mistake," "Falling and Failing," and "I'm Just Not That Into You: The Scale, the Mirror, and Another Salad" made me want to hug her. She left everything on the page about pride and guilt, shame and confidence, strength and power, and about feeling hopeless and feeling seen.

Cord stepped in and closed the door behind him. "You want to talk now?" He plopped into the chair.

"I'm meeting Britta at my place."

His jaw was set, and he gave a grunt in response and nodded before asking, "What are you going to do?"

"Are you asking if I can keep it in my pants?"

"No, jackass." He shot me a rueful look—one I deserved. "And don't act like I shouldn't. What is going on with you? Sleeping with a client? This is a big deal, and not just for the company. You're looking to be distracted so much, you put our company at risk. I've been your best friend for ten years, and you lied to my face."

"I'm sorry, but I swear she's not a distraction. I've never felt like this with someone." I met my friend's hard stare. "I know you warned me. I should have told you."

Cord's expression softened. "Well, tell me about her now."

"I can't believe she was writing about us the whole time."

"You said she told you she was a journalist this weekend?"

"She did, and I swear I thought it was for this one-and-done article. I thought she'd known for maybe a couple weeks. But six months?"

Cord looked thoughtful. "You love her?"

I had known the answer four hours earlier when I kissed her on the sidewalk outside my building. *Except we both lied for months.* I glanced at the pages and pages of the members of #TeamBritta without answering, but he must have read my expression.

He nodded, chewing on the inside of his cheek. "Thought so."

I glanced back at the screen, where I'd been scrolling through to a flood of comments on one of her posts—people saying how much they needed to hear about her struggles, how they'd thought they were the only one not knowing how to feel good about their body, with self-doubt and uncertainty, and that her posts made them notice warning signs in others. I pointed to the screen. "I can't shake the thought that if Libby had something like this, maybe she would have found other ways to cope, or would have felt she could ask for help."

"Maybe so."

"Like, these are the kinds of things I want our clients to be reading."

Cord was quiet for a few seconds. "I'm pretty sure she's going to have to choose between being with you and writing that."

"Yeah." I let my voice fade. Britta had reached so many people, and it clawed at me that I was the reason she might have to stop.

I glanced at the clock over his shoulder. "I gotta go, man." I pushed away from my desk and shoved my phone in my back pocket. "I know I fucked up, and I'll be careful, but I need to see her."

Cord nodded and raised his fist for me to bump. "Good luck."

I headed to the elevator with a sour taste in my mouth. I knew what I had to do. Britta was doing something important. As much as it made me want to punch a wall, I knew I wasn't worth her having to stop.

# 53

BRITTA

**User Bmoney34 not found**

BANNED FROM WRITING or posting, I couldn't focus. Eventually, I gathered my purse and walked toward the main entrance. I would have liked to say I walked with my head held high, but the entire company knew everything about me. So, I hung my head and pretended to be texting, praying no one would try to engage me in conversation. Though there were whispers, no one did. Claire hadn't so much as looked at me. I seethed at her betrayal and kicked myself for ever believing in her truce, especially after she tried to play innocent.

"Britta, a minute?" The voice stopped me in my tracks, and Maricela motioned from the doorway to her immaculately appointed office.

*Shit.* "Sure."

Maricela folded her toned arms on her desk and leaned forward. "How are you?"

I blinked back tears, drained, like someone had released the air from my tires. "Okay." I nodded too many times. "Maricela, I swear it's not as bad as it looks. We—"

She held up her palm. "Natalie told me already. It's not my immediate concern, the nature of your relationship with the coach. You've . . ." she trailed off. "The Internet can be a cruel place, Britta. We all know that—we deal with trolls, but you've walked into public scrutiny."

"I can handle it."

"I'm sure you can, and you will." She tapped at her collarbone. "You don't have a choice, but I have to think of our entire company, and we rely on readers trusting our collective voice. You've made a big mistake here."

I gulped. *No, no, no, no, no.*

"I need you to step back from Body FTW and writing. Maybe it's a good time to use some of your vacation."

My heart folded in on itself like Saran Wrap. "I thought the plan was to deny everything. You want me to take a leave of absence?"

"Nothing so formal as that, but I think it's best we put the project on hold. The concept was so solid, and you built it beautifully, but Claire can continue to talk about health and fitness on her own, in some other way."

The scattered and pulsing remnants of my heart shot outward in all directions. *Her own segment. Claire threw me under the bus to get her own segment, and it worked.* Tears pricked the back of my eyes, but I blinked them away, tapping my foot. I had no proof it was Claire, so there was no point bringing it up.

"It's not personal, Britta." Maricela reached across the desk to touch my arm. "I have to protect this company."

It was the best I should have hoped for. She could have fired me. "I understand. Should I . . . do I need to leave, then?"

"Take a week or two off, and hopefully things will blow over. Then you can start up again with solely your editorial assistant role."

*Not writing.* I nodded again. "Okay. Thank you."

I stumbled out of the building, my heel catching on the sidewalk. At least it didn't snap. *So, one win.* I traveled to Wes's apartment in a daze. *How could Claire do this? How mad is Wes? What am I going to do?*

I rode the elevator to his place, my heart rate bumping up with each floor. I felt as nervous as I had the first time we met at the gym.

*It's Wes. It'll be fine.* Over the weekend, he'd given me access to the building, saying he wanted me to be there a lot and planned to get a key made for me. Standing outside his door, knocking, I wondered if I should have just waited in the lobby. He didn't answer and still hadn't responded to my text. I glanced at my watch—it was twelve fifteen.

The weight of the morning fell on me as I fumbled with my phone. I accidentally tapped my notifications bar and was struck with post after post lambasting me, mocking me, calling me all kinds of names, and trashing FitMi. Memes with my face photoshopped onto lewd photos filled the screen. Unbidden, tears streamed down my cheeks, a sob wrenched from my chest. I stood in the hallway outside Wes's door, unable to look away from my phone and unwilling to stop scrolling.

The elevator dinged, and Wes stepped into the hall. He was looking down, hands shoved in his pockets. Air filled my lungs in a heaving sigh at the sight of his posture, the way he tensed his shoulders. He didn't look mad. He looked broken, and that was so much worse.

"Wes." My voice cracked.

His head snapped up, expression pained, but he closed the distance between us, scooping me into his arms. That he hugged me without question, brought me to his warm body, made me cry harder into his shirt, because I'd worried he'd hesitate, and of course he didn't. "It's okay," he said near my ear.

"It's not," I croaked, pulling back, and he searched my face before answering.

"Let's go inside."

"I'm sorry," I said, attempting to catch my breath as he guided me through the door.

"Are you okay?" He sat close to me on the couch, rubbing circles on my back.

*Taking care of me, because I found the world's most caring man and then this happens.*

I laughed. "No, I am decidedly not okay." I sucked in a deep breath, raising my gaze to meet his hazel eyes. "It's just . . . I thought you knew.

I wasn't trying to keep the truth from you any longer. When I told you I was a journalist, you acted like you knew. I planned to talk about it more, but I thought we had time . . ."

"I thought you were writing a short piece about mentoring for a kids' program I'm running. It was put in motion a couple weeks ago." He looked down at his hands. "I know you didn't intentionally mislead me about that, but you've been writing about FitMi and me since we first interacted. Britta, you have to know how shitty that feels. Why didn't you tell me sooner?"

I dropped my head to my hands. "At first, I didn't want my experience to be any different. I was trying to be an honest reviewer. Then I got to know you." I angled my body to him, looking up and wringing my hands. "And, look at you, you're . . . you. I had a crush on you, okay?" Color rose on my cheeks at the admission, even though he'd been inside me less than six hours earlier.

I peeked at his face, but his expression gave nothing away.

"But I couldn't scrap my project, my first real break at *Best Life*, for a crush." I paused for a second and reached for his hand. "I justified it to myself that I was focusing on my journey and that talking to you in person wasn't that different from online."

His eyes met mine again, his expression tired.

"I know. That's bullshit, but it's what I told myself. You didn't tell me the truth either, Wes."

He nodded, jaw flexed. "It's what I told myself, too," he conceded. "I convinced myself we could do both, coaching and being friends."

"This weekend, though . . . Wes, I couldn't let you say you . . ." I choked on the words, because I was about to remind him he'd said he loved me, and I hadn't said it back. I'd wanted to so many times over the weekend, but I wanted to work everything out at the magazine first. I wanted a plan before I admitted what I'd felt for him for a long time. He looked so tired, so betrayed, that I wanted to say it then, but that wasn't fair. "I couldn't let you say you felt the way you felt and have you not know."

"Britta, you . . ." He squeezed my hand but glanced away, his face fixed, jaw set. "What happened at work?"

"It's not good."

"They fired you?"

"No, I can go back to just being an assistant." My face fell again. "I should feel lucky I'm not fired, but I can't write anymore. I get it. I screwed up, and we're in a business where people have to trust us. I'm not curing cancer or anything, but I felt like I was doing something that mattered."

"I read the posts," he said.

"You did?"

"I think you're helping a lot of people."

Tears stung the back of my eyes. "I thought I was, too." My voice broke, but he didn't move to hug me this time. "Is it bad for you?"

"We're a trust business, too." He stared at me long and hard, and I saw his expression shifting, saw the frustration before he spoke. "Six months, though? What the hell, Britta?"

"I'm sorry, Wes."

"Stop apologizing." His voice was low and cold, and it startled me. "I know you're sorry. I'm just trying to understand. You could have told me. You knew I owned the company—you had to know how bad it could be if it got out, what that would mean for me. I'm just as much at fault for ignoring my own ethics. That's on me, but I never thought you'd lie to me. I realize that makes me a fucking hypocrite, but you have to know how coldcocked I feel right now."

He sat close to me, fuming, his frustration coming off him in waves, but he didn't back away.

"I know, and I'm sorry." I swallowed, wishing I could think of something better to say. "I was only thinking of my career, and . . . it was just business, at first. I'm sorry."

He stiffened next to me when I said "just business." Even being seen with me was going to hurt his business. How could I be the one to stand by and watch his reputation get destroyed? Wes could help so many people, and he was such a good man, and this business was all he had. His eyes dropped away from my face, and I knew—I just knew—he was thinking the same thing. *I should say it first.*

"I don't think . . ." My voice was soft, as if the tears I wanted to shed were seeping into my speech. "I don't think we should keep seeing each other."

"That's what you want?"

*No.* I swallowed my doubt, the anxiety coiling in my stomach. "It's the right thing for both of us, isn't it? We both held back the truth, and we both stand to lose a lot."

A muscle in his jaw ticked, and he stared straight ahead, not meeting my gaze. His voice was flat when he said, "Okay."

I had no idea if his intonation meant he was mad or frustrated or relieved. The energy between us felt sharp and difficult, and I drew in a shaky breath. "It's probably for the best. I'll just . . ." I glanced around his living room, a space I'd been so comfortable in twenty-four hours prior, but there was nothing for me to grab. I stood on unsteady legs and wiped at my eyes. "I'll go."

Wes didn't answer but dropped his head, his fingertips pressed against his temples.

My stomach clenched. Wes sitting there like that, not saying anything, was explanation enough of how much I'd screwed up this entire situation. I pressed my lips together to hold back a fresh wave of tears and stepped toward the door. I knew once I left, I'd have really walked out the door on any future with him. I inhaled the clean scent of his place.

Wes's hands wrapped around my shoulders and gently turned me so we stood facing each other. "Wait." His voice cut through the silence, and he dragged a finger along my jawline. His touch sent a rush through me so powerful, I closed my eyes trying to block out the sensation. "Not like this."

My voice was breathy from both his touch and the tumultuous emotions coursing through me. "It's for the best."

"Okay," he said, his voice low. "But not yet. Not like this. Don't walk out the door yet, please."

It was the "please" that got me, the rawness in his voice. When I returned his gaze, we were only inches apart, and the heat from his body surrounded me. I leaned into his hand, knowing this might be the last time he looked at me like that, the last time anyone looked at me quite like that.

"I just . . ." He searched my face, and his fingers trailed down my neck and over my shoulders while I clutched his shirt. "Not like this."

My eyelids fell closed and I breathed him in. "Wes," I sighed as his hands finished their path down my arm, then inched up from my waist in a way that was already so familiar and warm. When he kept touching me like that, the world would fade away and all that would be left would be me and him. "We shouldn't."

"I know we shouldn't," he echoed, dropping his lips to my neck. "I'm angry with you, and furious with myself, and I know you're right, but please don't make me let you go." He waited until I lifted my arms to wrap his own around me, holding me tightly. "Not yet."

"Wes," I murmured as he kissed my neck and his palms cradled my face. I heard what he hadn't said. He wanted that moment of the world fading away, and I did, too. "One last time," I whispered, my lips near his ear.

Wes groaned against my neck, the vibrations sending chills through me. He pushed forward, laying me back on the couch. The pressure of his hips rolling into me sent nerve endings popping, and our eyes locked as they had so many times in the last weekend. I wanted his look to say *No, we're not ending this* or *I need you in my life*. I wanted to convince him I'd never leave him feeling betrayed again, that what was between us was more important than our jobs. But he repeated my words, "One last time," and I knew it was.

---

HE'D TAKEN ME in every sense of the word, and I'd taken him right back. We lay on the couch, drained. His arms around me, my face on his chest—it was like when we'd run together side by side. Except this time,

I would leave, and I had to remind myself why it mattered. He deserved someone who would put him first, and I'd shown him that wasn't me.

"You should get back to work," I said, inhaling his familiar scent as fresh tears fell from my cheeks.

"I know," he said, voice husky and his chest heaving under my cheek.

He didn't move his hands from me, and I knew I'd have to be the one to walk away.

# 54

BRITTA SLIPPED OUT of my apartment when I went to the bathroom. I heard the click of the door, and that was it, she was gone. I wasn't sure what I had expected, but it was something more akin to a tearful good-bye. I'd known it was stupid to chase her, stupid to kiss her, and really stupid to sleep with her, but stupid was the only thing that made sense in that moment.

I'd thought if we had that last time, I could soak up her affection and it would sustain me. Maybe some part of me hoped she'd tell me she loved me, too, and that would solve something. Maybe she had the right idea, but getting ready to go back to work, all I thought about was her familiar scent and the taste of her mouth, and how everything about this decision to go our separate ways felt wrong. I also kept thinking about her posts and the comments and Libby. I had to keep reminding myself it was the right decision to end it, and that, despite everything else, we'd lied to each other for months. I glanced at my phone, hoping for even a hint of a reply from my sister. Instead, I had a message from Aaron. *School board put the brakes on the project. Call me.*

THE REST OF the week was a blur of Mason freaking out, Pearl looking concerned, and Cord *checking in for no reason*. I wasn't down for any
of it and left work with more pent-up frustration than I'd had in a long
time. I didn't want to talk about anything with anyone. I went for a long
run, letting the heat beat down on my shoulders and my muscles strain. I
tried to focus on my feet hitting the pavement, but it was no use. Later, I
sat at a bar in Pilsen alone, nursing what was left of my drink, pretending
to watch the game but lost in my head. On top of everything else, each sip
was tinged with the same guilt I felt every time I wanted a drink after a
hard day. I spent most of my life trying not to be my mom, but maybe I
was a hypocrite. Pushing the bottle away and throwing some bills on the
bar, I was turning to leave when my phone buzzed. I hoped it was Britta
calling to talk and figure out how to get back together, Aaron telling me
the school board had changed their mind, or Libby reaching out.

**Kelsey:** We need to talk.

The last person whose name I wanted to see. I couldn't imagine being
with Kelsey. Not anymore, not when I knew how good it could be.

**Wes:** I don't have time.

**Kelsey:** Make time.

Kelsey's clipped, entitled response pissed me off even more, because I
wanted the messages coming through to be from Britta. I'd even convinced myself that it was appropriate to send her links through the app
about self-care during stressful and difficult times, that a good coach
would still do that. When I clicked on her name at two in the morning,
a status window popped up: *Account not found*. I had her phone number
and her email, and I knew where she lived, but that digital connection
being severed, her account where she had logged so much progress and so

many accomplishments, her deleting that was a punch to the gut. Some-how, I knew her cutting that connection—that was the cut that mattered.

**Kelsey:** You'll be glad you did. Come over.

**Wes:** We're not going to happen, OK? I don't know how to make it any clearer.

There was no response, and I sighed in relief, climbing into the wait-ing car. Running wouldn't clear my head any more than beer had, and I was tired after tossing and turning all night in my empty bed. I'd just stepped into my apartment when my phone buzzed again.

**Kelsey:** I'm not trying to seduce you. You chose the chubby girl. I get it. Fact remains, the chubby girl screwed you over.

**Kelsey:** This is about business, and I have a plan that will benefit us both. You need me.

**Kelsey:** Get Cord. Come to my place.

# 55

## BRITTA

AFTER FOUR DAYS of "vacation" and living mostly unshowered in a rotation of sweats, yoga pants, and pajamas, I looked like hell, which my friends didn't hesitate to tell me.

RJ pushed into my apartment on Saturday holding iced teas and a bag of groceries, eyeing my outfit. "Is Del your stylist, or something?" Kat and Del followed her inside, each carrying canvas bags.

Del glanced over his shoulder. "I dress better than that."

Ignoring his casual appraisal, I settled on the couch. "My appearance slipped my mind, what with losing the job, losing the guy—oh, and the Internet collectively deciding I'm an untrustworthy slut." I hadn't run or gone to the gym since Monday morning, and my body wasn't used to being still for so long. The idea of putting on my sneakers and running without Wes made me sad, though. I'd gotten used to his strides matching mine.

"It's a small segment of the Internet." Del unloaded groceries, setting milk and vegetables, yogurt, and a bevy of food options in the fridge and cupboards. Kat and RJ shot him pointed looks, but I couldn't be mad at his honesty.

"Thanks," I mumbled, watching him opening and closing cupboards. "It was a substantial enough segment for me to lose my job, though."

"You didn't lose your job. You lost the job you wanted." RJ grabbed the other iced tea and sat next to me. "Still bad, but you're not unemployed." She fixed me with a to-the-point stare.

Kat was in her full elementary school teacher mode and patted my arm. "As for the guy . . ."

Del joined us in the living room. "B, you lied to him and put him at risk for some major shit. And it sounds like he lied to you, too. How was it going to last? You guys were a mess."

Kat and RJ shot him matching glares again, and Del held up his palms. "What? I'm just giving her the hard truth."

"You could be nicer about it," Kat scolded.

"I know you're right," I agreed, glumly. Wes had felt so perfect next to me, like all was right with the world. It didn't seem possible we weren't supposed to be with each other.

"But . . ." Kat's expression changed as she settled next to me on the couch. "You were *with* him. How was it?"

"I don't want to hear this." Del laughed and walked into the kitchen, hands over his ears. "I need more friends."

She elbowed me in the side. "C'mon, don't hold out on me. I'm old and married. I want details. He's a big guy?" Kat raised her eyebrows suggestively.

"Shut up," I said, pushing her away, but laughing in appreciation of the juvenile joke. "It's not funny."

"It's not, but we wanted to see you smile." RJ wrapped a protective arm around my shoulder. "How you doing?"

"I'll be fine."

"I was worried you'd be curled up in a little ball after the thing yesterday."

"What thing?" I'd been deep in a Netflix hole for most of the past two days so I wouldn't have to wonder what Wes was doing or whether he missed me. It hadn't worked. At one point, while binging a baking competition on Netflix in the middle of the night, I decided I wouldn't compete in the 10K. It would draw unnecessary attention, and I doubted I could finish the training on my own anyway.

"Oh. I figured you'd seen it." Kat's careful demeanor made me worry, but I was already feeling so low, I couldn't imagine anything fazing me.

"Seen what?"

RJ pulled her phone from her pocket with a sigh. "This came out yesterday. You don't have to read it, though."

Kat leaned toward me. "You really don't need to read it."

"After what happened this week, it can't be that bad." I took her phone and saw HottrYou's social media page. Photos of shiny people in small bathing suits filled the screen, but on top was a link to a press release.

*HottrYou president Kelsey Marshall responded today to reports that HottrYou coaches have been promoting unsafe and unhealthy practices.*

*"We train our coaches to use the utmost care with clients, and it is regrettable that allegedly some have interpreted our training to mean recommending crash dieting and dangerous exercise practices. We will suspend our coaching operation immediately to launch an investigation."*

*In response to the recent scandal involving competitor FitMi Fitness, Marshall stated she knows FitMi Fitness CEO, Christopher "Wes" Lawson, to be ethical and professional. Said Marshall, "It's a shame Body FTW turned into something ugly. We saw the two reviewers bring people together to reach their goals, and while we were, of course, #TeamHottrYou, both women should be commended on their efforts and for sharing their stories. We urge Best Life and FitMi fans not to let this blip sour you on two fantastic platforms."*

That was unexpected. I skimmed forward as she praised their innovation, the highly trained coaches, and the seamlessly integrated platform.

I was no business whiz, but when your competitor was down, it seemed prudent to strike versus sing their praises.

> *"I believe in the company and their mission, and that's why, in the coming months, HottrYou and FitMi will work together, combining the best of both programs to support the fitness and goals of all new and future users. The FitMi coaches are highly trained, educated, and professional."*

I looked up in disbelief.

Del had walked back in, holding a bottle of water and a banana and standing behind the couch. "What are you reading?"

RJ ignored his question and nodded to me. "Keep going."

I skimmed forward as they shared a few thoughts about the merger and then quoted Kelsey about the scandal with FitMi. Her answer left me rereading the sentence several times.

> *"Wes and I have known each other for years. We're close, and when you have a history like we do, successful business partnerships are only the beginning."*

I stared at the screen. The release included a photo of Wes and Kelsey from college. She was looking at the camera, but he was smiling at her, and it was his genuine smile, the one I'd thought of as mine. My heart stilled when another, more recent photo flashed on the screen. It was a selfie of the two of them, Wes's smile more of a wry grin, but that wasn't what held my attention. Scruff covered his square jaw—he'd told me after the wedding he never went out unshaven until I mentioned I liked it. That photo had been taken recently.

"It has to be a publicity stunt." Kat shoved her phone back in her pocket.

*His smile.* I couldn't get over him giving his genuine smile to her. "They dated," I said in a small voice. "They dated for years. He wanted to marry her."

I doubted all the things I thought I knew about him and me and our story. *Was he interested in Kelsey that whole time?*

RJ eyed the screen again. "Really?"

I nodded, nothing to add. *The things he said . . . they felt real, they felt more real than anything I've ever experienced.* I looked at the photo again, and my heart sank. I'd left Wes because I didn't want to hurt his company—it could help so many people—but looking at him and Kelsey . . .

"Still. I'm sure it's a publicity stunt," RJ added.

"It might not be," Del said, biting into the banana.

"Del!" Kat exclaimed, while RJ shoved him away.

"What? I'm not saying it's right, but if he'd do that, you're better off without him."

Groaning, I sat back on the couch and folded into myself, hugging a pillow to my chest.

RJ snatched the pillow out of my arms, throwing it at Del. "We're trying to make her feel better."

"Hey!" I tried to snatch it back. "I need that. I'm sad."

"You can be sad, but you're done hiding."

"I'm not hiding."

RJ fixed me with another decisive stare. "You have crumbled-up cheese puffs all over your clothes, and your hair is at least fifty percent bird's nest. You're sitting in your apartment glued to the TV and stewing. You're hiding."

I rested my head on her shoulder. "What do I do?"

Del ventured into the conversation again. "Get back up. That's what you said when my adviser told me to start over on a new research topic."

"And it's what you told me when I got in that fender bender and was so scared to drive again," Kat said, sitting on my other side.

"And it's what you told me after I slipped on the ice last January when we were running late for that movie."

Kat and Del gave her wary looks, but RJ shrugged.

I grinned in response. "You wore impractical shoes. It was your own fault."

"The lesson stands. Get back up."

I leaned against my friend, surprised at everything she'd said. "I don't know what to do, and I don't know if I can."

"Well, trust the people who know you best. You can," Kat said, joining the hug with RJ. "Now, go shower."

She shooed me off the couch, and I spread my arms to hug her and Kat before turning to Del. "You're good friends."

Del stopped me with a gentle palm to my forehead. "I will hug you when you're not disgusting."

# 56

## WES

KELSEY WALKED INTO my office without knocking. "Get my email?"

I'd been staring at it for a solid five minutes. I glanced up from the monitor and closed the browser window containing Kelsey's statement and HottrYou's post about her announcement. "What the hell was that?"

"What?" Kelsey grabbed a water bottle from her bag and sat back in the chair, crossing her legs. She looked bored, which gave my anger a more pointed edge. Against my better judgment, Cord and I had met with Kelsey after she'd texted me, and come to terms on a plan, but her smug expression reminded me of all the misgivings I'd had about it.

Cord slammed through the door of my office, features twisted in anger. "You implied our companies are *merging*?"

Kelsey rolled her eyes and took another sip from her bottle. "Calm down. We talked about this."

Her dismissive smirk set my teeth on edge, and I pounded my fist on the table. "You might as well have announced to the world it was a done deal. We *never* agreed to that!"

She pulled out her phone and thumbed over the screen. "You needed your asses bailed out. Did you see the positive response to my announcement? I have three major outlets ready to run positive, scandal-free stories about FitMi. You should thank me."

Cord paced. "We talked about *you* coming over as COO after you shut down coaching at HottrYou. That's what we agreed to."

She arched one eyebrow and shrugged.

"This is not happening, Kelsey. You need to put out a retraction." I slammed my fist on the desk.

"Okay," she said with an easy shrug of her shoulders.

I didn't believe she'd cave so easily. "Okay?"

"Sure," she said, setting the water bottle down and smoothing her skirt. "I'm sure flip-flopping on the heels of your CEO sleeping with a client paid to review the app won't bother your investors at all. I said we were bringing the best of both platforms together, but I'll just walk it back. While I'm doing that, why don't I tip off the press *you* were with her when she crash dieted into the ER. That'll speak volumes to your *superior coaching*, won't it?"

Her blasé tone and barely veiled threat hit me like a two-by-four. "Are you kidding me with this? You'd do all of this because I rejected you? In what universe do you think this would make me want to be with you, and when did you become this fucking vindictive?"

"I already told you, I'm not trying to seduce you. I'm just letting you know the score." Kelsey assessed my features and dragged a finger down my biceps. Her expression softened, voice shifting into a fake sympathetic tone. "You miss the fat girl. You really had it bad for her, huh?"

My voice was a growl. "You don't get to talk about her."

Cord stepped between us, and Kelsey gave me a pitying look but straightened. "Fine. It's not really about her, anyway, and I'm not being vindictive, Wes. I'm sure you don't believe it, but I'm being prudent and saving my company. Mixing up the heart and head was never my thing. That was always you." She smoothed her skirt again and stepped back. "I did want you back, Wes, and I am sorry for how I treated you four years ago. I really am. I truly hoped we could start up again, but you said no, and it sucked, but I'm not a thirteen-year-old girl. I listened, and I got over it. I do what I need to take care of myself. Survival is my top priority. You've always known that, and you know why." She held my gaze for a beat, and all the reasons I'd forgiven her crap for years washed over me. *The fucked-up families club.* This was different, though, and before I could respond, she waved over her shoulder and strutted out the door. "We can meet next week to hammer out the details. Take some time to think about the benefits."

I stared at the doorway, fists clenched at my side, my heart thudding in my chest with rage, a memory, and emotions I couldn't name.

Cord called out to Pearl, "Can you get Mason and legal and . . . I don't know, get everyone together ASAP?" He paced the small room. "What did you ever see in her?"

"She's changed," I muttered, leaning back against my desk.

"Are you serious?" He stared at me in disbelief. "Kelsey was always all about Kelsey."

"She has her reasons, but I never thought she'd pull something like this."

Years of memories crashed down on me. The eye rolls. The dismissive tones. The hundreds of small ways she'd reminded me I was expendable, so I had no upper hand. The way I'd thought I was saving her, even when she made it very clear she didn't want or need saving. Kelsey made sure she had control in every situation. It was something I'd admired in her at first.

"Well, sorry to burst your bubble." Cord kicked his feet up on the desk. "I should have known not to trust her on this. What just happened is pure Kelsey." He motioned around the room. "There's no fucking way we're going through with her asinine idea."

Pearl walked in with Mason, who clapped his hands together. "Okay, Pearl and I have been talking. We have some ideas."

## 57

BRITTA

WES AND I had never run together in Hyde Park, and I set off down the path, appreciating the dewy early-morning air on the cusp of a hot day, and the lack of memories. My feet hit the pavement, my mind ready to be out of the house and my body playing catch-up. I'd made a new playlist, and my footfalls matched the bass in the pop song. As I ran, I saw a few other early risers, and my mind wandered as muscle memory took over.

I hadn't talked to Wes in two weeks following our breakup sex, which had been intense and emotional and had lasted as long as we were both able. But it had ended, and I'd left. I wouldn't have been able to say a real goodbye to him. It had seemed easier. It hadn't been.

*Breathe. Breathe. Breathe.*

I'd been surprised that on top of missing Wes, I'd missed this. I'd missed that moment when I knew I was pushing myself a little farther, to go a little faster. I'd missed writing, too. I'd opened my journals and my laptop a hundred times, but I'd had nothing to say, so I stared at a blank screen. In a few days, I was going back to work, and my stomach hurt thinking about returning and facing everyone, especially Claire. I'd thought we were becoming friends.

*Breathe. Breathe. Breathe.*

A familiar figure walking nearby caught my eye. Skinny jeans and an overly styled mustache. Ben was walking down the street near the park, talking on the phone. With his painstakingly messy hair and trendy clothes, I had to wonder what I'd seen in him for so long. Thinking about how into him I'd been was like unearthing a relic, something worn from time and dust covered—I didn't recognize it. I slowed, not wanting to literally run into him.

I waited for the memories of that night to crash into me, for the shame of years of chasing a guy who didn't want me to hit. It didn't. Since him, I'd had Wes, who was a thousand times funnier and genuinely caring, not to mention sexy and generous and someone who believed in me. More than that, I'd had me! The last few months had given me countless opportunities to realize how much more I deserved than the scraps of time Ben had been willing to toss my way.

Ben shoved his phone into his pocket, head tipping up. That was the moment I could have met his eye and waved. I remembered Wes saying, *Anyone who makes you feel you're not good enough isn't worth the breath it takes to tell them to go to hell.* We could have had a friendly chat, or I could have told him off for ghosting me, but I filled my lungs with air, and neither option struck me as all that appealing.

The song switched to "Truth Hurts" by Lizzo. I smiled, returning to my run with the steady beat in my ears. In my periphery, Ben raised his hand and smiled, but I kept running. I had a race to train for, and I suddenly knew exactly what I wanted to write.

# 58

WES

MOM GREETED ME with a hug, and I wanted to sink into her like when I was a little kid. I'd spent a lot of time wondering how I'd look her in the eyes, what it would mean if she kept using. I still didn't know when I walked in the room, but standing there in her hug, I pushed my worries aside. I'd spent so much of the last six years running from guilt and pain, and trying to keep everyone safe, that it was almost a relief to just be there with her. When she pulled away, I breathed a little easier.

She was in rehab, which she'd agreed to at the hospital. I wanted to believe she'd stay clean this time. It sounded like she wanted to believe it, too.

"Chris." She said my name a few times while looking me over. "Sometimes I just can't believe you're a grown man." She glanced over my shoulder. "Where is your friend? Um, I can't remember her name. The one with the big tits."

I shook my head, a smile tipping my lips. It was reassuring in tandem with cringeworthy to hear my mom say "tits." "Her name's Britta."

"Oh yeah." Mom seemed so fragile sitting right next to me. "She's your girlfriend?"

"Not anymore." We'd never gotten around to labels, assuming we had more than forty-eight hours, but "girlfriend" and "dating" were so insufficient for what I felt for her. *Soul mate. Love. Ex.*

Mom grabbed my hand—such a small gesture, but I couldn't remember her doing anything that sentimental in years. "What happened to her?"

I shrugged. "Nothing, we just broke up."

She nodded and continued rubbing her palm over my knuckles. Her hands were tiny, thin fingers twining together. After a few beats, she looked up and met my eyes. "You should stop feeling guilty about what happened."

"Nothing happened to Britta, Mom. We're just not together."

"No. With Libby."

I stilled.

"It's not your fault, Chris."

I patted her hand, shifting to stand. "I know."

"No." She moved both hands over mine, holding me in place, her eyes widening in what looked like panic and her voice hardening. "No," she repeated, her voice returning to normal. "Don't walk away. You think it's your fault. I know you do, and I blamed you for being at school. I know I did." She chewed on her lower lip. "I . . . I've messed up a lot, and I know you took care of her the best you could, better than I did."

"Mom, we don't have to talk about—"

She held up her palm. "They make us talk here all the damn time, but there are things I want to say to you." She lowered her hand to mine again. "You couldn't help her. She grew up hard, same as you, but she wasn't ever tough like you. Libby ran away for a lot of reasons, and a lot of them were me, but none of them were you." Mom gripped my hand, clinging to me. "It wasn't your fault, baby."

I let her keep holding me in place, and my voice came out almost a whisper. "I could have done something."

"You couldn't."

"I should have tried harder to find her."

"You tried. I know you did. I know you still try." She swiped at her face, pushing tears away. "It's not your fault. I should have told you all this a long time ago, but I'm telling you now."

I bit the inside of my cheek and ran my free hand through my hair. "I do still try to find her, to save her."

"Maybe she doesn't need saving." Mom looked at her lap, then at our joined hands. "My responsible boy. Always taking care of things. Don't let it eat you up until there's nothing left. They make us talk about shit in here, so I don't have a choice, but maybe you should talk to someone out there." She squeezed my hand again and stood, eyeing the clock and knowing the time for visits was short. "I grabbed this for you. They had some lying around." She thrust a flier with AL-ANON printed across the top. "It's like AA, but for kids and families and stuff." She glanced away, uncertain or maybe embarrassed at handing it to me. "I don't know. Maybe it would help. I think you've got a lot in your head."

I tucked it in my pocket. "I'll check it out, Mom." I stood to leave, giving her a hug.

Her grip was weaker, and she kissed my cheek. "And bring that girl to visit again. I liked her."

———

AS I WALKED to the car, I chewed on what she'd said and opened the thread to Libby.

**Wes:** Mom is in rehab. She's actually doing okay with it.

**Wes:** You don't have to respond. You're an adult and you have your own life, and I know you don't need me and Mom, but no matter what, I'm here. I'll always be here, and I guess I just needed to say that.

In all the times I'd sent messages, it had always been about finding her, taking care of her, and trying to get her to come home or to accept money. I'd never said anything that plain. In my personal life, I'd looked for distraction after distraction to take away the guilt, but I'd never even considered forgiving myself. *If someone told me that by the end of the day, Mom could be pushing me to get professional help, I would have thought they were high.* I remembered how Britta's hand had felt in mine at the hospital, the way she'd known when to show me she was there.

> **Wes:** I miss you every day, Lib. I know you had to leave to take care of yourself, and I know you don't want to come back, but if you'll ever let me come to you, or know you, it would mean the world to me. There will never be a time I'm not there for you when you need me.

Bouncing dots I hadn't expected to see popped up.

> **Libby:** We're okay. I've been in California since November.

*We?* I leaned against my car, my eyes wetter than I wanted, a whoosh of breath leaving me. A minute later, she sent a photo, a selfie, the ocean in the background and wind blowing her hair around her face. She was smiling and squinting into the sun, and she was holding a baby.

> **Libby:** I've been busy. You have a niece. Hazel is eight months old.

I stared at the photo in disbelief, emotions I couldn't even name flooding my system. Libby was a mom. Had she been alone? Did she have support? I stilled my fingers, knowing me going into protective mode always scared her away. I zoomed in on the photo of the baby's tiny face. Her eyes looked like mine, like Mom's. A few texts and a photo wasn't much, but it seemed like everything in that moment. Those same feelings I'd had with Britta, of things fitting into place, returned to me.

> **Libby:** I'm not ready to come back to Chicago or see Mom, but I want you to meet her soon.

**Libby:** Let me do it my way, though, okay? I do better when I can control things.

**Wes:** She's beautiful, and I can't wait to see you both. Whenever you're ready, just say the word and I'll be on a plane. I won't push—I promise, but if you need help, you'll ask, right?

She didn't respond, so I let that question hang and added, I love you, Lib.

**Libby:** I'll talk to you soon. I love you, too.

Standing in the parking lot, holding my phone like it was a piece of fragile crystal, there was only one person I wanted next to me. Britta had held me so tightly at the hospital when she knew I needed it. I needed her.

The phone buzzed in my hand, a preview of a message from Cord scrolling over the top of Libby's photo.

**Cord:** You should see this.

I clicked on the link to a social media page, Britta's *Best Life* profile. Her profile photo made my chest feel buoyant. She was smiling, her hair resting on her shoulders and her soft brown eyes open wide as she made a funny face. She'd added a long post the night before, and I clicked to expand it. I read each word, feeling like she was saying it into my ear. I wiped the back of my hand across my face and stared at my phone.

**Cord:** Meet me at the bar?

**Wes:** Yes.

I needed a plan.

# 59

**BESTLIFEMAGAZINE**

**LIKED BY ETHELGIRLZ AND 962K OTHERS**

Hi, everyone. It's Britta, and there are a few things I felt I needed to say.

Some of you suspect I had ulterior motives, or believe I was trying to trick you. I wasn't, but I am sorry that I misled you. I started this journey for my job. I didn't really care about getting active, being fit, or anything else. It was a job. Sure, I wanted to look and feel good naked, but along the way, I stopped worrying about that and started caring about being strong. I uncovered new goals and I fell in love . . . with myself. Body FTW started out to review two apps, but it's been about the journey and the stumbles, mine and fellow *Best Life* staffer Claire's. I stumbled big. I lied, I had an unprofessional relationship with my coach, I lost the chance to keep writing for *Best Life*, I disappointed my readers, and I hurt someone I really cared about. In all of that, I learned four key things:

1. All those years I didn't move forward? The only thing standing in my way was me. Once I took a chance on myself, there was nothing stopping me. Looking back, there were things I didn't do, didn't wear, didn't try, and it wasn't my body holding me back, it was my fear.

2. My biceps are amazing. I always knew they were there, but now I can't stop flexing them, and they might be my favorite parts of my body. Sorry, boobs. You're bigger, but these, these I worked for. I wanted to look good naked, but now I feel good naked . . . and it has nothing to do with a guy and everything to do with me and my sexy flexed biceps. Side note: I look great naked, and it turns out I actually always did!

3. I'm still fat and still happy with me. For a lot of years, I believed it was wrong to be happy with this body. I settled for so much less than I deserved. No more, though. I love this body, and I won't ever be with anyone who doesn't love it as well.

   I learned those three things because someone believed in me even when I didn't believe in myself. Someone who pushed me to go one more mile, who picked me up off the floor, and who didn't let me get away with doubting myself or how strong I was. That person was my coach. I'm sorry I lied—I regret it more than you can know—but I'm not sorry I found him. Without him, I wouldn't have discovered how strong I am, how much I love my biceps, and what kind of relationship I deserve. That leads me to #4.

4. I can do it. I will show up for the 10K, lace my shoes, stretch, and I will run that race. It's no longer part of my job, and I

don't have my running partner anymore, but I worked for the opportunity to cross the finish line. When I do, it will be for me—not my coach, not my job, not the sponsors. But it will be for you, too—those of you who are reading this and think you can't do it. Whatever your 10K is, I'll cross the finish line knowing you can, too.

So, wish me luck, or better yet, wish me strength.

#TeamBritta #sorrynotsorry #curvygirlrunning

I SET MY umbrella against my cubicle wall on the way to the all-staff meeting my first day back. I walked in, head down, and took a seat near the door, prepared for this to be one of the lesser circles of hell despite the beautiful September weather outside.

A few minutes before nine, Claire slipped in. *The backstabbing snake.* Our eyes met before she cut her gaze from me and took a seat on the other side of the room. If I were a better person, I would have let go of the anger and let it fall away from me, but I wasn't *that* good a person, so I sat in my seat and stewed.

Maricela strode in chatting with her assistant and took the seat at the head of the table. I cast my eyes downward. I wasn't mad at Maricela—I knew why she'd asked me to step back, and I understood that it was the right decision from her vantage point—but I wasn't ready to meet her eye knowing I was back at square one. Only this time, I wasn't getting another chance.

"Good morning, everyone. It's that time again. I'd like to hear ideas." Hands sprang up around the table.

Maricela tapped her collarbone and her chin at good and bad pitches as the meeting progressed as it always did. I sketched in my journal, noting the pieces I'd been asked to assist with—a new line of gourmet dog foods, planning for retirement when you're just starting out, and a profile of a young up-and-coming politician. I drew a series of cubes in the margins while someone from HR discussed a change in reimbursement and expense accounts.

*I wonder what Wes is doing today.* I'd deleted his number from my phone and his Chat App ID from my contacts, but it didn't matter—I knew them by heart. For a few days, I'd opened the FitMi app. Logging exercise had become a habit, like drinking water or taking the stairs—like the workout didn't count if I didn't track it, but every time I did, I clicked on the mailbox icon, and my heart dipped at the empty inbox. I deleted the account, taking away the temptation, taking away the daily reminders we weren't talking.

"Finally, an update." Maricela's words snapped me out of my own thoughts, but I felt twenty pairs of eyes on me the moment the words left Maricela's mouth. "You're all familiar with Claire and Britta's excellent work, and I'm sure you've heard, or think you've heard, about the circumstances leading to its end. We won't rehash that here; however, I want to say one thing about the ethics of our work that I believe is critical for everyone in this room to hear."

I tensed my shoulders and hazarded a look in her direction. *She's going to tell everyone not to sleep with sources. Yep, got the memo.*

"I trust each of you to bring stories and information to light. Living one's best life is a trendy saying, but it's a philosophy I live by, and that means acting according to one's own moral compass."

*If I stare at these doodles hard enough, can I block out her voice?*

"Claire should be commended for her work revealing the issues with the HottrYou platform in the way she did. That is the decision-making I want from this team. She showed prowess in investigating the story and conviction in bringing it to light.

"I will support you when you're acting in the best interest of our readers, especially when it comes to health and safety." She turned to Claire, whose expression warmed. She was trying to maintain her cool exterior, but Claire was proud. Maricela addressed the group again. "I've offered Claire a permanent place writing features for our health and fitness section."

Applause sprang up from around the room. I willed the tears pricking the back of my eyes to still and joined everyone else in congratulating Claire. She got the job. I couldn't say that was unfair. Her work exposing HottrYou was arguably excellent—I wouldn't make the argument in her favor, but I didn't need to. She'd been thorough in her research and compelling in her writing, and she'd won. This personal and public humiliation was what I deserved.

I was gathering my doodle-covered notes to shuffle out at the end of the meeting when Maricela called me over.

"Britta. Can you hang back for a minute?"

Being in this room reminded of me the pitch for Body FTW back in February. As I walked to join her at the head of the table, I noted my body and how it felt to move in this room. My back was straighter.

"Welcome back. I wanted to check in and see how you're doing."

"I'm okay," I said, noticing how my hand looked against the smooth tabletop. I'd skipped getting a manicure to join Helen for an advanced hip-hop dance class the day before, and my polish was chipped, and the condensation from the water bottle that had replaced my morning coffee had left a small puddle near my pinky finger. I smiled to myself, taking in all the changes at once, and repeated my answer, but meeting her eye this time. "I'm okay."

"The post you wrote while you were out," she began, gesturing to her tablet.

I gulped and bit my tongue. I'd been banned from posting, but whoever was supposed to cut my access to our social media never did. I searched her expression, but it was the same professionally serene one she always wore. They didn't take it down, but probably by the time they noticed, it had too much traction already. *Did I get myself fired over this post?*

Maricela interrupted my stewing. "It was wonderful."

"Thank you." After I'd posted it, I'd logged off. I didn't want to risk seeing more hateful comments from trolls and disappointed comments from loyal readers, so I'd left it at #sorrynotsorry and had gone for a long run. My resolve to not check on it lasted only until the end of the run, and it had already exploded.

"It was tremendous, actually. It resonated with people, and I thought about passages days later."

"I'm glad."

Maricela eyed me, and a small crease appeared between her brows. "Britta, I'll be candid."

I swallowed. "Okay."

"Your ethical misstep was critical, and I can't ignore it. You will not write or post for us again. You've played fast and loose with our rules, and I can't allow that." The words hit like a hammer, but I couldn't say I didn't deserve them. "Please don't assume you shouldn't be writing *somewhere*, though." She tapped the screen of her tablet to wake it and then slid it to me, and I saw my post and comments. "And you should be writing things like this."

I needed to hear this today—keep running, Britta.

Thank you for sharing this. It makes all the difference in the world when you find your real motivation. We're cheering you on. Stay strong.

I hate that you lied . . . but it sounds like you're in love with someone amazing—both yourself and your coach. Keep going, Britta.

The comments went on and on, and emotion caught in my throat.

"You're a good assistant, and we'll keep you as long as we can, but this"—she tapped the screen again—"this is where you shine."

I pressed my lips together. Gratitude at the praise, sadness at the reminder I wouldn't move up at *Best Life,* and the realization I was in love with someone amazing . . . who I'd cut out of my life all hit me at the same time.

Maricela dropped her own perfectly manicured hand to mine. "I'm glad you're still going to run."

# 60

WES

"NERVOUS?" CORD GLANCED across the conference table after tucking his phone in his jacket pocket. He pulled at the sleeve and fiddled with a button. Next to him, Mason scrolled through his phone.

It had been weeks since Britta and I had split. Since then, I'd been a lot of things, but that morning, I was confident. "Not nervous."

Pearl strode toward us from the open door, stopping next to Cord, who straightened on her approach. "They're here. Ready?"

"Yeah, can you send them in?" I glanced at my notes, the condensed version of two weeks of planning, strategizing, investigating, and exploring.

Pearl nodded and ran a hand over Cord's shoulder, brushing off a piece of lint. "You look nice in a suit."

I'd known Cord a long time, long enough to decipher the flash of a goofy grin on his face.

He returned my questioning glance with a small shrug.

"Good morning." The three of us stood as Kelsey and two of her senior people entered the room. I'd asked her to meet privately, told her we were against exploring the merger and we weren't changing our minds, but she insisted she wanted her team there. She planned to steamroll us like I'd let her in the past.

"Morning," I said, extending my hand to greet them. Mason and Cord did the same, and we settled around the table.

"Let's get started," she said, resting both hands on the tabletop. "We've prepared a plan to—"

"That won't be necessary," I interrupted.

Her expression tilted in veiled annoyance. "I figured you'd want me to lead the planning, but by all means."

Cord cleared his throat. "As we've told you, we're not moving forward with a merger."

Kelsey's eyes narrowed, and she gave Cord a withering look. "I thought I made it clear why this was in both of our best interests." Her laser-like stare turned to me, and her two vice presidents exchanged their own worried looks.

"We never agreed to this." I examined her face, a cool and composed mask, but a muscle in her neck ticked. "And your intimidation tactics and threats will not work."

"Let's pause here," one of her vice presidents spoke up. "We believe this will be mutually beneficial, especially considering current . . . events. We've brought along some figures—"

Kelsey's expression shifted, her lips pursing. "Don't bother, Brad. This has nothing to do with business." She held my stare. "This is personal, and they're making a mistake."

The years of familiarity hung between us. The arch of her eyebrow and the set of my jaw held their own silent conversation.

Mason interjected with a chuckle, breaking the wall of tense silence and rapping his knuckles against the conference table. "Oh, man."

His interruption took her off guard, and her calculated stare faltered. "Excuse me?"

He flashed an easy smile. "I just appreciate your moxie. I might have enjoyed working with you."

"So, what's the problem?" Kelsey regained her cool composure.

Mason laughed again, and I knew Kelsey's teeth were clenched. I never imagined I'd appreciate the cocky way Mason carried on a conversation. "I just met you, so I can't speak for Wes and Cord, but there's nothing personal for me." Mason relaxed in his chair, his smile still directed at Kelsey. "But you've driven your profits into the ground, and you're about to be sued by hundreds, if not thousands, of clients for negligence or worse, and . . ." Mason paused his speech to slide a manila folder across the table with a smirk. "You should be more careful with your digital footprint."

Kelsey eyed the folder like it was covered in something vile. She turned to me. "Why is your communications person lecturing me about IT? I don't think you took my warning seriously, Wes. I meant what I said."

"Aww, don't be like that," Mason said with another megawatt smile. "They said you went to Northwestern. Me, too. I figured we'd talk MBA to MBA. Did you take Organizational Culture with Stronbacher?"

"Yes. So what?"

"Small world. You must remember the first thing he talked about was trust. It's present in a strong organization, and it's lacking in weak ones."

She shifted in her seat, pretending to ignore Mason. "We're adults, Wes. All of that was years ago."

"We happened years ago, but that—" I motioned toward the folder. She'd used an old account from college when identifying me as the person hugging Britta and implying we were sleeping together. "That was a few weeks ago. You trying to manipulate us to save your own ass? That was last week. And you threatening to hurt someone I love? That was about a minute ago."

Kelsey didn't reach for the folder, but clasped her hands in front of her. She'd flinched when I said "love." "How did you find out?"

Her two VPs looked like they'd rather be anywhere else.

"There's probably one person in the world who would remember that screen name. Unfortunately, he's in this room," Cord interjected. "What I don't get is why you would tank the *Best Life* project when it was helping you just as much as us."

"I had no choice," she said, voice clear and confident as ever. She met

Cord's eye and then mine, head held high. "When you told me you were seeing the fat girl from the park, I was surprised. She's not your usual type, but I didn't think about how she looked familiar until that photo went around."

I clenched my fist at my side.

"I wasn't going to do anything with the information. You shot me down and I got over it, but then the other writer started stirring up trouble and digging into the issue with our coaches. I had to protect my company and get that thing shut down. Linking you to this affair did that. People count on me, Wes. Anyway, I didn't make you sleep with a client. This isn't all on me."

"Damn." Mason's smug comment earned him a look so withering, my balls wanted to hide. "Much respect for your ruthlessness. Didn't you guys date for like six years, though? Cold. As. Ice. I admire that."

Color rose on her neck, and her two executives shifted away from her. Her fingers dug into her palm, something she only did when she was trying to hold in emotion.

I leaned forward, elbows resting on the table. "It doesn't matter anymore; it's all done. The key thing is that we are not merging, and you will not be joining us as COO. A statement will go out within the hour, and if you follow through with any of your *promises*, we will do absolutely anything we can to make sure your dangerous approach to coaching gets the attention it deserves. Actually, we're going to do that regardless."

Kelsey's eyes met mine. I hoped to see a flicker of apology in them, of sadness, of regret for this entire ploy, but I saw only the cool blue of her irises, fixing me with an icy stare. All I could see in her face was the person who sacrificed Britta and me for her own benefit.

One of the HottrYou execs pushed back from the table, breaking the tense silence in the room. "Well, then. I think we're done here, right?"

The rest of us stood to shake hands and share nods, but Kelsey didn't move. I saw her press her nails to her palm once more, then stretch and link her fingers. "That's it?"

The room stilled, and everyone turned to face her, silence hanging behind her question.

"That's it," I said.

She rolled her shoulders back. "Okay. Well," she said, her cool and professional mask back in place. She stood, smoothed her dress down, and strode to the door. Before stepping out, she turned to me, an apologetic expression painted on her features. "For what it's worth, I'm sorry, Wes. I wish things had turned out differently. It really was just business."

Cord shot me a look across the table, but I didn't need his warning. I actually believed her this time when she said it was just business, which made my reply even easier. "Goodbye, Kelsey."

WHEN THE DOOR closed behind them, Pearl slipped in, eyebrows raised. "She's a piece of work."

Mason slumped back in his chair. "I kind of admire her. I'd be curious what it's like to fu—" Mason stopped, catching the eyes in the room on him. "Sorry. I mean, what it's like to work with her." Mason pulled the folder he'd given to Kelsey back over and opened it, thumbing through things. "We *should* poach a few of their people before they fold—there's some talent."

"Wes. Are you sure you want to go through with the rest of your plan?" Cord slipped his jacket off. "With Kelsey no longer an issue, you don't have to. FitMi can go back to being the distraction it always was before."

"Absolutely." I watched Mason set aside the damning evidence of Kelsey's actions and skim the report we'd had compiled on HottrYou's finances. As he concentrated, there was a moment when the smug smile disappeared. He'd come through for us time and time again. Pearl, who'd first suspected the culprit might be Kelsey, was only my assistant because she refused every promotion I offered her, preferring to wait until she finished her degree. Cord was rolling his sleeves up. When we first came up with the idea for the company, he was skeptical. He didn't think he'd enjoy it and never wanted to be in charge, and now he was the one steering the ship. Looking around the table, I saw the embodiment of what Mason said about trust in organizations. Our organization worked because of the people around that table, and I knew I was making the right choice.

"You know, man, I don't think I need the same distractions anymore."

# 61

## BRITTA

A LIGHT BREEZE moved over the endless sprawl of runners as we gathered together in the sticky September air. Three people near me joked as they adjusted devices and clothing on their Lycra-covered bodies. I stole a surreptitious glance at the women to my left—two tall blondes in sports bras and brightly colored running shorts. My cheeks heated, and I rethought the race day outfit I'd spent so much time poring over. I wore formfitting black capri tights, but I wanted to feel as good as I could going into this. I pulled on a moisture-wicking running top and wore a T-shirt over it, one I knew would remind me I could do it. I brushed my hands down the worn, soft cotton.

> **RJ:** We're here!
>
> **Kat:** We're so proud of you! Are you ready?
>
> **Del:** Don't forget to pee first.

I smiled, reading the thread.

Claire stood alone twenty feet away under the Body FTW 10K sign. Natalie had emailed me saying FitMi had identified the person who outed Wes from the photo and that it had been taken care of. I didn't know what that meant, but I was sure it meant I'd been wrong about who it was. Like the blondes, Claire was in shorts and a sports bra, her toned body contorting as she stretched.

I looked back at my phone.

**Britta:** Already peed, ready as I'll ever be, and I love you for being here.

**Britta:** I'll talk to you after the race. Gotta do something before it starts.

I pulled up my mental big-girl pants and pushed through the crowd toward her as the heavy bass from the DJ rocked the ground beneath my feet. "Hey," I said with an awkward wave.

She eyed me coolly, a nod in my direction.

"This is wild, right?"

Claire checked her watch. "I guess." Her clipped tone made it clear we were back to being enemies, but I had to say something.

"Congratulations on your promotion." Her lack of audible or visual response made this so much more awkward. "I'm happy for you."

She arched an eyebrow.

"Fine. I'm super jealous, but also I'm sorry, okay?"

She straightened and crossed one arm over her chest, looking skeptical.

"I was wrong. It was unfair and out of line for me to accuse you of being the one who posted about the affair."

"It was." She switched arms.

"I was emotional and stressed, but that's no excuse. I was selfish and judgmental." My voice lifted, hopeful. "I was kind of enjoying being your friend, and you didn't deserve that from me."

She pulled her leg up behind her, considering my apology.

"You can take a shot back at me. Would that make you feel better?" I spread my arms wide, palms up in a universal come-at-me motion.

Her lips tipped up, and my heart rate slowed. "I'll save it for later. And for the record, I never said anything about you and your coach."

"I believe you."

She eyed me again, narrowing her eyes. "You don't want to hug or something now, do you?"

I laughed, the prerace tension that had been coiling all morning released. "No hugging. But we're okay?"

"Yeah, we're okay." Claire eyed the people near us. "You ready for this?" Claire looked as unsure as I felt.

"I've prepared myself to come in last," I joked, tugging the well-worn shirt down. "Anything better is a win." *Please don't let me be the last one across the finish line.*

A guy in a hoodie with shaggy blond hair and a tall Black woman with long braids cut through the crowd. "Britta?"

"I'm Britta," I said warily. Since the race was sponsored by FitMi, I'd been worried all morning that someone would recognize Claire and me.

The man reached out his hand, and I exchanged a quick look with Claire, who shrugged.

"It's nice to meet you in person. We've heard a lot about you. I'm Cord, and this is Pearl."

"Wes's friends?"

They both nodded. "I'm glad we caught you before the race. Do you have a minute?"

"Sure." I glanced around, wondering if this meant Wes was nearby. I'd talked a good game, even psyched myself up to come that morning after almost turning back three times on the way to the train, but I was panicking. *What if I can't do it? What if I mess up and everyone laughs? What if I finish and everything still feels the same?* As a swirl of questions twisted through my head, I knew if I could see him, talk to him, I'd feel better. I glanced behind Pearl and Cord but only saw more people in compression shorts checking their phones and jogging in place.

"First, thank you—you brought a ton of business our way." He looked over my shoulder to Claire. "Both of you."

"The last piece you wrote was so touching," Pearl said in a smoky voice that made me want to listen to her read the dictionary. "It embodied FitMi perfectly. Our users have been sharing it and posting their own lists. Despite the initial scandal, you've inspired people."

"Thank you," I said, still unsure what they wanted.

"Our VP of communications will reach out to you after the race to offer you a job writing for us. We think you'd be a good voice for FitMi Fitness, and we want to start an online community. We'd like you to head it."

"Is that a . . . joke or something?"

The two of them exchanged a knowing smile, and Pearl responded first. "Sorry, it's just that Wes told us you'd say something like that."

I pulled my arm across my chest to stretch, just to do something with my hands. My nervous energy was making me twitchy. "Wes . . . I don't think, um. I'm not sure how—"

Cord held up a palm. "Before you answer, read this." He pulled a folded piece of paper from his pocket and glanced at his watch. "You have a little time before the race starts."

I held the note in my hand. *What is happening here?*

Cord glanced at me, and his mouth twisted into a smile of recognition. "I like the shirt."

"Good luck with the race," Pearl said before they walked back through the crowd. After a few steps, she doubled back. "Keep an open mind. I know it's complicated, but he's worth it."

"That was weird," Claire said after the couple walked away. "What's in the note?"

I opened it to see Wes's blocky handwriting.

*Bubs,*

*You probably feel like you're not ready, but I promise you are. Get out of your own head. Take off your watch. Listen to our sweet Whitney Houston workout mix and push.*

*Pearl and Cord told you about the offer—I hope you'll take it.*
*You could do such good work at FitMi. You're a talented writer,*
*and you'll help move our platform to the next level. We need you. I*
*need you.*

*Keep stretching. It's about time to start. You don't need me in*
*order to cross the finish line, but I hope you'll let me meet you there.*
*I'll explain everything else after I get to kiss you again, if you'll have*
*me, that is.*

*I love you.*
*Now, go kick some ass.*

*Wes*

"What does it say?" Claire asked, half-heartedly jogging in place. "Is it from your guy?"

I reread the note. *I love you.* "Yeah, it's from my guy," I said. "He's going to meet me at the finish line."

A disembodied voice fell over the crowd from the PA system. "Runners, find your starting position."

Around us, bodies jockeyed for position. I'd planned to move to the rear of the crowd. *That's where the slow runners are. My people.* I worried Claire would make fun of me, but she motioned to the back, and we nestled between two elderly women and a couple bickering about going to pee one more time.

The voice came over the loudspeaker again before we could continue our conversation. I expected us all to lurch forward when they started the race, but from the back of the crowd, it was anticlimactic. The wave of people ahead of us started shifting forward, but we were still, waiting for our turn to launch. I observed my fellow runners. The older women next to us and the middle-aged couple—they forwent the extra pee break—had all trained, too. I felt a sudden soulful kinship with the back of the starting line crowd. *We can do it.* I wanted to shout out, to lead them in a cheer.

Claire had to yell to get her voice above the din of the waiting crowd and the Top 40 music blaring from the speakers. "Did you say he's waiting for you at the finish line?"

"Yeah."

Our area opened, and we started a slow jog along with the masses.

"I guess you'd better finish," Claire said before popping in her earbuds.

I popped in my own and hit play on my workout mix. "I guess I'd better."

# 62

## WES

I PACED BACK and forth in front of the registration tables, which were abandoned by the volunteers and covered in administrative flotsam. I glanced around and shoved my hands in my pockets. *This was such a big mistake.* My grand gesture had seemed like a good idea when I planned it. I was going to meet her at the finish line and tell her all the reasons I didn't want to live without her. As I stood in the early-morning sun alone, debating what to say to Britta, it seemed like a colossal mistake.

When I asked for a bouquet of sunflowers, peonies, lilies, ranunculus, tulips, and dahlias, the florist gently informed me they didn't go together. When I explained I needed to tell a woman I thought she was classy, bold, unique, cheerful, and smelled awesome, I earned a touched—if confused—grin from the woman. "Good luck," she'd said, handing over the wrapped bundle.

I glanced at the bouquet sitting on the table in the sun and questioned the decision. The florist was right; the flowers were a mess all together.

"Hey, man." Cord strode toward me from the volunteer tent, Pearl at his side. They both wore the staff T-shirts Mason's team had designed for the race. "You made it."

Pearl rolled her eyes and nudged Cord's arm. "Where else was he going to be?"

She ribbed him more than she used to, and he wasn't as quick to look away when she caught him looking at her.

I needed to focus on my own love life, though. "Did you give her the note? Tell her about the job? Did she say anything?"

Cord nodded, leaning against the table, one ankle crossed over the other like a smug bastard.

"And?"

"And . . . she listened."

"You're such a jackass sometimes." Pearl rolled her eyes again and looked back to me, her expression softening. "She didn't believe us at first, like you predicted, and I got the impression she would rip open your note as soon as we walked away. Girl kept looking over our shoulders for you." Her eyes fell to my clothes, and her smile straightened into a disdainful line. "Um, what are you wearing?"

I'd chosen a plain red T-shirt and gray track pants along with my favorite running shoes. "Not good?"

"It's a little casual, isn't it?"

"She'll feel self-conscious if I'm in a suit and she's in her running clothes." *Maybe I should have worn a suit. Maybe I should have planned to talk to her in a private moment without three hundred sweaty strangers around us.* "Won't she? Should I go change?"

Cord clapped my shoulder. "I've never seen you this nervous. Calm down, buddy."

"You know how my last grand gesture went." For the first time, I remembered my failed proposal to Kelsey without wincing and reaching for my pocket out of habit. Her dumping me had saved me from a lifetime of second-guessing everything.

"You're one of the best people I know," Pearl said. "And that woman is clearly in love with you. She'll think you're hot no matter what you're wearing."

"'Hot' is a bit much." Cord's smile betrayed his mock indignation before he turned his eyes back to me. "You gave her your shirt. The one with your number on the back?"

Britta had worn it home the day we got caught in the rain, and I'd told her to keep it after she said she'd fallen asleep in it. I loved having something of mine close to her while she slept. "How did you know I gave her my shirt?"

Pearl and Cord exchanged a look. Cord shrugged. "She's wearing it."

My chest swelled as a grin swept across my face. I'd told her compression gear and tight-fitting clothes were best, but damn it if her in my shirt didn't make me feel ten feet tall, my old number on her back. I grabbed the bouquet off the table.

"Okay. I'm ready. Let's get to the finish line."

# 63

BRITTA

I WILL NOT *pass out. I will not pass out. I will not pass out . . . yet.*

I glanced down at my running watch. *One more mile.*

Claire and I had started together, shuffling along at the back of the crowd. At first, I was content to stay with the other slow runners. Once we got going, though, I felt boxed in. Wes had pushed me to go a little farther and a little faster every time we trained, and soon I found myself passing people. Claire matched me step for step, and though we didn't speak, I enjoyed having her next to me. I was reasonably sure she'd call for help if I passed out. Even if she didn't, I'd kept up with her, and the foregone conclusion she'd come out on top wasn't so foregone. I went around a woman in her seventies and then two middle-aged men and through a trio of teens. My heart leapt with every person I passed, and I expected someone to pop out and say, *Hey! Get back to the end of the line. You can't cut it up here.*

No one did, though, and the first mile flew by.

After mile two, I stopped passing people, so I had to focus on something else. Music from my carefully orchestrated playlist flowed through my earbuds, and I remembered Wes handing them to me on the first morning at the gym. I smiled as I pictured the crooked grin on his face when he hit play, and remembered how I'd forgotten to feel self-conscious for just a minute on the treadmill.

Halfway through mile five, my breath came heavy and sweat poured down my body. Wes's shirt was soaked, and I almost regretted wearing it. My feet hurt, my body ached, and I was sure someone had turned up the temperature to something rivaling mid-July instead of September. *Why did I agree to this?* Several of the people I'd passed earlier moved forward—a little stab of failure hit me in the gut every time someone pulled ahead of me.

When I wasn't debating twisting an ankle as a gracious exit strategy, I thought of Wes. His smile, his voice, his bad jokes, and how nothing had changed—if anything, this job offer put us in a more precarious situation. I couldn't believe he didn't see what a conflict it was for him to not only hire me but create a job for me to do. I didn't want a pity job, but it was the kind of position I'd love. I wanted to build an online community, I wanted to write, and I wanted to do it in a place like FitMi.

My playlist ticked over to the audio file Wes had sent me when I was at the spa. His voice filled my head.

"Pick up the pace."

"Eyes forward."

"You're doing great."

"One more mile."

"I know you can do it."

"Push."

"I believe in you."

I shook off the self-doubt and picked up my speed, pumping my arms to pull forward, and moved from a jog to a run. I caught Claire off guard as I pulled away from her—I had a finish line to reach, no matter if I took the job or not.

That gust of adrenaline lasted until the six-mile mark, when I reclaimed my position ahead of many of my competitors. My lungs threatened to quit on me. *We're done with this shit.* My legs joined in with a chorus of *We're indoor people, remember?* and the rest of me wheezed and creaked.

I could see that the finish line wasn't far in the distance, and all around me, spectators cheered on the runners. The path was lined with tall trees, still full of wide green leaves with hints of orange signaling the onset of fall. *I'm so close.* My brain screamed at the rest of my body, but I slowed to a complete stop, staggering to the side to catch my breath. I bent with my hands on my knees, sucking in air. Running the last mile at that speed had been a mistake, but I was ready to go, ready to be there. Not just for Wes, but for me. I saw that finish line, and I wanted it.

Footsteps fell on the path behind me, and I moved farther to the side to let them pass. *Pass me. Just pass me.* I took in more breaths, gripping my knees. I closed my eyes. *Push, Britta.* I vowed to set my self-doubt aside until I finished, even if I was the last one to do it.

The footfalls I'd expected to hear fade as the runner passed stayed near me, and a deep, familiar voice pulled my gaze from the ground. "You've got a little farther to go." Wes jogged in place next to me. His hazel eyes were bright, and I fought the urge to leap at him. It had only been a few weeks since I'd last seen him, but it felt like forever.

"Thought . . . you were . . . meeting me . . . at the finish line." I struggled to catch my breath, but part of that was from being close to him again.

"I was." A sheepish look crossed his face along with his playful, crooked smile, and I melted.

"But . . . you're here?"

"It looked like you could use a coach."

"Always," I said, my smile growing through my heaving breaths.

He reached for my hand, his fingers surrounding my palm, and brought it to his lips, planting a soft kiss on my knuckles. Despite my exhaustion, the pain radiating through most of my body, my breathless lungs, and sweat-soaked . . . everything, a spark traveled from my hand up my arm and to every part of my body.

"Will you . . . go the rest . . . of the way with me?"

He met my eyes and shook his head. "Nah."

"What? I need you."

He let go of my hand and rested his palms on both of my biceps. "No, you don't." His hands were firm and warm against my sweaty arms. "Not for this."

My breath evened out, and I stared up at him as runners passed us in the morning heat.

"As the guy in love with you, I'm telling you you're perfect, and you can do anything you set your mind to." He rubbed his thumbs in small circles down my arms. "And as a coach, I'm telling you to get your pacing under control, pay attention to your breathing, focus on the finish line, and dig deep." Wes reached for my running watch and slipped it off my wrist. "When you get there, I plan to ask you to be with me, to trust me to share your heart and your life." His lips tipped up. "I hope you'll say yes, and we'll have lots of shared moments, but this one isn't ours. It's yours, and you're ready for it."

He dropped my watch in his pocket and brought my hand to his lips again. "You got this?"

I was, but before I took off, I met his eyes. "You know I'll say yes when you ask, right?"

The finish line loomed, a blue stripe painted on the road under an awning with a FitMi logo plastered on a wide banner. After ten thousand meters, six point two miles, and so many steps before that, I crossed that line. It wasn't graceful, but I didn't care, because I'd finished.

Struggling to catch my breath as a whir of emotion rushed from me, I looked around, wide-eyed. *I did it. I can't believe I did it.* Drenched and tired, already sore and exhausted, I'd never felt so alive and like I could do anything I set my mind to. Stumbling to the side of the path, I wanted to high-five every inch of my body—the body I'd tried to camouflage for so much of my life—for getting me here. RJ, Kat, and Del yelled my name and waved signs nearby, and tears welled in my eyes. I wanted to tell my high school gym teacher to shove it. *I wanted*—Wes wrapped his dry, clean-smelling body around me and kissed the side of my head—*that.*

He spoke close to my ear, still holding me tight. "I'm so proud of you."

"I have to stretch," I joked.

"Priorities, woman." He still held me close as other runners sped past us. He wrapped his long fingers behind my head and pulled me to him.

"I'm all sweaty and gross," I protested, without protesting at all as our lips moved closer.

"I've always liked you sweaty and gross. You can shower when we get home."

"We?"

"Will you come home with me?" His breath brushed my lips, and the surrounding noise disappeared as I looked from his eyes to his lips before letting my eyelids fall closed. He tasted like mint and possibility, and I sank into the sweet kiss.

"Thank you for coming to my rescue," I said as we pulled apart.

Wes drew back, holding my shoulders and bending to look me straight in the eyes. "Thank you for coming to mine."

I met his gaze, taking in the rich gold-green of his irises as my heart and lungs battled to regain their normal rhythm. *Lungs, you'll get there. Heart, you might be out of luck.*

Claire's voice broke the spell, and I turned to face her. "Thanks for leaving me in the dust, Britta." She pulled her earbuds from her ears and looked Wes up and down, assessing. Claire's cheeks were flushed, and she gulped in a breath. "I'm Claire," she said. "You must be the coach."

Wes shook his head. "Just the boyfriend, I hope."

# 64

## WES

TWO HOURS LATER, Britta lay on my couch, wrapped in my thick terry cloth robe after taking a shower. Her hair was piled on top of her head, and I held her feet in my lap, pressing my thumbs into her arches. I looked up to see her smiling, eyes bright, and it reminded me of the first time I'd sat on the couch with her, except everything was different now.

"What?" she asked, after letting me stare at her for a minute.

"I like how you look in my robe," I said, squeezing her heel to elicit a little moan. *Her sexy noises. Damn, I'll never get tired of them.* "And on my couch."

The bouquet of her favorite flowers was propped in a water glass on my kitchen counter along with her racing bib and medal. When I'd handed them to her, she'd laughed and smiled this wide Britta smile, and she'd kissed me again. Next to that was the letter outlining the formal offer of employment Mason had handed her before we left the race. Now, Britta was at my place, her feet in my hands, and I couldn't imagine anything that felt more like home.

"Can we talk about the job?" she asked, pulling her lower lip between her teeth. "You know I can't work for you."

"Technically, you'd report to Mason."

"And he reports to you," Britta chided.

I ran my fingers down over the back of my neck before meeting her eyes again. "Not technically."

"Not technically?" She arched a brow in that sexy way she had, and I dragged my fingers back to her feet, beginning a slow journey up to her ankle.

"He reports to the CEO, but I don't really want to talk about Mason while you're practically naked." I loved the way she inhaled sharply when my fingers skirted up her calves. "Do you have anything on under this robe?"

"Wes," she said in a slow, breathy tone that left me at full attention. I let my hands dip under the edge of the robe to stroke the soft skin on the backs of her knees. She let out another little moan, and I felt the heat from between her legs as I shifted to lay next to her, fingers dancing up her thighs. I didn't expect her to still my hand.

She looked at me with those big brown eyes, and I waited. "Don't distract me with your sexy fingers," she said, pushing my hand down but not away.

I chuckled, making circles with my thumb on the outside of her knee. Her body was pressed to mine, and I'd already forgotten what we'd been talking about. "But you like my sexy fingers."

"You're the CEO. Why doesn't he report to you?"

Trailing my hands from her knee up the outside of her thigh, I toyed with the belt holding the robe together before meeting her gaze. "I stepped down."

"What?" Britta jerked up, her face almost colliding with my head. "You own the company. You quit? Is that because of me? Because of . . . us and the scandal?"

"I still am a part owner, but do you know the thing I was most upset about after everything happened, second only to losing you? That mentoring program with the high school—they canceled it."

"Wes, I'm so sorry," she said, running her fingers over my hairline.

"I loved working on it. Doing that, playing football with your nephew, teaching Aaron's daughter how to play basketball . . . I was happier doing any of those things than running the company. And, honestly, I wasn't good at being an executive. So, I stepped down, effective next week."

She bit her lip again.

I paused my intended journey under the robe and instead cupped her face. "I thought about what makes me happy. My mom is doing okay, and Libby is talking to me again." We'd spoken a few times, and I'd already shown Britta the photos of my niece. It was harder than I'd thought, but I'd even started going to a few Al-Anon meetings and researched potential counselors—Mom was right, and I had a lot in my head to sort out. "I think it's the right time to do what makes me happy."

"I like you happy," she said, cupping my face the same way. "I—"

"Hate me?" I dipped my forehead to hers, and she puffed out a breathy little laugh.

"I was going to say I love you, but yes, that, too."

"I love you." Holding her playful gaze, I drank in the warmth of her mahogany irises. "Coaching you—being with you—helped me realize I needed to make a change."

"What will you do?"

"I'm going back to school to be a teacher. Working with the school and the kids on this peer education thing, it reminded me. I've been thinking a lot lately about my high school coach and all he did for me. I want to be that kind of teacher, you know? It's a big jump, but I think I can do it."

Britta trailed her fingertips over my biceps, and my body lit up with her touch. "You'll be a great teacher."

I brushed my lips to hers, unable to hold back from kissing her any longer. "So, will you take the job?"

She toyed with a lock of my hair, and a grin played across her lips. "Try the sexy fingers again. See if you can convince me."

I tugged on the belt of the robe and moved over her. "I'll try my level best."

# Epilogue

## THE FITMI FITNESS FORUM

### *The Curvy Girl's Corner*

PREVIOUS POST: SAVE CHEATING FOR MONOPOLY: WHY I NO
LONGER BELIEVE IN CHEAT DAYS

### The First Boy to Push Me Out of a Plane

Britta Colby, FitMi Fitness

APRIL 12

Longtime readers will remember that one of my goals when I first
signed up for FitMi was to jump out of a plane. That was well before
I came to work with this tremendous online community. It was before I discovered a love of running. It was before I lost some weight,
then gained some back, then lost some again before I finally listened
to my coach and stopped counting. Just like so many of you, I listed
a goal when I was just starting out, not convinced I'd ever reach it.

I could write for days about my first skydiving experience, but I'll
distill it down to nine main points.

1. Do you know how many ways there are to injure oneself or die when jumping out of a plane? I do. After signing that waiver, I knew I could do anything.

2. I did what's called a tandem jump, where an experienced and highly trained (I checked!) professional straps you to themself like a newborn and jumps with you. Here's a picture of Jerry and me. I wrote his name on the back of my left hand to make sure I remembered it. Readers know I have an amazing boyfriend, but Wes didn't control the parachute from the ground, so I committed myself to Jerry.

3. It's cold that high in the air. Freezing. When the door opened, I forgot it was spring. I was so focused on the cold and the wind and, you know, being 15,000 feet in the air, that when I heard Jerry yell something, by the time I asked "What?" we were airborne.

4. I thought it would go in slow motion. It didn't. Here's a photo of me screaming obscenities right after we started free-falling.

5. I was certain I would die, but then I didn't. Here's a photo of my dopey grin right after Jerry yanked the cord to open our parachute.

6. Did I mention that I love Jerry? I do. The man gave me a THRILL. Don't tell Wes.

7. I could see for miles beneath me, and it was incredible. Our state is beautiful, and I can't wait to try this again with mountains or the ocean in the distance. See the photo of me dumbfounded by the view.

8. Landing was basically sitting on Jerry's lap as we cruised to a stop—again, don't tell Wes. Or do. I guess he needs to know he's sharing me from now on. It all happened too fast! Soon I was getting untangled from the chute and unstrapped.

I did it! A year and some change after deciding to join FitMi, going through a ton of ups and downs, starting a new career, and learning so much about myself—but not what I thought I'd learn—I reached one of my goals. I jumped out of a plane.

See the photos below of me landing and celebrating. You all know what it feels like to reach your goals, or you soon will. I couldn't do this before because I was heavier than they allowed, but more importantly, I was weighed down by all this negative stuff I didn't even realize I carried with me. I'm glad I waited until now to do this, because I feel good about my body and I know what it can do. I jumped out of a damn plane today.

One more thing happened this morning . . . see the photos below.

9. I didn't know how much of a dork I'd look like in all my gear with my hair going in every direction after I removed the helmet. In sharp contrast, Wes was wearing a suit when he met me in the middle of the field. Turns out, he wasn't planning on me having another man's name written on my hand when he asked me to marry him. See my expression go from confused to surprised to tearful when he dropped to one knee, said beautiful things I'm going to keep private, and put a ring on my finger.

We (and Jerry) will be very happy together.

NEXT POST: THE CURVY GIRL GOES WEDDING DRESS SHOPPING

BRITTA AND WES finally found their paths. If their story has raised concerns or questions for you about your path or the path of someone you love, the resources below may be helpful.

**NATIONAL EATING DISORDERS ASSOCIATION** |
nationaleatingdisorders.org

**AL-ANON/ALATEEN** | al-anon.org

**NAR-ANON** | nar-anon.org

# Acknowledgments

The idea for this book came to me when I sat in a room full of strong, caring, purposeful people of color where I felt safe to be vulnerable and brave enough to tell this personal story. First and foremost, thank you to people who give others the strength to feel that way. I count myself lucky to have so many of them in my life.

My husband and my sweet tiny human, thank you for always cheering me on, encouraging me to write, and offering up needed distraction in the form of a Netflix binge or dance party. I can't imagine spending my life with two more perfect dudes. Tiny Human: You can NEVER read this book, either.

This book came to fruition during the pandemic, and though that meant being apart from my family for a long time, their care stretched through the phone and over Zoom. Thank you to my parents, who have always pushed me to do better and had a hug or high-five no matter what. Thank you to my brother. I could share a quote from our orthodontist, but I think you know what you mean to me. To Amanda, Mike, Melissa, Jean, Bruce, Barb, Tim, Aretha, Allison, Kaitlin, and all my aunts, uncles, and cousins, my niece and nephews, and my friends, thank you for listening to me talk about writing for years, and for endless support.

I highly recommend having talented publishing professionals in your life who happen to also be strong and kind. Thank you to my wonderful agent, Sharon Pelletier, for always being in my corner and making me feel seen. Thank you also to Lauren Abramo, Andrew Dugan, and Cat Hosch at Dystel, Goderich & Bourret, Kristina Moore at Anonymous Content, and Eleanor Russell and the Piatkus team.

Thank you to my editor, Kerry Donovan. I can't imagine working with someone else—my soul and my book have so much more sparkle because of you. Also thank you to Dache' Rogers, Tara O'Connor, Bridget O'Toole, Natalie Sellars, Mary Baker, Lindsey Tulloch, and the rest of the Berkley and Penguin Random House team for bringing this novel into the world. The cover for this book was designed by Farjana Yasmin, and I am in love with the beautiful representation of the book that includes a sky full of possibilities.

Bethany Moore has read this book more than anyone and was the very first person to fall in love with Wes and Britta. More than that, she's my sister in every way except blood, and one of the strongest and most beautiful people I know.

I don't know if I'd have made it through 2020 without the Better Than Brunch crew. Charish Reid, Taj McCoy, and Cass Newbould, you are my rocks. The laughter and love in our Sunday writing session fills my cup, and I love you three.

Katie Golding, you are amazing, affirming, and the ultimate cheerleader, but also the ultimate friend. On top of writing captivating stories I can't get out of my head, you are a beautiful, strong woman who makes me feel like I can do and be more. Thank you for being part of my world, Eagle!

Allison Ashley, I will always trust you with my messy drafts, knowing you will make the book better. Thank you for loving Britta and Wes from the beginning!

Rosie Danan, you are a ray of sunshine and I am so glad we are friends. You haven't convinced me to watch *Speed*, but you have impressed and inspired me at every turn with your talent, care, compassion, and humor.

Jen DeLuca, Libby Hubscher, Priscilla Oliveras, Tova Opatrny, and

Sarah Smith, thank you for always being there with encouragement, advice, humor, or the perfect GIF (and sometimes all four).

Thank you, Kenyatta, Jacki, Jasmine, Jalen, Wonjae, Jen, Racheal, Jathan, Matt, Tera, Emily, and the rest of my ISU family for celebrating bookish wins with me. It means the world to me to be able to share my love stories and accomplishments with colleagues I so admire and cherish.

Thank you also to Robin, Kat, Alex, Brenda, Yesenia, Haley, Emily, Brian, Tara, Nicole, Carolyn, Alissa, Rena, Ambre, Lisa, Janet, Salem, Diane, Miranda, Laynie, the rest of #TeamCarly, Natalie, and all the other friends who shared your time and suggestions for this book.

Finally, a huge thank-you to everyone who has let my stories be part of your life. I am endlessly grateful.

Keep reading for a special preview of

# DO YOU TAKE THIS MAN

by Denise Williams, coming in fall 2022!

I COULDN'T BLAME Maddie Anderson for scowling at her soon-to-be-ex-husband.

He appeared calm and collected in a bespoke Italian suit, remaining quiet, deferent, and reasonable. He almost looked bored by the proceedings, about the minutiae of his marriage ending. I made note of the gray at his temples and supposed it was easy to look dignified as a fifty-seven-year-old sitting next to one's twenty-three-year-old wife, and probably easy to be bored when you'd done this a time or two before.

Behind the makeup, Maddie's eyes were puffy, and the cuticle on her thumb looked shredded, like she'd been nervously scratching it. Since walking in on her husband with not one but two women during their son's first birthday party, she'd been through a lot. The hurt and embarrassment were clear in the woman's mannerisms, but Mr. Anderson didn't seem to care. Granted, my client popped her gum and huffed any time opposing counsel spoke. She rolled her eyes again, and I glanced at the clock on the far side of the wall. Despite the eye-rolling, the gum-popping, and the faint smell of perfume I could only assume was Kardashian-inspired, Maddie Anderson was going to leave a very rich woman. Her husband didn't want to leave this room without a settlement, and I suspected he and his attorney underestimated how well we understood that.

Twenty-five minutes later and before rushing back to my office, I smiled at Maddie, whose philandering ex-husband was not as covert in his affairs as he'd hoped. He'd chosen the wrong woman to underestimate.

"Everything should be finalized by the end of the month." I shook Maddie's hand to interrupt the hug coming my way and shared her smile. One point for the wronged woman and one more win for me. I popped a Butter Rum LifeSaver in my mouth and rushed down the hall, trying not to look like I was rushing, even though it was four fifteen and there was no way I was going to be the usual fifteen minutes early I considered to be on time. The candy gave me the quick rush of sugar I'd wanted all afternoon and a brief moment of bliss. The moment didn't last long.

"RJ." The smoky voice of one of the senior partners left me cursing in my head as I turned to greet her. Gretchen Vanderkin-Shaw would have scared the crap out of me if I didn't admire her so much. Okay, she still scared the crap out of me, but as a named partner before forty with a success rate through the roof, she was a force to be reckoned with, and she liked me. Gretchen was the lawyer I wanted to be, and I was gathering my courage to ask her to be my mentor.

She nodded toward the conference room. "The Anderson case?"

"We were able to come to a resolution that worked in our favor." That was code for crushing them like tiny little bugs and then doing a victory dance that involved some light professional twerking.

She nodded, a faint smile on her lips, because I'd learned the victory dance from her. "Excellent. Eric mentioned you wanting to talk to me. I have a free hour now."

I stole a quick glance at my watch, because nine times out of ten, if Gretchen asked to meet, we did. Hell, if she'd asked me to hop, I would have.

"Do you have somewhere to be?"

I could have lied and said I had a conference call or a client meeting, but what was the point? Everything I was doing was because the firm wanted to keep a client happy. Well, mostly. "I have to be downtown at five."

Her mouth formed into a thin line, and I knew she'd decoded my reason for needing to be downtown. She nodded. "Well, you better go. You know how I feel about this, though, RJ. You're better than some publicity stunt."

I fumbled with a response, biting my lower lip. That wasn't characteristic for me—I embraced the power pose, I held my shoulders back and chin up on the regular, and I never backed down from anything. I made powerful people want to cower, and I was good at it. She was right, I was better than a publicity stunt; but I had to admit, I enjoyed this particular stunt. "Thank you for checking in. I'll talk to your assistant and make an appointment."

I hurried into the back of a waiting Uber, with plans to change clothes modestly in the back seat. Was I telling myself I would be modest knowing that I was about to give anyone looking a bit of a show? Absolutely.

**Penny:** Where are you?

**RJ:** On my way. There's traffic.

**Penny:** You're killing me.

I sent her the knife emoji. *This is my life now. Event planners harassing me as I strip down in the back of an Uber.* I was going to have waffles for dinner, my favorite, and I had a bottle of special maple syrup a client had given me as a thank-you. I had to get through this thing, and a relaxing night was ahead of me. My phone buzzed again from the seat as I brushed powder onto my cheeks and checked my edges in a compact.

**Penny:** But I love you.

**RJ:** I know.

**RJ:** You have the mic set up how I like?

**Penny:** Yes, but if you're late, you're getting a handheld with a tangled cord.

I pulled out the binder where I'd prepared my script. All the pages were in plastic covers, a copy of all pertinent information in the back folder and a Post-it note reminding me of everyone's names tucked in the front. I climbed from the car and repeated the opening phrase to myself as I hurried toward the stairs of the venue. I spoke part of the line to myself. ". . . the promise of hope between two people who love each other sincerely, who—"

Without warning, I was hurtling toward the sidewalk, not sure whether I should try to save myself, my bag, or the notes. I clutched the binder to my chest as I hit the concrete, my leg scraping and my palm stinging with the impact. The clothes I'd hurriedly shoved in my bag after changing fluttered around me, and I took in the large form of the man who'd run into me.

In a movie, this would be a charming meet-cute. The tall guy, his features obscured by the sun at his back, would lean down and help me up. Our eyes would meet. He'd apologize, I'd take note of something like the depth of his voice or the tickle of the hair on his forearms, and we'd be off. That might have happened for other people, but I was not in the market for cute, and now I was about to arrive late and bruised to perform this couple's wedding.

DENISE WILLIAMS wrote her first book in the second grade. *I Hate You* and its sequel, *I Still Hate You*, featured a tough, funny heroine, a quirky hero, witty banter, and a dragon. Minus the dragons, these are still the books she likes to write. After penning those early works, she finished second grade and eventually earned a PhD in education, going on to work in higher education. After growing up as a military brat around the world and across the country, Denise now lives in Iowa with her husband, son, and two ornery shih tzus who think they own the house.

## CONNECT ONLINE

DeniseWilliamsWrites.com

🐦 NicWillWrites

📷 NicWillWrites

f AuthorDeniseWilliams